Lisa,

Please enjoy the book.

Animal Dances

Jim Saunders

D0814955

Published 2018 by Shorehouse Books
Printed in the United States of America

Cover Design by Dwayne Booth

ISBN-10: 0-9994127-4-4
ISBN-13: 978-0-9994127-4-9

Cover:

Privates Harry C. Edwards (left) and Steve Hughes; Redon France, July, 1918, 2nd Squad, 3rd Platoon, Battery B, 315th Field Artillery Regiment, 155th Battalion, 80th (Mountain) Division of the National Army. The men are standing in front of a photography shop in Redon, France.

Dedication:

To Aunt Emily (1899-1990). Without your wonderfully quirky ways and obsessive need to save everything, this would not have happened. And to Elaine, who endured more versions of this book than anyone else. Her critical editorial eye, that proved invaluable to the final product, was a wonderful new discovery in a woman whom I thought I knew everything about.

MAP OF MEDIA/MARPLE AREA

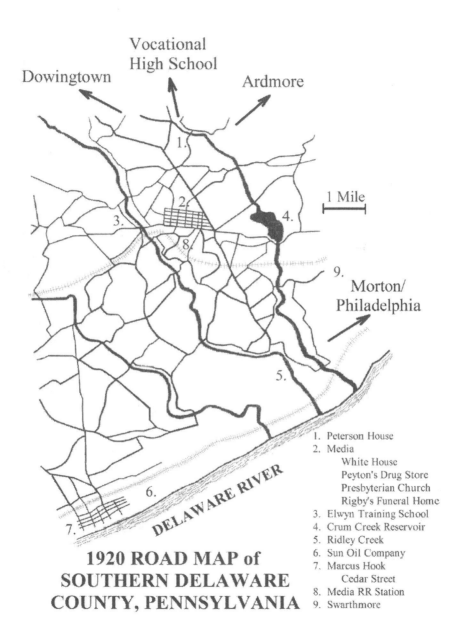

Vocational
High School

Dowingtown

Ardmore

1 Mile

Morton/
Philadelphia

DELAWARE RIVER

1. Peterson House
2. Media
   White House
   Peyton's Drug Store
   Presbyterian Church
   Rigby's Funeral Home
3. Elwyn Training School
4. Crum Creek Reservoir
5. Ridley Creek
6. Sun Oil Company
7. Marcus Hook
   Cedar Street
8. Media RR Station
9. Swarthmore

1920 ROAD MAP of SOUTHERN DELAWARE COUNTY, PENNSYLVANIA

iv

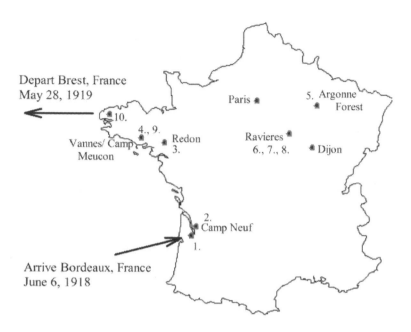

Depart Brest, France
May 28, 1919

Paris

5. Argonne
   Forest

10.

Vannes/ Camp
Meucon

4., 9.

Redon
3.

Ravieres
6., 7., 8.

Dijon

2.
Camp Neuf

1.

Arrive Bordeaux, France
June 6, 1918

CHRONOLOGY of HARRY EDWARDS TRAVELS in FRANCE

1. Arrival in Bordeaux, June 6, 1918
2. Depart Camp Neuf for Redon, June 13, 1918
3. Depart Redon for Camp Meucon, August. 17, 1918
4. Depart Meucon for the Argonne Forest, September 14, 1918
5. Depart Argonne for Ranviers, November 30, 1918
6. Depart Ranviers for Paris Holiday, March 11, 1919
7. Depart Ranviers for Dejon Holiday, March 27, 1919
8. Depart Ranviers for Camp Meucon, May 8, 1919
9. Depart Meucon for Brest, May 12, 1919
10. Depart Brest for Newport News, Virginia, May 15, 1919
11. Arrive at Camp Lee, Virginia, May 28, 1919

80ᵗʰ DIVISION OPERATIONS DURING the MEUSE ARGONNE CAMPAIGN of 1917-1918

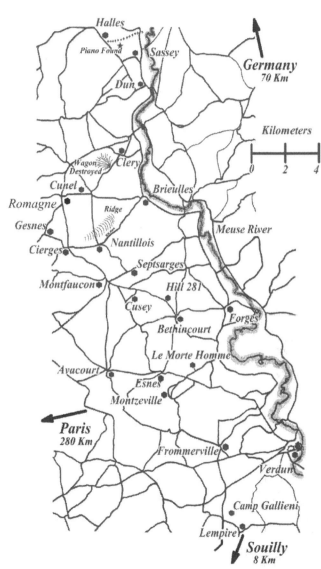

1 meter = 39 inches
1 kilometer = 0.62 miles
1 yard = 0.91 meters
1 mile = 1.61 kilometers
1 kilogram = 2.2 Pounds
1 pound= 0.45 kilograms
1 liter = 0.26 gallons
1 gallon = 3.79 liters

PART ONE

CHAPTER 1. Recollections

May, 1682; 500 miles east of Liverpool, England.

An eddy in the howling wind caught the ship. The Lyon listed dangerously to the port as the helmsman desperately struggled to bring her into the wind. Just in time she righted, but not before a wall of water washed over the deck, found a loosened hatch, and poured into the hold below. Ten year old Madeline crawled across the soaked oak floor toward her mother. Jane gathered close the terrified child. "We'll be alright, we will be safe," she uttered with wavering conviction.

Harry C. Edwards imagined the plight of the Lyon, as vivid now as the first day he'd heard the story.

∽

January, 1969; Walnut Street, Morton, Pennsylvania.
My bed sheets shared the chill in the air, and my frigid nose made it hard to drift off to sleep. We were in a freeze for over half a month and the temperature hadn't risen above 28° since Christmas Day. I wanted to get out of bed and turn up the heat. Harry, you've got to brave it out. You can't afford the luxury, I thought..

I found sleep only by burrowing deeper into the blankets and forcing the cold from my thoughts. Night after night I ran through a litany of past events. Why do I keep dredging up these old memories? Was it really just to get to sleep, or the ramblings of a deteriorating old man? Maybe it was the way I forced the loneliness from my heart? Or perhaps it was just to listen to myself tell a long story, my story.

Mid December, 1908; Rose Tree Road, Lima, Pennsylvania.
I remembered again Father's voice. "Sally, wrap the blanket around you; children, use this one." Morris and George, my younger and older brothers and Emily, my sister, and I pulled the cover around us in the rear. Father jiggled the reins, and flicked the whip. The "crack"

had Jock up to a smart trot, pulling the buggy through a crisp Saturday morning in December of 1908 to spend the weekend with Nana.

A heated cup of apple cider waited our arrival. It soothed cold hands, and fanned our desire to gather around grandmother. Nana was old and gnarled. It didn't matter, she was gentle and we loved her all the more for it.

"Nana, tell us a story? Please, please," we chimed. Emily begged, "Yes, now," as she grabbed a wrinkled hand and tugged it toward the living room. The old woman was a natural story teller, and this time she resurrected William Edwards, his wife Jane, and their children, Katherine and Madeline.

I remembered how Nana painstakingly painted the scene as our Quaker ancestors embarked for the New World in 1682. I patiently waited till the good part of the story emerged. A boy of ten needs action: pirates, a whale, a storm.

Nana soon enough had the wind blowing more solidly, the sails ceased to ruffle, stiffened, then billowed. The sky darkened as a light rain washed over the hull. The old lady raised her hands to her face with concern as the wind grew to a howl and the ship listed to port. Nana leaned to the left and the three of us tilted with her.

Nana told us Madeline and her mother huddled in the stalls calming frightened animals from the roar of thunder and the rolling ship. We learned that sea water from a huge wave washed over the deck splashing into the stalls soaking everyone. The old lady cupped her ear. "Listen, the men are tightening the hatch. You hear? It's fixed. We're safe." Nana added, "Katherine was also frightened but she comforted a trembling lamb by herself. Katherine was older, and able to rise above her fear."

"Nana, what do you mean, 'Rose above her fear?'" I asked.

"She forced herself to be brave, Harry."

"But how do you force yourself?"

Nana just looked at me and smiled. She just smiled.

After all these decades I still recall how I imagined myself on that ship, bravely facing those dangerous seas. It still amazes me how Nana's story foreshadowed my own future on a storm-tossed ocean.

It was then that I recalled my most favorite part.

"One day a year later found Catherine and Madeline alone in the cabin," said Nana. "That's when they heard the ruckus from the chickens." The old woman brought to life the snarling beast. The fur covered marauder drooled saliva, dripping in anticipation of a tasty hen. I still imagined its lips curled back revealing sharp teeth ready to rip flesh into chewable morsels. Quickly, Katherine walked to the mantle, removed the heavy flintlock and cocked its hammer. Madeline tip-toed to the door, ready to open it on her sister's signal. They'd been told stealth was essential, that noise from the house might unsettle the beast and send it running. With a nod from her sister, Madeline pressed the latch and quietly opened the rear door. Katherine silently stepped onto the back porch."

I imagined Katherine as she set the stock to her shoulder, took aim, and squeezed the trigger gently. Nana had the beast turn its head toward the house and momentarily freeze, startled by the unexpected presence of a person. William taught his daughter well, for the ball, true to its aim, laid the fox to the ground at the entrance to the hen house!

Excited by her story, I'd raise an imaginary gun to my shoulder. "Blam" I'd exhale and jerk back in a fake recoil. It's what boys do.

Even in my cold bedroom more than 60 years later, I shared Katherine's feeling of satisfaction. It's what happened next that echoes loudly down the corridors of time. I'd always ask Nana what made those settlers so brave.

"They were Quakers, Harry, they believed in their providence."

"What does that mean?" I would ask.

"Harry, one day you'll understand."

I now see myself at a party, dancing with one of my girlfriends. Which one this time? I don't focus so easily any more. It does not matter, they were all fun. The music had us giddy from the exaggeration of our dance moves, and like our friends, we're having a swell time.

On reflection, I'm embarrassed by the need to party in my young life. With the wisdom of age I now understand how the dances helped ease the toil of the farm on a Friday or Saturday night. Most farms out our way had an inexpensive Victor Talking Machine, what we called simply the "victrola." At parties, my friends and I danced with abandon to its scratchy music. Our favorite records were the Animal Dances. They were one-step routines that originated in the bordellos of San Francisco and danced to a ragtime beat. During the three minutes the record spun, the drudgery of my life evaporated. I felt free, I felt rebellious. The Animal Dances caught the spirit of the changes blossoming in the teen years of the twentieth century and the freedom to step out of the norm swept me along with them.

As a young man, three serious girlfriends passed through my life. The first, beautiful and smart, captivated me when we cavorted in the Grizzly Dance. I saw myself sharing her life, but she followed a path that didn't include me. An enchantress followed, and finally a child-woman seductress. I gave my heart to them all, but only one lived in my soul all these years.

My health is failing now. It's harder and harder to force the air out. The docs think it's something to do with the war. They might "think" it, I know it. That damn war cost me dearly, and now it's taking my breath. How I despised what it did to me.

Chapter 2. Valentino

Late March, 1918; Paxon Hollow Road, Marple, Pennsylvania.
   "Damn," I mumbled, when the letter arrived, three months shy of my twenty-first birthday. The government compelled me to register back in October of '17. Having heard nothing for months, I figured they'd forgotten me. Ha, I'm prone to wishful thinking.

   23 March 1918
   Mr. Harry C. Edwards
   R.F.D. #1, Marple, Pennsylvania
   *   Re: Selective Service No. 61175682*
   Mr. Edwards,
   *   By order of the President of the United States of America and pursuant to the Selective Service Act of 1917 authorizing the United States to identify citizens for military service, you are hereby ordered to report to Camp Lee, Petersburg, Virginia, on or about the morning of 6 May 1918 for induction into the United States Army. Should there be some reason you cannot comply with this order you are to contact your local Selective Service Board, No. 267, Ridley Park, Pennsylvania, immediately.*
   *   Instructions are contained in this letter for obtaining a travel voucher for transportation to Camp Lee on or about Sunday, 5 May 1918. Failure to comply with this order is a Federal offense punishable by fine or imprisonment.*
   Walter H. Bradley, Chairman,
   Selective Service Board, Number 267
   Ridley Park, Pennsylvania

February, 1915; Paxon Hollow Road, Marple, Pennsylvania.
   Dick Mulholland had rolled his 1914 Ford into a ditch in February of '15. The impact snapped the engine mounts, and the front fenders crumpled. His daddy bought the spoiled son a new car rather than fix the old one. With money I'd saved, I could afford a damaged car. Set me back forty dollars, and with the odometer showing about 500 miles, I saw a good deal.

"Say, George, help me get the car home?" I asked my older brother.

"Yeah. Well, guess so." George avoided any show of enthusiasm, especially if it was something I suggested.

We talked loud to George because of hearing loss from meningitis suffered when he was fifteen. Fortunately, George was really good at reading lips and body language, and with the companionship of a small ear trumpet he could follow conversations. He knew how to talk by the time he lost his hearing, so he had no problem speaking.

George and I jimmied the car back on its wheels, hitched it to the family horses, hauled it out of the ditch, and then towed it two miles back to the barn.

"George, help me get the Ford fixed. You're better at that than I am. Besides…," and I knew how to sweeten the pie, "You can drive it when she's running."

The major repairs were completed within days. Had a devil of a time getting the engine tuned, but George soon enough set it right. Amazed me how he fiddled with the idle control to smooth the engine while feeling vibrations through his hand on the fender. I faced George with a grin. "Damn, you're good." He read my lips over the engine noise and nodded. George hammered out the dents and I gave the Ford a new coat of paint.

We taught ourselves to drive, but not before I yelled a dozen times, "Let it out slowly, s-l-o-w-l-y," as the car jerked forward. I wasn't going to let George see it, but I was damn proud when he finally got the hang of the clutch. A month later the mailbox presented us with our 1916 Pennsylvania driver's licenses.

May 4, 1918; Paxon Hollow Road, Marple, Pennsylvania .

I cleaned the car for my date. Worked at it all afternoon, everything had to be perfect. It was Saturday, May 4th, and tomorrow I'd be leaving for the army, and didn't know when I'd see Fannie again. Me and my Ford had to look sharp.

The brown seersucker suit went well over the blue and white striped shirt with the starched collar. A brown bow tie, black suspenders and polished black patent leather shoes completed the outfit. I convinced myself they complimented my pale blue eyes and light brown hair. Dashing, but not overtly so, I thought. "Yeah!" Examining myself in the mirror I combed down my hair and decided, I looked pretty spiffy. That girl won't be able to resist.

I bounded down the stairs, paused at the ice box for a leftover piece of ham, and hollered from the front door, "I'm going to a movie in Media with Fannie."

"Don't be late, Harry," Mother called from the parlor. "Big day tomorrow."

"I know," I shouted back.

With the ignition engaged, gears in neutral, choke set, and the brake tight, I exited my Model T and stepped in front of the radiator, stooped and grabbed the crank. A handle twirl and a minute later my machine sped down Paxon Hollow Road.

Fannie lived three miles away in the heart of Media, about 25 miles south of Philadelphia. She lived with her aunt and uncle, Cliff and Janet White. I knew she'd come north from the family farm in Virginia after her father died some eight years ago. She saw herself as different, and that was her most attractive feature. Well, she was also beautiful. Her jade eyes and chiseled cheek bones demanded attention. Fannie was brash, and played on what remained of a cute southern drawl to enhance her appeal. At eighteen she was a year older than most of her classmates, and her enthusiasm bubbled over at being a high school senior this coming fall. She had told me she was doing something special for tonight's outing.

∾

May 4, 1918; Jackson Street, Media, Pennsylvania.

I listened as Aunt Janet removed the curlers and combed out my hair.

"Oh Fannie, this looks better than even I expected." She smiled at me and added, "Who knew I was so good at styling hair?"

"Maybe there's a new profession for you," I said. The style was indeed a new look.

Hmmm... Thoroughly modern. Harry's going to love it, I thought.

I applied a hint of makeup, a touch of rouge to enrich my complexion. I had to be subtle. "Women shouldn't get gussied-up. Gives 'em a harlequin look," Uncle Cliff would lecture me and my aunt. I rolled my eyes at the thought and pulled a sandy colored silk blouse over my shoulders, then stepped into a new dark blue skirt. I loved its shorter hem length; it's that new voguish look I liked because it revealed my ankles. As I slipped a light pink cardigan sweater over my shoulders, I heard Uncle Cliff's call. "Fannie, Harry's here."

I glanced at the clock. How nice, he is right on time.

"Be right down," I hollered.

～

My car stopped in front of the White's house. The gleaming columns and railings were newly painted, and the white wicker chairs and double swing on the porch looked like a catalogue advertisement. With the daffodils I'd picked from Mother's garden in hand, I tapped the door knocker. Cliff answered with a warm smile and outstretched hand.

"Come in Harry."

Cliff called, "Fannie, Harry's here."

"Be right down," I heard.

Janet came out of the kitchen, and removed her apron. "Nice to see you, Harry. Tomorrow's the day, isn't it? We're going to miss you."

"Well....Ahhh.....Yes. Thank you, Mrs. White."

"You want to stay for supper?"

"That's kind but, no. We're meeting Ernie and Margaret at Payton's. We'll order something to eat with them." Ernie Gillespie and Margaret Moore were our best friends.

"You boys going to show that Old Kaiser what for, eh, Harry?"

"Sure try, Sir."

"Not try. Hell, you get over there an' damn well kick his ass."

Janet shook her head.

"I'll do my best, sir."

"Hi, Harry." I faced that sweet voice. God, she looked beautiful. Something's different about her, I thought.

Fannie blushed as I handed her the flowers. She sought their subtle fragrance, smiled, and without taking her eyes from mine, handed them across to her aunt.

Cliff broke the spell. "Harry, have Fannie home by ten-thirty."

"Come on, at least eleven. It's Harry's last night home," Fannie pleaded.

"Well, all right, but girls shouldn't be out past ten."

"You're so old-fashioned," she chided.

Janet laughed, and asked "What are you seeing?"

"It's a double feature Valentino night. The Strand hired a new piano player and his music sets the mood just right," answered Fannie.

At the end of the walkway, I tilted the handle and opened the car door for my lovely lady. Fannie took her seat, and as we pulled away, I realized. "You changed your hair. I like it."

CHAPTER 3. The Elwyn Training School

May 4, 1918; Payton's Drug Store, Main Street, Media, Pennsylvania.

"Hi!" Fannie called, as we approached the soda fountain booth.

"Wow, I like your hair. You're looking so svelte," said Margaret.

"My aunt cut it for me this morning."

"I think she's looking pretty svelte also," I replied to Margaret.

"You ready for tomorrow?" asked Ernie.

"Nope."

We took a seat opposite our friends and Margaret set the conversation, avoiding any mention of the army. "Catherine Walker saw "The Married Virgin" last week. Said Valentino was delightful."

Fannie added, "He's so handsome I could eat him."

"I think he'd taste greasy with all that oil in his hair."

"Ernie, stop, what an awful thing to say," chided Margaret. Fannie giggled.

I ordered a cream soda for Fannie and a cola for me. We shared a ham sandwich. The four of us chatted for twenty minutes, when, glancing at the wall clock, Margaret interrupted, "Time to feast on some Valentino."

Half-way through the second feature, Fannie leaned over to me and whispered. "Let's go, I'm bored." As we rose, Margaret wondered why we were leaving. Fannie said she wasn't feeling well.

May 4, 1918; Ridley Creek, Media, Pennsylvania.

I knew where to go, a pull-off north of town, alongside Ridley Creek, out near the Elwyn Training School. I parked and switched off the car lights. Fannie and I were alone, lit by the soft lamp-light flickering through the trees from the distant school. The only sound was the bubbling water as it washed over the rocks. She faced me and we embraced. I sensed her passion.

Suddenly she pulled away. "I don't want you to go."

"I don't want to leave either."

"Then, let's run away, right now."

I didn't want more talking and pulled her toward me. When we separated, my eyes followed the outline of her face in the dim light. My fingers brushed tenderly across her cheek. How soft her skin, how beautifully smooth, like the feel of her silk blouse. Her graceful smile was lovely in the flickering light. She relished my gentle stroke, and leaned into my hand, seeking its touch.

"I'm going to miss you," she said.

The sadness in her voice gripped me. We gave ourselves to one another as desire grew. Fannie squirmed to get closer—one arm circled my neck while her other hand caressed my face. I watched as she unbuttoned her blouse. With no restriction my hand found the satiny skin of her stomach. Hesitantly, it wandered upward. My God, how soft…. how smooth. Her hand held my head as she pushed back.

"Harry, we must go. If I'm not home by eleven there will be hell."

Despite the plea, her other hand slid from my neck, found my hand under her blouse, and pressed it against her skin. We kissed again. The embrace ended and my hand slowly withdrew.

∽

May 4, Jackson Street, Media Pennsylvania.

When we stood at the front door, Harry wrapped his arms around me and drew me to him. He seemed different. There was a tenderness about him, or was it sadness? A wave of emotion washed over me followed by an urgency that filled me with need. As I pressed into him a well of desire erupted. Harry pushed me back, staring into my teary eyes. I held his gaze, then needed to feel him again, and burrowed my head into his chest. He shared my anguish and I heard his soft whisper, "It's tough for me too." I couldn't let go. Out of nowhere, a horrid thought flit through my mind: This embrace might never be repeated. I may never see him again. A dreadful notion, and to make it go away, I wrapped my arms ever more tightly around him.

As Harry bid me good-by I promised to write. I waved as he pulled away from the curb. The tail lights disappeared when he turned onto Providence Road. It was over. He was gone. I stood alone on the front stoop and that awful thought returned.

CHAPTER 4. Departure

May 5, 1918; Paxon Hollow Road, Marple, Pennsylvania.

I switched off the rudely ringing alarm clock, and sat at the edge of my bed fighting a stomach of dancing butterflies. A sudden compulsion forced me to open my top dresser drawer and touch every pair of underwear, each individual sock, even my Long Johns. Mindlessly, I ran my hands over the handkerchiefs. With all accounted for, I closed the drawer. Why the hell'd I do that? I asked myself.

I straightened the bed sheets, tucked-in their folds, and pulled the bedspread over the pillows, and sitting, I sat motionless on the edge of the bed trying not to think of anything. The butterflies continued their dance as I lifted a small suitcase onto the bed. With the lid pushed back, two folded towels and a washcloth went inside. A small kit bag with my toiletries followed, along with a razor sharpening strap.

Last night I had taken the pictures of my mother and father out of their frames and placed them on the dresser. To these were added snaps of my soon to be eighteen year old sister, Emily, and fourteen year-old brother, Morris, as well as others I'd taken in early April with George driving the buggy. They were secured in a cloth pocket sewn into the lid of the case.

A picture of Fannie, Fannie and I with our arms around each other, and another of us standing in front of my Ford, were protected by the pages of my bible. With greater care I packed the one taken in March of us kissing. Could I imagine how I'd cling to those pictures months from now? A change of underwear, an extra pair of socks, a pair of trousers and a work shirt carefully surrounded the other contents. Cripes, not much to go to France with, I thought.

"Harry, come down to breakfast, before it's cold," I heard Mother call.

When I entered the kitchen all but my mother were seated.

"You ready, Harry?" asked Father.

"I got my room picked-up and I'm all packed." I couldn't tell them how I really felt.

"Do they give you a gun right away?" asked Morris.

"Don't know."

Father glanced toward Emily. "Would you pour the coffee, Em?"

She rose and fetched the hot kettle. I luxuriated in the smell of the roasted brew, especially when it mixed with the sweet odor of the golden hotcakes sizzling on the griddle.

"Just the way you like them, Harry," said Mother, as she slid four onto my plate. The butter and syrup were passed, and for a moment the only sound was the clink of knives on dishware.

"Harry, I've decided to stay home," said Father. "All of us can't fit in the Ford."

"It's okay, I'm just getting on the train. Ernie's going with me."

"You got the tickets through to Petersburg?" asked Emily.

"Not yet, they're at the station in Philly. We're meeting Ollie and Jake in Washington to board the evening train to Petersburg. I hear it's a four mile walk to Camp Lee from the train station."

"Why are Ollie and Jake in Washington?" asked Mother.

"They went down couple of days ago to do some site-seeing."

After a pause to eat, I faced George. "Say George, you be sure and run the Ford's engine now and then. Drive it back and forth. It'll keep oil in the cylinders. The clutch might act-up also. Heck, George, just take her out whenever you want."

"Harry, you've said the same thing three times already. Don't worry, the Ford will be ready for your return."

The conversation fell silent. 'Your return,' a phrase with meaning no one around the table wanted to contemplate. I sensed the awkwardness, and took a sip of coffee. Breakfast ended and my brothers and sister excused themselves, and Mother muttered something and left the kitchen. I collected dishes, placed them in the sink, and faced my father. "Say, Dad come with me to the barn."

He adjusted his cane, and came out of the chair. "Is something wrong?"

"No," I answered.

The screen door opened and our dog, Charlie, burst out of the kitchen. Toby and Fritz stirred as we entered. They whinnied in anticipation while I filled their feed buckets. I handed one to Father for Fritz, then hung the other one around Toby's muzzle.

My mother's passage through the change of life was a difficult one for the whole family and I needed to say something to my father about it.

"Dad, I'm unsettled about leaving for the army, and don't know when I'll be home. Worse, I hate to leave Mother, though it looks like she's doing much better. Emily's able to look after her, but you'll have to do the same. You'll have to watch her closely."

He shrugged. "Harry, with the Americans entering the war the whole affair will be over. You'll be home before you know."

"We can hope for that. Most likely I won't be back before Christmas.

Marple Township in 1918 was a sparsely settled area southwest of Philadelphia. The modest farms, like the one we lived on, were carved from the Quaker land grants of the late seventeenth century. The owners now were mostly wealthy gentlemen from Philadelphia who saw their farms as a summer retreat. We lived on a farm owned by a family named "Peterson," located on Paxon Hollow Road. My father managed the day-to-day activities of the farm and his industry and reputation were well known. He was paid reasonably well to maintain the property, and we kept the earnings from farm product sales. My brothers and I were the engines that kept the place running.

It was a three-mile buggy ride to the borough of Media, the county seat and hub of the district. My mother, a successful seamstress, sold dresses and women's undergarments through a ladies shop in Media. At least compared to other farm families, we prospered.

Father disagreed with the war declaration, likely something to do with his Quaker upbringing. But he prided himself on being informed, and six months ago he had subscribed to the *New York Times Mid-Week Pictorial*. The family waited on the mail to read this weekly review of the world at war. I knew more facts about the Great War than needed, and understood the carnage on the Western Front. I never liked the graphic photographs of horrid battlefield scenes and maimed soldiers the *Pictorial* portrayed, but at the same time I couldn't put it down. My concerns were fanned by more than the *Pictorial*. My friend Jake Osborn loaned me a book in February of '18.

"Harry, it's really popular," Jake told me. "Read it and learn what we'll face over there."

Arthur Guy Empey's "*Over the Top*," with its visceral description of British Tommies in the trenches upset me. The book made me question how I'd react in similar circumstances and left me wondering what sort of soldier I'd make. It so unnerved me that I hid the book from the rest of the family.

∽

Just before we left the house Mother called me to the kitchen and handed me a paper bag with food for the train ride: an egg salad sandwich and a piece of Emily's pie. A moment later she reached into the cupboard and removed a small tin box. Told me it was filled with writing material, everything I needed, stamps as well. She pleaded with me to write her. That she'd be worried sick over me if I didn't. I promised to write, and reached out to hug the lady that gave me life.

In the driveway, Father wished me well. We clasped as he fumbled for words, "Keep safe, Son. We need you home." Mother, Emily, and Morris got in the back seat. George spun the crank, and I drove.

My mind pushed aside the fact that I was leaving home. I focused instead on the beauty of the spring day with its brilliant blue sky and soothing warmth signaling the coming summer. I noticed the tree buds of spring had grown into leaves, but not yet reached full size. I saw how the growing roadside sunflowers and foxtails along Paxton Hollow Road waved in the spring breeze. Was there a sweet scent from the morning glories in the air? The promise of new life blossomed all around me, and I reckoned it odd these things were not obvious to me before. I don't want to leave this, I thought.

May 5, 1918; MediaTrain Station, Media, Pennsylvania.
When we arrived at the station, Ernie, his family, and Margaret were already on the platform. Everyone turned as the locomotive

rumbled around the bend and I shared farewell kisses with a tearful Emily and my mother, then shook hands with George. My little brother hugged me.

From behind I heard a shout, "Harry wait!"

Fannie careened around the corner of the station house and ran to me.

"I had to say good bye," she said, trying to catch her breath. Before I could say a word she kissed me.

"Hey, kid. This train don't wait," shouted the conductor.

Fannie brought her cheek to mine and whispered, "Come back to me, Harry. Promise me."

I nodded my head, "I will."

As the train pulled from the station and Fannie disappeared from sight, I wondered if I'd ever see her again?

CHAPTER 5. Camp Lee

May 6, 1918; Camp Lee; Petersburg, Virginia.

In the middle of the night the southbound train approached a siding outside of Petersburg. The conductor shouted, "Camp Lee, all out, boys." Seventy-seven conscripts scrambled wildly for their suitcases and tumbled out of the coaches. A sergeant waiting our early morning arrival shouted instructions in the muggy night air and proceeded to line-up his conscripts on the road. He addressed the kid alongside me.

"Where you boys from?" Thank goodness he didn't pick me, went through my head.

Out of the corner of my eye I watched as the draftee raised his right hand to his forehead and saluted the sergeant in the manner of a Boy Scout. He confidently replied, "We're from eastern Pennsylvania, Sir," and his arm came down.

The sergeant glared. "One, you call me sergeant. Two, you don't salute sergeants. An' three, that's not an Army salute. The only thing saving your sorry ass is you aren't a soldier, yet."

At that moment a cavalry trooper sauntered up the road on a magnificent stallion branded with the letters "U.S." on its flank.

"Sergeant, don't be too hard on them boys. They're still dumb as rail posts. You'll have your way with them soon enough."

"You can bet on it," the sergeant snickered.

"Follow me you gobs," ordered the trooper

I grumbled to Gillespie, "You think they would have trucks or something."

"What the hell are gobs?" asked Gillespie.

An hour and fifteen minutes later, two lines of hot, sweaty men came round a bend and confronted the lights of Camp Lee. The Trooper dismounted at the guard station, saluted, handed papers to an officer, remounted his stallion and trotted away. The Lieutenant beckoned a corporal and ordered him to escort us to the Induction Center. The corporal replied, "Yes, Sir," with a smart salute.

"Follow me," he said to us.

"Hmmmm, are we always following someone?" I murmured.

"Must be the army way," whispered Gillespie.

The column passed through the gate and proceeded up the main roadway. The humidity worsened and my forehead dripped with sweat. We walked about ten minutes when the corporal stopped beside a huge field. "There's the parade ground. You men will get plenty of practice out there." He pointed across the street. "That there's the Induction Center and next to it is the Division Command Post."

Osborn called out, "How come the only lights in this camp burn in the Command Post and the Center?"

"Soldier, them's the generals in there planning how we're going to beat back Kaiserism. And the Center, well, that's where your lives will change."

Inside the Center I raised my right hand, repeated a simple oath that, at 0240 hours, changed me from free citizen to U.S. Army property. We were immediately directed to the rear of the Center where an imposing man with two silver bars on his shoulders ordered us to strip down to our skivvies and form two lines for a physical exam. I don't know what the cough test showed; surely never experienced anything like it before. At the next station I watched as two orderlies, on the left and right side of the soldier (three in front of me) seized each of his arms. Then with a deft move, each shoved needles into his upper biceps and pushed the plungers. Damn if the man didn't faint right out. Quickly righted, the orderlies shoved him back in line.

I'm next. Damn. This is going to hurt. It must have been the anticipation that played with my head, 'cause it really didn't. I shuffled to the next station, which lined us up in front of three barbers. Horrified, I realized what was coming.

"Hey, do you have to cut off my mustache?" I heard one of my compatriots complain.

"Look soldier, regs say short hair on head, no hair on face," replied the barber.

On the road behind the Induction Center a new soldier met us dressed in an immaculately pressed uniform. He wore a wide-brimmed hat set squarely on his head. On the upper arm of his tunic, stitched on each sleeve sat an insignia of three gold chevrons, underscored by a single curved gold rocker bar. He ordered us to line up in the middle of the street, four abreast.

The escort stepped back. "Staff Sergeant, these new recruits are yours."

"Do they belong to the army now?"

"Yes, Staff Sergeant, they do."

"Good, return to the main gate soldier. Okay, you gobs. My name is Staff Sergeant Pitt. You never salute me, and you always address me as Staff Sergeant. Now, let's start turning you into soldiers."

Pitt ordered the front of the line to turn around and step across the street toward the Quartermaster Building. Inside, disgruntled privates, annoyed at having to outfit new recruits this early in the morning issued us toiletries and summer khaki uniforms: a drab brownish green cotton tunic, matching trousers, and a soft felt hat. Army green underwear and socks completed our gear. Russert boots would come later. Pitt ordered us to dress quickly in our new duds and put on our old shoes.

On the street Pitt yelled orders and ranks were formed. His voice, now filled with power ordered, "Ah-leffft face. Now move out." I don't know what got into Baker, but in a sing-song voice he mocked Pitt from the line of soldiers, "Ah-leffffffft face."

"Halt," yelled Pitt. Somehow the Staff Sergeant identified Baker among the throng of men.

How the hell did he know it was Baker, I wondered. Pitt didn't even look in his direction.

Two inches in front of Baker's face, Pitt yelled, "Soldier, are you a funny man? That was an order. Do you not understand what an order is?"

Baker stammered, "I....Yes....Sergeant." The veins in Pitt's neck expanded, and even in the dark I saw the deepened color in Pitt's face.

"It's Staff Sergeant, soldier! One more word out of you, or any of you gobs, and you'll be running till daylight."

Dead silence followed as we walked to the Depot Brigade where we were assigned temporary barracks. I lay between the sheets by four o'clock in the morning.

Next afternoon I wrote postcards. One to Mother telling her I arrived in Camp Lee and that the army rousted us out of bed at five in the morning to drill us for four hours. Another to Fannie saying they shaved my head and removed my moustache. Said she'd hardly recognize me, and if she did, she'd laugh. Said I missed her, and asked her to write soon.

Before entering the mess hall for supper Captain Reed addressed the new recruits. "Gentlemen, welcome to Camp Lee. Our job is to make you soldiers. Your training won't be completed here, that'll happen in France. However, never forget, every man must work hard for his country, his comrades and himself. You are embarking on a great adventure and each of you is expected to bring honor and glory to your unit, the Division and the Army. Nothing less is demanded if we are to win this war." We'd hear that refrain again and again in the coming weeks.

Several days later I was equipped with a rifle, helmet, backpack, and boots. My boots hurt like hell, but they eventually wore in. A guy named Phil Doyle, a couple of bunks away, had the worst time. Exchanged his first pair for a size larger, but not before his heels got some awful blisters. Doyle, a tall Irishman, told me he worked the Philadelphia docks. He had a big mouth, a pushy personality, and a brash sense of humor.

Mid-morning on May 9th we were ordered to meet with the assignment officers. My line advanced until I handed my papers to a bored lieutenant.

"Private Edwards, you're to be assigned to a regiment in the Eightieth Division. Currently we need men in the 315th Field Artillery Brigade. You okay with this?"

"Ahh....Yeah....I guess so, Sir."

"Well. Are you or aren't you?"

"Yes, Sir, I am."

He asked me if I knew much arithmetic. I told him I could add, subtract, multiply, and divide slowly. He wanted to know if I knew any trigonometry. I didn't.

"Says here you work on a farm. Know much about horses?"

I told him I could ride 'em, bridle 'em, hitch 'em to wagons, shoe 'em, pull a plow. That I knew how to feed and breed 'em, and if I had to, I could rid 'em of worms.

"You got what I'm looking for. You're assigned to the Supply Section of Battery B. They need wagoners. Say, I also see here you've some experience with plumbing."

"Yes, Sir. Been apprenticin' back home."

"I'll add that. Regiment may call on you if they need plumbing help. You right with this, soldier?"

"Yes, Sir."

The Lieutenant leaned over and filled in some blanks, and told me to move on to the next desk. "Good luck, soldier."

"Thank you, Sir." I saluted, and moved on.

Inside, I jumped for joy, thinking, hot damn, the artillery. What could be better? I'll work with horses. The horrid images of squalid trench conditions, maimed, battered, and disfigured soldiers and the gut wrenching orders to "go over the top" in Empey's book about British Tommies, were still fresh in my mind.

Ernie Gillespie, Ollie Baker, Jake Osborn, Will Adams, Phil Doyle, Charlie Powell, Bill Ford, Jim Nightlinger, and I were all assigned to the Supply Section. Most likely because we were standing together in the same line. I knew Ernie, Ollie and Jake from back home. The rest were strangers. We changed barracks, and it turned out a fellow named Steve Hughes, the final man in the squad, occupied my lower bunk. The ten of us were now the Second Squad of the Third Platoon of Battery B, in the 315th Field Artillery Regiment.

Hughes and I were the same age. He was the only child of Welsh immigrant parents. Born upstate in Scranton, Pennsylvania, he, like his father, had toiled in the coal mines outside of town. A man with a muscular build and brown eyes set on a handsome face. His hair was the same color as his eyes and he parted it on the left and combed it to the right. Hughes rarely spoke up, but never said anything he didn't mean.

We had our differences, and I'm not talking about disagreements, though enough of them followed. I yapped more, said what I felt, and pretty much did what others told me to do. I also had the unfortunate habit of believing anything told to me. Likely, the result of growing up around honest folk. I disliked the army and complained more than warranted.

As it played out, I made Hughes think by challenging him with new ideas. He wasn't accustomed to that, and it created an unexpected experience. At the same time, Hughes kept my distaste for the army in check. He kept me out of trouble. We settled easily into a camaraderie that led to friendship.

Oh, another thing, both of us liked to watch the girls but Hughes certainly could be smoother around them. As far as the ladies were concerned, my new friend had a problem back in Scranton. It seems he married early and just before his conscription he and his wife agreed they were not compatible and filed for divorce. It was not yet finalized by the time we met in Camp Lee.

I wrote a letter to Emily on May 15th. Told her I had a uniform and my boots were now comfortable. I complained the army only provided one bale of straw as a mattress for our bunks. It had to be shared among ten fellows, and that our food was barely edible. Also noted we now had a Sergeant named Jozef Sedelsky.

Our Lieutenant, a man named John Harden conducted an inspection on the afternoon of May 21st, the fifth one in as many days. Harden found Jake Osborn's rifle dirty and admonished the squad for it. Said we had dirty rifles for a second time. That meant all of us were confined to quarters. There'd be no YMCA Canteen for us tonight or tomorrow night.

After the Lieutenant left, a forlorn Osborn sat at the edge of his bunk looking at his rifle. "There's no dirt in this gun. I just cleaned and oiled it. What the hell's with the Lieutenant?" Gillespie told us he heard from a buddy in fourth squad that the Lieutenant does the same to them, and we concluded he simply liked to rake us over. One of the guys also learned that Lieutenant Harden had just graduated in early May from West Point.

"Jeez, he's as green as we are," said Baker.

"Guess he's tryin' to make a name for himself for bein' tough," added Hughes.

"Who the hell do we complain to? Sedelsky just goes along with him," said Charlie Powell.

I noticed Doyle. He sat on his upper bunk, legs dangling over the side staring at Osborn with tight-pursed lips, a reddish tint grew on his Irish face. He cracked his knuckles, not once, but over and over. Suddenly he hopped to the floor and approached Osborn's bunk.

"Shit Osborn," he said in a thick Irish brogue. "If you had your damn rifle cleaned, I'd be at the canteen tonight instead of sitting in these barracks."

I'd seen this happen a few days earlier when Doyle got excited at evening mess. He'd decided the food wasn't fit for pigs. Made a stink to Sedelsky, who quickly set him straight.

"Doyle, I don't plan it, I don't cook it, and I don't serve it. All I do is eat it. You expectin' your mothers cooking? Hell, go complain to the cooks." Sarge did not stop, "Tell 'em you ain't happy. You'll be peeling potatoes for a week. Otherwise, youse got two choices: starve or eat."

Doyle went back to picking at his chow.

"So, Osborn, you get fun out of keeping me here? Everything you do gets screwed up. At the range you proved you can't shoot worth a damn, and two nights ago you failed to relieve my watch on time," blurted an angry Doyle.

"What the hell you saying? Maybe I don't handle a rifle like you, but my weapon's clean. And I was late because Sarge stopped me on my way to post."

Doyle wasn't listening. "It's always the same with you, Osborn. I'm going to take you out back and beat the crap out of you if you don't shape up."

The room went dead silent.

"No, you're not," came from another bunk.

Doyle faced the voice. "What? You going to stop me?"

"Yeah. I'm tired of your big mouth," said Hughes.

Doyle's fists clenched as he headed toward Hughes. I stepped in front of him.

"Leave it alone, Doyle."

Doyle's arms cocked back as he made ready to shove me out of the way. From behind, Jim Nightlinger grabbed his arms.

"That's enough. Let it go, Doyle. Ain't Osborn's fault. The damn Lieutenant's messing with us."

"Nightlinger's right," said Gillespie.

Nightlinger must have been roiled by this episode. The largest man in the squad, he had a huge chest with arms like logs, likely from tossing cases from his delivery truck. Nightlinger kept mostly to himself. Not this time.

"Doyle, I'm tired of you pushing your weight around here. If you don't get over it, I'll take you out back myself, and you'll get a whipping so bad you won't sleep well for a week." A murmur of surprise passed through the squad. A defeated Doyle jimmied through the crowd and slunk out the barracks door.

Couple of hours later Hughes and I were drawing on cigarettes out front before lights out. "What the hell had Doyle so riled?" I asked.

"Well, I saw him hitting on one of them canteen chickens. The girl that seats us before a show. One with the flamin' red hair."

"Yeah, she's a looker alright."

"He's always talkin' about gettin' under any skirt he can find. Being cut out of canteen tonight probably put a dent in his plans."

"Jeez Hughes, I didn't see any of that, you're quite the observer."

He jabbed my ribs, followed by a know-it-all smile. "Edwards, just ask me when you want to know what's going on around here."

CHAPTER 6. Instructions

May 22, 1918; Camp Lee, Petersburg, Virginia.

Reveille had us up at 0600 hours. Breakfast followed after half an hour of calisthenics. Morning drill practice, rain or shine, kept us busy for two more hours. Another two hours were spent in cleaning our barracks or memorizing army regulations.

It was quickly apparent to me that Camp Lee had no artillery ordinance or supply wagons. Just a few antiquated two-inch field pieces, and rickety two-wheeled carts, each drawn by a single horse. I counted only three trucks in camp. The more experienced hands said nobody knew if the supply units were to be horse-drawn or motorized outfits. I hoped for tractors, but figured I'd soon enough be driving wagons. A persistent rumor spread through camp that conscripted divisions, like us, got second rate equipment when compared to the enlisted divisions. I didn't know how true that was, but it certainly seemed so when I saw how few howitzers, wagons or trucks were in camp.

After lunch we attended lectures on how to load 75- and 155-millimeter shells, powder bags, and fuses into wagons. Practice with dummy munitions followed. My God, did the army think we're so stupid to need lectures on loading wagons? Demonstrations on how to hitch-up horse teams and care for horses were new to many of the men. I knew most all that stuff. They also showed us how to grease wheel bearings with petroleum jelly. It smelled more like rendered animal fat to me, and certainly wasn't the kind of grease I used on my Model T.

However, I have to admit that I was surprised by the difficulty encountered in hefting those shells into the wagon bed. The damn things were heavy, especially the shrapnel shells.

After mounting a shell in the wagon, I heard Baker ask the Lieutenant:

"Sir, are them shells in there dangerous?"

"Are you joking me, soldier?" he replied. "You do know they got one purpose, to kill. But don't worry, they're safe as lilies, as long as there's no fuse in 'em. You don't attach the fuse, that job's for the artillery boys."

Baker looked relieved, for that matter I think we all felt the same.

"One thing though," added the Lieutenant. "Don't ever let a shell get in a fire. When hot enough they'll blow, even without a fuse. If a wagon's burning and you can't put the fire out, get the hell away."

∽

Afternoons were spent in additional drill practice. Occasionally, the army provided live-fire instruction at the rifle range. I enjoyed the range and also the week of First Aid training. Thought it might be important one day. The army also provided me a gas mask that was carried in a pack on my chest. I never had it on for more than a few minutes and mostly to practice positioning it quickly over my face.

Map reading came the week after First Aid training and conversion to metric distance scales confused the hell out of me at first. The generals were hedging their bets because a few late afternoon discussions focused on tractor engine maintenance. Now I really enjoyed that. After all, a combustion engine's the same in a car or tractor.

The lectures on avoiding the clap or crabs caught my attention. Jeez, was I naïve. At first I hadn't a clue what they were talking about! The lieutenant told us the surest protection was abstinence, which produced a snicker from Doyle.

After three weeks, just when army life appeared routine, reality jolted the squad. On May 25th the four hundred troops of Battery B were ordered to assemble in the Mess Hall. I watched as Colonel Williams stepped to the platform.

"At ease, men," he began. "Your great adventure is about to begin with the next stage of your training. Training that will bring honor and glory to your country. May 29th the Regiment departs Camp Lee for Newport News where you'll board ship. At our final destination overseas your work begins. Artillery units can expect live fire exercises and supply units will carry live ammunition. The country, the 80th Division and your loved ones demand the utmost from each man. Nothing less than your total effort will win the war. I expect this to be the best damn artillery brigade in the division. Now, Major Shaw has additional remarks, so listen up."

I leaned over to Hughes and whispered. "How many times do we have to hear this pep talk?"

"Shhhh, I want to hear the Major."

Shaw assumed the podium and called for ship-board volunteers. He emphasized volunteers were given coffee in the galley after their shift.

"Hey that's what we want," said Hughes.

Ernie Gillespie nudged me in the back. "What are you volunteering for?" he whispered.

"Nothing."

"You should. My friend over in fourth squad said he had a letter from his brother-in-law saying he would be bored as hell on the crossing if he didn't volunteer for something."

"Well, I don't want to start volunteering. Do it once, and they'll likely never stop pestering."

Suddenly I heard Hughes' voice. "Put Hughes and Edwards down for nest duty."

"What the hell'd you do?" I asked.

"I volunteered us for 'nest duty.'"

"You did what? What's nest duty?"

"Something to do with watching for submarines. Hell, can't be that hard, besides, you get coffee at the end of the watch."

I heard Gillespie snicker. "Now they'll be pestering!"

"Yeah. Well stick it where the sun don't shine. Both of you."

May 29, 1918; The Port of Newport News, Virginia.

Just shy of noon Hughes and I ascended the gangway to the *Tenadores*. I glanced at my billet card: "Compartment 1, Hatch 1, Bunk number 36, forward bulkhead." Hughes was bunk number 35.

❧

Built in Belfast in 1913 for the United Fruit Company, the *Tenadores* had sailed as a "banana boat." The Navy commandeered her in 1917, refitting the ship to carry troops. Refitted's an exaggeration. Hemp hammocks were installed in the frames that once carried banana bunches, creating row upon row of bunks. Extra heads were installed, and the galley and mess rooms enlarged.

∾

"Hey, this isn't so bad," I said as I shimmied into the hammock.

"No, it ain't," Hughes replied. "These bottom bunks make it easier to reach the head if we gotta pee. Better yet, we're away from the engine room. It'll be quieter."

"You got that right, long as we're not torpedoed and go down front first."

"Aren't you the cheery one," Hughes shot back.

By mid-day one thousand two hundred and twenty-four men were stowed aboard the *Tenadores*. Many of us were assembled on deck and watched as lines were cast. Powerful tugs nudged the ship into the channel. Concern washed over me when the decking shuddered as the engine came to life. Concern switched to amazement as I watched the huge ship glide through the water. The tugs released us when we reached the deeper water of Hampton Rhodes Bay, and now, under its own power the *Tenadores* rounded the point into the open channel of the Chesapeake Bay. I grabbed my hat in a sudden gust of wind.

The throbbing engine created a rhythm that pulsed through the decks, and as we steamed beyond the coastline, the ocean swells added to the concert. I'd never before experienced a rolling sensation like this, and my head and stomach were not happy. Worse yet, for us nautical novices, memory of the Titanic was never far away.

Still within sight of the coast, the *Tenadores* joined a circling convoy of fourteen troop and cargo carriers. The whole 80th Division, plus the supplies to make us an army, was on the ocean. As if on cue, a sudden rush of seamen fanned out across our ship, sealing portholes against light leaks. Word passed that we could sleep on deck or below, and Hughes and I decided we'd be more comfortable in the hold. Fortunately, my head and stomach calmed as I learned to shift my body against the rolling deck.

"Nest" volunteers were ordered to report to the foredeck at 1400 hours for instruction and training.

"Hughes, you figured out what this 'nest' thing is?" I asked.

"Think so." He pointed upward to a small platform welded some thirty feet up the shaft on the forward mast. "They called it the crow's nest on older ships."

Lieutenant Harden, accompanied by a seaman, took roll call and began his spiel. Told us our four hour shift began exactly on the hour. We were to scan the sea—horizon to horizon—in the direction the nest faced, looking for anything out of the ordinary. Binocular use was required, even at night. We might catch an unexpected flash of light. He explained how to communicate with the bridge using a push-button on the mast and listening for return buzzer signals. His most stern warning was not to smoke in the nest.

"A light could give away our position. I catch you smoking up there, it'll be KP duty for the rest of the voyage."

Harden then stepped aside. "Gentlemen, this is Master Seaman Bargel. Pay attention to him."

Bargel, a short, stocky man with a dark complexion, had massive forearms exposed by rolled up denim shirt sleeves. A weathered face reinforced the impression that you didn't mess with this sailor. He showed us the safety belt with its large metal clips, and demonstrated the way it went over our heads, and how, when positioned at our waist, it could be snapped to brackets.

"Be sure it's secure, your life depends on it."

Bargel drew us to the base of the mast and gestured upward. He pointed to a steel plate welded at the end of a ladder about 10 meters above the deck. "That plate up there is the nest," he said.

He told us there were metal brackets and hand grips welded onto the mast, and that the belt clips attached to the brackets. Small steel blocks on the plate, gripped by the heel of our boots, helped wedge us against the mast. Posts about the perimeter of the plate supported a rope railing, and grabbing the rope or hand grips could steady us when needed.

Similar brackets and hand grips at the base of the mast allowed us to practice at deck level. When it was my turn, I pulled hard on the belt to be sure the clips were secured.

"That's good, soldier, Understand men, if your belt somehow comes unclipped up there, and the ships in bad weather, with the mast tossing about, you're likely going to die."

That sent shivers through me.

Harden took over. "Okay, we're going to practice climbing till chow time. Teams one to eight go with the Master Seaman to the aft mast, nine to sixteen will stay with me. Oh yes, the nest duty roster is posted on the board outside the mess hall. Memorize your shifts."

Hughes was concerned about the climb. The first time he clung so close to the ladder and moved so cautiously that I thought he was going to crap his pants. For me it was nothing. I'd been climbing ladders into barn lofts since a kid. I must admit, though, the barn ladders never rocked back and forth. After practicing over the next hour, Hughes decided it wasn't so bad.

With evening mess completed, Hughes and I joined the other troops milling about the deck and watched as three destroyer escorts joined the flotilla. Blinking lights from Aldis lamps indicated a flurry of messages relayed back and forth. The messages resulted in a course change as the ships reorganized into a convoy heading away from the coast.

Suddenly, one of the destroyers broke from its position at the rear of the convoy. "Edwards, looks like one of them destroyers is coming right toward us!"

"Good Lord, Hughes, that ship's moving fast; she's going flank speed."

"What the hell's 'flank speed?'" Hughes asked.

"Steam's pumped up and she's flying over the water, fast as she can. Read it in the magazine we get at home."

"Jeez. She's doing that all right," said Hughes.

We saw the enormous "57" painted on the bow as the destroyer overtook the *Tenadores*, not more than a hundred meters off the starboard side. Its wake tossed us about some as it settled in position at the head of the convoy.

"That was pretty exciting," I said.

Hughes and I found ourselves against the stern railing just before sunset. I watched the water swirl away from the stern as the

Tenadores ploughed forward through calm seas. On the western horizon the golden orb of an oversized sun silently slid from sight. The lights of America winked on, and then disappeared into a hazy line with an uncertain separation between sky and water. Each of us were lost in our thoughts. Hughes whispered, "Good-bye," just loud enough for me to hear, as he flicked his smoke over the side. I mouthed to myself, "I'll return, Fannie." In the growing dusk we worked our way along the deck to the forward hold, and descended to our bunks.

CHAPTER 7. Squall

Early June, 1918; Mid-Atlantic on board the *Tenadores*.

The routine was boring and the only thing I looked forward to were our trips to the nest. Seven days after our departure—just before lights out—I leaned over the bunk and, quite unsettled, whispered to Hughes. "Say, you heard the rumor?"

"No. What's it this time?"

Was there a hint of sarcasm in his voice?

"There're big ugly spiders in here, called Tarantulas. They climb out of the bilge at night. I mean big, three to four inches across! You're dead if they bite. Remember the scream the other night?"

"Yeah?" Was it a snicker I now heard? He was my friend and all that, but why was he always so skeptical?

"Well, everyone thought the guy had a nightmare, but Gillespie told me what really happened. He heard from a guy who's friends with the guy who bunks next to the guy who screamed, that he woke up with one of those bugs crawling up his blanket."

Hughes shifted to the side of his hammock and looked up at me.

"Edwards, sometimes you're so full of shit it scares me. Do you believe every piece of nonsense told you from a friend of a friend who knew somebody who thought they heard something? Worse, do you believe everything Gillespie tells you? The man's in a perpetual tizzy. Where the hell do you think them bugs came from?"

"This ship used to carry fruit. Those bugs stowed away on the bananas, and hid-out down in the bilge," I replied.

"Edwards, will you stop believing everything you hear? The bilge is six feet below us. The floor's sealed with welded steel plates. Now go to sleep."

"You'll be damn sorry if one of them bites you," I said.

I lay in the hammock for a while thinking. Maybe I did exaggerate some things. I thought a little bit more and came to another conclusion. Perhaps I needed a distraction to keep my mind off the fact that we'd soon be arriving in France where I'd be another step closer to what I dreaded.

I had never seen the ocean before and no matter how many times I came onto the deck or sat in the nest, the sheer vastness of the sea overwhelmed me. I kept remembering Nana's story of how my ancestors sailed this same ocean in flimsy sailing ships. I had a new appreciation of their venture across the sea.

Seven days since our departure, on June 5th, the well-coordinated zig-zag course placed our small armada south of the Azores islands. I never saw the islands and only knew they were there because Osborn found a map pasted to the top of a life vest locker and did some mental figuring. Jake Osborn is one smart guy.

The ship steamed ever eastward in that torturous manner for another thousand kilometers until the flotilla shifted course again. Osborn had another look at that map and likely guessed correctly from the change in the position of the sun, that we were steaming to the north, up the coasts of Portugal and Spain.

Rough seas were encountered on June 7th. It tossed the *Tenadores* about some, and caused me and others to visit the railing where we participated in an unpleasant ritual called "feeding the fish."

Although we were never threatened by submarines, there was one short-lived event off the coast of Portugal that scared the daylights out of everyone. It started innocently enough on June 8th when Hughes and I drew the evening watch on the aft mast.

We ascended the ladder and inched our way onto the plate. The hard metal offered little comfort as I wedged my back against the steel shaft and secured the safety belt. I thought I'd be clever on this trip to the sky and had tied a sweater around my waist. The plan was to use it as a cushion. In fact, the plate felt almost comfortable with the sweater under my bottom. The *Tenadores* was running with the wind and the seas were calm. The mast rocked in the gentlest manner. I reveled in the semi-tropical warmth as we steamed toward nightfall. In the fading light I watched soldiers mill about on the deck below. They seemed distant, detached from the reality that defined Hughes and me on this small piece of metal. From my lofty throne I felt like the exalted ruler of those below me.

The white wake stretched out behind the ship, creating the only blemish on a greenish-blue ocean whose tint ever deepened in the dimming light. Troop carriers, freighters, and destroyer escorts were visible in the distance, seemingly immobile, as if part of a picture post card. Out beyond the convoy, the ocean's far horizon formed an arc with the sky bright to the west, in the direction of the setting sun. When my gaze rotated to the east, the sky darkened toward the oncoming night. Distant lightning exposed clouds. I marveled at the scene around me, with its gorgeous changing colors. It held a poignant beauty, yet the vast expanse before me was humbling. I felt small and insignificant against its grandeur.

Hughes also sensed the overwhelming feeling of smallness, for out of nowhere he asked. "Say, Edwards, do you think God forgot about us up here?"

"Do you mean you and me here in the nest? Or everyone else in this horrid war? Either way, I hope He's not forgotten us."

He laughed. "I hope I live long enough to experience a beauty like this again."

"We both will," I answered.

"Hey, tell the bridge we're here."

I flexed around and pushed the button five times. Five buzzes came back.

"Look there," I said, pointing to the northwest. The darkness settled around us and the flashes of distant lightning streaking across distant clouds was more obvious. It was far ahead of us and slightly to the port. I counted seconds till thunder rose, but no rumble came across the sea.

"I don't hear anything. Must be a long way off," said Hughes.

"You got that right. It's well beyond the ring of our ships."

The *Tenadores* continued to roll in the Atlantic swells as she steamed forward, and the gentle sway of the nest relaxed and soothed us. Hughes and I scanned the sea for submarines and time passed. The sky grew black revealing a canopy of stars that painted a glow across the heavens. The flashes drew nearer.

"Why the hell are we here at night?" I asked. "I can't see a damn thing. Those subs can't see anything as long as the portholes are covered. This is crazy."

I couldn't see it but Hughes probably rolled his eyes as he did every time I lodged a complaint.

"Edwards, that's the fifth time you've said the same thing. Do you like being a needle stuck in the groove?"

I chuckled. "Hey, at least I've got you to get me unstuck!"

"Yeah, that's rich. You gotta stop being so pissed, Edwards."

"Cripes, Hughes, you my mother, or what?"

A bolt suddenly escaped through the clouds to the northwest. Our heads snapped in its direction.

"Hey, that's closer." I said.

"Sure as hell is," Hughes replied, as a low rumble passed through the nest half a minute later.

Neither of us spoke for the next hour. The stars winked out as cloud cover shrouded the ship. The distant flashes neared and brightened. Thunder grew steadily louder, and the wind built, gradually at first, and then more briskly. The nest, as though on a long lever, began to rock. I wouldn't say we were concerned. Nevertheless, Hughes remarked, "Wow, haven't felt it sway like this before."

"A bit more exciting 'eh," I said.

A shaft of blinding light suddenly stretched in a torturous path from the heavens to the sea. The brilliant stroke lit the sky, releasing frightening tendrils that radiated overhead from the main bolt. I began counting, "One, two, three, four, five," at six, thunder roared.

"What's it, Edwards, little over four seconds to the mile? Shit, it's only a mile and a half away."

In the darkness I reassured my foothold on the plate and wedged my back against the mast.

"You tight?" Hughes asked.

Before I could answer a burst of shouting came from below.

"Everyone, back to your bunks, right now. Get moving. This is not a drill," yelled an unseen voice. I heard rapid shuffling as men jammed the stairwells and heavy metal doors slammed shut. A moment later only the wind and more frequent thunder rolls filled the air. Abruptly, the buzzer blared three paired pulses, paused and repeated the sequence, paused and repeated a third time; the 'Warning' signal. Hughes and I instinctively tugged on our safety belts and pushed our bodies against the mast.

"What's all that commotion about?" asked Hughes.

"Damned if I know. Maybe something to do with the lightning."

The night protected me, for I'd have been terrified if there were enough light to see the wall of water barreling toward us, pushed by a malevolent swirling black cloud at the front of the squall line. Moments later the *Tenadores* plowed headlong into the maelstrom. The bow, awash in ten feet of water, thrust upward as the giant wave rolled under the ship. The mast shook and my back crushed against the shaft as we crested the mound of water. Just as quick the bow settled into the trough behind the wave, causing the mast to jerk forward sharply. I'd have been catapulted into space were it not for the belt. I grabbed for my sweater as the bow rose again, but it was gone. My hands thrashed about to grasp a hand grip, but missed as the ship rolled into the trough of the next wave. The safety belt held, and when the bow rose again, I slammed back against the shaft with an impact that drove the air from my lungs. Gasping, I found a grip and struggled to hold tight.

The full fury of the squall descended on the ship. The violent stem-to-stern yawing and extreme rolling threw Hughes and me around like weightless sacks. The nest leapt upward then plunged downward, and just as suddenly veered to the left or right, while at the same time thrusting forward and backward. The wind howled in our ears. Hughes must have sensed a shift in wind direction and yelled. "The Captain's bringing us into the wind."

"Hold on!" I yelled back, not knowing what else to say.

The ship struggled to change course as the wind drove rain drops, like tiny darts, into my exposed face. I ducked, tried to shield myself. It didn't help. Droplets forced themselves under my tunic, drenching my shirt.

The demonic lightning flashes followed by thunder claps so deafening I felt them slam into my chest, consumed me with terror. My grasp on the grips now so tight my finger nails sliced into the skin of my palms. Hughes and I were clinging precariously to life as the tempest grew. In a response of madness that showed complete separation from rational thought, I forced every ounce of breath from my lungs in a fruitless cry. "Stop this!" I yelled. My voice, absorbed in the swirling vortex assured that no one heard, no one answered, no one cared.

Suddenly, Hughes' body flipped to one side. I heard him shriek above the roaring wind,
"THE CLIP BROKE!"

His legs tossed outward as he clung to the grips. The nest jerked back just in time, and a flash of lightning revealed the broken bracket and unconnected clip. The next flash made visible the look of panic on Hughes' face, as he desperately sought to secure his hold. A moment later the ship rocked back and his body slammed against mine. He screamed: "EDWARDS, GRAB ME." I clutched at his jacket. One end of Hughes' safety belt still held, and when the mast rocked forward again, I pulled hard on him. Guided by the lightning flashes, my hand lunged for the intact clip bouncing at the end of his belt. Hughes saw what was happening and with all his strength pulled himself tighter to the mast, as I snapped his clip to my bracket.

"The bracket broke," I shouted.

As the maelstrom raged, Hughes jerked on his belt. Assured of its security I could barely hear him say, "How the hell'd that happen?"

The two of us clutched at the grips as the storm raged.

The squall passed as suddenly as it had begun. The tumultuous sea calmed and the nest, as if by a miracle, returned to its gentle sway. The violent shifts and their sudden cessation churned our stomachs, and we both leaned over the edge of the plate and retched. Our "technicolor yawns" plopped onto the wet deck below. Out of the dark I heard the buzzer signal from the bridge asking if we were still there. Hughes reached around and coded the "Acknowledge" reply.

Thirty-five minutes later the relief crew came up the ladder. A voice in the darkness announced, "Reston reporting for watch." Reston changed positions with Hughes, and asked, "How did you guys do in the storm?"

"It was interesting," I replied, not in the mood for more.

Still unnerved, Hughes grunted, and finding the ladder rungs, disappeared into the black. I followed.

With unsteady steps we crept along the railing to the mess hall. In the darkness, just before entering, Hughes reached out and gripped my shoulder.

"Hold up, Edwards. I thought I was finished up there. I owe you one."

"Hey, you'd have done the same for me."

"Maybe I'll get the chance."

I closed the door to the galley behind me and stepped through a slit in the curtain. The coffee smelled especially good and I felt invigorated. Surviving that wild ride and keeping my friend safe seemed like fate had tested me. I had acquitted myself well and a new sense of confidence surged in my blood.

❦

The destroyers broke contact with the convoy on the morning of June 9th as troop carriers and supply ships entered the mouth of the Gironde River. Particles of silt leached from the plains of Aquitaine colored the river chocolate-brown. A deeper ruddy tint emerged when the flow of the Dordogne, draining the ancient French landscape to the east, joined the flow. Tidal action, strong currents, and the narrowing gauge of the river made the 105 kilometer trip up-river tricky.

By 0500 on the morning of June 10th the four cargo ships tied-up at the port of Bassens. The troop carriers continued upstream another seven kilometers and docked along the quay of Bordeaux.

The finest wines in the world, for centuries, had journeyed forth from this ancient Roman port. Now the finest blood of America arrived at the same place. Harry Edwards's life had undergone more changes and adventure in the last month than in all his twenty-one years, but he couldn't anticipate in his wildest imagination what lay ahead.

PART TWO

CHAPTER 8. Camp Neuf to Brittany

June 10, 1918; The Port of Bordeaux, Bordaux, France.

The ten troop carriers docked in single file forming a line of ships that extended one and a half kilometers along the Bordeaux waterfront. *Tenadores*, the second in line, berthed opposite a building with an imposing façade that was set-back from the river's edge. The *Place de la Bourse* dominated the riverfront. To the left and right of the *Bourse* were the wine warehouses whose storerooms were filled with barrels of expertly aged vintage waiting to be rolled to the freighters that arrived between American convoys.

In front of the warehouses, and paralleling the waterfront, coursed the *Quai des Chartrons*. The road teemed with strange looking motor cars and trucks. They scooted among horse drawn vehicles blaring horns that demanded their slower brethren get out of the way. A flimsy wooden barrier, on the river side of the road, separated the debarking troops from hundreds of gawking school children, riveted by the early morning flurry of activity. In the distance, the *Pont De Pierre* served as the bridge that connected Bordeaux to towns on the eastern side of the river.

⊷

I lifted the forty-five pound pack over one shoulder, and wiggled my arm through the other strap. Hughes and I climbed out of the bowels of the *Tenadores* at 0730 hours into a humid, overcast morning, I felt solid ground for the first time in days, and Hughes commented, on stepping off the gang-way, "At least I ain't 'feedin the fish' anymore."

Sergeants shouting along the quay struggled to get men in formation, and somewhere in the chaos the regimental band struck up a tune. Columns of men formed four abreast and snaked southward along the muddy quay. Hughes and I flowed with the column toward the bridge. Mid-way across the river the elevation afforded a dazzling scene. The space between the *Chartrons* and the waterfront was alive with troops disgorged from the ships. I could see that cranes were already unloading the stuff that would make us an army.

Thousands of men wound their way toward the bridge. Framing the spectacle, the red rooftops of the city skyline rose above the riverfront buildings, and beyond them church spires thrust into a cloudy sky. Like a gaping mouth, the river stretched in a straight line downstream to the point where land and water disappeared in the mist. Ahead of us men stepped off the bridge on the eastern side of the river, greeted by a large sign that announced the town of Cenon. Coming off the bridge the column veered north, and the troops walked on the *Quai des Queyries*, which paralleled the river.

June 10, 1918; Quai des Queyries, Cenon, France.

I heard Gillespie spell-out, "C-h-a-r-c-u-t-e-r-i-e" from a sign he spied above a shop.

"Must be a butcher shop," I said.

"Can't be, Edwards," said Hughes, "Those are sausages hanging in the window. Looks like blocks of raw bacon beside 'em."

"Look, back in the corner, it's a shank of ham. This place just sells pork," offered Charlie Powell.

"Edwards, open the left side pocket of my pack," Gillespie interrupted. "I've a French to English dictionary. Get it out, we'll figure out what's going on."

I reached around, unsnapped the pouch and removed a small brown book with gold lettering on the cover.

"Hey, look there," said Ollie Baker, pointing at a basket filled with bread sticks.

"B-o-u-l-a-n-g-e-r-i-e," I spelled from the sign painted on the shop window. Gillespie looked in his book. "Bread bakery."

"Like you couldn't tell from the window," I said.

The line came to a halt. At that moment an old lady abruptly stepped out of the storefront door, grabbed a number of bread loves from the basket. The woman had tears of what I assumed were joy streaming from her eyes. She took several loafs and shoved one into Jake Osborn's hand, then handed out the others along the line.

"*Pour les Américains. Merci! Merci!*" she shouted, happily waving at the troops as we moved on.

"Well. Ahh, that's damn decent Ma'am," Osborn called back to her. He sniffed the loaf, broke off a piece. "Jeez, this sure smells good."

Osborn handed the loaf to Hughes who broke off a chunk. He passed it to me and I tore off another piece, and sent it along to Gillespie, who passed it back to Doyle.

After taking a bite, I exclaimed, "Tastes great. It's even a bit warm."

"Wow, 'bout the best damn bread I've ever had," said Doyle.

I nodded in agreement, while compelled to add, "Yeah. Well anything would taste good now. When are they going to get us breakfast?"

The column passed its first café with morning patrons seated around little outdoor tables.

"Vive les Américains! Vive les Américains! Vive l'Amérique!" they shouted.

"Jeez," commented Baker. "They're drinking booze and it's not even noon."

"Don't think it's hard liquor, just wine," added Jake Osborn.

"Maybe these Frenchies are more civilized than we think," said Goldrick.

A grizzled looking man, couldn't be younger than fifty, sat opposite a very attractive young woman. Unkempt hair and stubble on his face suggested he hadn't bathed or shaved in days. The stump of an unlit cigarette dangled from his mouth. He tenderly stroked her hand.

Doyle caught me looking. "She must be his daughter," I said.

"Damn, Edwards, you live on a farm or somethin'? You ever seen a father and daughter hold hands like that?"

One of the guys gave the 'cat call' whistle to the young woman. She glanced at the line of troops and smiled. Her disheveled partner sharply raised his right arm with a closed fist in the universal gesture. They both began laughing and shouting while waving at the new arrivals.

"How the hell that old guy find such a good looker?" wondered Hughes.

"Maybe he's loaded," Doyle replied. "But if she's after looks, I'd make the perfect replacement."

The man abruptly pushed back his chair, caught hold of the wine bottle,and limped to the line of soldiers. The bottle was quickly passed around, and the fourth man only tasted dregs.

"Hey, c'mon, pass the bottle back here," Hughes shouted.

"You need to be quicker," I told him.

"Damn," he responded. "I was hoping for some French civility."

The squad walked on.

"Hughes, did you see the damn road sign? Its name just changed. Now this road's called something like *Rue Lecocq.* "What kind of a street name is that?" asked Doyle.

Baker didn't miss a beat. "This street must attract the ladies."

Hughes and I laughed. *Rue Lecocq,* it was too much.

Our line wound slowly out of town and entered the countryside. After a while, Bill Ford asked, "Say, you guys notice anything different back in town?"

"What the hell you talking about Ford? It was all strange!"

"Hughes, I know it's all weird. But did you guys see it? No young men. There were kids, women, old men. No young ones."

Hughes looked at his watch. "They're at work, maybe out in the fields."

"Or, maybe something else," I said.

Step by step, each pace carried us ever northward.

June 10, 1918, Camp Génicart, France.

Six kilometers from Cenon, Camp Génicart was a sprawling complex of rest stations, and we were headed to called Camp Neuf, the ninth rest station. The barrack was a mess and it stunk like the toilets hadn't been cleaned. We selected bunks, and groused. Just then Sedelsky entered with Lieutenant Harden behind him. "Ah-tenn-tion," Sarge shouted.

"At ease. Men, this camp's a hole and you all see that. Major says we're here for three, maybe four days till we get transportation out of here organized. Clean this place up; make it livable. Sergeant, assign details." They saluted, and Harden walked out.

Before Sedelsky could issue instructions, Jake Osborn asked, "Sarge, when's the chow served?"

"Not till this place is cleaned. There're buckets, brushes, and brooms in the back. Baker and Edwards, get the heads and the showers cleaned. Adams, Nightlinger, I want those windows washed so I can see in!" Sarge pointed at Ford and Gillespie. "You two, find the quarter-master depot and get sheets. The rest of youse gobs get these bunks outside, air out the mattresses, shake the blankets, get this place swept out. The quicker youse get this done, the sooner we get to the mess hall. Now get the lead out, I'm hungry."

"Hell," I muttered, "Why do I get the crap jobs?"

"Hey, Edwards, aren't you the who wants to be a plumber?" responded Baker

The morning of June 13th the First and Second Battalion of the 315th retraced their steps to the rail head at Bassens where troop trains waited our arrival. They'd carry us to our training camp in Brittany, four hundred and fifty kilometers north. Forty men in the four squads of the third platoon of Battery B were assigned to train number eleven. I saw large, white letters painted on the dark red sides of our boxcars: "*Hommes 40, Chevaux 8.*"

Gillespie consulted his dictionary. "Hey. That means that it's forty men or eight horses per car."

"Jeez," Doyle lamented. "We'll be jammed in there like sheep. There'll hardly be room to breathe."

Sedelsky shouted to the men. "Word's come down we've a long ride. Major says three squads to a car. That way you gobs can lie down."

"Don't tell me the army's showin' good sense!" said Hughes.

"They tell me these cars carried horses," Sedelsky added. "Be sure you get the floor cleaned or you'll stink to hell, or be sick by the time we reach Redon."

Osborn couldn't contain himself. "Sergeant, where's this Redon?"

"I've no idea," he replied.

First, second and third squad climbed into the car. We kicked at the urine-soaked straw and horse droppings. The car still stunk of horse pee, but it was tolerable. Twenty-six hours after leaving Bassens, and within a half kilometer of the town center, three squads of hungry and grumpy men climbed out of the box car and walked into Redon.

CHAPTER 9. The Chateau

June 14, 1918; Redon, France.

Redon was a small town in the region of France called Brittany. It nestled among gentle, rolling hills at the junction of the Oust and Villaine rivers. Over millennia the rivers had carved a deep estuary to the Bay of Biscay, twenty  kilometers to the west. In 1811 the rivers were diverted to supply water to a canal system that served many towns in Brittany.

Redon warehouses once teemed with goods off-loaded from ships arriving in the bay. The war changed all that, and a casual visitor would never know that Redon had once enjoyed importance as a shipping port. The only current activity came from lighters ferrying US Army materials from freighters in the bay.

By June, the Americans commandeered every vacant place in town where men could sleep or war material stored. Some of Redon's citizens complained their new visitors were disrupting their quiet town. However, the pragmatists won the day. Americans were going to save France, and they had lots of money. This was our training base for the next two months.

Second Squad billeted a kilometer west of town in a small barn. It was one of many buildings spread in a half-circle behind a large manor house. Le Chateau Mongeort lay in disrepair. One old man lived in the basement and cared for the building as best he could. Word had it the owner left for the front in 1914 and hadn't been heard from since.

The officers and non-commissioned officers of Battery B billeted in semi-comfort in the Chateau, while the platoons slept on the floors of surrounding barns, storehouses, or cottages. The main road out of Redon passed in front of the Chateau and connected Redon to the western towns of Brittany. Drill practice, horse training, and wagon maneuvers occurred on a large open field across the road from Mongeort.

∾

Second squad entered the barn and explored the digs.

"This ain't so bad," said Phil Doyle. "There's plenty of dry straw to sleep on."

While the guys explored below, I clambered into the loft to check it out. After a quick look around, I hollered down. "Hey. Lots more clean straw up here and plenty of boards."

Ernie Gillespie spied a wood stove in a small rear room.

"Sarge. There's a stove back here with lots of firewood. We can warm coffee on it."

"Okay, youse gobs get yourselves fixed up in here. I'll be back at 1200 and we'll head to the mess hall." Sarge walked through the large barn doors. A moment later he was back. "Oh yeah," he called out. "No smoking inside. Should be obvious why."

Jake Osborn placed his bed roll near the barn door.

"Why the hell are you sleeping there?" asked Powell.

"This barn's a damn fire trap and the closer I'm to the door, the happier I'll be," Osborn shot back.

"Well, blame yourself if you get stomped on in the middle of the night when one of us races out to pee."

During mess Sedelsky was bombarded with questions.

"Say, Sarge when are the wagons arriving?" Doyle asked.

"When you make 'em. We start building the first one tomorrow morning."

That took us by surprise.

"Sarge, so after we assemble the wagons, where are the horses?" Ford asked.

"There're on the way," is all Sarge told us.

"From where?" I asked.

"Look, Edwards, when I know, you'll know," he snapped, annoyed at all the questions. Sarge then he eased back, "Listen up, men. If you guys want to get into the action you'll need to look sharp over the next week or so. Lieutenant's going to pick the driver and brakemen for the three rigs. All the supply sections in the company will receive instructions for two weeks starting as soon as we complete the wagon assembly. That's when you'll learn what's needed to do your jobs."

"Edwards, we want a wagon," Hughes whispered to me. "Then we'll get some action. We gotta look sharp."

CHAPTER 10. Wagon Assembly

June 16, 1918, The Wagon Assembly Warehouse, Redon, France.

Parts for two hundred wooden combat wagons were off-loaded from freighters in the Bay of Biscay. The parts were ferried up the estuary, and hauled by locals to the assembly warehouses. There'd be enough parts for three wagons per supply squad in the whole regiment. The wooden pieces were painted army green, while the cast-iron fittings that held the wagon together were black. There were no predrilled holes for the bolts or screws. Worse yet, we had no instructions, just a drawing of what a finished wagon looked like. We worked blind on the first one.

Sergeant Sedelsky, a regular army vet with thirty-two years of service, had grown up in a North Philadelphia, Polish neighborhood. In 1886, at sixteen, he had enlisted to escape an abusive father. He served first in a cavalry unit posted to the Nebraska Territories. Reassigned to the Second Artillery Regiment in 1897, he landed in Cuba in the summer of '98. Sedelsky remained garrisoned in Havana for several years before being transferred to the Panama Canal Zone. Promoted to Sergeant in '08, he was reassigned in 1912 to the Twelfth Cavalry in Texas commanded by "Black Jack" Pershing. Sedelsky arrived at Camp Lee in early 1917, charged with taking draftees and turning them into solders for the 80th Division.

He was a stocky man with a long deep scar running the width of his forehead. He never talked about how he got the scar, and none of us had the grit to ask. His appearance broadcast a man you didn't trifle with. Curt and crusty, he never wasted words. Sarge doled out work duty and punishment fairly, offered public praise, and criticized in instructive ways. Over campfire coffee he laughed and swore with the best of us. We saw him as experienced and wise. We trusted his judgment, and beneath a gruff exterior was a surrogate father for rambunctious young men.

∽

After breakfast on June 12th, Second Squad entered the wagon workshop. A continuous stream of orders flowed from Sedelsky that kept us busy for the next three hours. Row upon row of preassembled wagon beds, stacked three or four high, covered the supply room floor. Sarge had us get our hands under the bed of one and lift it off the pile. The damn thing was made with thick oak planks and certainly was sturdy. Must have weighed over 150 kilograms. Assured of a firm grip, the ten of us carried it to our assembly station.

The station—nothing more than four large wooden blocks—held the wagon bed half a meter off the ground. Sedelsky barked orders that sent pairs of men rushing to the stockroom for parts, and gradually the assembled wagon emerged until only attaching the wheels remained.

"Okay, Gillespie, Osborn, start rolling the wheels over here." The two men hustled to the front of the supply room where a collection of wheels lay on the floor. The supply officer pointed to the ones they needed. For some reason the dirt floor at the front of the supply room was wet and slippery. They struggled to lever a wheel off the floor, into a vertical position.

"Damn. This thing's heavy," said Osborn.

When half-way up, Osborn's left boot lost its grip on the wet floor. For a moment the whole weight rested on Gillespie.

"Shit, Osborn, get a hold, I can't manage by myself."

While Osborn struggled to regain his footing, Gillespie's boots also slipped.

"Look out!" Gillespie yelled, as the rim slipped from his hands and dropped to the floor. Osborn leapt back and the wheel hit with a loud thud, narrowly missing his boot. Sedelsky rushed over, mad as hell.

"You damn jerks. Be careful. I don't need one of youse idiots in the hospital because a wheel fell on ya? Watch yourselves!"

"Sarge....Ahhh.... The floor was slippery," stammered Osborn.

"Don't give me excuses. Now, get the wheel over to the wagon."

The two men levered the sixty kilogram wheel into an upright position, and rolled it toward the wagon. As the rest of the wheels got propped-up nearby, Jim Nightlinger got a tub of axle grease and a brush.

"Okay. You two," ordered Sedelsky. "Go over to the stockroom and get four jacks."

Charlie Powell and Phil Doyle retrieved the jacks, wrestled them into position, and the frame was soon higher off the floor.

"Edwards and Baker, get under the wagon. Secure the front axle and swivel. Ford and Hughes, attach the rear axle mounts. The rest of youse gobs surround the wagon and grasp the edges to steady the bed."

"Edwards, you sure those jacks are safe? We'll be crushed under here if they aren't," said Ford.

It was a bit scary every time the wagon wobbled, but twenty minutes later, with axles in place, the four of us scooted out.

"Roll over one of the rear wheels," Sedelsky instructed.

Hughes and Powell, on either side at the rear of the wagon, adjusted the jack height so the wheel hole and axle rod were aligned. Nightlinger swabbed a generous helping of grease onto the shaft while four of the guys wiggled the wheel back and forth, and, by brute force, lifted it slightly and shoved it onto the shaft. Ollie Baker slipped a retaining plate over the protruding end, reached into his pocket to retrieve a large cotter pin, and secured the wheel. Within half an hour the other three wheels were attached.

Sarge told two boys to retrieve the wagon pole, and it was bolted to the tongue. When the assembly was finished, Jim Nightlinger positioned stencils and Ollie Baker dabbed paint over them. The rest of us admired the bold red lettering on the wagon's side: *315th Field Artillery, Battery B, No. 20.*

Sedelsky faced the Squad. "Okay, boys, she's looking good. Everyone pulled together. I'm proud of youse gobs, you did a nice job. Now let's load her up and push it back to the barn."

We agreed that it was one fine-looking wagon. Sedelsky had us load tack for four animals, lengths of rope, horseshoes, tools, and other wagon supplies into the bed. Forty minutes later, the wagon was pushed to the field behind the barn, and everyone collapsed to catch their breath.

"Damn, pushin' that was work," griped Hughes.

"Okay, boys, we're not done yet. Got two more to finish tomorrow. Now, let's get those supplies into the barn. It's off to supper at 1230, so get cleaned up."

Two days later three new war wagons sat behind the barn. There were no horses in sight yet. Meanwhile, Lieutenant Harden had selected Hughes and me as one of the three pairs of driver and brakeman, and Sarge assigned us to Wagon Twenty. The other teams were Gillespie and Doyle and Adams and Powell.

After morning calisthenics, breakfast, and drill practice, the squad spent the next three hours in instruction. They were mostly easy with the exception of map reading. I slowly gained a feel in my head of how long a kilometer was, and Hughes got better at reading the names of French roads and interpreting road signs. Like back at Camp Lee, we had practical training on loading, securing, and unloading dummy artillery shells; the proper way to handle and secure powder bags, and where to stow fuses.

On the first day of instruction Lieutenant Warwick, a man with a rounded face, protruding ears, and slicked back blond hair, entered the room. He had a presumptuous air about him. Sedelsky called us to attention.

"Good morning, gentlemen. At ease." Warwick introduced himself. He was a no-nonsense, to the point, and too-much- information kind of guy.

"The war wagon you drive carries a maximum of 1,363 kilograms. That's close to 3,000 pounds of artillery rounds, powder casings, fuses, emergency tools, and two men." He added that each wheel had a 5.0-cm wide steel band bolted to the rim. This made the wagon more stable in mud. He emphasized that the wagons were strong, but with a full load, they could break an axle or shatter wheel spokes when driven hard on rough ground.

We learned that field repairs were our problem. A disabled rig was as useless as if it had been blown up. Each 155-mm shell weighed forty-three kilograms (ninety-four pounds) and was color coded. One, two or three red bands indicated a charge of tear, mustard or phosgene gas. A single green band signaled chlorine. A blue band meant high explosive, and yellow contained a shrapnel charge. Shells with a White Star on the casing contained a mixture of phosgene and chlorine.

"Your wagon can carry 22 shells, and they are mounted in a pair of parallel, grooved racks on the wagon bed. A strap, drawn tight over the rack, secures the shells. Be sure that strap is tight," added Warwick. "Last thing you want is a shell bouncing in the back of the wagon. They won't explode, but get knocked by one and you're likely dead."

Outside the classroom, we practiced loading and unloading the dummy shells, and Warwick insisted we wear gloves. "Powder bags could burn your hands if you make contact with them," he said.

"I don't understand," said Ollie Baker. "You wouldn't be holding those bags if they were on fire."

"No you wouldn't. I mean a chemical burn," added Warwick. "The skin will blister up if you come in contact with the powder inside the bags."

"Oh," responded Baker.

CHAPTER 11. Andalusians

June 22, 1918; Le Chateau Mongeort, Redon, France.

Nineteen train cars carrying over 150 Andalusian stallions arrived in the railroad yard this morning. These gorgeous animals were distributed among the thirty-six supply wagons of Battery B. The unconfirmed rumor was that these horses had been smuggled across the Spanish border. Regardless of where they came from, there was little 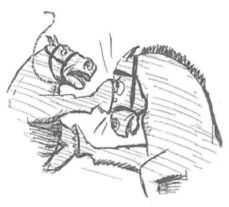 doubt that these were the finest animals in the Battalion. By 1300 hours, twelve of these studs were assigned to our three wagons.

❧

"Okay, men. We need a picket line. Make it long enough for six staggered animals on each side. Tie loops in the line at two-and-a-half meter intervals."

"Where do you want it, Sarge?" asked Baker.

"There's an apple tree behind the barn, Baker. Tie one end of the rope to it. Baker and Hughes, go search for something to use as a stake for the other end."

"We're on it, Sarge," said Hughes.

Meanwhile, I helped tie loops onto the picket line rope. The loops provided places to clip the lead line from the horse's bridal.

"Sarge told us to tie the loops every two and a half meters," said Jim Nightlinger. "Let's make it every two meters, then we don't have to move around so much."

"I'm not so sure," I said.

"Sounds good to me," offered Charlie Powell.

What the hell would a truck driver and a railroad guy know? I had never set a picket line so I really couldn't argue either way. We tied the loops at two meter intervals. Within an hour, six horses were tethered on one side of the line, six on the other, in a staggered fashion. The animals, exhausted from their travels, stood quietly.

Right after breakfast next day Hughes and I harnessed our four Andulusians and mounted the other tack to mate them with the wagon pole. It was obvious these animals weren't too happy with their new restriction, and they were slow to calm after they were hitched to the wagon. With the first team ready to roll, Will Adams called out, "Edwards. Did you see what your horse just did?"

"Yeah. He tried to bite the tail of the animal in front of him. Damndest thing I've ever seen."

"Me too," replied Adams.

With the stallions hitched to the wagon, each brakeman walked his team down the Chateau driveway and onto the training field. We drivers held the reins lightly. Once on the field, I began to train the team to pull the wagon on command.

Hughes and I happened to glance toward Wagon Twenty-Two. Adams and Powell were at the back of the rig when, suddenly, the left front and rear horses started a raucous whinnying, shaking their heads up and down. The lead horse shifted position to raise its rear left leg, and a moment later slashed its' hoof backward, just missing the chest of the Andalusian behind it. It happened in a blink.

"What the hell?" I shouted.

Hughes also saw it. "Hey, Adams," he called. "One of your lead horses just tried to kick the one behind it."

Over supper Will Adams voiced his concern. "Sarge, there's something with those animals. I swear they look like they're attacking one another. Ain't ever seen anything like that before."

"Don't worry about it," Sarge said. "Those animals are agitated because they've never been hitched-up. They need gettin' used to it. Besides, Spanish stallions are high strung, just as rambunctious as youse boys. Just keep a watch on 'em."

Each animal was again hitched to the wagon pole by mid-morning the next day. Some still struggled with the confinement, but soon all accepted their fate. By the end of day they were acting as a team, pulling our wagons and responding to commands. As the training intensified, they had little time to play dominance games.

Nevertheless, the squad again reported peculiar behaviors. Sedelsky finally witnessed an event with the rear two horses of wagon twenty-one. One of them leaned over and bit the neck of his neighbor.

"Gillespie, what the hell did you do to get them horses riled up?"

"Nothing, Sarge. They just started acting crazy."

Sedelsky shouted. "You crews be careful. They ain't trained yet, and there's something goin' on. I don't know if it's us or them."

I was jolted awake at 0330 hours on June 23rd when Lieutenant Harden and Sedelsky burst into the barn. Harden's lantern cast flickering shadows across the walls as Sedelsky yelled. "Out of bed youse gobs. Form up, now!" We shrugged off sleep, squirmed out of our sleeping rolls and stood in line.

"Ah-tennn-shon!" shouted the Sergeant.

"At ease," ordered Harden. "Why are those horses carrying on out there? The Colonel can't sleep with that racket. Now get out there and quiet those damn animals." He faced Sedelsky. "Pronto!" Harden handed him the lantern, and walked out the door.

Sedelsky instructed his startled squad, "Listen up, men. The tie points are too close together and the lead line's too long. The damn stallions can reach one another and they're fighting over who's boss. Youse need to widen the tie points and shorten the lead line. Grab the extra lanterns so you can see what you're doing. Let's go."

The stallions were at war. Along the picket line, nostrils flared, and black irises, dilated with rage, swam in a sea of white. We heard snapping teeth and whinnies that sounded more like shrieks.

Will Adams hollered, "Sarge, be careful. They'll nip at anything that comes between 'em."

"Come at each animal slowly from the side," Sedelsky shouted. "Don't get behind or in front of 'em. Move up slowly, grab the lead rope, control the head and pull it down. Unhook the lead from the picket line and get 'em separated."

Ernie Gillespie approached the horse's head. As he did, the raging horse threw its' head to the side. Startled by the sudden shift, Gillespie's hand lurched for the lead rope. As he grabbed the line, the animal's head shot down and bared teeth clamped shut around his palm.

A blood-curdling scream erupted from Gillespie's throat, and he slammed the horse's head with the palm of his other hand. The shocked animal opened its mouth and jerked away, before it clamped down hard. Gillespie jumped back, shaking his hand.

Jim Nightlinger saw it and ran to Gillespie . "Sarge! Sarge!" he yelled. "Gillespie's got bit."

Sedelsky rushed over. "What the hell happened?"

"Damn horse bit me. Christ. It hurts like hell."

"Let me see. Yeah, it's discolored, but no bleeding. You got a nasty pinch."

"Sure as hell did," Gillespie replied.

"It'll be black and blue for a few days. You'll live. Okay, men, back to it."

Bill Ford grew up in the city. He'd never been around horses, and those huge stallions scared the hell out of him. He'd been telling me as much over the past two days.

Ford approached an animal at the far end of the line. His steps were cautious as he approached the side of the animal. With trepidation he advanced slowly till he could grab hold of the lead line and pull the animal's head down. In doing so, Ford unfortunately stepped in front of the horse. The Andalusian on the opposite side of the picket line rose on its hind legs, its eyes blazing with rage. The stallion lashed out with its front leg, and the edge of its hoof slashed down, slicing into the side of Ford's thigh. Howling in pain, he fell to one knee and rolled to his side.

"Help! Help me!" he cried as he struggled to crawl away.

I ran to Ford.

"Edwards, the horse cut me. Jeez, it hurts."

I rolled him onto his side.

"Oh my God, it hurts."

A vertical slit had opened the pants over the muscles of his upper leg, a red piece of meat protruded from the wound. Blood spurted into the air, a gush with each pump of his heart. Ford's eyes rolled into his head and he passed out. Adams and Powell were at my side in seconds.

"Edwards, he's going to bleed out. Do something," shouted Doyle.

I grabbed Doyle's hand and forced the palm over the wound, "Put pressure on it."

"Get me a stick," I yelled to Powell. "This long. This thick. Now. Now."

I pulled off my undershirt as Powell took off at a dead run for the tree line. The rest of the squad rushed to us. Sedelsky sized up what had happened and knelt down beside me.

"Baker, run to the Chateau and get Doc. Quick!" he shouted.

I used my penknife to cut the shirt in half, then rolled it up into a long tube.

The cloth roll looped around Ford's upper thigh, above the gaping wound and blood-soaked pant leg. I tied it into place with an over-hand knot. Powell returned with the stick and I said, "Put it here." Using the ends of the shirt, I tied another knot, then rotated the stick to tighten the shirt roll against Ford's leg. After a few turns, the tourniquet drew tight.

"Take your hand away, Doyle," and with another half turn the blood flow stopped.

"What time is it?" I called. "0347," said Osborn.

"Everyone, remember that."

Five minutes later, Doc arrived in his night shirt and unlaced boots. "When did the bleeding stop?" he demanded.

"Five minutes ago," I replied.

"We need to return circulation. Loosen it slowly, soldier." Doc compressed the wound, as I turned the stick in reverse.

"Sergeant, send one of the men to the first aid station. Tell them we need a litter immediately."

Two orderlies, carrying a stretcher with a Red Cross nurse in tow, arrived twenty minutes later. I helped get Ford strapped on the stretcher, and Doc accompanied the orderlies, as the nurse, holding a lantern, led the group away.

Next day, before supper, Sedelsky entered the barn and announced Ford would live. He had surgery, a blood transfusion, sixteen stitches, and was now conscious.

"The muscle's torn badly and he's headed back to the States," Sarge said. "You saved his life, Edwards."

A few days later I wrote a long letter to Mother. I didn't mention the dust-up with the horses, no need to concern her, and most likely the censor would black it out. Otherwise most everything in the letter was true.

Somewhere in France
June 27, 1918
Dear Mother,

I am well and hope all of you are the same. They finally paid me all of seventeen dollars in French money. Mother, the paper money is colorful, but some of it's so tiny, more like tobacco tags. I spent my tobacco tags on pictures, food, and souvenirs in town.

The town we are in is beautiful this time of year and all the Chestnut trees along the streets are heavy with nuts. Well Mother, they are harvesting the spring wheat now. The women help mow with a scythe, same as men. Some use oxen to pull their mowing machine.

I haven't seen a wooden house or barn. Every building is made of stone and certainly put-up to stay. The town square has very old, lovely buildings. Mother, friends and I are granted leave in the evening to visit town. You can buy almost anything, and a fresh Lady Finger in the market costs five cents. We soldiers buy figs, cherries, dates, oranges, nuts, and candy. All kind of junk to eat. You will be pleased to know they don't sell tobacco or cigarettes at all. Mother, there are many cafés where my friends and I stop for supper. The French food is different with some meals delicious.

They do lots of fishing in the canal, and I have been in town Monday evening when they have a very good meat and fish market. Mother, they sell everything, right out on the street: pigs, chickens, cows, oxen, carp, dry goods, everything imaginable. The beer and wine flow more plentiful than water, but I don't drink any.

My friend Steve Hughes and I have good times together. All my friends are like brothers to me. We loan each other anything we have. Tell Emily in my next letter I'm going to send her some pictures of Hughes and me. I am going to drive a wagon and our horses came the other day. They are beautiful animals.

You ought to see them fellows running for their mail. I run to get mine and I received your welcomed letter yesterday. Would you mail me some pictures of Emily as my friends want to know what she looks like? Ask Emily to tell me how Fannie is when she writes next. I suspect she's gone to Virginia for the summer. Mother, you should invite the Whites and Fannie over for Sunday dinner in the fall, so you could know them better.

Well, I guess I told you all the important news. I will stop now as I want to write Fannie. I hope you will try and not worry about me and not take it so hard that I am away. I will be with you all soon. Take best of care of yourselves, and I will do the same.

Your loving Son,
HCE

Sedelsky entered the barn just before dinner on June 26th. He had a soldier in tow named Joe Goldrick. Second Squad had to be brought up to strength after Ford's departure, and they'd found a man in a reserve unit. He was one of us now. We welcomed him and Hughes suggested he use Ford's old sleeping spot. I learned that Goldrick was a carpenter. Another journeyman, and that made him right by me. He was about my age, slightly shorter, with an oval face that showed his front teeth when he smiled. Had brown eyes, lighter hair the same color, and a nose a little too large for his face. Goldrick was somewhat overweight. He did his job, did it well, and his most notable feature was that he could tell jokes. That he knew so many amazed me. Goldrick was as good a replacement as we could hope for.

CHAPTER 12. Blue Moon

June 27, 1918: Le Chateau Mongeort, Redon, France,

Throughout the day and night, soldiers rotated through three-hour sentry duty at the entrance to the Chateau, alongside picket lines, or in other locations scattered around the compound. Weapon inspections were randomly conducted by junior officers, or out of nowhere they'd approach a sentry and start bombarding him with questions about army regulations, or challenge signals. An evening pass was denied for failing a question. A weapon that failed inspection brought extra sentry duty. You'd end up in the brig for failing to know the daily challenge and reply words.

At 0800, after returning from morning chow, Lieutenant Harden entered the barn with Sedelsky.

"Ah-tenn-tion! Prepare for inspection," bellowed the Sergeant.

Rifles gathered, the squad formed ranks, and stood to attention. Harden found grease in the chamber of Doyle's, Powell's and my rifle. He ordered Sedelsky to cancel our town passes for the next two days, and had us stand extra night sentry duty.

That night I walked down the driveway to the intersection with the road from Redon, relieving Powell for the three-hour post beginning at 2400 hours.

"Halt. Who goes there?" challenged Powell.

"Private Edwards reporting to post."

"Advance one and be recognized."

I stepped forward a pace and Powell again said, "Halt." He offered the challenge.

"What's your reply?" I gave it.

"Okay, Edwards. It's all yours."

Powell lit a cigarette as he walked back up the driveway. I shouldered my rifel and began pacing.

The night air was warm and still. Shimmers of light from the street lamps around the *Hôtel de Ville* registered Redon in the distance. Across the road the huge training field sloped gently downward. Two hundred meters away a tree line hung low against the night sky. Like a painted canvas, brilliant pinpricks of light peppered the night sky, while the Milky Way cast its soft, incandescent glow.

I paced back and forth across the driveway, six steps each way. At the end of each pace I'd lift the right foot, place the toe behind the left heel and rotate. Two boots snapped together, parallel, facing the opposite direction. I stepped forward, retraced the path, only to repeat the turn. Back and forth, over and over, again and again.

Damn, the only value in pacing is it keeps me awake, I thought..

Six paces forward, turn, and six back. Back and forth, over and over, again and again. The boredom was excruciating. As I fought to keep my eyes on the road, my anger grew. My Enfield was clean, I thought. What the hell do I have to guard anyway? We're at least 400 kilometers from the front. In my anger I lost focus on the guard duty, and it was further distracted by something else.

A soft yellowish glow began to grow above the distant tree line. It slowly resolved into a huge moon, rising steadily over the tree-tops. The white orb captured me, and the back and forth pacing became a reflex-like behavior that completely faded from consciousness. Only the rising moon captured my attention. I don't know where the thought came from, but wasn't this the second full moon of June, a Blue Moon? Another thought rose in my head: Is Fannie looking at this same moon? Suddenly, she and I were connected through that bright ball.

Back and forth, over and over, again and again, but the moon saved me from boredom. I drafted a letter in my head.

Somewhere in France
June 27, 1918
My Dear Fannie,

I hope this finds you well as all is the same for me. I was on sentry duty in the middle of last night because the lieutenant said my rifle wasn't clean. That's wrong, I always keep a clean rifle. After midnight a huge full moon, a Blue Moon, rose over the distant trees. So dramatic, so huge and beautiful, that all I thought about, as I paced, was you. The possibility, that even though we're so far apart, you might also be watching the moon made me feel so close to you.

Remember the night you and I swam at Crum Creek Reservoir after the Compton's party, when another full moon rose over of the water? We held onto each other and watched the weightless orb float higher into the sky. There was just you, me and the moon. The three of us, bound to each other. I wish you were here with me to see this moon. I feel so far away and fear I'll never get home to watch another moon-rise with you. I miss you so much.
With affection,
Harry

CHAPTER 13. Is There a War On?

July 4, 1918; Redon, France.

Life in Redon followed a rigid cadence from the crack of dawn till lights out. The best part of the day came in the afternoon. It might include first aid instruction, practice at the rifle range, grooming horses, or best of all, visits to the canal for a bath. Free time was after supper, between 1830 and lights out. That's when I wrote letters home, or requested a pass to town.

Hughes and I frequented the YMCA Canteen in Redon, which brought a bit of America to us boys. They served free American coffee, sold American tobacco, candy, newspapers and magazines, organized outdoor movies and occasionally presented vaudeville performances. My friends and I took supper in the local bistros, posed for photos, shopped for souvenirs, or ogled the passing ladies from outdoor café tables. It was all surreal. We repressed the fact that four hundred kilometers north, men were slaughtering each other by the tens of thousands.

At breakfast July 4th, 1918, Sedelsky announced that everyone was granted town leave.

"Begins after the review and extends till 2200 hours."

The field in front of our chateau was the venue for the review. Late morning the regiment marched before our commanders. Afterwards a tug-o-war competition among platoons commenced, and despite the cheering, Third Platoon lost after we'd advanced two rounds. I must admit, everyone had a good time at it.

With the competitions concluded the battalion cooks served up hamburgers and hotdogs. There was fresh salad and the army offered a new thing called potato chips. After lunch, the boys over in Battery A carried a victrola to the south end of the field. Soon enough dancing with the local ladies began. I guess the brass had lifted the ban on fraternizing for the day.

"Come on guys. I'm going to grab me a woman," shouted Phil Doyle.

"Sounds good to me," said Jim Nightlinger.

"Naw, not interested," I replied. I wasn't in the mood.

"I'm going with them. See you later, Edwards."

"Jeez, Hughes, you don't dance."

"No time like the present to watch and learn." Hughes caught up with Doyle and Nightlinger, and joined by Goldrick, they walked toward the revelry.

"Say, Edwards. Not into dancing?" asked Gillespie.

I told him no, and reminded him there would be fireworks later on, and that the canteen was putting on a show.

"Want to walk into town?" he asked.

"Sounds good. Don't much fancy standing here watching them have fun. Reminds me too much of Fannie."

"Yeah, same for me with Margaret."

Ernie Gillespie and I collected Adams, Powell, Osborn and Baker, and the six of us set off for town.

We wandered the shops, hunting souvenirs until late afternoon. That's when we began scouting cafés to find a free outdoor table. When seated, wine was ordered and we watched the ladies walk by, talking about each one. We decided to stay for supper and Gillespie ordered Coq-au-Vin. I ordered something from the *Fruits de Mer* section.

"That's seafood, Edwards," said Gillespie.

"You still studying your dictionary?" I asked.

When the waiter arrived, I pointed at a menu entry in complete ignorance. He broke into a broad smile, "*Il est très bon, très bon. Un bon choix.*" I nodded affirmatively as though I knew what he said.

We shared three bottles of wine, two reds and a white. Gillespie seemed to know what to order. My dish had the most delicious crunchy crust and savory center, aided by crisp vegetables. A delicious sauce drenched everything. Problem was, I hadn't a clue what I was eating. As my fork pierced a last piece, a section of the crust broke off. On its way to my mouth I noticed a strange texture to the meat beneath. Looking more closely, there was a round sucker-looking thing staring back at me.

"What the hell's that?" I said.

Gillespie looked at my fork. "I think they call it calamari. I had it last week. The waiter called it 'squid' in English."

"What's a squid?" I asked.

"You got me. But how's it taste?

"It tastes great, but looks like hell."

We were quite mellow on the wine as we ambled to the canteen to buy cups of ice cream. With cups in hand, we sought our chairs. A YMCA man walked onto the stage and introduced himself as the MC; told us there'd be some patriotic speeches, singing by a lovely American lady, and some racy dancing, which inspired cheers and whistles. He added that the show would end with a comedy sketch.

I spied a small band in the corner with only four players. The musicians were introduced, and the attractive piano player was Miss Charming Edwards of Knoxville, Tennessee. The boys leaned in and teased, "Is she your cousin?"

"Of course she is," I replied.

Another very attractive lady kicked things off.

"Hello, I'm Roxy from Virginia," she shouted and the audience hooted in reply. She pointed to the piano player. "Hit it, Edwards." Miss Charming's fingers danced over the ivories delivering the ragtime opening for, 'There'll be a Hot Time in the Old Town Tonight.' On cue Roxy hit the lyrics, continued through the chorus and dove into the second verse. She stepped briskly across the stage, and when the chorus returned, she encouraged us to join in:

> When you hear dem bells go ding, ling ling,
> All join 'round and sweetly you must sing
> When the verse am through, in the chorus all join in,
> There'll be a hot time in the old town tonight.

A third and fourth verse followed and when she finished, we gave Roxy wild applause. The 'Hot Time' set the tone for the next thirty minutes. She closed with a melody everyone loved, 'I'll Wed the Girl I Left Behind.' The lyrics brought a tear to my eye.

After a ten-minute intermission, the second half began with rather risqué dancing by very pretty ladies. They kicked up their ruffled skirts a mite high. "It's the French style," said Jake Osborn. Now, how the hell'd he know that? Regardless, cheers and hoots accompanied their steps. Following the dancing, a circus man performed all sorts of amazing balancing feats.

Finally, a stage troupe presented a short skit that had us holding our bellies from laughing so hard. Seemed this feller came home to his wife after being away in a war. He walked into their cottage dressed in a fancy red uniform, and said to her, "Goodness, things look the same in this old cottage since I've been gone."

He moseyed over to an end table and noticed a cigar lying in an ash tray. Picked it up, and looked it over. The poor man was quite perplexed.

"I'll be damned," he said. "It's my same cigar in the same ash tray I left it in four years ago. It's still lit!"

He took a deep puff and exhaled the smoke upward. Another draw, and would you know, he blew smoke rings, perfect donuts that flowed upward from his mouth.

"How can it be?"

Chuckles flit through the crowd, as they sensed what was coming. The ex-soldier's eyebrows rose, and he suddenly understood. He turned to his wife.

"You're still my wife aren't you?" She didn't say a thing.

The audience heard a rattle off-stage.

"What's that sound, Dearie?" The wife didn't even look his way, though she quickly moved toward a large armoire. The husband asked, "Why can't you look at me?"

"I've a confession to make," the wife said.

"And what would that be, Dearie?"

"Take back your ring. I love another."

"What's this I hear? What's his name?"

"He's your old friend, Colin," she said. "You aren't going to kill him are you?"

"Hell, no. I just want to sell him the ring!"

At that, the door to the Armoire burst open and out stepped Colin.

"How much?" he asked.

Still laughing, we walked to the canal to watch the fireworks. After the *Grand Finale*, which was not as *Grand* as back home, we hiked back to the barn, checked in with Sedelsky, and hit the sack.

⁓

July 16, *Point de la Glequelais*, The Canal, Redon, France.
The Nante-to-Brest canal passed through the center of Redon. Twenty-five meters in width and three meters at its deepest, the canal accommodated two barges passing in opposite directions. On one side, the *Rue du Canal*, a well-kept carriage path traced the waterway. The grass was neatly trimmed, and mature chestnut and oak trees formed a shaded promenade. On the opposite bank, an overgrown tow path followed the canal.

Fifteen hundred meters to the west of town, *Le Pont de la Glequelais* passed over the waterway. The rickety old metal suspension bridge hung across two stone pillars, high enough so barges could pass below.

After lunch on July 10th Sedelsky announced we were headed to the canal for a bath.

"Take a towel and soap. It's wash time boys. God knows, youse gobs need it. Ladies in this town been complaining; they don't like stinky men!"

Second Squad crossed the bridge to the bathing area along the tow path. "Jeez! I can't wait to get in the water. I haven't swum since last summer," said Jim Nightlinger.

"Yeah. Well you certainly need a bath," shot back Ollie Baker. Some pushing and shoving followed, to be cut short by the Sarge.

"OK children, that's enough."

We clambered to the tow path, and settled on the bank.

"All right boys, strip down and in the water with youse. We've half an hour here," ordered Sarge.

Eagerly, I got into the buff. The bank was slippery, and half of us jumped in while the others slid down the grass into the warm water. Everyone except Joe Goldrick.

From the water, Sedelsky spotted him and bellowed. "Goldrick, you got a problem?"

"Sarge. I don't have a bathing suit."

Sedelsky looked at him in total disbelief.

"You can get in here fully clothed for all I care. Now get moving. We don't have all day."

I watched as Goldrick hesitated. Sarge yelled again, and he reluctantly unlaced his boots, shed his pants, then tugged on the band around his skivvies—all to a rising tide of cat calls from the water.

Baker's shout, "You got something to hide?" had everyone laughing.

"I'm impresssssssed!" shouted Phil Doyle as Goldrick shielded himself and slid down the bank into the water.

"Oh. This is great," hollered Hughes. A soap bar made its rounds; bodies and hair were washed, and rinsed. Soon everyone was engaged in a splashing war.

"Hey, Edwards, can you swim?" challenged Jim Nightlinger.

"Yeah. Likely better than you," I taunted.

"Race you to the other side and back."

"Go." I shouted, and jumped to an advantage. Nightlinger took off after me. Despite my bravado, I was less accomplished. Nightlinger had smooth form. He took a double stroke before tilting his head to the side for a gulp of air. His hands were cupped and he swam with powerful kicks. He easily passed me, reversed back across the canal, and finished a good two lengths ahead. "Yes!" He bellowed at the finish. The squad cheered. They'd known from the start that Nightlinger never issued a challenge unless he was confident of the result.

"Bath time's over. On the bank with youse gobs," shouted Sarge.

I struggled up the slope helped by the hands of those who had reached the ridge first. Along with their sergeant, ten men, fit and trim, graced the grassy ridge, naked as the day they were born.

Phil Doyle was the first to spot the group of young ladies strolling from the direction of town along the carriage path. They were not more than sixty meters away. There were four of them, all fashionably dressed. One pushed a pram. Two twirled parasols to shade from the noon sun. Who knew why they were there.

Doyle's response was at the core of his nature. I heard the loud shout, "*Bonjur Mesdemoiselles*," and saw his towel slip to the side. Nine pairs of eyes traced along Doyle's line of sight. The ladies no doubt saw us from some distance back. They surely watched as we climbed naked to the tow path, but it didn't deter their stroll. With the exception of Sedelsky, the ten of us faced the opposite bank, exposing ourselves in unabashed glory.

"Ahhh-bout face," Sedelsky bellowed. "Now! You're embarrassing the army and I'll have none of that."

"Sarge, shouldn't we show the local ladies just how outstanding us Yanks are?" asked Doyle. A big grin hung on his face. The Squad smiled and agreed.

"Enough!" snapped Sedelsky, but not before I caught a grin on his face.

Jake Osborn glanced back. "Hey, something's happened. Looks like the one pushing the pram slipped or fainted."

Across the canal the three women leaned over and helped the fourth. Even at our distance, it seemed more like they were consoling her. Just as quickly the ladies reversed direction and walked back toward town.

Sedelsky snickered. "God, Doyle, one look at you and the poor woman fainted!" Without hesitation, Doyle replied. "Ohhh noooo, Sarge. You got that wrong. It was the sight of Goldrick that took the air out of that lady!" Everyone but Goldrick agreed with Doyle's assessment.

As we retraced the path across the bridge, Hughes spoke to me. "Wow, I feel better. We need to do this every day."

"You got that right," I said.

CHAPTER 14. Rifle Range

August 9, 1918; The Rifle Range, Redon, France.

Located a kilometer-and-a-half from the barn on the north side of town, the rifle range had been constructed out of a large, flat field. It accommodated two hundred shooters at a time. After considerable practice, some of us guys in the supply units could hit a target at one hundred meters. I 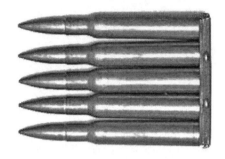 figured I'd be a fair shot from the time spent back home plunking varmints with Father's rifle. My job had been to keep groundhogs out of the garden and foxes out of the chicken coop.

Just before lights out Sedelsky announced that we'd be heading to the range tomorrow afternoon. Next day, Sarge entered the barn. "Okay, men. Get your rifles and move out." Half an hour later we were at the range. It was huge; a single long line of 30 blocks. Each block had five firing positions. A position consisted of a raised mound of compacted clay and was where a shooter positioned himself.

A lieutenant, with a range instructor in tow, strode over. The lieutenant spoke. "You men ready to do some shootin' today?" We nodded in response as he spoke to the instructor. "Well, Sergeant, it's time you teach these men how to shoot."

The Sergeant told us that we'd be shooting from the prone position for this practice session. We paired up with one man the shooter, and the other the coach. The coach helped the shooter sight his rifle and counted the hits. Our five teams settled on positions numbered twenty-six to thirty.

"Remember," said the Sergeant. "Never release your safety unless you plan to shoot or are so ordered. Never point the rifle at anything other than what you plan to shoot. Be constantly wary, there may be a cartridge in the chamber you forgot. You're holding a lethal weapon. Treat it as such."

One hundred meters away sat a red target disc, fifty centimeters in diameter. The disc looked as if it floated on the embankment behind it. Above the target was a large painted number corresponding to the firing position. The range sergeant told us, if we put a bullet through the target, a small white disk would be raised.

"Okay, men, let's begin. I'll call your position, one at a time. You fire on my order. Position twenty-six, insert the stripper clip."

Gillespie pulled the bolt back as far as possible, and loaded a clip into the magazine. With a push he reset and locked the bolt. This action stripped a cartridge from the magazine, slid it into the chamber, and cocked the firing pin at the same time. The weapon was ready to fire.

"Release your safety." A faintly audible click followed.

"Position twenty-six, take aim… Fire."

All eyes were on the distant target where a burst of dirt flew upward, about a meter to the right of the target.

"Damn," said Gillespie.

"Next shot compensate your sight two clicks to the left. Engage the safety, twenty-six."

The Sergeant shifted to the next position. "Position twenty-seven, load your weapon."

Doyle charged the magazine. The sound of bolt movement was again heard as a cartridge rammed home.

"Release the safety, take aim… Fire!"

This time the dirt puffed right above the target.

"Good. You're on target but over compensating for elevation."

So it went. At one point the Sergeant had to correct Ollie Baker when the rifle barrel shifted upward as he pulled the trigger.

"What's your name soldier?"

"Private Baker, Sergeant."

"Well, Baker, squeeze the trigger. Don't pull it. Squeeeeeze."

Baker never quite got the concept.

The sergeant stepped behind me. I went through the moves, put a bullet into the chamber, and released the safety when ordered.

"Position thirty, take aim…Fire." I squeezed off the round slowly, with care, like my father had taught me. A white disk thrust upward.

"What's your name, soldier?"

"Private Edwards, Sergeant."

"Think you can do it again, Private?"

"Sure like to try, Sergeant."

"That's what I like to hear."

The Sergeant roared, "Position thirty, reload."

I pulled back on the bolt and the chamber disgorged the spent casing. The hollow, hot brass tube gave a distinct "clank" as it hit the hard ground. I chambered the bolt, and a new cartridge slammed home.

"Position thirty, take aim." The Sergeant hesitated, and I took a deep breath.

"Fire."

I squeezed again, and a moment later a white disk danced at number thirty downrange.

"I'll be damned. An artillery supply man who can shoot! Now re-engage the safety, private."

The guys in the squad murmured. Sedelsky had a huge smile on his face, and said loud enough to be heard, "Who'd of figured that."

"Second Squad, you've four shots left in the clip. On my command, empty the magazine. Then, reload with a second clip, and continue firing. You have six minutes to expend nine shots. Take your time, think about what you're doing Concentrate, put those rounds through the target. Coaches, tell the shooters where their rounds went. Help 'em compensate. When finished, re-engage the safety and lay your rifle down alongside yourself. Any questions?"

Baker called out, "Sergeant, what if the gun jams?"

"Just set the safety and place the weapon down."

When the Sergeant was sure all the firing positions were ready, he instructed: "On my command. Load… Release the safety… Take aim… Fire."

Later, the Sergeant announced that there'd be a qualifying round of ten shots in five minutes. The coaches kept tally of the number of hits and I finished my rounds in just over three minutes. Sedelsky filled in a sheet and called out the results. "Position twenty-six, four hits; twenty-seven, zero hits; twenty-eight, seven hits; twenty-nine three hits; and thirty, ten hits."

Shooters and coaches exchanged positions. In the new group Jim Nightlinger put nine shots into the target on the qualifying rounds. I held the squad record.

CHAPTER 15. Leaving Redon

August 17, 1918; Redon, France.

Orders arrived: We were pulling out of Redon. The new deployment relocated us to the artillery range at Camp Meucon. Meucon, about fifty kilometers to the west, near the town of Vannes, would take us three days to get there.

The first night's bivouac lay outside a town called Malonsac. Months earlier the army had prepared a large field and the Service Brigade installed temporary mess tents and latrines. On entering the bivouac area, Third Platoon was directed to its assigned site and our wagons were soon arranged neatly alongside each other.

෪

"Osborn, get the stakes. Nightlinger and Hughes, find the sledge hammer and rope in wagon twenty-two. Set up the picket line in front of the wagons," instructed Sedelsky. "The rest of you men unhitch the horses. Place the tack in the wagons and put a canvas over everything. When you're finished, take care of the horses. When you are done, set your tents in a circle in this area."

Baker asked if we could light a fire after chow, and Sedelosky said it was okay. Told him to take three other guys and fetch some fire wood, and that we needed to hustle because there'd be other squads thinking the same. While the rest of us tended the horses and raised our pup tents, Osborn, Powell, Hughes and Baker hustled toward the tree line. Half an hour later they returned with plenty of kindling—large sticks, and a dried tree trunk—enough for a respectable fire. After mess, Second Squad sat around the fire and enjoyed the aroma and taste that flowed from a coffee pot.

෪

Joe Goldrick innocently asked Sedelsky, "Sarge, I never slept out in a tent before. Will bugs climb all over me?"

Sedelsky smiled, "You can reckon on it."

"Jeez," muttered Goldrick as he passed along the coffee pot.

"Sarge," asked Ollie Baker. "You got any info on how the war's going?"

"Not much more than you know. The non-commissioned officers in the chateau overheard the brass talking; we're headed for the

Argonne Forest near Verdun. Pershing won't let the Americans serve under the French or Brits. We'll stay together under our own command. We move up sometime in September."

Ernie Gillespie said that he'd heard from a friend in the HQ Battery that the Germans were about wasted, and that the Brits and French were no better off. The arrival of us Yanks may end the war."

"I hope so," said Hughes.

"It won't happen before we experience some bad shit," offered Osborn.

"Hell, us guys got it easy," I replied. "We're behind the lines."

Will Adams shifted the conversation.

"What'd you think of the food in the cafés?"

"Any of you guys have *Boeuf Tartare*?" asked Hughes.

"Cripes," answered Jim Nightlinger. "You seen that shit? I ordered it when Powell and I had supper at the Auberge. I couldn't believe it when it arrived. Nothing but a piece of raw meat with a fried egg plopped on top. Well, I told the *garçon* to take it back and cook it properly."

"What happened?" I asked.

"The waiter disappeared. Returned, maybe three minutes later. He's got the plate in hand and the beef looks exactly the same. Maybe a little warmer. Like someone breathed on it." We laughed at that.

"I complained like hell because I'm getting pissed. The owner comes over flapping in French. Nobody understands anybody. An officer steps up who speaks Frog and he translates."

"So did you get your steak?" I asked again.

All ears were following the story now.

"Yeah. After ten minutes it comes back, and now that *garçon* plops the plate in front of me. He turns away in a huff."

"Well?" asked Gillespie.

"Well what?" responded Nightlinger.

"How did it taste?"

"Oh. You mean the steak? It was still rare, but at least not raw! Damn if it wasn't delicious. There was a sauce on it the likes of which I never tasted. Oh La La!" Nightlinger raised his fingers to his lips, with a snap he sent us all a kiss.

Charlie Powell added a thought. "What I liked best was sitting outside and watching them French women. Those ladies know how to carry themselves."

"Terrible how the army keeps us away from them," Hughes complained.

"The young ones look *magnifique*, and I like how they dress. I'd like to get my hands on one," added Doyle, mimicking Nightlinger's snap to his lips.

"Hey, wait, Doyle, you can't go out there and fiddle a French maid," said Jake Osborn

"Why not," replied Doyle.

"Because the army's got a rule against fraternizing, that's why," Sedelsky responded sternly.

The banter continued until Sarge announced, "lights out." Will Adams stomped out the fire and we shuffled off to our pup tents, lit by the last rays of the fading day.

"Goldrick," Sedelsky called out."Be sure and pull your bed roll up tight so the bugs don't get in. But don't worry too much. Ain't likely many bugs left on the ground after all the troops that been camping here."

"That true, Sarge?"

"Don't I always tell it like it is?"

CHAPTER 16. Camp Meucon

August 20, 1818; Camp Meucon, Vannes, France.

On Monday, slightly after 1400 hours, the Battalion arrived at Camp Meucon. Sarge told us we were six kilometers northeast of the railhead at Vannes. Once again I had no idea where we were.

Sedelsky barked directions. "Listen up boys, we're assigned to Building Eight. Looks like its four barracks further along."

I slapped the reins and the rig moved on. Hitching posts, already set for a picket line, were behind our quarters. Sedelsky organized the wagons parallel to each other, then ordered us to tend to the horses.

Thirty minutes later, Sedelsky barked again. "Get your packs boys. Let's go inside."

The third and fourth squads were billeted on the second floor, and our quarters, along with the first squad, were on the ground floor. Sedelsky assigned the bunks.

"Wow, a real mattress," I heard Ollie Baker say.

I pressed on mine. "Damn. This is soft."

After supper Battery B was told to assemble on the field in front of the barracks. Major Shaw called us to attention, and Colonel Williams stepped to a makeshift platform and spoke.

"At ease, men. This is our final staging area before we leave for the front. It's the last training you'll get. Everyone must know their jobs. Your lives and those of your comrades depend on it. Artillery units will start live fire exercises, and our supply wagons will practice with live ammunition within three days. We'll be heading north most likely within a month. Good luck to you all. Honor and glory await you and every man must do his unit, the division, the country and his loved ones proud. Everyone must give their utmost to win this war."

I was getting settled in my bunk, when I looked over and saw Jim Nightlinger and Charlie Powell break out a deck of cards. I hoped they'd invite me. As Powell shuffled the deck, Lieutenant Harden entered with Sedelsky in tow. Sarge called us to attention and the Lieutenant set us at ease. The Lieutenant laid out the plan. We were to get our equipment in order over the next two days and memorize our maps.

Harden handed Sedelsky sheets of paper with our orders. Next Wednesday morning we were to report to the ammunition dump at the edge of Camp, take on a load of shells, and deliver them to the gun emplacements. Harden said that the sergeants at the dump would stamp our orders with a time-out, and that we'd find the time needed to reach our destination written on the orders.

"You can't follow another wagon since each is assigned a different location, anywhere from three to twelve kilometers from Camp," said the Lieutenant. "Evening leave would be granted to any wagon team that delivered their load on or before the designated time." Harden warned, "If you take longer than the listed time, leave will be denied."

He looked around the room all serious like. I thought he was joking, was this a game?

It was as if he read my mind.

"This is not a game. Your job's to figure out the best route to deliver your shells. Study your map, memorize it. Plan for what you'll do if the map gets lost or otherwise destroyed."

He let that idea sink in before continuing, "We'll soon practice deliveries at night. Oh yes. Sergeant, make sure every wagon carries a back-up man. He'll ride buckshot and help the brakeman navigate. You backups need to know how to operate the wagon in case a replacement is needed."

Just before Harden left he faced us, "Tonight you gentlemen have a two hour leave. Enjoy the canteen, might be a while before you visit again. I want a good show from you men. For now, study those maps."

"Hot damn," said Phil Doyle. Fifteen minutes later Second Squad headed for the door.

Next day, August 20th the horses were groomed, the map memorized, and rifles cleaned. Late afternoon a guy from First Squad called out, "They're delivering mail, out front."

We all ran. Emblazoned on the canvas of a covered wagon was: "US ARMY MAIL."

"Edwards!" came the call. I pushed my way to the front of the crowd to find two letters: one from Emily, the second from Fannie. I tore open Fannie's first. She had mailed it from the farm in Virginia. Her words warmed my heart, and the way she signed the letter popped my eyes.

> *August 2, 1918*
> *Culpepper, Virginia*
> *Dearest Harry,*
>
> *I am in Culpepper and will return to Media in three weeks. Uncle Cliff forwarded your recent letter about the night you were on guard duty watching the moon. I also saw the full moon last month. The blue moon matched the way I felt.*
> *It was well past one o'clock in the morning. I was sound asleep but the window was open on account of the heat of late. The moon's pale white face lay low in the sky and the light flowed through the window and spread across my bed. I woke, disturbed but not knowing why. It took a moment to shake off the sleep, then I saw it. The brilliant old moon filled entirely the lower half of my window, and its face looked down on me just like you described. As the moon rose, my room darkened again. But in those enchanting moments my thoughts reached to you. Though you could not know it, you and I crossed the gulf separating us and were magically joined. When I received your welcome letter, and realized the connection that night was mutual, I felt so close to you. What a wonderful thought. I miss you so, hurry home to me.*
> *Love,*
> *Fannie*

She had signed it "love!" A tingle spread over me. I caressed the letter, absorbed its message, and longed to be beside her. For the next two hours I floated in a dream. The world outside the letter ceased to exist, and I forgot to open Emily's note.

August 21st was our second preparation day. The Army expected our wagons and horses to be in tip-top shape, and there were map exercises to test our knowledge. Just after breakfast a siren went off.

"What the hell's that?" asked Hughes.

A loud steady wail came from the camp center. Sedelsky yelled, "Gas! Gas, get your masks on!"

I grabbed at the soft pack on my chest, ripped open the buttons, and fumbled with the mask. A hose connected it to the charcoal filter particles in a chest pack. The straps had been adjusted earlier, so a quick motion across the top of my head, followed by a downward pull, was supposed to place it tightly over my face. Hughes had his mask out, straps across his head, and had easily pulled it over his face. Jeez. How the hell did he do that so quickly? I wasn't as coordinated, and failed to get the straps properly placed. When I pulled, my mask slid to the side. This is not good, crossed my mind.

"Edwards, take it off and start again," Hughes called in a muffled voice.

Thirty seconds later I had my mask properly positioned. Back at Redon, the instructor had warned us half a minute could mean the difference between survival and death. Sedelsky went from soldier to soldier and checked the seal. He tightened mine and the damn thing felt terrible. I was sure it cut into my face. Oh well, this drill will be over soon enough, I thought.

Sedelsky's voice sounded weird through his mask, "Okay, boys, time to get back to work. Listen for the all clear. Do not remove the mask till you hear the siren. Anyone looking for a breather will have hell to pay."

Three hours later the all clear sounded. We'd never worn the horrid things for so long before.

"Jeez, Hughes you got a red ring around your face. Do I have one? God, my face hurts."

"Yeah, you do. Hell, I've needed to scratch my nose for an hour."

"My God that was awful," added Joe Goldrick.

CHAPTER 17. The Game

August 22, 1918; Camp Meucon, Vannes, France.

Next morning, with a solid breakfast under our belts, the rigs were ready to roll. Sedelsky got the squad lined up and ordered Goldrick to ride with our wagon.

"If you gobs want canteen tonight you need to work as a team. Okay, off with you, and keep sharp."

Thirty minutes later, our wagon bed held six high explosive shrapnel shells. The sergeant at the ammunition dump handed me our destination orders with the stamp-out indicating 0810. "Get on it boys," he encouraged. "There's some great singing by pretty ladies tonight. If you don't get lost."

Hughes opened our map.

"We're headed to Range Three. Edwards, turn around and exit through the north gate, turn left and continue for two kilometers. You agree, Goldrick?"

Hughes traced the route as Goldrick watched over his shoulder.

Goldrick sat quietly for a moment eyeing the map. "Hughes. Show me how you are going again."

"What'd you see?" I asked.

He studied Hughes' route. "Look, this symbol indicates a ford. If we continue along this road, we'll have to cross a stream. It rained pretty heavy last night and the creek's likely swollen. There'd be a hell of a time turning the rig, if we had to backtrack. If we follow this route, we could loop around and avoid the crossing. It's longer, but we'll be sure of reaching the guns."

Hughes concentrated on the map. "Jeez, Goldrick you're right. Edwards, let's use the longer route. It's a safer bet."

"Hughes, you got to think of these things."

"Hey, don't hound me, Edwards."

"Look here," and I pointed to the map. "There are some fairly straight roads. I could get the team to trot. We'd make-up time."

I shook the reins and the horses circled on the wide gravel road in front of the armory and headed toward the north gate.

Forty minutes later we drew to a stop at the entry post of Artillery Range Number Three. The duty officer took our orders and stamped us in, then directed us to Battery B, Howitzer Number Four.

"Jeez, that was a piece-a-cake," said Hughes.

"Well, the roads were dry, the horses were fresh, and we didn't have a full load. And we avoided that ford. Let's hope it's always like that!"

"Hey, we'll be singing at the canteen tonight," said Goldrick.

"Hot damn, you got that right," I said with a big grin on my mug. "Yeah," Hughes added.

We were instructed to drive toward a dense copse of trees and follow the road through the thicket. On the other side a huge space opened before us extending down range to distant hills. A supply road ran along the edge of the woods, and across the road were the four guns of each of the regiments six batteries. The barrel tubes of all twenty-four howitzers faced down range and each weapon was manned by a team.

We found gun number four in Battery B, and Hughes and I unlatched the rear door, while Goldrick rolled the first shell across the wagon bed to the shelf. The two of us hefted an end, and the gun boss told us where to stack the shells alongside the weapon.

I'd never before been this close to the 155-mm howitzer. It was monstrous. "What's it, about four meters from the barrel tip to the end of the trail?" I asked a corporal.

"Close enough," he replied.

"Is it easy to move?" wondered Goldrick.

"Takes eight horses to pull it. Damn thing weighs 3500 kilograms," replied the corporal.

The three of us were admiring the gun, when a sergeant came running over to the gun crew.

"Men, orders just came down. Shift Gun Four two hundred meters to a new firing position. You boys in Wagon Twenty have the only horse team available, so use them help move the 155. Follow the gun crew's instructions. You men got thirty minutes to get this weapon relocated. Get crackin'."

"Unhitch the horses, and move them to the gun carriage," ordered the gun boss. "When we attach a limber to the trail, you'll hook the horses to the limber pole."

The limber was a contraption that provided another set of wheels allowing the howitzer to be pulled. As we readied the horses, two guys in the gun crew brought a limber to the trail.

The trail was a long metal extension attached to the rear of the gun to help stabilize the weapon. The end of the trail could be mated to a hitch on the limber. As the limber was positioned, a soldier hastened to the side of the gun and spun a wheel that lowered the tube elevation until the barrel was horizontal. This brought the center of gravity of the gun over the axel of its wheels, and with the trail now serving as one end of a long lever, four men—two on either side—could easily lift the trail off the ground and mate its end with the hitching post on the limber. When correctly aligned, the trail was lowered and locked to the post.

The front of the limber had a pole that attached to the harnessing system on our horses. It took five minutes to get the team lined-up and secured to the pole. With the horses, limber, and trail in place, the gun crew positioned themselves around the howitzer. I jumped onto the limber seat, while Hughes and Goldrick grabbed hold of the bridal of each lead horse.

I looked around to be sure everything was ready. "Let's go," I called, and slapped the reins hard. The horses strained, the limber pole tightened, but nothing happened.

"Come on team. Hey, pull hard on the bridal." The horses snorted. I felt the strain. Again, nothing.

The gun boss hollered, "The wheels are stuck, boys. On my command everyone push on the carriage. Okay, on three. One, two…three. Heeeeave."

"Come on horses show me what you can do," I yelled. "Move out, move out," and added the loud crack of my whip just above their heads. Hughes and Goldrick pulled on the bridals.

The howitzer broke free with a sudden jolt and began to roll. All of us erupted in a cheer.

The horses pulled the 155 along a hard dirt road, and at the new location I pulled on the reigns so that the team swung the howitzer around, positioning the weapon with its barrel pointed down range. We unhitched the horses from the limber pole and walked the team back to our wagon. Once the rig was set, we recovered the six shells left behind. As our wagon approached Gun Four, I heard the range sergeant dressing down the crew.

"You got the gun over here and set up in twenty-five minutes. That's excellent. But you dumb gobs forgot to place the shells in the limber and left them at the old location. The wagon team had to go back to retrieve them. Pull a stunt like that again and you'll be doing extra duty for two weeks."

"Yes, Sergeant," the boss replied sheepishly.

I felt sorry for him. One of the guys on the crew said they'd never been ordered to shift the howitzer on such short notice. In the excitement the shells were forgotten.

"Say, when you gonna fire?" Hughes asked the gun boss. "Can we watch?"

"Sure. Don't matter to me. You got the time?"

"We're okay," I said. "We've a couple of hours to kill."

"You should move the rig over there." He pointed a good distance behind the howitzers.

"The guns have spooked horses before. Order to fire might come down in fifteen minutes, so stick around. The Gun Boss faced me before returning to the weapon. Say, the name's Corporal Wilkes. The boys in the crew appreciated how you helped shifting this 'Little Bertha.' Can't imagine what it'll be like for real. We hear that the roads up north are nothin' but mud and ruts."

"Thanks," I said. "We'll know soon enough about those roads, and I suspect we'll be helping you again."

I repositioned the wagon about 30 meters behind Gun Four, and took in the bigger picture. The four howitzers of Battery B formed a line in front of us, each manned by a crew. A sudden flurry of activity occurred as gun crews checked or adjusted their trail and tube. The gun boss stood alongside our weapon wearing a pair of headphones. Suddenly he shouted some numbers, and two men shifted the trail to the right by small increments by levering a handle back and forth.

"What the hell are they doing?" asked Goldrick.

"They're setting the direction using a compass bearing."

"Jeez, Edwards. When'd you go to artillery school?" Hughes smirked.

"Direction set," I heard the guy with the compass holler.

The gun boss barked another order, and one of the crew began spinning a wheel. The tube elevation rose as he looked intently through some sort of eye-piece set on the side of the weapon. He stopped spinning, made some minor adjustments on the wheel, then stepped back and yelled. "Elevation set 48 degrees. Elevation confirmed."

The gun boss spoke into a microphone hanging from a loop around his neck. The crew was now motionless.

"Order to set six rounds," the boss shouted.

He hollered more numbers, and while one member of the gun crew steadied an upright shell, another screwed a fuse into the nose. Next, he twisted the fuse with a strange looking tool, moving from one shell to the next. Once all were set, he repeated the numbers back to the gun boss, and shouted, "Munitions set."

"Commence loading," shouted the boss, and a massive, grooved, round block of polished steel, at the back of the gun, opened. The breach man activated a firing mechanism in the center of the breech, securing it by what I thought—at our distance—was some sort of a safety plate. Simultaneously, one of the gunners cradled a 155-mm shell in his forearms. He placed it on a tray aligned to the tube opening while two soldiers, on either side of the weapon, lifted a T-bar secured on the trail. They positioned the head of the bar at the back of the shell, and—using the T as handles—rammed the steel projectile into the tube. As the bar drew back, another gunner, his arms sheathed in heavy leather gloves, shoved a cylindrical white cloth bag into the tube, pushing it up hard against the projectile.

"Lock the breech," the gun boss shouted, and the massive block rotated again on its hinge.

"Gun Ready," shouted the breech man.

"Firing positions. Arm the weapon," shouted the boss. The crew stepped back, crouched and covered their ears.

The man at the breech pulled back the trigger and locked it in place, after which, he rotated away the safety plate exposing the firing cap.

"Weapon set for firing," he said.

This was a perfectly orchestrated performance with every step executed with errorless timing. Jeeze, this gun crew's been practicing these moves a long time, I thought.

All movement suddenly ceased. I glanced along the line. The gun crews of the other howitzers were in the same positions.

"Fire!" yelled the boss and the breech man triggered the gun.

A blast of smoke and flame gushed from the mouth of the tube. The barrel recoiled, and smoothly slid back into position on its well oiled rails. The strength of the blast caught me off guard. I felt as if something slammed into my body, and my ears hurt like hell. Hughes stumbled backward in surprise, bumped the edge of the wagon, lost his balance and fell. Goldrick flinched, and then belatedly covered his ears.

"Hey, Hughes, you okay?"

"Shit," he said. "I didn't expect that. Yeah, I'm OK."

The startled horses shrieked at the roar. Almost immediately we scanned a hillside, many kilometers down-range. Huge balls of smoke and orange fire burst ten meters in the air. The ground beneath erupted in a shower of splayed dirt, as the shrapnel balls slammed home.

Before we fully recovered our wits, the process repeated itself. Another shell rammed into Gun Four, and the order to "fire" came again. Although I could barely hear him over the din, Hughes yelled, "Let's get outta here!"

We jumped on board, and Hughes released the brake. As the rig approached the guard post, the firing stopped. Goldrick looked at his watch, "Damn, that only lasted five minutes."

"Jeez," said Hughes, "How the hell does the gun crew tolerate those blasts? What if it goes on for hours?"

"Must turn their ears to mush," said Goldrick.

"Or their brains," I added.

"Did you see down range?" asked Goldrick. Those six 155's fired thirty-six rounds in five minutes. I did some figuring," and he pointed to his head. "Each shell has around five hundred shrapnel balls.

That's more than eighteen thousand balls slamming into the hillside. God, I wouldn't want to be under that."

"How the hell'd you know that?" I asked.

"Lectures back at Redon," said Goldrick

"I'm surrounded by experts," muttered Hughes.

At the debriefing I handed Sedelsky our stamped orders. "Well. I'll be damned, you boys in Twenty were the only team to clock-in under time. Only one other rig in the platoon made it. Nice going. You get leave tonight."

CHAPTER 18. The German POW

Mid August, 1918; Camp Meucon, Vannes, France.

Our rig carried ever larger numbers of shells and sometimes we delivered loads twice a day. Hughes, Goldrick and I were getting good at this, and were on-time twelve of sixteen runs. I lost control of the wagon twice on muddy roads during heavy rain. The rig slid into a ditch, and we had a hell of a time getting it back on the road. Fortunately, the horses weren't hurt.

When we weren't hauling a load of shells Sedelsky made us practice one hundred and eighty degree turns on narrow roads; a difficult maneuver, but not impossible. Sedelsky would not give us a break on the practice. Jeez, we get it, I wanted to yell at him.

Late August, 1918; Camp Meucon, Vannes, France.

Our first night run began on August 27th, with the rig rolling at 0230. We now had to get from the gates of Meucon to our destination by sun up. There were new challenges. If the rig drove under a heavy tree canopy, or if night clouds covered the stars, the roadway was nearly pitch black. The map was hard to see, even when lit by the glow from a cigarette lighter. There were frequent wrong turns and muddy ruts were difficult to avoid. The possibility that our horses might suffer injury worried me. But to the surprise of the three of us, we gradually got better at it. It was never totally dark, and you could visualize the outline of the road and its direction easily in starlight. I also learned to "feel" the road from the slip-sliding of the wheels and the sloshing sound of hooves when we drove in wet or muddy conditions. The application of braking pressure to maintain control of the rig came more naturally to Hughes and me.

Fortunately, between the day and night details the army squeezed in enough sleep and food to keep us from total exhaustion.

One evening Hughes asked, "Say, Edwards, I'd like to drop your sister a letter. What's your address?"

"What you going to say to her?"

"Well. I'll tell her how damn pretty she looks in the picture you showed me. Then, I'm gonna tell her how us boys are holdin' up and what a good guy her brother is. In fact, I'll also tell her we're like brothers to one another. That way I'll call her sister. And if she's my sister, I'm gonna give her hugs all the time. When I end the letter, I'm gonna to ask her to write me back. I might even suggest when the war's over, I'd visit her and your family."

"Jeez, Hughes, now don't you be coming on to my sister. You can't sweet talk her till you get your divorce matter cleaned up." I gave him the address anyway.

September 4, 1918; Camp Meucon, Vannes, France.

Hughes and I were grooming the horses after breakfast waiting for the order to hitch-up, when Sedelsky and Lieutenant Harden rounded the barracks.

We saluted and Harden spoke. "Edwards. Your file says you've experience with plumbing. That true?"

"Yes, Sir, was an apprentice before the Army took me."

"Battalion's looking for soldiers who do plumbing. Seems they're installing a new water line and need someone to connect pipe sections. Can you handle that?"

"If it's coupling pipe sections, Sir, yes I can."

"Okay, I'm assigning you temporary duty in the Engineer's Section. Here're your orders. Report to Lieutenant Lilly. You'll be on assignment for three days beginning right now. The work's on the western edge of camp. Sergeant will tell you where."

"Yes, Sir."

Harden handed me the orders, and returned my salute.

The water line project was at the far end of the camp. New barracks had been built at the base of a large grassy hill. A three hundred meter long trench, more than a meter deep, and at least half a meter wide, snaked around some large boulders down the hillside, ending at a barracks complex. The trench started three-quarters up the side of a hill, beginning at a newly constructed, wooden water tank. The tank was filled with water pumped by one of those new electric pumps from a well dug into the side of the hill. Uncoupled, cast iron pipe sections lay at the bottom of the trench.

I pulled back the flaps of the engineers' tent. "Lieutenant Lilly?" The Lieutenant looked up from his desk and I saluted.

"What is it soldier? I'm busy."

"I'm private Edwards, Sir. My CO sent me over, said you needed some help with plumbing." Lilly looked up. "About damn time they found someone. Can you connect pipe?"

"Yes, Sir."

"Well, we'll see. We're behind schedule. You need to join the detail immediately. We use Krauts as helpers, can't take more of our boys off their training. Half those Huns are still in shell shock and the rest are dumb shits. They're under guard, but you keep your eyes open around 'em. There's been no trouble, but I'm taking no chances. You know any German?"

"A few words. Went to school with some Pennsylvania Dutch."

"Good. Corporal, take Edwards over to the works."

The Corporal introduced me to Sergeant Amick.

"Glad you're here, Edwards. Those sections need coupling, starting at the bottom of the storage tank. There are tools in the shed over there, and those boxes contain couplers. You need to connect to the tank first and when that is finished, join-up the sections." Amick continued, "You'll work with Corporal Ellis. We use German prisoners to help, and I'll get a couple of Krauts over here that understand some English."

He introduced me to Ellis, and added, "You boys get set-up. We've two days to finish this job. And, don't go talking with those prisoners."

"Where you from, Edwards?" Ellis asked as we walked to the shed.

"Place called Marple, South of Philadelphia. You?"

"Bluefield, West Virginia, west of Wheeling."

Jeez, that boy's got some drawl, I thought.

"You a plumber?" I asked.

"Yeah. Got my license late '17. Didn't do much good. Early '18, I'm over here."

We cut, threaded and coupled pipe sections to the tank discharge valve, so that the line reached the trench bottom. The first long section was ready to be attached, when Amick appeared with two prisoners in tow.

"Change of plans, boys. Ellis, you and one of the Germans work on the other end of the pipe. Get the fittings set so they mate to the barrack lines. Seems it's more complicated," Amick said. "Edwards, you stay here with this Kraut and start coupling the sections."

The German and I were alone. I climbed out of the trench and pointed to myself, "Edwards," I said. "And you?"

"Klinghoffer," he replied.

I pointed and he jumped into the excavation. I passed down the tools, then hopped-in the trench.

We joined the elbow from the tank fitting to the first section of pipe. I showed him how to use the wrenches, and then we walked down the trench to the next junction and repeated the process. It took thirty minutes to get the first two sections joined, and it surprised me how quickly Klinghoffer got the whole idea. I suspected he knew more English than he let on.

"Only two hundred and eighty meters to go," I said. Klinghoffer nodded affirmatively. "American, you do this before?" he asked in a thick accent.

Sneaky bastard, he did understand more than he let on, I thought.

"Yeah, but never on pipe this big," I said.

We retrieved our tools and walked down the trench to the next section. Curiosity was killing me.

"Where'd you learn English?"

"*Meine Großmutter*," he responded. Klinghoffer hesitated, saw I understood, then continued. "*Mein* grandmother, she talk me English all time when *ich ein Junge war*. When I small. I slowly learn."

"*Mein Großvater*…, ahhh, how you say, *mein* grandfather sell *schriebemachine* in England before war."

"*Schriebemachine*? What's that?" I asked.

"He thought a moment, and imitated a sound. "Chic, chic," paused, and repeated the "chic, chic, chic" rapidly. Another pause followed by another "chic, chic," all the while moving his fingers up and down in time with each "chic." Klinghoffer stopped, reached up with his left hand and pushed an imaginary lever from left to right, while melodically intoning, "Zing."

"A typewriter."

"*Ja. Ja.*"

"Your grandfather sold German typewriters in England! He met your grandmother, they married and she came to live in Germany."

"*Ja. Das ist recht*. Err... *Ja*, correct."

We walked to the next section.

"*Haben Sie ein Mädchen?*" asked Klinghoffer.

"*Mädchen?*"

"Ja, e*in frau. Ein damsel.*"

"Ahhhhh. You mean a girlfriend... *Ja*."

"*Und ihr* name?"

"Fannie," I replied.

"*Fannn-ie*," he exaggerated.

I laughed. "*Ja,* Fannn-ie. And you?"

"*Meine Frau est Katia.*"

"*Frau?*" Glancing down I saw a ring peaking through the dirt on his hand.

That's when I learned he had two children, Victoria and Lydia. Klinghoffer levered the pipe end and I spun the coupler on the threads. He stared into the distance, with a look that revealed his sadness.

"Klinghoffer. You're alive. You'll see them again."

Deep heartache etched his eyes, and the muscles of his face sagged.

"Yes, I alive. So many others are *todt*. I will see Katia, Lydia *und* little Victoria, if they live the war."

"What do you mean, if they live?"

A while later Sergeant Amick looked into the trench. "Everything all right down there? Were you talking to that Kraut?" Before I could answer he ordered, "Leave him alone. Your job is to finish this pipe. I need ten more sections coupled before 1700 hours." And just as suddenly, he left us to our work.

"Edwards, you get in trouble?"

"No, sergeants don't bother me."

That made Klinghoffer smile.

Our work finished for the day, I climbed out of the trench and reached out a hand to help the German out. Sergeant Amick approached us. "Okay, Kraut. Over there," he said, pointing to a collection of prisoners.

"Good job, Edwards. Be back here by 0800. We have to finish this job tomorrow, then test the system to be sure it's okay. The Krauts will fill in the trench."

"Yes, Sergeant."

❧

Later, over supper, Hughes asked, "Where were you today?" I told him about the new water line and the German who'd worked with me. This was something new and all the guys wanted to hear more. I described how the German prisoners had dug a trench down a hill.

"Hell of a job. Hill's full of stones and boulders. Soil's all clay. The prisoners had laid uncoupled pipe sections in the trench and my job was to couple the sections together."

"Hard work?" asked Ernie Gillespie.

"More tedious than hard. I had a German prisoner helping me. Had a huge PW stenciled in white on the back of his denim jacket. Same thing on the butt side of his pants." Now they were listening closely.

"Interesting guy. Knew a fair bit of English and since no one could see or hear us in the trench, he talked-up a storm."

"What'd he say?" asked Hughes.

All the guys leaned-in, even Sedelsky tilted an ear. I recanted Klinghoffer's story.

"So, how did he get here?" asked Ollie Baker.

"Marines captured him in a night raid in the Belleau Wood sector. He's sleeping in the dugout when they burst in. After the interrogation, they sent him to a POW camp about ten kilometers east of here. Discovered he spoke some English, so they assigned him to a work detail here."

"How long was he at the front?" Osborn wanted to know.

"About two years."

"He tell you about it?" asked Will Adams.

"Yeah. He survived the bombardment on the Somme in September of '16. His unit had just arrived at the front and was settled in their dugouts when the shells started falling. The way he tells it, his whole squad was blown to bits or buried in mud. He survived because an officer ordered him to carry a message back to the command post just before the barrage."

"Lucky bastard," said Gillespie.

"He was reassigned to a new squad, but they were all wiped out, except him, by shrapnel shells, when they went over the top this past June. Got reassigned again and that's when the Yanks picked him up in the Belleau Wood raid."

"Jeez, that Hun's got nine lives," said Jake Osborn.

Next day Klinghoffer and I finished the coupling job. I saw him in a different way. Sure, he was the enemy, but we both shared a common desire to go home. Home to people we loved and missed, who loved and missed us in return. We both wanted to return to a life that, for me at least, was becoming a distant memory. Klinghoffer's tale of survival, and the fact that he didn't fit the evil Kraut of our propaganda stories, complicated my view of the war.

Chapter 19. The Oliver Number Three.

September, 1918; The Peterson Farm, Marple, Pennsylvania.

The pumpkins ripened slowly in the cool September air, but by the end of the second week of September they had yet to turn completely orange. There were still streaks of green on the rind. When I tapped the largest—must have been twenty inches in diameter—it resounded with a healthy dull "thump."

"Emily, Don't harvest them too early," Mother instructed. "They'll have a bitter potato-like taste. Be patient."

The rest of the garden yielded a late summer bounty and every afternoon I picked fresh vegetables for dinner. By the end of September Mother and I would be able to harvest a whole new crop of green tomatoes, more than enough for canning.

I had convinced myself my pretty face didn't need makeup. Besides, I couldn't afford it. I wore my long auburn hair either down or in a bun depending on my mood, and dressed as well as we could afford. When necessary, I made my own clothes. I had a good sense of design, and friends often complimented me on my outfits. Talking was a skill I cultivated, and with friends around me, we could quickly create gossip. I loved going to the parties and thrived on having a good time. My junior year in high school was difficult because of the extra time I had to take to help Mother in her passage through the change of life. Often, I prepared dinner and did all the washing and ironing on top of my other chores. Fortunately, by the summer of 1918, her health improved, and I looked forward to a less stressful senior year.

I returned to school in September and my brother, Morris, joined me as a freshman. Mother insisted I graduate high school, likely because George and Harry had only completed eighth grade. I'd always liked school and looked forward to my typing classes. With Harry away and Morris in school, George and Father worked the farm together. Toward the end of the summer I noticed that George's mind seemed elsewhere, and I assumed it was because he had this fancy for fixing cars. I couldn't know it yet, but George had another fancy, and it would create a big problem.

Morris and I trekked down Paxon Hollow Road to the intersection with Providence Road. Early every weekday we waited on the corner till the school wagon arrived to carry us, along with Edith Worrell, Fannie White and Anna Moore to the Marple-Newtown Vocational High School. We girls were the best of pals. Fannie and I, at eighteen, were a year older than most of the other kids in our class. Me, from starting school a year late, and Fannie, because she was placed a year back when she came north from Virginia. She said it had something to do with catching-up in her schooling.

One morning Anna Moore mentioned that she'd seen a typing machine for sale in Media. When next in town for the Saturday market, I wandered over to Wallace's hardware store and snuck a look at it. What a lovely machine; I had to have it.

After two weeks of constant nagging—I kept insisting that Father at least come with me to examine how it worked—he finally relented. He won't say it, but I secretly believe that he doesn't want me to become a secretary. I don't know why that is. Fannie says parents can be so old fashioned. She's quite right. Saturday morning Father got the buggy set, and we trotted into Media to examine the Oliver Number 3.

Mr. Wallace showed us the used machine; a handsome Oliver 1914 front-strike model. It came with its own carrying case. Front strike typewriters are a strange design. The keys approach the strike zone from the sides. This creates two pods of keys at the sides of the machine. I liked its unusual appearance. It set it apart from other typewriters. The problem with this particular Oliver was that the strike rods for the letters "f" and "g" jammed occasionally. Mr. Wallace said it had something to do with the fact they were adjacent to each other on the keyboard. Otherwise, it worked well. He wanted the machine out of his store. It'd been in the window too long, and he explained that with a little mechanical skill, the problem key shafts could be bent inward and all would be fine. In fact, he had a letter from the Oliver

Company describing how to perform this repair. Father insisted that I try it. With the typewriter placed on a table I sat down, inserted a paper sheet, and thought about a line without an "f" or "g".

"Hmmm, let me see…." I quickly produced a line: "Sally sells sea shells at the seashore." No hang-up in the rods.

Father said, "Try this. 'Glowing goblins found frolicking in Halloween fun.'"

Everyone laughed when every "f" or "g" key-stroke got stuck.

Father offered five dollars less than what Mr. Wallace was asking. He thought a moment, shaking his head. "You always were a hard man, Frazure Edwards. It's a deal."

They laughed and shook hands. I owned a typewriter.

My brother George had the hammer action repaired by evening supper.

∾

Whenever the weather was bad, George drove Morris and me to the corner, and waited until the school wagon arrived. George would wave and flirt with the other girls as they looked out the window. Despite his hearing loss, George had a handsome face and my friends never minded his attention. Of course, we always accepted his offer to drive us somewhere, like the soda parlor at Payton's drug store in Media.

George had a certain shyness around people he did not know. It likely grew from his hearing loss and the failure to understand everything said to him. Nevertheless, my brother had one remarkable talent. On the dance floor his shyness disappeared. He blossomed and looked confident. The transformation was amazing to witness. George's rhythm was graceful and seamless and he guided his dance partners in the gentlest manner. He took control, mastered his partner's movements and molded her into him and the music. The girls loved it, and I relished every chance to dance with my brother.

It's a mystery how he could dance so well; he could hardly hear the music. Harry once told me that George felt the music. Its rhythm pressed on his chest or vibrated his feet through the floor. George's awareness of his partner's body position was so sensitive he could sense—likely through his finger tips—the most subtle of shifts in balance. He immediately applied gentle pressure on hands or hips to reassert control. When the music stopped, George's nervousness returned. But while the turntable spun, I marveled how he lived in a different place.

❧

Though I was close to my friends and they were interesting, and despite the excitement of my last year at school, Media remained a sad place, so empty of young men. Harry was gone, and all the boys my girlfriends and I knew—at least those we wanted to be seen with—were off to war.

"Sometimes I feel so sad," I told Mother. "There's no men around to show off for."

"Now Emily," she replied. "In the first place you shouldn't have to "show off" for anyone. And it's not right to be feeling sad for yourself. You should be feeling for your brother over there. Living in them horrid conditions, facing death, and who knows what else."

CHAPTER 20. To the Front

September 12, 1918; Camp Meucon, Vannes, France.

We'd had plenty of practice delivering munitions in the month since our arrival at Meucon. Our wagon navigation skills had improved greatly, and night supply runs were not as intimidating as they first seemed. The area around Camp Meucon had good roads. But our ability to negotiate on very muddy roads, like we kept hearing about up north, was yet to be tested. It was not clear when we were leaving for the front, but the rumor mill was rich with one word: imminent.

Joe Goldrick and I carted camouflage supplies from the quartermaster depot this morning and Sedelsky had us practice setting it up all afternoon. We must have installed and removed the netting at least ten times. Somewhere around the fifth time, Ollie Baker caught hell. As he unhooked the camouflage from one of the poles, the mesh caught on a pin. We all heard the ripping sound, and of course Sedelsky never missed a thing.

"Baker, what the hell'd you do?"

"Ahhhh…Sarge. The twine caught. I pulled too hard and it gave way."

"Damn. How many times do I have to tell youse gobs? Be careful! This camouflage is not made with rope. It's delicate. You can't pull on it."

"Sorry, Sarge. I'll be careful next time."

"You certainly will. Now get the repair kit and retie the split."

Sedelsky kept pushing us until the netting could be mounted over the wagons and horses in fifteen minutes.

∽

On September 14th the order arrived.

"Listen-up men. We pack for the front immediately. Get your gear stowed and get the wagons ready. Baker, you be the last man out. Check around the bunks and be sure nothing's left behind. Goldrick, Adams, do the same in the toilet and shower stalls. Osborn, check the closets. Shake it up boys, everyone outside in five."

By 2010 hours the horses of Battery B were walking at a good pace, closing the distance to the rail junction at Vannes. Darkness overtook the column and our advance slowed, but we easily followed each other since every wagon carried a lantern. A chill filled the air, and dampness cut through my tunic. Unexpectedly, every time the column broke out of the trees a strange pall of light grew in front of us, unusual and bright.

"Edwards, where the hell's that light coming from?" asked Hughes.

"You got me. It's not fire, there's no flicker."

"Whatever it is, we're headed toward it," said Goldrick.

Just after 2100 hours the rig rounded a sharp bend and came upon a huge, brilliantly lit field. The open space glowed with dozens of spotlights lighting the staging area. A modern miracle—daylight at night. The din of a generator joined the bustle. There were three parallel railroad tracks that ran the length of the field. Long lines of those small French box cars were interspersed with a number of flat cars. Sedelsky got directions, then shouted to the rest of us.

"Okay men. Head toward Track A."

He directed us to a flatcar. A ramp led to the bed of the car.

"Edwards. How the hell is this loaded wagon getting' up the ramp?" asked Hughes.

"Ha. You kidding me? The army way, by pushing and pulling it."

By the time we secured the third wagon and covered each with canvas, we were pretty well spent. But no rest followed. The horses had to be coaxed into the boxcars, organized eight to a car. This was a tricky maneuver, since those Andalusians were just damned reluctant to walk up a ramp, and when they did, they hesitated at the door.

Two men accompanied the horses in each car. Their job was to calm the animals. We'd rotate 'horse detail' at each stop along the trip. Four squads were assigned to a car; thirty-two men, less the eight guys watching the horses. It was cramped, but there were benches along the wall, and if you didn't sit, you could lie down.

The engine whistle shrieked into the night at 0030, and the train began its long journey to the war. There were five station stops, each long enough for us to change horse detail, stretch our legs, have a cigarette, and relieve ourselves. At one layover, we had plenty of time for a sandwich and a coffee. Otherwise, the squad was cooped-up in that boxcar for over thirty-two hours.

CHAPTER 21. War Bonds

September 18, 1918; Marple, Pennsylvania.

The school wagon arrived at the stop. I stepped aboard and sat next to Edith. Fannie and Anna were in the seat behind us. It was the third week of September and I couldn't wait to tell them my idea.

"Girls!" I said. "The paper says that girl scouts are selling Liberty War Bonds all over the country. I thought we ought to do the same thing. What do you think?"

"Emily, why ever would we do that? We're not even girl-l-l-l-l scouts," said Edith.

My Daddy Bought Me a Government Bond of the **THIRD LIBERTY LOAN** Did Yours?

"What a silly question. To help the war effort, why else? My brother's over there, and I don't think writing letters is enough." I became more insistent. "Fannie, you've got two brothers in the Navy, and Anna, your cousin's in the Army. That's why!"

"There's a point there," said Fannie.

"First, you get permission from the county court house in Media to sell the bonds," I said. "They check to make sure you're legitimate. Next, you approach a local bank for a war bond sales' kit."

"But we're not part of any organization," said Anna.

"Say, here's an idea, why don't we ask Principal Janson if we can represent our school? If he agrees, we'll put up a table on State Street and sell bonds to the Saturday morning shopping crowd in Media," I offered.

"Oh, I like it," said Fannie.

Edith changed the subject. She wasn't convinced, yet. "Emily, have you received any more letters from Mr. Hughes?"

I blushed.

"Oh. You have. You Have! Come on, tell us, tell us," said Anna.

"Yes, Yes," chimed in Fannie and Edith.

I admitted he'd written four letters and wanted to know all about me. He said my picture makes me look 'tall' and 'lithe,' even 'sensuous.' A jealous Edith thought I should be flattered, whereas, Fannie concluded that it sounded quite racy. I retrieved a picture of Harry and Mr. Hughes from my book bag and showed the girls how handsome Mr. Hughes was. Anna examined it with a critical eye and agreed. Said she'd do the Grizzly Bear with him anytime.

"If anyone rubs bottoms with Mr. Hughes, it'll be me," I told Anna. Fannie noted that Harry had sent her the same picture and that they looked brave with their guns. Why didn't she mention the picture before? I wondered.

The following Saturday morning, the four of us stood behind a table in front of Payton's Drug Store. Chits purchased from us could be converted into Liberty Bonds at the local bank. A sign propped on the table proclaimed: **UNITED STATES LIBERTY BONDS, Sponsored by Students from the Marple-Newtown Vocational High School**. It looked quite professional.

The four of us were dressed in white full-length dresses. The white was Fannie's suggestion; she said we'd stand out in the Saturday crowd. A great idea, but I had to alter one of mother's dresses, because I didn't have a white one of my own. I thought we looked rather chic.

At first folks just walked by. After half an hour, no one even stopped to look.

"Ladies, this is not going well," Fannie announced. After a quick huddle, and a consultation with our war bond sales' kit, we shifted our pitch. We drew a new sign indicating that a twenty-five dollar bond bought two hundred rounds of bullets; a hundred dollars guaranteed three Enfield rifles; while five hundred dollars bought four 155-millimeter shells.

Now, customers bought bullets to defeat the Kaiser. That had oomph!

Later in the morning a reporter from the *Delaware County Times* stopped at the table. He took some notes and a photographer took our picture. We couldn't stop tittering about how we'd be in the paper.

When the shops closed at one o'clock, we stored our table and took stock.

"Wow! We sold over eight hundred dollars in bonds. Not bad for a morning's work," I said.

"You're all coming to the party at my place tonight, aren't you?" asked Edith.

"Yes, my brother will drive me over. What time should I be there?"

"Oh, tell George to stay. We need all the men we can muster, and he's such a good dancer. Six-thirty would be fine."

"Fannie, how about if I ask George to swing by and pick you up when he drives me over?"

"Oh, that would be great."

I said my good-byes, hitched-up my dress, and began the three mile ride home on Harry's old bicycle.

CHAPTER 22. First Action

September 14, 1918; Souilly, France.

      Just after sunrise a weary Second Squad and their sergeant jumped out of the box car and stretched their legs at their final destination. The town of Souilly was twenty kilometers southwest of Verdun. Untouched by the war, the railhead bustled with the delivery of American troops and their supplies. Our first job was to unload the wagons from the flatcars.

      "Come on boys, up the ramp," hollered Sarge. "Adams, Baker, Doyle, Goldrick, get the wheel clamps opened on the rear wagon. The rest of youse gobs reattach the wagon pole."

      With the pole in position, Baker asked, "Sarge. You want the wagon pole down so's we can steer?"

      "Yeah. Okay, she's loose. Now keep a tight grip. Baker shift to the right, toward the ramp. Little sharper. Okay, cut now!" I watched as the rear wheels came to the edge of the ramp.

      "Edwards, Powell, Doyle, get to the rear and push back as we start down. Osborn and Hughes, use the brakes" instructed Sedelsky. "I don't want this thing gettin' out of control. Okay, boys, ease her down."

      As Doyle, Powell and I pushed at the rear of the wagon to control the descent, I heard Charlie Powell mutter, "This damn thing's heavy." Then Powell shouted, "Hughes, brake tight, it'll run right over us if she breaks loose."

Twenty minutes later all three wagons were on the ground. The horses came next, and they were more than eager to get out of the boxcar.

By 0710 the three wagons of Second Squad advanced north on the Souilly – Verdun Road. The three of us in Wagon Twenty were exhausted, and it took complete concentration to keep from dozing off. The horses stepped along at a modest pace for more than an hour. We talked to each other to keep awake. I was confused because all the roads at the front were supposed to be muddy dirt, but this road was macadam. The other strange thing was the constant rumble. Hughes said he'd been hearin' it since we unloaded the horses.

"Do you think it's artillery?" asked Joe Goldrick..

"I think so, but I'm not sure," I replied.

Goldrick ignored me and kept looking up at the sky.

"You hear that buzz? It's louder one moment, softer the next, sometimes it disappears altogether. There, there, hear it?" he asked.

"Sounds like an airplane," I ventured.

The distant drone suddenly grew much louder as a biplane tore over the road in front of us, not more than a hundred meters in the air. The trees on the sides of the road blocked the view, so I never saw it coming till the engine roared overhead. I only caught a fleeting glance, but Hughes declared it was one of ours. Said he saw circles on the wings. Goldrick wasn't sure.

The horses pulled us another kilometer or so when a deep staccato thud, thud, thud, thud, echoed through the trees. Alarmed, I shouted to Doyle on the wagon ahead, asking if he knew what it was. He hollered back that Sarge called it an 'Archie,' anti-aircraft fire.

What were they shooting at? We again searched the sky. The whine of an aircraft engine returned, and the Archies stopped. A sound of a second engine was heard, and high overhead two planes came into view. They banked, dived, and climbed in a torturous duet, dancing a ballet of follow-the-leader. Bursts of rat-tat-tat-tat-tat-tat were heard over the straining whirr of engines. The lead plane rolled over and screamed towards the ground, the second in close pursuit. Both disappeared behind the trees, their sounds muffled. A moment later, two planes banked over the road and headed in our direction. The lead craft was flexing left and right, while the one behind mimicked its evasive actions. It all happened fast, and in the next moment I heard a different pitched machine gun. Brilliant white flashes spit from behind the propeller of the lead mechanical bird. Macadam and dirt spit upward in a trail of pock marks that sped toward us, shifting rapidly back and forth across the road. I sat frozen in the driver's seat. Pieces of road burst into the air, when the bullets hissed passed the wagon. The aircraft roared overhead, and disappeared.

"Jeez," I yelled. "Did you see the black cross?"

"Yeah, but the Frenchman was on its tail," added Hughes.

Before Goldrick could get a word out, a new machine-gun sound began, interrupted by a distant explosion. We heard cheering from the troops on the road behind us.

"He got the bastard," shouted Hughes. Goldrick and I were all smiles, busily congratulating each other. We'd just won the war. Hughes kept his wits and prodded me to pay attention to the road.

A hundred meters ahead, at the side of the road, two horses lay beside an abandon wagon. One lay still on the ground while the other struggled to lift its head. One leg was grotesquely twisted, and blood seeped from a wound on its neck. An officer stepped up, took out his revolver and shot the animal in the head. Just like that, no fanfare, no hesitation: barrel to the skull, he pulled the trigger. The three of us flinched at the report. "Damn," muttered Hughes. My heart would soon harden. A dead animal's better than a dead man.

Some meters further, we came to another stalled wagon. A pair of medics attended a soldier lying in the wagon bed. I saw a pair of boots hanging over the back shelf. They'd removed the man's jacket and a medic worked on his chest. A moment later, the jacket was placed over the soldier's head. The medic sat back, dejection on his face.

Without being aware of it, my senses began to change. My hearing grew attuned to the sounds of war. The distant thunder grumbled in a cloudless sky, but I realized that it rolled over the ground rather than coming from above.

Goldrick and I were able to control our anxiety, but Hughes' agitation grew. Over the next few hours every airplane he heard signaled a Kraut aviator with us in its sights.

"Edwards, do you see it?" He implored. "Do you see it?" He squirmed in the seat turning side-to-side, eyes searching for what was not there.

"Christ, Hughes. Get a grip."

"Edwards, one of 'em could sweep down this road. Shoot the hell out of us. Why the hell are we here? We're in the open, exposed." Hughes suddenly pointed, "Let's pull under those trees. Over there."

"Goldrick, talk him down," I said.

Goldrick reached from behind, grabbed Hughes' shoulder, and shook sharply.

"Hughes, Calm down, relax, you're in knots. Keep on and you'll go nuts."

"Hell, I gotta get a grip." Hughes had trouble looking at us. He struggled to control himself. Unfortunately, his anxiety slowly infected the three of us, and the road congestion that slowed our advance did not help matters.

Nearly a million American soldiers flowed into a 120-kilometer-wide wedge of the Argonne Forest. The troops of the Eightieth Division would soon occupy a landscape only twenty-five kilometers wide, centered on a hill the French called *Le Mort Homme*. We were stopped at every intersection by the huge numbers of French soldiers that trudged westward, as we advanced north.

Sedelsky passed the word that at 1345 hours we were to find shelter and bed down till nightfall. Good news, because I was exhausted. But it wasn't all good since no chow wagons were in sight.

The driver in the platoon's lead wagon pointed to a large clearing up ahead with a tree-lined perimeter. Sedelsky motioned us off the road and our wagons nestled in among the trees. We shrouded the wagons in camouflage, and then tended to the horses.

"This is good," said Sarge. "Youse gobs bed down here. Weather's warm, it's dry, no need for the tent. We'll be pulling out by evening."

Hughes and I got the horses unhitched and set a makeshift picket line. The distant booming did not let up. I found a soft spot, under one of the trees, collected some leaves, lay my ground cloth over them and spread my bed roll over it.

"I'm wasted," said Hughes.

"Me, too. Wonder what's next?"

"Right now, it's sleep for me," said Goldrick.

"You got that right." I rolled on my side and drifted off.

Sedelsky rousted us at 1800. I shook out the ground cloth, folded my blanket and secured both to the pack. Hughes grumbled something incoherent. We both needed more sleep. Goldrich's stomach growled so loud it caused me to smile. "Damn, Goldrich," I told him, "I'm hungry as hell, but at least my belly ain't talking to me."

"Well, me and my stomach have a good relationship," he replied.

Fifteen minutes later, I clambered onto the wagon seat and took the reins. Daylight was nearly gone, as our wagons joined the road column. Two hundred meters later we entered a small village with just enough light to read the sign: Lemmes. It was only half-a-dozen stone houses with thatched roofs. Not a light was seen from any window, and no one was on the street. The last building had a sign, "*Brasserie la Julian*," and every window was lit.

It started to rain a few hours before sunrise, sometimes quite hard, and by first light on September 15th the three of us were soaked through. We'd advanced only five kilometers. Two kilometers north of a town called Lampire the squad's wagons shifted off the Verdun road into a dense forest. We were assigned an area at the far perimeter called the *Bois de Chapitre*. With camouflage positioned, Hughes and I pitched our pup tent in a downpour. I dug a small ditch around the perimeter with our trenching tool to drain water away. Fortunately, the packs stowed under canvas in the wagon were dry, and that meant that our ground cloths and bedrolls were also dry. It was fully light now with low clouds approaching from the west.

By 0830 the heavy rain had changed to a drizzle. Doyle collected some firewood, and as he leaned down to put a match to it, Sedelsky stopped him. "No fires. Smoke would give away our position. Besides, the wood's soaked. It wouldn't catch anyway." Jeeze, that's obvious, I thought.

Adams and Baker and I fitted a large tarpaulin under the camouflage to keep the rain out and Sedelsky gathered the rest of the squad under it.

"Listen up, men. We'll be hauling shells in two nights. Tonight and tomorrow night the guns of Battery B are advancing into position on the south side of Dead Man's Hill. Hill's about nineteen kilometers due north of us. We're now in a place called Fort Gallieni. It's a major ammunition dump."

"Do we haul them shells from here to the Hill, Sarge?" interrupted Baker. "That's a long trip."

"No. There're secondary dumps up the line. They tell me we'll be bivouacked about four kilometers from the guns. Today and tomorrow we rest here in Gallieni. You'll have map study and other prep work to do tomorrow. We won't likely be in any fixed location. We follow and supply our battery, bunk under tent, under the wagons, in dugouts, or in the open. You might have to carry shells, help move the guns or dig their emplacements. Always, we'll be resupplying ammunition. There's a morning briefing, but for now youse gobs know as much as I do."

A commotion rose behind the sergeant as a chow wagon approached. It was about time. We hadn't eaten in almost thirty hours. The hot corn beef hash, known as Corn Willie, tasted horrible. At least it blunted my hunger, and anything digestible was better than nothing. The hot coffee warmed cold hands.

Breakfast next morning was a plate of creamed beef on toast. I remarked that if I closed my eyes and concentrated, the creamed beef tasted like scrambled eggs!

"Guess you're really concentratin'," snickered Hughes.

Hmmmm. Seemed more like the old Hughes. I wondered if he's got himself to a place where he can handle the fear he had yesterday.

At 0930 Sedelsky had the squad studying maps, and by 1300 Hughes spoke what we all felt.

"Sarge, I'm sick of readin' these maps. It's burned into my head."

"Well, it needs more burning. Youse gobs understand this, where you're going there ain't no street lights. You've seen how black it gets, especially when overcast. Youse need to know where you are, up here in your heads," as he pointed to his skull. "If youse get lost out there, there's no rescue squad. Our job is to deliver shells, and it won't help if you're riding around willy-nilly totally lost. Yesterday, the captain described everything north of here as a wasteland. It goes on for more than eighty kilometers."

"What do you mean wasteland?" asked Baker.

"Captain said the land's blasted bare. You can hardly find a blade of grass let alone a road." Sarge added. "Look boys, I don't like saying this, but youse need to get your heads set for misery."

After that cheery talk we went back to the map.

At 1800 hours Sedelsky rounded us up again. "Check your canteens and the wagon water barrel. Be sure they're full. Lieutenant says water's sparse where we're going. Remember, don't ever drink the water in a shell hole. You've no idea what may be rotting in there."

"What do you mean rotting?"

"Cripes, Baker, what the hell do you think I mean? Rats, dead mules, horses, Germans, Frenchies, our own boys. Water'll kill you just the same as a bullet through the head, only it'd be a whole less pleasant! You get it now, soldier?"

Starlight on a clear night provided enough light to see my way. But in a landscape devastated by war, with an overcast sky, I saw only the outline of the horses directly in front of me. Nevertheless, as we traveled further north, the night sky was peppered by distant flashes. They were too distant to see the explosion. Just a flash on a barren horizon that silhouetted distant hills, outlined shattered tree trunks, and briefly revealed the wagon in front of me. These flickers of light set my bearings. But they were frightening; we were headed straight toward them.

CHAPTER 23. Le Mort Homme

September 17, 1918; Camp Gallieni, France.

At 1835 hours the wagons of Second Squad left the gates of Gallieni. The air was raw, and darkness was soon upon us as we rolled along in a steady, cold downpour. Chilled to the bone, I wore my helmet over a tightly drawn poncho hood. Water still seeped into my tunic. Vague outlines of horses, like ghostly apparitions, jostled in front of the wagon. Hughes and Goldrick took turns pulling the lead animals. Their vigilance kept the wagon from slipping into the depression on the right side of the road. The only thing I heard were horses stepping and the wagon wheels, as they sloshed through the mud or crunched over road gravel. The macadam roadway was far behind us now.

Occasionally, there would be a shout of "Pull-up," and the wheels of the wagon ahead went silent. I'd tighten the reins and pull on the brake handle, and shout, "Pull up," to the wagon behind. Calls echoed down the line. A minute, two minutes, five minutes, maybe as much as an hour later, came the call, "Move out."

Sedelsky's voice came out of the dark. "Edwards, been a change of plan. Captain thinks he's found a less congested route. About three kilometers ahead we'll reach Frommerville. At the main intersection turn west, continue till you reach Bethelainville, then turn north for about two kilometers to Montzeville. That's our new bivouac." Sarge shouted to be heard above the drumbeat of rain.

"How long you reckon?" I shouted back.

"Don't know. Lieutenant says the road's congested all the way to the intersection." Sedelsky's boots sucked mud as he sloshed to the wagon behind us.

Gallieni, the Meuse River, the Argonne Forest, or all those "ille" or "court" villages, they were just words to me. I knew their locations, but they were dots on a piece of paper. I had no idea where I was. Sedelsky, even if privy to useful information, had no time to explain. All night he tromped back and forth between wagons, shouting instructions, and encouraging the rigs to keep tight. Where'd that old man get the energy? I wondered.

At the first hint of dawn on September 19th, the ruins of Montzeville emerged from the fog. The wrecked village was set back on a loop from the Chattancourt Road. Once it must have been well wooded for there were tree stumps all over. The squad got lucky and found a relatively flat space to park the wagons. I figured we were in a churchyard, because the adjacent pile of rubble had a broken stone cross protruding from one side. Phil Doyle raised the concern that our tents might be pitched over an old graveyard.

"What, is the brave Doyle scared of a graveyard?" asked Powell.

The squad had no time to think of anything other than raising the camouflage. With the rigs secured, Sedelsky ordered the pup tents set-up under the netting.

"Under the netting. Now!" Sedelsky yelled. The Lieutenant thought he heard an aircraft motor. We listened intently. The sun had barely risen, but the morning light revealed an overcast sky with dense, low-lying clouds. There was no plane.

"That was dumb," muttered Jake Osborn. "Planes don't fly when it's cloudy. They can't see the ground."

The interruption gave me a chance to look around. To the south, from where we came, I could just make out trees with leaves. In the other three directions there was nothing. I mean nothing. The landscape was stark and empty, and wherever a stand of trees had been, there were now only lifeless stumps. Shattered naked shafts of wood thrust upward, top branches sheared off, and only fragmented shards of leafless lower branches spread outward. Other than the occasional distant boom, we were enveloped in silence. The churned earth stretched outward until shrouded by haze. Not a bush, a weed, a blade of grass existed. The startling feature of the land were holes in the ground, all perfectly round. The bottom of almost every hole was filled with water. About fifty meters away, to the north, a single chimney thrust upward from a mound of rubble. The chimney widened at the base to reveal the fireplace, and within the opening a rusted iron pot dangled from the remains of a spit.

"That's Le Mort Homme," said Sedelsky, pointing to the north. In the far distance, a hill peeked through the morning fog.

By daylight the chow wagons arrived. Why were they exposing themselves in the daylight? Well, they had to be or we'd be starving, I concluded.

Then I remembered what Osborn said. "Planes don't fly when it's cloudy."

Not long after the chow wagon, the engineers arrived in motorized trucks. Fifteen men jumped out equipped with picks, shovels and rakes. Feverishly, they smoothed the deeper ruts and filled cratered holes in the road. Their work concentrated to the north, toward Dead Man's Hill. It was still overcast with low clouds and the road work crews worked out in the open with no worries about Kraut airplanes. The German spotters—wherever they were—tried to target us with their 88-mm guns. They weren't very good at it, because the occasional shell just whistled overhead to detonate out there in the devastation. If they were aiming for Montzeville or the road, they sure as hell couldn't shoot worth a damn.

At 1500 hours Sedelsky assembled the squad. "Boys, orders have come through. Ammunition delivery starts after dark. Captain's ordered at least two, maybe three runs a night. We're to load Battery B with 1000 rounds for each of our four guns. Two hundred meters up the road, beyond the ruins of Montzeville, there's a munitions dump. It's under camouflage, and you can just make it out in the distance." Sarge pointed in its direction. "We'll be hauling shells for as long as it takes to stock the guns. Youse drive in a loop, and Pioneer Guides will show us the way till we know it."

"How long for each trip?" Hughes asked.

Sarge said the round trip was five, maybe five-and-a-half kilometers. But there were two complications; the road might be jammed with night traffic, and the gun emplacements were located two hundred meters up the south side of the hill. We'd have to hand carry the shells up the hill.

Ollie Baker leapt in. "Jeez, Sarge, those damn things are heavy!"

A collective groan came from each of us.

"And twice a night?" asked Doyle.

"You got it. Maybe three times if you hustle!" added Sedelsky.

Another groan.

"It's not as bad as it seems. The gun crew helps carry the shells and two platoons of engineers are being pulled from the echelons for additional help. Lieutenant Harden said there's some kind of contraption to help carry them."

"Can't we just empty the wagon and leave?" asked Will Adams.

"No, the shells have to reach the guns, and the engineers won't be in position for three days. For now, you'll be making at least two deliveries a night and as many hikes up the hill."

"Is there a trail? How steep's the climb?" asked Ollie Baker.

"Don't know. Lieutenant checked the hill yesterday. He said it's muddy and that they've cut an up and down route. Youse won't be bumping into anyone. Lieutenant said to be sure and stay on the trail. Either side's pitted with craters."

At 1900, with darkness on us, the rigs were ready to roll. Final instructions came from Sedelsky. "Okay, boys, this is it. I've been ordered to stay at the ammo dump. Pay attention to the pioneer, he'll keep you from getting lost. Oh yeah, Harden said to watch your time. Youse must be under camouflage before dawn. Can't risk a Kraut plane spotting us. Lieutenant said to call off a run, if you can't make it back before sunrise. It's the wagon driver's call. Okay, men, pull-out."

I slapped the reins and the wagon blended into the road congestion. Twenty minutes later twenty-two shells were secured in the wagon bed. We were the lead wagon, and a Pioneer Guide now sat between Hughes and me. He told us his name was Hank Jackson from

Vermont. I never got a good look at Jackson in the dark, but I had the impression he was older than Hughes and me. Jackson told us to keep our eyes peeled. The engineers had placed white marker posts alongside the road. They'd keep us on track and were easy to see, even on overcast nights.

The intersection with the east-west road was jammed with infantry and supply vehicles. I halted the rig, and waited while a whole company of doughboys trudged westward toward Esnes. Jackson said he'd overheard they were going to occupy old French trenches in Malancourt. After crossing the intersection, we rode on an empty road as Jackson pointed out marker poles. I'd have driven right past the damn things. So much for "easy to see."

"Turn left in another twenty meters," Jackson instructed.

The turn marker was barely visible, but not so the two MPs who suddenly called out, "Halt, identify yourself."

I pulled on the reins. "Private Edwards with Second Squad, 3rd Platoon delivering munitions to Battery B." One MP shined a light in our eyes, while the other scanned the wagon bed.

"Okay, in fifteen meters, you'll see lights on the ground."

There were lanterns ringing a large area, shielded so that their light diffused over the ground. The light had me looking down, and it took a moment to realize that there was a camouflage shroud above us. Other wagons ringed the perimeter, and shadows of men hustled back and forth. Muffled voices came from all directions.

Jackson called out, "Who's here from Battery B?"

"Over here," came a voice.

A pair of hands beckoned the rig forward. I drew the horses to a stop, tied off the reins, and got out of the wagon. Hughes had already unhooked the rear wagon gate. Goldrick see-sawed the first shell from the wagon deck to the rear shelf.

"We've been waiting for you," said a guy wearing a uniform streaked with mud. "I'm Wilkes from Gun Crew Four. When we get up top, the rest of the crew will come down and help carry the remaining shells. You ever carry a 155 before?"

We'd met Wilkes back in August at the artillery range of Camp Meucon. Wilkes told us we'd be using a wooden frame to carry the shell. The frame hooked over our shoulders and the shell fit in a channel behind our shoulder blades. We'd have to lean forward to keep our balance or we'd topple over.

"You'll get the hang of it fast, or get hurt real bad!" he added.

I didn't quite share his humor. The crude carrier had no straps or padding, it just rested on my shoulders. However, my tunic and poncho fortunately kept the edges from biting into my skin. The shell in the channel did not need to be strapped in, as long as I leaned slightly forward. With the frame in position, I backed up to the wagon. Goldrick and Hughes lifted the casing onto the frame, and jiggled it to adjust the balance.

"Damn," I complained. This is clumsy." I took a step and almost fell over backward catching myself in the nick of time by grabbing the edge of the wagon. After some practice, the four of us and the rest of the men in the squad were ready to began our trek up the hill. There was a steady rain and I pulled on the strings to tighten my poncho hood. It didn't help much.

Wilkes's voice came out of the night. "Follow the boot steps in front of you. I can use a lantern tonight 'cause it's overcast. Keep your eyes on the light and stay at least a meter apart. If the shell slips out, it won't hit the guy behind you."

Soon, the only sound was that of boots wallowing in mud and heavy breathing. We all sucked wind. It wasn't the slope or the mud, but the weight.

My God, my legs are going to give way, I worried. What the hell am I doing here?

"Keep with me," Wilkes encouraged.

Fatigue built, and I felt like I'd collapse. Sooner than I expected Wilkes told us we were just thirty meters from the top. Only thirty meters, how the hell'd we get here so fast? I wondered. Next thing I knew, someone lifted the shell from the harness, and it felt like I'd float away. A quick swig from my canteen soothed my dry mouth and throat. A new voice shouted for us to have a smoke. We'd be headed down in five. I squatted down, still breathing heavily.

"Shit. That was rough," said Goldrick.

"Hughes, you here?"

"Yeah, right behind ya."

"All right men, time to start down," called an unknown voice.

The tips of three cigarettes came to a bright glow with a last drag. A lantern led the way as we descended. A swinging lantern and the labored breathing of another crew passed us on their way up.

Back at the wagon I counted seven men from the gun crew that had come down with us. It took eight minutes to transfer another load of death to our shoulders. A moment later, we were on our way up the trail. This time the shell fuses were added to our pockets. Round-trip took thirty-five minutes. The gun crew returned to the wagon a second time, then trudged up the hill with another load. The gun boss, who came down with the crew, told me to unload the wagon placing the remaining shells and powder bags under a tarpaulin.

"Why aren't we going up again?" asked Hughes.

"They want us to deliver another load before dawn," said Adams.

Gillespie's rig led on the return with Jackson now guiding us back to Montzeville. This trip took less time, because we rolled against the traffic that streamed westward from Verdun. The cutoff back to Montzeville had no traffic at all. We made two more deliveries that night, and by the time the last rig parked under the camouflage, daylight glowed on the eastern horizon.

"That was close. Don't begin a delivery unless you have at least three hours to dawn. Can't have Krauts catching youse in the open." In an exhausted stupor I muttered, "Yes, Sergeant."

I felt like I had to tell one leg to move in front of the other. The chow wagon arrived, and half an hour later Hughes and I headed to the tent.

September 26, 1918; Montzeville, France.

On the first run, slowed by a traffic tie-up, we didn't reach Dead Man's till well after 0130. I trudged up the muddy incline twice, and by the time our wagon returned to the ammunition dump for a second load it was 0315 hours. Sedelsky decided there was enough time for a second delivery, but when the squad's three wagons arrived at the bottom of the hill, the drop-off area was deserted. There weren't even MPs at the turn. Confused, and with the time to sunrise getting tight, we decided to place everything under a tarpaulin, and begin the trek back to Montzeville. My rig was in the lead. The Verdun-Esnes road seemed unusually empty. Only ambulance vehicles passed us heading west. As we turned onto the by-pass road, I was concerned about the hint of daylight on the easterly horizon.

"What time you got, Hughes?"

He held his wristwatch up to the dim light. "0525," he said. "Damn, Edwards, we need to hustle."

I pushed the team as hard as the rutted road allowed, but the effort was unsuccessful. Three hundred meters from the safety of our bivouac, the sounds of snorting animals, the swishing leather tack sliding on horse flesh, the crackling of chains, the muffled splash of hooves and the squish of turning wheels suddenly disappeared, replaced by a roar from Hades. The twelve horses of Second Squad lurched at the sudden thunder. I struggled to control my team and yelled, "Pull up."

At 0530 *Le Mort Homme* came alive as our guns began a barrage, flinging their deadly projectiles toward the German lines. I realized from the roar of the 155's and steady drumfire of the French 75's, that there were many more heavy guns on that hill than just those of Battery B.

Second Squad came to a stop. We stood in our wagons and tried to take it in. Spitting forth from all the hills as far as I could see to the east and west were flashes of cannon fire. Our eyes and ears shifted to the north as the deadly force of the barrage slammed home. The distant front blazed with a deep orange glow.

Like deer caught in bright lights, we were transfixed by this spectacle. That is until, Adams shouted above the din, "Come on, Edwards, roll out. It's getting light." I flicked the reins, and the squad's three wagons continued their trek across the barren landscape.

Chapter 24. Clutch

September 26, 1918, The Peterson House, Marple, Pennsylvania.

I'd been driving Harry's car for just under five months. There were some problems that needed attention, particularly in the clutch mechanism. I'd rolled the front wheels onto 12-inch wedges to raise the car. In that way I could crawl under it to work.

Father found me under the car. He tapped on my boots till I crawled out. My old man was angry.

"George, are you foolish enough to trust those wedges? Jeez, Son. If the brakes slipped, you'd be crushed."

I didn't understand him at first.

"Say that again." I'd left my ear trumpet on the kitchen table. He repeated himself, and this time I looked closely at his lip movements.

"It's not a problem. I put braces under the rear wheels, so she won't roll."

Father exaggerated his lip movements as he spoke. He went on with something about how the farm would suffer if I got injured. I wasn't sure what he said, because I wasn't concentrating. I wanted to crawl back under the Ford. He asked what I was doing.

"I've installed new clutch plates," I told him. "Problem is, there's a strange vibration when driving in low gear. I don't know what's causing it. Far as I know, I put everything back together correctly."

Father asked me if I had any parts left over after I reassembled clutch.

"You're making a joke, aren't you?" I asked somewhat annoyed at his comment.

He smiled and said, "George, why don't you take the car down to Mr. Thompson's garage? Ask him what he thinks the problem is. Could save you a lot of time. Tell him I suggested it. Oh yes, tell him the welding job he did on the plough is doing right well."

Next day I drove over to Thompson's.

"Hello, Mr. Thompson. You remember me? I'm George Edwards, Frazure Edwards' boy."

"Oh yes. George. How's your Father? I haven't seen him in …well, must be a year now. So, what can I do for you?"

"Could you speak up a bit. I don't hear so well." I got the trumpet pointed in his direction, and he repeated.

"Doc says he's got some arthritis growing in his knees. Otherwise, quite well. Thank you for asking. My father suggested I come see you. My brother's over in France and left his Model-T to my care. The clutch plates needed replacing, and I decided to do it myself. Got the repair manual from the library, and sent a mail order for the parts. Put the car on some blocks and changed-out the plates. Everyone says there's this ting, ting, ting sound when I drive in low gear. I can't hear it, but I do feel a vibration in the car seat. Father says it worsens when the car speeds up. Strangely, there's no problem in high gear. Took it apart a second time but it didn't help. I'm not sure what to do."

"Did you have any parts left over when you got it all back together? "

"Ahhh… No, Mr. Thompson." Did my old man put him up to this? I wondered.

"Just pulling your leg, George. Let's take it for a short spin, I'll drive."

"Okay, here's the keys."

"Will you crank?"

"Don't need to. It's got one of them electric starters," I said.

"Damn, who installed it?"

"I did." Mr. Thompson looked surprised.

He kicked-in the engine and drove it a block, then did a U-turn.

"I know the problem, George. Seen it a number of times."

"Do I have to tear out the whole gear box again?"

"No. The clutch fingers aren't adjusted right." Mr. Thompson told me how to set the fingers. "Oh, and be sure and replace the cotter keys. Say, I'm impressed George. Never had a young feller in the shop who took the time to understand these machines."

"Well, I like working with them Fords. Taught myself everything about 'em. I want to learn body work. Maybe one day, I'll open a business."

"Hmmmm, competition eh. Let me ask you something, George. My business is boomin' lately. More folks are buying cars, and soon there's going to be a lot more than just Fords. When the war ends, them boys'll be coming home looking for a place to part with their bonus. A new car'll look real attractive. I need help in the shop. What about you come work for me? I could pay you $2.50 a day. I want to expand into body work, so you'd learn that also. What do ya say?"

"Ahhh... Mr. Thompson... I hear you right? You offering me a job?"

"That's right, son."

CHAPTER 25. Hill 281

September 26, 1918; Montzeville, France.

The roar from our guns prevented any of us from turning-in, and the squad just sat under the netting engaged in small talk. At 1000 hours the firing abruptly stopped and we experienced an eerie silence. I looked northward toward Dead Man's Hill and saw Sedelsky running full-tilt down the road from the ammo dump.

"Hughes. Something's up. Sarge is hightailing it this way."

Sedelsky entered camp. "Okay men. Turn out," he gasped. "Command's ordered us to break camp. Battery B's relocating to a position further north. The attack was a success. Caught the Krauts off guard. They're pulling back all across this sector and Battery B's shifting immediately to a more forward position. The guns are coming off the Hill as we speak. We're headed to Hill 281. Pack up and fast. Leave the camouflage behind."

"What? No camouflage?" asked Baker.

"No need for secrecy anymore. Now get the tents down and gear stowed in ten minutes. Pack the wagons, so you can carry a load of shells. We'll be heading westward toward Cuisy. Hill 281's about a kilometer west of Bethincourt. Lieutenant said we can drive right up to the emplacements. Brigade supply is already stocking a new ammo dump. Oh yeah, keep together, the road's congested."

"What about being out during the daylight?" asked Powell.

"Yeah, that ain't good. Them Kraut planes may harass us. Keep your rifles on hand. Shoot back if the bastards come in low. Now set to, men. Hustle."

Twenty minutes later, with each wagon carrying twenty-two shells, we merged onto the Esnes-Bethincourt road. Glancing back, I saw Le Mort Homme behind us. It was silhouetted in the morning light, and in that moment I realized that this caper was just beginning.

Hill 281was in sight by 1430 hours. It was not as high as Le Mort Homme, and more important, the wagon rigs could drive right up to the gun emplacements. The big howitzers had arrived half an hour ahead of us. Lieutenant Harden ordered Third Platoon to help Battery B dig in the guns. Hughes and I shifted dirt for more than four hours to set the beasts. We excavated three to four meters into the hillside, and then laid down a wooden path for the gun wheels and trail to roll on. This made it easier for the gun crew to position each weapon. We supply boys pitched in pushing and pulling the howitzer.

"Okay men, listen up," said Sedelsky. "We need to find our new bivouac, set camp and be ready to resupply our 155's. Lieutenant says there's a new ammo dump just this side of Malencourt. Our bivouac is close by. Gillespie, I'll ride in your wagon."

I pulled hard on the reins and four horse heads shifted left. Sixteen legs strained on the ground pulling the wagon and its three weary passengers away from the emplacements. At that moment an incoming Jerry screamed overhead, followed by a deafening explosion two hundred meters to our side. Shells started dropping all around us! I heard someone yell, "Gas!" I reached into my chest pack, fumbling to position the unruly mask over my face. My God, I thought, this is for real. The body language of Hughes and Goldrick revealed they were as scared as I was. For a few moments I thought I saw Hughes' hand shaking.

Fortunately, the German fire was ineffective, with most of the shells impacting some distance from us. Nevertheless, the three of us saw a yellowish mist drifting nearby. The squad escaped unscathed this time, but the three of us in Wagon Twenty convinced ourselves we had a metallic taste at the back of our throats.

Our wagons delivered artillery shells to Hill 281 for two days. The Battery fired salvos, but they were never sustained. A single gun might deliver rounds for two hours, unleashing one every five minutes or so. After which another gun would take on the job. Who knew if they fired blindly, or if they had a spotter directing their action? Sedelsky called it "harassing fire," designed to disrupt German lines of communication or lessen their ability to organize troops. Did that really work? It seemed more like wasted ammunition to me. After all, Jerry's harassment fire on us had no effect.

Late afternoon of September 28th, Hughes and I were the last wagon to return to the bivouac. Sedelsky gathered the squad. "New orders men. We're shifting to the hill called Montfaucon. Our new bivouac's at the base of the hill. Battery B is relocating to Septsarges, about six kilometers northwest of us. We'll resupply them from Faucon."

"How far in front of us are the doughboys, Sarge?"

"Don't know, Baker. Maybe four, five kilometers to the north. We're closer to the enemy than ever. Lieutenant says be careful. Kraut stragglers could be lurking. They could be dangerous."

We broke camp and were on the road in fifteen minutes. By 1850 hours Hughes and I had our tent set in the skeletal remains of a forest near the intersection of the Bethincourt-Avocourt Road. We lay in the shadow of Montfaucon, only half a kilometer from our position. The hill rose sharply over the surrounding fields.

Adams hollered the welcome cry. "Chow wagon!" Ten hungry men and their Sergeant rushed over to get some eats. As we ate, Sedelsky laid out the plan. "Okay, men," he said. "Youse get three hours shuteye. Then, it's back to hauling shells. Septsarges will be a short run up and back. For now, review your maps, and hit the sack."

CHAPTER 26. Stragglers

October 2, 1918; Cierges, France.
Early in October the squad shifted location again. We were now bivouacked two kilometers north of Montfaucon, along the Faucon-Romagne Road, in the ruined town square of Cierges. It looked like a tractor had come through and pushed all the ruble aside, creating a large clean space, big enough for tents, wagons, and horses for the whole platoon. We even had a mess tent. I guessed access to the well water and hand pump in the middle of the square was what the army wanted. Ammunition stored in the armory at Montfaucon supplied our wagons, and the 155 howitzers were never satisfied no matter how many rounds we delivered.

With the Cierges camp established, orders to resupply Battery B arrived. It seemed crazy to back-track to Montfaucon to load our wagon, then ride north passing the bivouac to the new gun location. But, that's how the army organized it. The howitzers were now located east of Romagne, nestled below a ridge adjacent to the village of Cunel, seven kilometers north of Montfaucon. There was unconfirmed talk of stiffened enemy resistance, but no counterattack had occurred yet.

The ammo runs from Faucon to Romagne used four different routes. At least we had options, when road congestion became unbearable. All army supplies flowed from southern railheads, and traveled north over the same routes our wagons drove. Fortunately, the more use a road had, the more the engineers kept it repaired. Regardless, road congestion would have driven us to drink, if we had any.

A warning came from the gun boss in Battery B during one delivery.

"Edwards, Hughes. Hold up. The Lieutenant wanted me to warn you guys. You need to be careful on your trips here and back. We've advanced fast and pockets of Germans have been skipped over. They've holed up in dugouts along old trench lines, particularly on roads less traveled. Most times they don't know they're isolated. Infantry, supply crews, even us artillery guys pick up stragglers all the time. Mostly, they just rise up shaking something white and surrender."

Hughes asked. "What the hell do we do if we capture one?"

"That's not the point, some of 'em are loyal fanatics, sneak out of their dugout and ambush our guys. One of our boys, Corporal Wilkes, took a round in his side two days ago from one of them. Lieutenant got an infantry platoon to clean out the bastards."

"Jeez, I know Wilkes. Is he okay?" I asked.

"Yeah, bullet passed clean through."

"Any way of knowing where them stragglers might be?" asked Hughes.

"No. Lieutenant says use caution. Especially, if you're passing old German trenches, or you're on a road you don't know. Keep sharp eyes for anything that don't look right. Keep your rifles close."

"Jeez, I'm so tired, I don't know if I'll be able to see anything unusual," said Hughes.

"You're not the only one," added the gun boss.

I unhooked the reins, and got the animals engaged. The wagon reversed direction and headed toward Montfaucon. Traffic jammed the road south of Romagne.

"Jeez, we'll be forever getting back to camp," I said.

Hughes checked his map and suggested an alternative route. "Edwards, we could go west, through Gesnes. Might take us out of the way a bit, but we'd bypass this mess." He traced the route with his finger. "They captured the area more than two weeks ago, should be safe now," he added.

Half a kilometer south of Romagne we found the intersection and I shifted the rig to the southwest, out of the congestion. The whole area had been shot-up, and the muddy, rutted road was barely passable. The detritus of recent fighting was all around, accompanied by the horrible stench of decay. The bodies hadn't been buried yet. Bloated corpses were scattered along the road or hanging grotesquely out of trenches. Body parts stuck out of dirt mounds.

"Damn, must've been a lot of fighting here," said Hughes.

At one point we passed eight bodies laid out parallel to each other at the side of the road. They were covered with American ponchos, and behind each a rifle was stuck in the ground by its bayonet. A helmet and ID tags draped over the end of the stock. Their boots had been removed, and a yellow tag, tied to the big toe, fluttered in the breeze.

"Looks like the burial detail tagged 'em," I said. "Jeez, Hughes, let's get out of here."

Forty minutes and three kilometers later, we entered the rubble of Gesnes. The stone work of a few shattered house walls still stood, and long lines of rubble outlined the course of what once was a stone fence. We came to an intersection and Hughes pointed, "That's our way back."

I was about to turn the horses when movement caught my attention out of the corner of my eye. A loud "crack" and a "whoosh" cleaved the air. A "thud" shook the seat back. I glanced down and saw a perfectly drilled and blackened hole, the diameter of my pinky, between me and Hughes. A waft of smoke came from the hole. Recognition took a few seconds longer. I yelled, "Jump!" Hughes had the sense to set the brake before he tumbled from the wagon. Another "crack." This time the bullet ripped overhead.

"To the back," hollered Hughes. The rear of the wagon afforded pitiful shelter. Crouching, I opened the rear door and Hughes crawled into the wagon bed. Keeping low, he squirmed over the empty shell mounts, grabbed my rifle, passed it back to me. Hughes cradled his own rifel, and clambered to the rear. Another "crack" echoed off the crumbled walls. We felt the shudder when the bullet slammed into the wagon side wall.

"Christ, this wagon ain't any shelter. If that Kraut gets any sense he'll shoot low. Get us in the legs," said Hughes.

"Be safer behind that," I said, pointing to the ruined stone fence. "Can't be more than five meters."

"Okay. You go first. I'll keep him down. You ready?" I nodded.

"Go!" said Hughes.

I took off toward the wall at a crouched run. Hughes popped up over the rear gate, took aim at where he thought the rifle sound came from, and pulled the trigger. I was over the stone mound, and safely protected by it. The shooter popped up and discharged another round. An undisciplined shot. I indicated with a hand signal for Hughes to go. He kept the wagon between himself and the shooter and sprinted toward the rubble. This time, I popped up and fired a shot. As Hughes dove over the top, another "crack" ripped through the air. Stone shards burst from the impact next to his boot.

I was peering through a slit in the debris. "I know where he is."

I gave Hughes the approximate location. "I'm going to creep off to the right," I told him. This rubble goes for another twenty meters or more. You keep him busy. I may get a clear shot at the end of the wall. He'll be looking in your direction."

"Be careful," he said.

I crawled on the ground, carefully negotiating the stone rubble.

Easy does it, don't dislodge any stones, I warned myself..

Hughes shifted behind the mound, two or three meters to the left and right to make the German think both of us were together. Since the Kraut never knew where Hughes would pop-up next, his return fire had no effect. Nevertheless, he was a persistent bastard, and matched Hughes round for round.

At the far edge of the pulverized wall, I peaked around the corner. Sixty meters in front of me I saw the Kraut as he bobbed up and down. His focus was on Hughes and an easy target from my angle. I shouldered my rifle, took aim, and waited. Hughes let off another round and the German rose to fire back. I squeezed. His rifle flipped in the air. I heard a grunt and a "clank" when his weapon hit the ground. His body stiffened, arched backward, and fell from sight.

"Just wait," I shouted.

There was no movement, only silence from where the German had concealed himself. My mouth was dry. My hand trembled, as I chambered another round and fingered the trigger.

"I don't see anything." I called.

I inched around the corner of the ruble, rose slowly, looked around, and stepped cautiously onto the road. My heart was pounding. Hughes climbed over the mound and approached the German. I advanced more slowly, scanning the ruins.

"Edwards, you gotta see this."

Jittery, I eyeballed the ruined walls, and approached Hughes with half steps.

"Shit," I uttered.

The figure below me was dead. Strands of severed cloth and a red splotch ringed a tiny hole on the front of his tunic. A growing red pool from beneath him spread on the brown earth. His open eyes stared up at me.

"Damn, Edwards. It's a boy!" said Hughes.

"God, he can't be more than thirteen or fourteen. Those damn Krauts sent a boy off to war. Help me look for his papers."

"No, don't. Come on, back to the wagon," Hughes insisted. "We're outta here."

He grabbed my arm and pulled me toward the horses. I fought to go back to the body, but he pushed me away. Reluctantly, I climbed onto the seat and sat there staring into the distance.

"Edwards. Snap outta it. Come on, move out!" I sat frozen, the boy's piercing eyes seared in my mind.

Hughes saw it first. From the crumbling remains of a wall across the road, behind where the dead German lay, a rifle barrel poked out from the edge. A white handkerchief tied to its tip shook back and forth. "What the hell?" Hughes said as he cradled his gun, and with his other arm, jolted my shoulder. That returned me to my senses. I grabbed my rifle, jumped off the wagon, and leveled it at the fluttering rag.

"*Kamerade. Kamerade. Kamerade,*" was the cry.

"Come out," I yelled.

Hughes scooted to his right, kept his weapon leveled, and quickly scanned the front of the ruin. A solitary figure came around the corner of the house. I gestured with my rifle tip for him to put his arms up. His hands rose in the air, but he still carried the rifle. I brought my weapon up and sighted on him, fingering the trigger. The German faced around for a moment and said something. From behind the building another figure emerged. Then another, and another, and another still, their hands in the air.

"*Hände upp!*" I uttered in broken Pennsylvania Dutch.

"Over here," said Hughes.

I kept a bead on them, as Hughes approached and relieved them of their guns.

"Jeez, Edwards. They're all kids!"

I gestured for them to remove their cartridge belts. They unsnapped the buckles, and belts fell to the ground. We loaded the boys into the bay of the wagon and the German lads sat quietly, a look of relief on their faces.

The dead boy in the ditch entered my head as, half-heartedly, I flicked the reins. The horses trod at a even pace as we followed the road out of Gesnes, carrying me away from this depressing place.

"Damn, Hughes. Why the hell didn't he surrender?"

Hughes replied, but I was beyond listening. I couldn't stop thinking about those eyes. Tears formed, then silently streamed down my cheeks. There wasn't supposed to be any killing in artillery supply wagons. At least none like this.

CHAPTER 27. Dinner Party

October 15, 1918; The Peterson House, Marple, Pennsylvania.

My son had been away for five months and by October we were experiencing cooler fall nights. Monday evening, while preparing supper, Emily asked me if she could invite Fannie White to stay over this Friday and Saturday night.

"I think that will be all right," I replied. "Let me ask your father. Say, Emily, I just had a thought. Why don't you invite the Whites to join us for dinner on Sunday? Ask them to come over around one o'clock. I'd like to meet them."

"Oh! I think Fannie would like that. Let me ask her," said Emily.

That night, before turning out the light, I told Frazure of Emily's request. "Emily asked Fannie White to spend the weekend with us. She'll come home after school on Friday. I agreed, and suggested she invite the Whites to dinner Sunday afternoon. It's time we meet this Fannie and her parents."

"Why's that?" Frazure asked.

"Goodness, you do realize that every letter from Harry mentions Fannie. There's something serious between them."

"Sally, you're reading too much into those letters."

"You didn't see what happened at the train station when he left for Camp. The way they kissed."

"Sally, Harry's twenty-one years old for goodness sake. So, what if he gave her a big smooch."

"Well, I feel strongly about this, Frazure. Are you all right with the dinner?"

"Yes," he replied. My son had a crush on this young lady. Am I the only one to see it? Indeed, the show at the train station told me all I needed to know. It was high time I learned more about this girl.

❧

October 18, 1918; The Peterson House, Marple, Pennsylvania.

Fannie met my mother several years ago when all us kids were attending the Cedar Grove Literary Club. Friday after school, I re-introduced Fannie to Mother.

"I'm so glad your parents are joining us Sunday, I look forward to meeting them. Will you girls help me prepare the meal? I heard Mother ask.

"We'd love to," I responded, and Fannie nodded with enthusiasm.

Fannie and I were headed out of the kitchen when she twirled around. "Hold up a moment, Em. Mrs. Edwards, you should know the Whites aren't my parents. Clifford is my Uncle and Janet's my Aunt."

"And your parents?" Mother asked.

"My mother's still alive, she lives in Virginia. Father passed away years ago. I've eleven brothers and sisters and momma couldn't handle all of us. I was sent to live here in Media. So, here I am."

Did I catch a look of surprise on Mother's face?

Three years ago Father placed a double sized bed in my room. He told me a young woman needs to have a nice place to sleep, and that my brothers would do quite well in their single beds. I am glad he sees it that way. Father did not favor me often, and I certainly wasn't going to complain about the lumpy mattress. When she slept over, Fannie shared my bed, and we talked and giggled till midnight.

Next morning, Fannie and I helped with Saturday breakfast by mixing batter for a whole rack of flap jacks. Midway through breakfast the phone rang. Mother answered, and I overheard her say to Aunt Ella that my school friend was spending the weekend with us. After a pause, Mother turned to us and announced that my Aunt was inviting us over for lunch.

"When do you want them, Ella? Around noon? Okay, George will drive, but they can't stay all afternoon. The girls have to help me prepare for tomorrow. We're entertaining the Whites for dinner Sunday. Okay dear, speak to you soon. Love to Albert."

October 19, 1918; Ardmore, Pennsylvania.

George drove us to Ardmore. Morris sat up front while, in the back, Fannie and I kept up a barrage of girl talk to annoy the boys. Well, It didn't annoy George, he couldn't hear a thing.

During lunch Uncle Albert happened to mention that he'd just bought an electric table saw. Fannie overheard, and told Albert her Uncle taught woodworking in Media High School, and that he'd recently been talking about those new saws at supper.

"Could I see it Mr. Long? My Uncle'd be so jealous of me."

"Sure," said Albert. After lunch he ushered us to the basement to see his current woodworking project, and the saw.

"Can I cut a piece of wood, Uncle Albert?" asked Morris.

"Yes, but let me show you how. You need to be careful," he said. "This machine can be dangerous." He switched on the saw and gave Morris a demonstration on how to use it. Albert let him cut a piece of wood as Fannie and I covered our ears to shut-out the roar. Uncle Albert flipped the switch and the saw settled down.

"Can I try Mr. Long?" asked Fannie.

"That's not a good idea, Fannie," said George. "Your frilly cuffs could get caught in the blade."

"No they won't, I'll roll 'em up."

"I think George is right, Fannie," said Uncle Albert.

Fannie offered her best pout, but with no success.

She climbed the cellar stairs ahead of George, halted at the top, and faced him. I heard her say, "It was so sweet of you to care about me, George. Thank you."

Aunt Ella, Fannie, and I cleaned up from lunch and chatted about how my mother was feeling and if Fannie's Uncle had a woodworking hobby like Uncle Albert. In the parlor, the men discussed the farm, Harry and the war. At 4:30 George announced, "Aunt Ella, we need to start back."

George asked Fannie to sit up front with him.

"Would you mind, Emily? Cliff never lets me sit up front."

"It's okay," I replied. The October afternoon was cool and George got two blankets from the seat locker; one for Morris and me in the back, and the other for Fannie and him up front. We waved good-bye and as George drove away, I noticed Fannie snuggling over toward him.

❦

October 20, 1918; The Peterson House, Marple, Pennsylvania.

Sunday, at one o'clock the front door knocker announced our guests. Mother and I were in the kitchen. She dried her hands, and hurried to the front door. "Frazure… Frazure," I heard her call. "The Whites are here."

From the kitchen I listened. "How nice to meet you folks." Introductions followed, and Mother ushered everyone into the parlor. When seated Mr. White offered. "Please call us Clifford and Janet," and Mother and Father reciprocated the gesture. The atmosphere relaxed.

Fannie and I joined the group and I noticed that Clifford had a receding hair line which he tried to hide by letting his remaining hair grow long. A brown beard and neatly trimmed moustache covered his face. He was dressed in a grey suit, and a watch fob extended to the vest pocket beneath his jacket. Janet was prim looking with trimmed short brown hair, rather prissy looking glasses, and dressed in a plain beige fall dress whose hemline went to the floor. A large shiny gemstone band adorned her left index finger. Both reminded me of schoolteachers.

Fannie and I listened to the conversation.

"Have you heard from Harry?" asked Cliff.

"Yes. He's in northern France, around the Argonne Forest," said Father. "Went to the Front from their French training base about a month ago. We don't learn much from Harry because of the censorship. Every time he writes something about the war there is a black line over it."

"You must be so worried, Sally," Janet said.

"You can't know how much."

"Harry was off to the Army in early May. Did some training in Virginia," said Father.

"Yes, I know. He was over the house the night before he left for camp. He seems like a nice boy."

Mother and Janet weren't interested in war talk. "Janet, where do you live in Media?" asked Mother.

"Two houses up from Jackson, on Third Street."

"Been there long?"

"Clifford, how long have we been in the house, thirteen or fourteen years?" I heard Janet ask.

"Excuse me, Frazure. It's thirteen this November, Dear."

"Fannie told me you have two other sons?"

"Yes, George and Morris. The boys should be in any moment."

"And you, Sally, how do you keep busy?"

"Well, I take care of the house. But, I have fun making under garments for ladies. I sell them in the Pink Parasol, on State Street.

"That's a nice shop."

"Yes it is, and you, Janet?" asked Mother.

"Mostly volunteer work in the Episcopal Church."

Mother excused herself to return to the kitchen to finish preparing dinner and directed us girls to join her. Janet asked if she could help, and in the kitchen she diced parsley for the potatoes. Mother prepared gravy from the lamb drippings. Fannie cut the bread loaf into slices, while I placed butter on the table, and filled the water glasses. Mother called Morris to the kitchen and asked him to remove the leg-of-lamb from the spit. He placed it on a cutting board and carved it into dinner pieces. It simply amazed Janet that Morris knew how to carve.

With our guests seated, Mother arranged boiled potatoes and onions around the lamb cuts, then sprinkled them generously with Janet's diced parsley flakes. I carried the serving platter to the table. When Mother entered the dining room, carrying the gravy boat, she beamed as everyone praised the delicious looking platter. She was quick to point out that we girls had helped her.

Pleasant talk complimented the dinner. At one point I heard Clifford ask George about working at Mr. Thompson's garage. He mentioned that he was thinking of installing an electric starter in his car, and Father told him that George had installed one in Harry's Ford, and that it sure beat the crank.

"Say George," asked Clifford. "Could you do the same in my Buick?"

"I don't see why not. It might cost twenty-five dollars, plus the cost of a car battery."

"Is that all! By George, I'll give it serious thought," said Cliff.

We all laughed at Cliff's pun, and I overheard Fannie comment on how clever George was. He acknowledged her compliment with a head nod.

"How did you become the shop teacher at Media High School?" asked Mother. The explanation of his path from the Peach farm in Culpepper, Virginia to Media High school consumed the next half hour.

"Uncle Clifford, tell them about the peach farm," Fannie said. "It's so beautiful there."

"You never talked to me about it," I said.

"I know, Emily, but I didn't think you'd understand. It's so different and peaceful. There's none of the bustle of Media."

"Why don't you describe it, Fannie?" Cliff asked her.

"Well… On a clear day you can see the mountains in the west. In the spring, when the trees blossom, the whole valley is this shade of pink. I return home summers to help pick the crop. The peaches drip with nectar, and I swear, they're so good I could eat one for every one I pick! My grandmother and older brothers and a sister live there and they're such fun. We help mama make delicious peach jam. The winters here are so miserable, and I don't like the cold and snow. But at the farm, it's much warmer. After high school, I may go back for a longer time. Momma's getting frail now and she can use my help."

"But don't you want to do something with what you learned in school?" I heard Mother ask.

"I'm taking typing like Emily, but I also love picking peaches, Mrs. Edwards."

Everyone laughed.

"I'd hate to see you waste that typing skill," Cliff said.

Emily helped me with the dishes and by six-thirty the kitchen was cleaned. I had settled myself into my favorite chair to do some darning. When the clock chimes rang nine my husband announced it was time to retire. He switched off the lights and ascended the stairs behind me.

As I pulled up the bed covers Frazure said, "What a nice afternoon, Sally. The meal was wonderful. Interesting folks, those Whites. I'm glad we got to know them, and Fannie seems a sensible young woman, though I hate to see her spending her life picking peaches."

"I am troubled, Frazure," I said. "Fannie says she wants to go back to the peach farm. She clearly loves it there."

"What's wrong with that?"

"What if Harry comes home and marries Fannie? The girl will convince him to move to Virginia. Where does that leave us?"

"Sally, I think you are just jealous of another woman in Harry's life," Frazure said to me. After that he reached over and switched off the light.

CHAPTER 28. False Alarm

October 14, 1918; Cierges, France.

Hughes and I worked round the clock. There was hardly any sleep to be had. Day or night we helped set artillery pieces, hauled them from one place to another, or carried-out endless ammunition details.

German shells rained down incessantly even though we were behind the lines. Our platoon hadn't suffered any casualties, but there were increasing reports of men in the supply section killed, wounded, or even gassed by the German shelling. I wrote Father that Hughes and I were pretty good at dodging Jerry's shells, and wondered if my lines had escaped the censor. It was the uncertainty of the German harassment that terrified me. I never knew when or where the next shell would land.

My fatigue grew as days and weeks blended together. I couldn't anchor the immediate past, and the future didn't have any certainty. Worse, that image of the boy I killed never left me. I couldn't shake it. Blood oozed out of the bullet hole, and his stilled, staring eyes haunted me. I forced myself to think about Fannie, the folks back home, my car, anything else. But my thoughts always circled back to his lifeless body. I shot him through, as if he were nothing more than a gopher in the garden. I kept telling myself that he tried to kill us. That damn kid had no business being there. It wasn't my fault the lousy Kaiser sent him to war. Yet, I could not dismiss the fact that it was my finger that pulled the trigger.

It became harder and harder to face the next detail. Hughes kicked me out of my bedroll, forced me to get my leggings on and boots laced. I could hardly muster the desire to do anything, and a little more of my vitality drained from me each day. That kid's death wouldn't leave me alone. It kept churning in my brain.

We'd just returned to our bivouac at 2300 hours on October 15th and I'd hoped for an early night. No such luck. Sedelsky, ordered us on an additional supply run to Cunel.

The horses pulled us out of the Montfaucon depot just before midnight and headed north. The road wasn't that crowded, and the engineers now maintained the Fucon-Cierges-Romagne Road as a two-lane drive covered with crushed stone. It only took us an hour to reach Battery B and unload the wagon.

I was about to snap the reins and get the rig headed back to Cierges when a commotion erupted behind us. In the dark, sergeants ran around rousting everyone. "You guys in wagon twenty, stop! Tie-off the horses. Grab your rifles, collect every cartridge you got an' follow me." The sergeant led us around the howitzers. I stumbled in the dark as we climbed the hill, and had to grab Hughes when he slipped in the mud. The starlight lit our way to an abandon trench line along the crest. Everyone was ordered into the trench. I knew these had been German trenches, because of the wooden duckboard floors and with walls reinforced by oak slats. French trenches were much cruder.

"On the firing step with you," yelled the Battery Sergeant. "Command's reported a German break-out, maybe four or five kilometers to our north. A whole Hun regiment may pour down on us after daybreak. Reinforcements are coming, but we're to slow 'em down, protect our guns. Those are the orders, boys; set yourselves for it."

"Shit, Edwards. Looks like we're in a pickle," said Hughes.

"You got that right," I replied.

Forty-five artillery men and Wagoner's lined this section of trench, all pointing rifles into the black of night. The only sounds came from the occasional Jerry whistling overhead followed by a distant explosion. The sporadic shelling stopped around 0400. Dead silence followed.

By 0430 clouds rolled overhead, accompanied by a cold mist. The black quiet of the starless night pressed in on me. I could hardly get a breath through a dry mouth. My stomach was tied in knots. I was alone, suspended in a void. My hands trembled with fear.

"Hughes, you there?"

"Right beside ya," he replied.

At 0540 the sun lit the horizon to my right. From our location on the ridge, a valley of desolation emerged in the growing light. The view before me revealed a terrain of shell holes, mud and shattered tree trunks. Row upon row of barbed wire stretched into the distance with dead and decaying bodies "closelined" over the wire. What a horrible term for dead men so grotesquely displayed. Some faced away and others toward us defining them as French or German. Pockets of hoary mist, condensed from the cool night air, settled in shell craters across the valley floor. It produced a surreal polka-dot scene. In the shifting light nothing so much as quivered.

By 0730 the word quickly spread that it had been a false alarm. There was no breakthrough. Relieved artillerymen and wagoners removed their fingers from the trigger. Expressions of relief were passed from man to man, until I heard a lieutenant shout, "Everyone, back to the guns." Hughes and I climbed out of the trench and scurried down the hill. As we approached our wagon, I hailed the gun boss. "We're heading back to our bivouac."

"Okay. Guess we cut a lucky break with that false alarm this morning."

"Yeah, hope the luck holds," said Hughes. It wouldn't.

CHAPTER 29. No Men Here

October 18, 1918, Cierges, France.

After two ammunition runs, Hughes and I returned to our bivouac at 0800 hours. With the wagon parked, and the horses freed from their tack, we gave them fresh water and what meager food was available. They were hungry, and given how we had cut their rations, they were slowly starving. You could see their rib cages. Lieutenant Harden said additional feed would arrive any day. Ha! Empty words.

"Long night boys," Sedelsky told us. "Clean yourselves up. You're both filthy. Get some chow, be back here by 1000 hours to review tonight's mission. Then, get some shuteye. Youse need it. Oh, Edwards, a letter came for you yesterday."

Hughes and I retrieved our kits and walked over to the mess tent. Scrambled eggs, shriveled, burnt brown sausage links, and a boiled potato filled my tin plate. This shit looks revolting, I thought. However, the rumble in my stomach overrode my disgust. I slathered a piece of stale bread with strawberry jam, and filled my cup with coffee. Fatigued legs carried Hughes and me to a table.

"You got a letter from Emily?" he asked.

"Yeah."

I opened Emily's letter, and scanned its contents.

"Well. What's happening?" Hughes asked.

"Tell you later," I answered.

After the briefing, I crawled into my damp sleeping roll and laid there rereading, trying to make sense of Emily's letter. I thought about Beatrice. I wanted to reach out and comfort her. I rolled on my side in a useless attempt to get more comfortable. Ha, comfort, what a quaint concept.

Beatrice kept reappearing in my head, forcing away the need for sleep. I had received a letter from her back in June, when we were stationed in Redon, and recalled every word of it.

Media, Pennsylvania
Sunday May 25, 1918
Dear Harry,

I received your letter, and although we have been separated a long time I was very glad to know you're still thinking of me. I want to tell you right here that there are no hard-feelings on my part in any way. I was also glad to hear that you arrived safely. I knew when you left for camp, and also when you departed for France. The weather here keeps very cool for this time of year, but today is one beautiful day. Edith Worrell and I are going to spend the day together, or rather the afternoon. I went to Sunday school this morning, as I did not have to work today. I am still a telephone operator at the Swarthmore office. You were right, it's rather boring, but at least it's work.

I remain involved with the suffrage movement and organizing chapters. You remember Alice Paul? Well, she's invited me to Washington next week. I am so excited to meet her.

Yes, Media is deserted at night, as there are no men here I want to go out with. Only young boys or old men. It makes you begin to realize what is going on. The girls look lost. You see a lot of girls going around without a boyfriend (myself included) just because all that are left are only children or else ones you would not like to be seen with.

Harry, just one personal question. Has anyone else been lucky enough to take the place I once had? I must close now, as my time is growing short. Hope to hear from you again in the future. May you be one of the lucky ones.

Best wishes and regards for your future from a onetime sweetheart.
Love,
Beatrice

My relationship with Beatrice was romantic history, yet I carried her memory with affection. I replied to her letter in early June in a way that was honest and not hurtful. From the distance of a few years I could see the indelible mark she left on me.

Here in this damp tent, so far removed from everything once dear to me, Bea's haunting blue eyes flooded my mind. I conjured her shapely body and hair styled after Mary Pickford. Her hair always smelled of honey and had the most wonderful silky feel. Beatrice dressed well, and the deep red lipstick she wore added a snappy look. She was a bit older than me and unquestionably more mature. I had fallen madly in love with her after a dance party in mid June of 1915. Exhausted as I was, I fought off the need for sleep and let my mind drift back to a church basket social.

❧

May 15, 1915; Media Presbyterian Church, Media, Pennsylvania.

I had bid 75 cents on a basket offering that caught my attention. The high bidder acquired not only the basket but the company of the lady who made it. After the bidding, a lovely girl with a perky hair style walked over to me.

"Beatrice. Is this your basket? What a nice surprise."

"Hi, Harry. I'm glad you won. We haven't talked in a long time. Say, I put a blanket in the basket. Can we eat outside? It's warm enough, and I'd like that."

Our families were members of the same church, and we'd known each other since we were kids. Her father owned Wallace's Hardware store. I'd seen Beatrice from time to time, but we hadn't talked in several years. She had to be eighteen now.

I spread the blanket under a Maple tree. Across the drive, stone pillars marked the entry to the church cemetery. Bea held her hand out, and I steadied her as she sat on the blanket. Glancing up, she saw me looking at the cemetery and asked if I ever walked through there. I joined her on the blanket and told her that I'd been in the cemetery last when my grandmother died.

Beatrice said her great grandfather was buried there. He had died at Gettysburg, and her great grandmother insisted the army return his remains to Media. Somehow she prevailed, but the family always wondered if the body in the coffin was actually great grandfather.

"Maybe it's empty," I said and Bea chuckled with me.

She reached into the basket and brought out plates, flatware, cups and some red and white checkered napkins. Dipping into the basket again, she removed crispy light brown chicken thighs and a tub of potato salad. I salivated. Finally she produced an elongated, round container with a red cap on it.

"What's that?"

"It's new from the store," she said. "It's called a thermos jug, keeps drinks cold." She popped the top and filled my cup.

"Oh. It *is* cold," I offered after a swig of lemonade.

We lay back on the blanket and talked as we ate. I complimented her on the fried chicken and how the crunch was just right.

"Thank you," she replied. "Say, what keeps you busy these days?"

I told her I still worked on the farm. "But I'm learning plumbing. I apprentice two days a week, learning from a guy named Alvin Morell," I said with enthusiasm. "He's a friend of my father's, and last week he had trusted me to do a sink installation in a farm house. I really enjoyed that."

"You sound ambitious."

"You got that right," and my zeal came pouring out. "Those old houses will all be needing new plumbing; showers, tubs, toilets, sinks, service and drain lines, septic tanks, water heaters, boilers, radiators, and the like. That new plumbing will come about because electricity will reach into the countryside and new electric pumps will be installed in farm wells. It'll be a booming business one day."

Beatrice nodded. I wondered if she really understood what I was saying.

"So, what about you? Aren't you graduating in a few weeks?" I asked.

"Yes, I can't wait to get out."

"What then?"

"Father wants me at the hardware store to work the counter and handle accounts. I'm not too keen on that. There's openings for operators at the telephone exchange in Media, and I'm going for an interview this week. Pay's good, but I can't say I'm excited about being an operator."

"Yeah, saying, 'How can I help you?' all day could get boring pretty fast. How'd your father feel about you not working at the store?"

"He said it would be all right. He wants me to be independent."

"Well, if the store or the phone company aren't appealing, what do you want to do?"

Bea's expression stiffened. "Don't laugh!" she said. Quite spontaneously I told her that I did not laugh at pretty ladies. She smiled and said that most folks thought her silly when she told them.

"Well, go on," I urged.

Beatrice described how women focused on temperance after the Civil War. Their efforts to reduce the amount of drinking fizzled. Men just didn't listen to women, and being ignored angered them. That anger kindled a growing effort for women to gain the right to vote.

"Do you think women should have the right to vote?" I asked. Wow, that changed her mood.

"Should women have the right? What a silly question, Mr. Edwards." Bea was animated now. "Of course they should. More women are completing high school, holding full-time jobs, and paying taxes from money earned by their own effort. Why shouldn't we vote? Women need a say in how the government's run, how our money's spent. Why should men have all the power?"

"You ask a lot of questions," I said. "My father believes that men should dominate in the public arena, while women should properly influence the home."

Bea reminded me that she had heard that my father was raised a Quaker and that Quakers believed all people were created equal. "Your father should see women in the same light as men."

"Jeez, how'd you remember that? I don't know much about what Quakers believe. We don't talk religion at home."

"Seems your father forgot his Quaker roots, or your mother's learned to use 'the power.' Maybe she's read about Josephine Drudge."

"What do you mean, 'use The Power?' What power? Who's this Josephine Drudge?"

"Now who's asking the questions?" she said with a smile.

I learned that Drudge was a silly, rich lady who was against suffragettes. Drudge argued that women should influence politics from behind the scene. No one quite understood what she meant by that. However, Bea's girlfriend, Emma Watson, said it likely meant women should withhold pleasures from men, if they don't pay attention to them.

"That's clever," I said. It certainly would be power! But I still don't see why women should get the vote."

"The world's changing, Harry. I see it all around us. We talk to one another on the telephone. The telegraph gets news to us faster than ever. And there's that new radio thing? Electricity lights our houses, and gas motors make work easier. Airplanes are beginning to deliver the mail. Cars and trucks will need new roads. There'll be jobs for all. You said as much in the coming plumbing revolution." She paused to catch a breath. "The fact remains that women won't have a say in any of this progress till they get the vote."

"So, where's this taking you?"

"Be patient," she said. Bea took a bite of chicken and chewed slowly. After a sip of lemonade she was back at it.

"I'm interested in the ideas of Alice Paul. Paul has plans on how to change the argument."

"How's that?" I asked. "From all I've heard, suffragettes just try and embarrass men on the basis of equal rights, or matters of justice."

She argued that I didn't see the issue correctly. That if I believed—as my parents do—that a woman's place is cooking, cleaning, and raising babies, nothing would change.

I was getting jack of this conversation, so I interrupted her, saying again how delicious her chicken was. Beatrice thanked me, but was undeterred.

"Dr. Paul believes suffragettes need to change their approach. They need to be politically involved, become more aggressive."

"But wouldn't this hurt your cause?" I asked. "My father says woman's efforts to embarrass President Wilson show disrespect."

She put down her cup and told me not to buy what my father said.

"Figure it out for yourself, Harry!"

She argued that more than "equal rights" or "women's compassion" was needed, and then blurted out, "I want to get involved with Paul's movement." Beatrice hesitated for a moment as if maybe she'd pushed this suffragette thing too far.

"But, enough talk about female emancipation."

"That's a good idea," I replied.

Her passion and dedication, more than the cause, is what impressed me. When our picnic was over, I invited Bea to meet me at Payton's Drug Store for an ice cream. We agreed on two o'clock the next Saturday afternoon. I looked forward to seeing her again.

CHAPTER 30. The Bunny Hug

May 20, 1915; Payton's Drug Store, Media, Pennsylvania.

I sat in a booth at the at the soda fountain and watched as Bea walked toward me.

What a lovely sight, I thought.

"Hi Harry, sorry I'm late. Father had me at the counter and I couldn't get away."

"Don't worry. I'm just glad you're here. Come, sit down, how have you been?"

"Getting ready for exams, and you?"

We shared a pint of chocolate ice cream and some soft drinks. Bea and I talked for at least two hours. Her conversation returned again and again to Alice Paul until she glanced at the clock above the counter and realized how late it was.

"Harry, I must run. We're having guests for dinner, and I told Mother I'd help."

"Can I see you again?" I asked.

"Emma Watson is having a dance party next Saturday night at her place. Would you take me there? We'd have a swell time."

"Wow, Yes, that'll be fun. What time shall I pick you up?"

May 27, 1915; Emma Watson's house, Media, Pennsylvania.

Next Saturday evening my Ford and I escorted Bea to the Watson house. I couldn't take my eyes off her. She looked so alluring as she flitted about the room chatting and laughing, fixing me a plate of goodies, swaying her hips to the music, and tossing me the occasional "let's dance" look.

When Emma's Mother and Father finally went to bed, things got interesting. Bea scanned Emma's record collection and asked: "Say. Who knows the Grizzly Dance?"

"I do," said Florence Weaver.

"Want to show the boys how it's done?"

"Sure."

"Hold on a moment," said Emma. She inserted a new needle in the phonograph reproducer and tightened the motor spring with cranks on the handle. With the disc spinning, she placed the needle over the starting groove. A moment of scratchy sounds preceded Sophie Tucker's throaty voice tumbling out of the brightly colored honeysuckle horn speaker. I watched the two girls, and listened to the words.

> *Out in San Francisco*
> *where the weather's fair.*
> *They have a dance out there*
> *They call the Grizzly Bear.*

They hooked their fingers, claw-like, over each other's shoulders, bent over to support each other while pushing their bottoms out. They rocked to the beat taking two sliding steps to one side, four back to the other, and two steps back to the start position. They stretched their arms apart, separating their shoulders from each other. What followed was a sudden inward pull on the upbeat to rub their breasts together, all to the beat of the music.

"Good grief," Jake Osborn called out.

The girls stepped to the beat as they circled the room. Abruptly they stopped, unhooked their "claws," and raised their arms above their heads. Turning around, they vigorously shook their raised arms with a shimmy of hip shaking, accompanied by an intricate sashay around each other until they were back-to-back.

"Oh my," I muttered as they backed into each other's rear ends and rubbed their bottoms together. Back and forth, and up and down in a crude imitation of a bear scratching its backside on a tree. Just as quickly they resumed the "shouldered claws" position, and then repeated the whole thing while singing the chorus:

> *Hug up close to your baby.*
> *Throw shoulders t'ward the ceiling.'*
> *Lawdy, lawdy, what a feelin','*
> *Doin' the Grizzly Bear.*

We gents watched, spellbound.

"Jeez. I've never seen anything like that," said Ollie Baker.

When the song was over, Emma lifted the player arm, and Bea asked breathlessly, "Okay. Who's ready to try?"

"I'll give it a go," I said. I grabbed Bea, and loudly instructed Emma, "Crank that machine."

Ten seconds into the music, all the couples were fast stepping, twisting, shimmin,' shakin.' and rubbin'. The infectious laughter and carrying on got to all of us, and the girls were enjoying it as much as us guys.

When the music stopped, a breathless Bea browsed through the records again. She started laughing and asked Emma, "Where did you get this one, 'The Bunny Hug?'"

"My mother bought it. She likes the song. I've never played it."

Bea asked, "Anyone know the "Bunny Hug" dance?"

"Well, I know about it," giggled Margaret.

"Do you know how to do it?"

"Mostly, Bea," she replied, an impish smile on her face.

"Where do you girls learn these things?" asked Ollie. Bea just winked at Ollie.

"Give these ladies room," I said.

As the music began, the two girls faced each other and placed their hands on each other's hips. The scratchy sound of the William Jerome score filled the room. Off they went to the beat of the music: Step, step, step, step, step, step, step step. Bea stepped forward and Margaret backward. They rotated slightly to a side-by-side position. Step, step, step, step, step, and then back face to face: Step, step, step, step, step, step, all the time skillfully circling to keep within the confines of the narrow room.

Bea and Margret came to a full stop, now moving just their hips to the beat, shifting left and right, four times. My mouth fell open as they pushed their pelvises together tightly and stepped side-to-side with the beat several times in a crude imitation of what bunnies do so well.

> *Float me honey 'round the hall.*
> *Bounce me like a rubber ball.*
> *Squeeze me, tease me, please me*
> *while we glide along.*

The five guys in the room could hardly believe what they saw. These girls were steamy. They picked up the one-step again, flowing around the room. All eyes were riveted on the girls while the lyrics played-out.

> *Tell me that you're glad you found me.*
> *Come on, sweet. Oh-sweetie, won't you come, oh sweet!*
> *There's honey in the air.*
> *Oh babe, I'm there, there, there!*
> *Hold me fast, hold me tight.*
> *Close as a kitten that lays on a rug.*
> *That's the Bunny Hug.*

It didn't take much imagination to know what they were imitating when they brought their pelvises together.

"Oh yeaaah," Ollie Baker hollered. "That's tops. You ladies are headed for jail!"

Half an hour later, a breathless Beatrice whispered in my ear, "I need some fresh air. Let's go outside."

Out on the porch she asked me."Do you have a cigarette?"

"Girls aren't supposed to smoke."

"Oh, Harry. Are you still listening to your mother?"

Bea and I strolled down the driveway. She held onto my arm. Her head burrowed into my shoulder. That feels good, I thought.

"Remember what I told you about Alice Paul?"

"Your hero?"

"She's giving a lecture at Swarthmore College next Wednesday evening. I know I'm presumptuous Harry, but you have a car. Would you take me there?"

I didn't hesitate, "Sure thing."

"Oh, thank you." Beatrice whipped around and kissed me full on the mouth. Well, that was a pleasant surprise. I definitely wanted more.

Chapter 31. Alice Paul

May 30, 1915; Swarthmore College, Swarthmore, Pennsylvania.

A week later, I came by to pick up Bea and learned she'd invited Emma and Florence to come with us. Half an hour later I found a space in a parking lot packed with buggies, wagons and cars. The lawn in front of the lecture hall bustled with women. Some waved placards reading, "Women Work, Women Vote," or "Women Bring all Voters Into the World." Others held large banners and one caught my eye: "If We Can't be Citizens at Voting Time, We Won't be Citizens at Tax Time." In the distance I heard ladies chanting, "We want action… now."

I led the girls inside and ushers directed us to seats in the balcony.

"This is good," said Emma. "We can see the whole stage."

"Did you expect it to be this crowded?" I asked.

"Never," answered Florence.

I scanned the balcony, and looked over the edge at the throng below.

"I only see maybe ten other men!"

Beatrice looked at me, raised her left eyebrow ever so slightly, rolled her eyes, and looked coyly askance. She said, with more than a measure of sarcasm, "Harry, you do realize, this is a woman's suffrage meeting?"

Within minutes a portly gentleman, dressed in a dark jacket and tie, sporting a well-trimmed beard, strode to the podium. He raised his arms to quiet the crowd.

"Welcome ladies, and those few brave gentlemen to Swarthmore College."

A chortle passed through the crowd.

"My name is Dr. Joseph Swain. I have the privilege of being the president of this fine institution. It's a great pleasure for me to welcome

Dr. Paul. She graduated with highest honors in 1905 with a major in Biology… and never looked back on that subject again."

Laughter again flitted through the crowd.

"She has worked for the suffragette movement in the United Kingdom, and currently plays a major role in the effort for women to gain the right to vote. Since the founding principle of this Quaker College is equality for all, it is indeed a pleasure to have her as our speaker this evening. Please join me in welcoming Dr. Paul."

A tall, spindly lady, with a round face, and deep-set eyes, dressed elegantly in white, and wearing an eye-catching silver locket necklace, stepped to the podium. Her brown hair, perfectly coiffed was piled in a bun. The crowd jumped to their feet cheering and clapping. She shook hands with the President, kissed him on the cheek, and scanned the crowd, waving to those she recognized.

What did she do to command this adulation? I wondered.

"I am so pleased to be back at Swarthmore where I have such wonderful memories."

In the speech that followed Paul told her audience about the woman's movement in America and England. Her strong voice spoke with clarity.

"There are those who fervently believe the fundamental issue of equality alone is a sufficient argument justifying the vote for women. Others believe that the moral authority of women gives us compassion, and that this will offset self-serving political behaviors. Others believe voting women will cause a revolutionary improvement in political civility. All are valid concepts. But ladies, they will *never*, I repeat *never,* sway the entrenched political power to grant us access to the ballot box. I propose a different route. One that stops the effort to justify ourselves and looks more at how we get there."

The women sat in rapt attention as Paul lectured them about "how to get there." The pitch of her voice rose, suggesting urgency, accompanied by a subtle quickening of her pace. One after the other, she hurled new ideas at her audience, lifting the crowd from their seats with cheers of approval.

"The National Women's American Suffrage Association has worked with state legislatures to advance laws granting women the vote. This effort has had success in the west, where the spirit of pioneer women still echoes across the landscape. Unfortunately, it has gotten us nowhere in the Midwest, South, or here in the East. A new path is needed. One that is more active. We have to organize."

A crescendo of cheering rose from the crowd as Paul continued to speak. The power in her voice seeped into the soul of those wildly cheering women. I have to admit, even me.

"Our message must be forced on Washington. I am announcing tonight, for the first time, that like-minded women have formed the National Women's Party. Our single goal is to gain a constitutional amendment for women to vote."

The women went wild. Paul, once again raised her arms to calm the crowd. "The Fifteenth Amendment asserted that the right to vote shall not be denied by any state on the basis of race, color or creed. It forgot to add women. We need our own amendment."

If I didn't know better, I could easily have believed that the building itself shuddered its approval. Paul guided her audience with her words, building to a final crescendo.

"I call for volunteers to serve as Silent Sentinels. The White House must be picketed around the clock in a new form of civil disobedience. President Wilson needs to be embarrassed. We will throw his noble words back at him. He tells Americans the light of freedom is being snuffed out in Europe, that Germany is oppressing everything in its path. Well, Mr. President, what about the oppression of half our citizens here at home? The women of America tell you, Sir, America is not yet a democracy. Twenty million of your citizens are denied the right to vote." The crowd was now hysterical.

"Volunteers are needed immediately," she announced. "We must organize women for the Party in this corner of Pennsylvania. All of you must come forward to help. I expect the vote for our generation, not that of our children. My mother always said, when you put your hand to the plow, you can't put it down until you get to the end of the row. We've started tilling that furrow, and we won't stop till it's finished!"

She concluded with the cry, "We must organize, organize, organize!"

The auditorium erupted, roaring the cry back to her. Beatrice, Florence, and Emma jumped and yelled with abandon. I was overwhelmed. The ardor of these women flowed into me, and I chanted with them, "Organize, organize, organize!" With each chant I pumped back and forth an out-stretched arm and clenched fist. Mindlessly, I was swept into the frenzy.

As we drove home, the girls couldn't stop talking.

"Wasn't she great, Harry?" asked Beatrice. "And to have been there when she announced the new Party."

Emma bubbled with enthusiasm, "We must busy ourselves and organize a chapter here in Media."

"When can we get started?" asked Florence.

I didn't say much, but as I listened to the passion in Bea's voice I couldn't help but wonder, where's my place in all this?

CHAPTER 32. Fannie

December, 1915; Media, Pennsylvania.
 Before December was half over Beatrice had organized twenty-two women into a Media chapter of the new political party. After that, she recruited women into half a dozen new chapters scattered across southeastern Pennsylvania. My Ford, in this effort, was her mode of transportation. More and more, my only role seemed to be as her chauffeur. Is that all I am?

Early May, 1916; The Peterson House, Marple, Pennsylvania.
 I was peeved because it was harder and harder to find time to be alone with Bea. Throughout the winter of 1915 and into the early spring of 1916, we went to the occasional party. Her sultry self emerged and my interest rekindled instantly. From time-to-time Bea agreed to attend a picture show and afterward, if the weather was nice, we'd park along Ridley Creek. But she was too committed to her work to let herself be overcome by passion.
 "Harry, you have to stop. Isn't just kissing me enough?" she'd plead. "I'm worried when your hands start wandering. I can't do this," she protested. "It could ruin everything."
 "Don't you care about me?" I asked in frustration.
 "I'm not sure you respect me or what I am doing any more. I can't jeopardize everything that matters to me for a few moments of pleasure."
 "What in the world do you mean "I don't respect you?" That's not fair. Beatrice, you don't leave any time for us. This suffrage thing consumes you, and nothing else matters. Where's the "we" in all this?"
 "I can't help it," said Bea. "Action on the amendment is moving fast. I need to be ready. Look, next Saturday there's a basket social at the church. We'll be together all afternoon."
 I cranked the engine and drove her home in silence.

 She didn't answer my question. Why am I putting up with this? Maybe it's time to move on. But I can't put her out of my mind. She's so beautiful, and when we kiss I can't get enough. When we dance, there's an angel floating in my arms. And she has shown me so much more about life. But it's all about her. She has no interest in my life, just my car. Am I looking for something she can't give?

**May 13, 1916; Media Presbyterian Church, Media,
Pennsylvania.**

Bidding on the baskets began at noon. Ollie Baker, who was mulling over the baskets, spotted me. "Hi Harry. You picked one to bid on?"

"Yep."

"Say, mind if we sit with you guys when I get mine?" I agreed, without much enthusiasm.

The auction started at twelve fifteen, and I paid $1.25 for Bea's basket. We had agreed earlier that hers was the one with the blue ribbon. With the bidding over, Reverend Hartley told the ladies. "All right, now is the time to retrieve your baskets. Introduce yourselves to those lucky gentlemen."

A pretty girl approached Ollie.

"Hi, Ollie. Thanks for buying my basket. I don't know if you remember me, but I'm Fannie White."

"Oh yes. Didn't we meet at Florence Weaver's back in April?"

She smiled, "I'm impressed that you remember."

Bea joined us. "I see you have bought my basket, Mr. Edwards."

"Ahhh, Miss Wallace, how nice to meet you," I said smiling.

The four of us collected chairs from the Sunday school room and sat out on the lawn.

What followed was inevitable.

"What do you think of the woman's movement?" Bea asked Fannie.

"You mean the effort to get the vote?"

"Yes."

"Well, what have women done to earn that right?"

"What in the world do you mean?" asked Bea.

"I live with my Aunt and Uncle, and they extended me privileges. I tell them where I'll be when I go out. I come home on time, do my homework, and complete my chores," Fannie told Bea. "In return I'm allowed to entertain friends, I receive a small allowance, I can play the victrola, and other things. I have these privileges, not because I'm me, but because I've earned them. So, again I ask, how have women earned the privilege to vote?"

"Women should be granted the right because they are half the population," answered Ollie.

"What a silly argument," responded Fannie. "A large part of the country is perfectly content with women remaining the lesser half. Besides, what does calling out the President and embarrassing men at every opportunity get us?"

"Fannie has a point," I said, clueless about the toxic brew I stirred.

"No she doesn't," Beatrice snapped. "Women don't have to earn the right to vote. It should be inherent in the fabric of the country."

"Wait a moment," Fannie protested. "We women have demonstrated enormous commitment to society. That's not in question. Women's involvement in the abolitionist movement is not viewed well by one-third of the country. The temperance effort made women seem like a bunch of "do gooders." And, the aggressiveness of that Paul lady provokes more resentment in men than anything else. So again, what have women done to earn the right to vote?"

Ollie tried to make peace. "Ladies, let's enjoy our food."

Beatrice fumed, and Fannie appeared more than a tad smug. Fannie's words certainly impressed me. In fact they were the first sensible ideas I'd heard in a long time.

At two o'clock Beatrice, abruptly said to me. "Harry, I have to go. I'm meeting people at our house in half an hour.

"I'll walk you home."

"That won't be necessary."

Beatrice packed her basket and said curtly, "I'm off."

"I've got to run too. I'm meeting some guys to plan the summer sports festival," said Ollie.

With strained smiles the girls bid each other goodbye.

"Guess that leaves us!" Fannie said to me.

"I think you upset Beatrice. Did you know she's very involved in the suffrage movement?"

"Yes. I recognized her from a picture in the *Delaware County Times* a week or so ago. Maybe I just wanted to goad her 'cause I'm not really sure Paul is correct in what she's doing. Don't get me wrong, women should have the vote. But Paul's path may be wrong."

"Fannie, can I drive you home?"

"You could walk me. I live off Jackson and Third Street. It's only half a dozen blocks."

She packed her basket, as I returned the chairs to the church.

"Say, Harry, aren't you Emily Edwards' brother?"

"Yes, how do you know Emily?" I asked.

"From school. We take the wagon bus together each morning. I've been trying to place you, and it suddenly came to me. You drive Emily to the corner when it's raining."

"Wow, me too. I've had this nagging feeling that I'd seen you before," I said.

'Edith Worrel and I are hosting a dance party this Saturday at Edith's house. Emily's been invited. Why don't you come too."

"That would be great," I said.

"So, I'll see you Saturday? It starts around six o'clock. Oh, and bring something, a dessert."

October 19, 1918; Cierges, France.

Lying on the damp ground in my tiny pup tent, along side the shattered remains of Cierges, I read Emily's letter again.

> *September 29, 1918*
> *Media, PA*
> *Dear Brother,*
>
> > *We are well here but hints of the coming fall are settling in. I saw Emma Watson in town today and learnt some news you might want to know. Beatrice Wallace lives in Washington and works for Alice Paul and the suffrage cause. In late June she met an Army Lieutenant. They married in August, and shortly afterwards he shipped out to France. Emma told me he was killed in the battle of Saint-Mihiel just after he arrived. I think it's near where you are. Beatrice took the news terribly. Lost the baby she carried. She's recovering and will go back to work week after next. Emma gave me her address. It's enclosed on a slip of paper, if you want to write her. The news here is buzzing with rumors the war might end soon. I hope so. I must go now and help Mother pick the last of the green tomatoes. Keep safe, Harry. We miss you so.*
> *Your Loving Sister,*
> *Emily*

Keep well Beatrice, I thought. Fatigue forced sleep on me and the slip of paper with Bea's address must have slipped from my fingers and fluttered to the wet ground. I woke next morning to find that the dampness had smeared the ink. I never did write her.

CHAPTER 33. Lives Saved

October 20, 1918; Nantillois Ridge, Nantillois, France.

We had completed our last ammunition run to Cunel and were heading back to camp for some food and sleep. Unfortunately, two burly MPs stopped us at the intersection of the Romaigne-Montfaucon road.

"Sorry boys, can't let you through. Army's restricted the road to northbound traffic only."

"What's up?" Hughes asked.

"Don't know. All they tell us is no southbound traffic."

"Well how the hell do we get back to our bivouac at Cierges?" I asked.

"Best bet is to head east and take the Cunel-Nantillois road. That will take you back to Montfaucon. It's the only way I know for movin' south. Most supply units are just pulling off the road until traffic reopens late this afternoon."

"We hear ya," I said.

I pulled off to the side, as Hughes retrieved his map. "I see what he's sayin.' Map shows a short cut from Nantillois to Cierges. I've seen engineers workin' on that shortcut. Might be passable now and it'd save us time. Either way, it'll take us more than two hours to get back. We could also return via Gesnes." Hughes traced out the route on the map.

"No, I won't go there again," I said. "We could just bed down here till tonight."

"I'd rather head back. There'd be warm food and sleep," said Hughes.

"Sounds like a good idea," I said.

Fatigued, we rode in silence. An hour later the rig crested the ridge above the ruins of Nantillois.

"Say, Edwards, pull-up. I gotta take a crap. Is there any paper?"

I pulled on the reins and Hughes set the brake.

"Yeah, it's in the locker."

I rose to stretch my legs and surveyed the valley below. I could see the outline of the wrecked village in the distance. There were four roads that converged on Nantillois. From high on the ridge it looked just like the map. The road to the south would take us back to Montfaucon. The path to the southeast was the Sepsarge road, while the extension to the northeast would end near the current front at the village of Brieulles on the Meuse River. The road we were on came up the ridge and snaked its way to the turn-off leading to Cunel.

As I watched below, a company of doughboys caught my eye. They'd entered the intersection from the direction of Montfaucon, and stopped. Most likely reinforcements moving toward the front at Cléry, I concluded. From our position on the ridge I could make out officers pouring over a map. One of 'em pointed in the direction of Brieulles.

"Why are they going that way?" I mumbled. Suddenly, something else that caught my attention.

I felt the wagon jiggle as Hughes returned.

"Whew, I needed that. What were you muttering?"

"Look," I told him. "Those Doughboys are taking the Brieulles road. Why the hell they doin' that? All the troops we've seen have been headed north. They'll be shifting too far to the east."

"Damned if I know. It's their problem; let 'em figure it out."

"Wait, there's something else. Look further up the Brieulles road. 'Bout half a kilometer beyond the intersection. You see what I mean?"

I pointed as Hughes shaded his eyes with his hands and stared intently.

"Jeez! That trench's filled with men. Maybe twenty of 'em," said Hughes. "It's hard to tell from here, but looks like they're all crouched down. What the hell they doin'?"

"Must be Kraut stragglers. Bastards are laying an ambush!"

"Shit," said Hughes.

We stood on the wagon seat, shouting and waving our arms to alert the doughboys. At our distance, with a wind in our face, it was too far to be heard. Besides, the company had already begun walking toward the Meuse. No one looked back in our direction.

"Grab your gun."

"Huh? What you got in mind?" asked Hughes.

"Follow the ridge line, its shorter. We'll get behind them Krauts, pick off a few. It'll warn 'em."

"Hell of a long shot," said Hughes.

"Yeah. But we'll be looking down on 'em. Come on."

I grabbed my rifle and flipped the other one to Hughes. We scrambled along the crest, and soon looked down on the trench, maybe a hundred and twenty meters away from our perch. As we positioned ourselves on the ridge the Americans continued their advance along the Brieulles road, advancing ever closer to the waiting Germans. I quickly charged the magazine and assumed a prone position on the ridge. The rifle strap tightened around my wrist, as I set the butt to my arm pit, and took aim. Hughes did the same.

"You ready?" I asked.

Our weapons barked. I saw one Hun fall backward. The rest looked around, unsure what had happened. We shot again and two Krauts fell back. The Americans heard the shooting and dove for the roadside ditches. Hughes and I let off another volley, and one more Hun fell. The Krauts huddled into the bottom of the trench. I waited for the opportunity for another shot. Minutes passed until a white cloth poked up, waving back and forth from the tip of a bayonet blade.

Yank officers saw the cloth and ordered the doughboys back onto the road. Hughes and I stood up and began shuttling down the barren hillside. At the same time the doughboys scurried to the trench and disarmed the Germans. We clambered the rest of the way down and were standing above the trench, when a major and a captain approached on the other side. Both of us snapped a salute.

"Which one of you is in charge?" asked the Major.

"Well, Sir," Hughes said. "We're artillery supply wagoners. That's our rig up on the hill." I pointed toward the hill and wagon.

"Who's in charge?" he asked again.

That'd be me, Sir."

"Who's 'me'?"

"Private Edwards, Sir. Supply Wagon Twenty, Second Squad, Third Platoon, Battery B, 315th Field Artillery Regiment. This here's Private Hughes. He's the brakeman." I tilted my head in his direction.

"That's better soldier. Where in the hell did you boys come from?"

"Well, Sir, been on a supply run to our battery positions at Cunel. The Romagne-Faucon Road's closed to southbound traffic and Nantillois is the only way back to our unit. Our rig came over the ridge, and we saw your men. I spotted the Germans. Had to do something, didn't we?"

"You sure did. Damn fine thing, saved my men from being shot up. To boot you captured twenty-one Krauts."

"Perhaps it's our providence to be here, Major," I said.

"Perhaps so, Edwards."

"Captain, get the names of these men and remind me of this when we're settled."

"Ahhh, Sir," ventured Hughes.

"Yes, Private?"

"Sir, ahhh… Begging your pardon. This road's not gonna take you north, if that's where your headin.' I can show you on my map, if you like, Sir."

"We're ordered to join up in Cléry. You say this road won't get my men there?"

"That's correct, Sir. You see our wagon up there. If you follow the road it's on, keeping straight ahead, maybe five or six kilometers, it'll get you to Cléry. Can I show you on my map, Sir?"

Hughes and I clambered to the other side of the trench, and indicated on our map where his men needed to go.

"Well I'll be damned. You men not only saved us from an ambush, you kept us from getting lost. Maybe it was providence!"

An hour later, our rig pulled into the Cierges bivouac. Sedelsky, concerned by our late return, forced the story out of us. "Hell. You boys had a time of it. Three deliveries, a big detour, you saved a whole Company, and captured a bunch of Germans. Not bad for one day! Youse gobs better get some chow and shuteye. There's a lot more to do!"

"Surely you joke, Sarge," muttered Hughes.

CHAPTER 34. The Letter

October 20, 1918; The Peterson House, Marple, Pennsylvania.

"Emily, a letter arrived for you," said Mother. I'd just come in from school, retrieved the envelope and saw the return address from Jake Osborn. Jake had written me weekly since his call-up. I brought the envelope upstairs and placed it on my dresser.

In the year before he'd been drafted, Father gave Jake permission to call around. He escorted me to the picture show, church socials, had even driven me to a number of parties. Jake was certainly handsome enough. He was always gracious, and the perfect gentleman. Introduced me to his friends as the "lovely" Miss Emily Edwards. Well, I certainly am "lovely." Although Jake knew how to reach a girl, he never spoke to my heart. He had a high-falutin' way of speaking and acted like he knew more than anybody else. With a pipe dangling from his mouth he'd talk plumbing with my brother, horse care with Father, on how to keep a sewing machine oiled with Mother. He even had the gall to tell me about a recipe for pecan pie he'd found in an old cook book. Said it came from a Georgia plantation. Well, it didn't look special to me. The nerve of that man. He knew I cherished my own recipe.

His patronizing attitude drove me to distraction, and when Jake left for the army, I'd have to say that I felt glad to be away from him. Oh, what an awful thing to say. He writes regularly, and I feel obligated to write back. I mean, it's my patriotic duty isn't it? Well, maybe I'll be glad when he comes home. At least I'll be escorted to the parties again.

Problem was, I had a new suitor, Steve Hughes, Harry's army friend. Near as I could gather, Harry and Steve worked together. My brother told his friends about his eighteen-year-old sister. He likely told them how pretty I am, showed them my picture. Well, next thing I know, Harry wrote, imploring me to send additional pictures of myself. Seems his friends wanted to see more of me. Against my better judgment, I did send a picture. Well, actually several. Okay, I sent five. No doubt, Harry gave one to Mr. Hughes, who now writes me letters as often as does Jake. Between writing Jake, Mr. Hughes and Harry, my pen never knows dry ink. I run out of things to write about, and half the time I just make up news. My news is quite creative, if I do say so. However, my friends on the school wagon have berated me for this. They've argued it's my duty to write, but not with made-up tales.

"Our brave boys want letters. They want to know what's happening here at home. It keeps 'em happy. Lets them know what they are fighting for," said Anna.

Well, I hope they aren't fighting for me. But I keep writing.

Mr. Hughes' letters have a raffish quality, and the phrase, "My dear Emily" occurred far too often. I couldn't tell if he was being dramatic, or charming. The latter, of course, was perfectly acceptable. However, it was his level of familiarity that unsettled me. The man took liberties on the edge of impertinence. I concluded that Mr. Hughes was not well schooled in the social graces. Yet, he did use interesting words. I couldn't deny their earthy quality, it was part of his appeal. Indeed, I looked forward to his letters.

Mr. Hughes' letters couldn't have been more different from Jake's. He kept returning to this strange idea that the boys in Harry's squad shared everything, whatever that meant. I guess they told each other their most personal stories, and I dare say, I had this image of Mr. Hughes swapping his underwear or toothbrush with Harry. Oh, how naughty of me.

In another letter, Mr. Hughes described how the boys in the squad are so close they're like brothers to one another. From this he drew a nutty conclusion. If he and Harry were brothers, and they shared everything, then I must be one of his sisters. Thus, Harry had to share me with him and that means he would give me hugs all the time. That was such nonsense. Where does he get such silly ideas?

Last Thursday's letter, for example, was downright risqué. He wrote that after the war, he was going to drive to Marple dressed in his best suit and operating a new car bought with his war bonus. He'd bring me fresh flowers and whisk me away for dinner at a fancy restaurant in Philadelphia. At first this struck me as brazen. I mean the man had never met me. He went on to write that we'd share a wonderful dinner in a candle-lit alcove, sipping a glass of freshly opened Bordeaux wine, while listening to the soulful strings of a violin. Well, Mr. Hughes does tickle my imagination. Jake would never think of taking me to a dinner like that. I thought it over for all of three minutes and, without hesitation, wrote to Mr. Hughes telling him I looked forward to our dinner.

As I worked in the kitchen, the notion of that French restaurant played in my mind and I forgot all about Jake's letter. After supper, with the dishes washed, I retreated to my bedroom, and changed into my night shirt. I decided to open Jake's letter after my homework to prevent spoiling my "restaurant" mood.

Northern France
26 September, 1918
Dear Emily,

All is well with me as I hope it is with you. Us boys are exhausted with all the work we do. We are fed more than enough food, and while it rains too much, the days are still mild. Your Brother Harry is in good spirits and I see him every day. We're on different wagons so he may be coming while I'm going. We're pleased with our effort over here, but our current location can become quite noisy. Much more than the fourth of July down on Media green. We have been lucky so far.

His best buddy is a guy named Stephen Hughes. Lives up in Scranton. He's Harry's brakeman. Our horses are mighty fine animals,

Harry keeps pushing us to write our girls back home. Let 'em know we're okay. You know I don't have anyone else to write, so I'll write to you. He's constantly writing Fannie White. Must have something going there 'cause he never stops talking about her. Drives us to distraction. Harry tells me Steve Hughes is writing you regularly. That's nice, but I sure hope he writes his wife back in Scranton as much.

Well, that's all from me and there's not much time till the next detail.
Your Friend,
J.F. Osborn

I stared at the letter and felt as if a lance had pierced my heart. The impertinence of the man, writing and inviting me to a French restaurant when he is married! I was certainly going to give Mr. Hughes a piece of my mind. I looked carefully at the censored lines, tilting the letter to the light, unsuccessfully trying to read under them. Then, I started to cry.

CHAPTER 35. Pushed to the Limit

Late October, 1918; Cierges, France.

The squad had bivouacked in Cierges since the first week of October. Despite our fixed location, the doughboys slowly pushed the Bosch back toward Germany. The front now lay fifteen kilometers away, and that placed our artillery battery as much as ten kilometers to the north of Ceirges. This meant supply details could be a round trip of twenty kilometers or more. That was a challenge.

The hill named Montfaucon dominated this sector. Rumor had it that the German Crown Prince watched from its summit during stages of the battle of Verdun. On September 27th, 1918, doughboys in the 157th Brigade had taken the hill. They gained a crest peppered with booby traps and mined dugouts. It took almost two weeks to sanitize the place. Limestone caves at the base of the hill were stocked full of German munitions. None of the thousands of rounds fit our guns, with one exception. The capture of Le Mort Homme in late August recovered three Kraut 88-millimeter howitzers. Four-thousand rounds of 88-millimeter shells and fuses were discovered in the Faucon armory. The Colonel ordered a special detail to make the 88s "Fit for Duty." The irony of returning the Kaiser's pills to his own troops seemed like good medicine. However, I saw a problem.

"Yeah, it sounds good," I said. "But it won't work."

"Why not?" asked Jim Nightlinger.

"How's the Hun going to know that his own shells are being returned?" I asked. "There's no tiny message on shrapnel saying "Made in Berlin." There's no satisfaction unless the Kraut knows he's receiving his own pills. Air Service should drop messages over their trenches telling 'em what's up."

Jake Osborn grinned. Hell, every time I see that look he's on to something, I thought.

"They'll know soon enough," Jake said. "Those Kraut shells are full of duds. Most likely the Hun will find them and realize it's their packages being 'returned to sender'".

The Army decided Montfaucon should be retained as an ammunition dump. It was impregnable, even to Jerry's largest shells. But another, more serious issue, demanded our attention.

"Hell. Our trips are gettin' so long there'll only be one delivery a night," said Hughes.

"You're right, and worse, it'll wear out the horses," agreed Will Adams.

"Why the hell don't they just move the damn ammo dump?" asked Doyle.

"From what I hear the Army won't use transportation equipment to supply new dumps because we're steadily losing wagons, horses, and crews," offered Sarge.

"Worse yet, there isn't enough food for our animals," added Will Adams.

"Lieutenant says motor transports for supply units and tractors to shift the howitzers are on the way. But they ain't here yet. And the Generals have assigned all possible wagons to ammunition details. The big guns come before all else," said Sedelsky.

"That might be true, but what happens when the chow wagons are pulled out of service?" asked Joe Goldrick.

"Won't happen," Sarge assured us. "All our water and chow wagons are flimsy carts pulled by one or two horses or donkeys. They're no good for hauling shells."

"Sarge, I'm betting that even those will be pressed into service in a pinch," said Osborn.

"Those trucks better get here fast," offered Adams. "Our horses aren't going to last much longer."

"Okay boys, enough talk," said Sarge. "There's work to do. Our pressing problem is to keep the animals in shape."

"Yeah, that's fine, Sarge. But where's the feed coming from?" I asked.

Sedelsky had no answer.

Most ammunition deliveries, now took place during the day, which meant we spent more nights in our pup tent at the Cierges bivouac. There were harrowing times, when I'd wake to the drone of a Gotha bomber, easily recognized by its low, moaning multi-engine growl. There'd be a flash in the distance, a boom, and a moment later the tent canvas would shake. The Gothas only flew during clear or moonlight nights, and none of us understood how they navigated. We suspected they hadn't a clue where they were.

One night I lay in the pup tent. My blanket, pulled tight to my neck, didn't relieve the usual chill in my chest or the dampness crawling through my feet. The blanket stunk of mold, and only the sound of a bomb made me forget my discomfort. The Hun did something to the fins of their bombs to make them whistle when dropped.

"It's comin' toward us!" yelped Hughes, as the whine of the falling projectile got louder. "Listen! Oh, my God!" The poor man was in a panic. An explosion shook the tent violently and it surprised me that the damn thing wasn't blown over.

"Hughes, we're okay." It took discipline to be reassuring without exposing my own fear. In the dark of the tent I heard the hum of another plane motor draw near; its bombs certainly seemed to march toward us. I shivered in the chilled air, and prayed fate would grant me another night. Soon, I couldn't take the stress.

"I'm going outside," I told Hughes. "Lying here's driving me crazy."

"Bad idea, Edwards. You could get cut through by a scrap of shrapnel."

I crawled outside and found an unexpected light show.

"Jeez. Hughes. Come out. You've got to see this."

"What is it?" he grumbled, as he squirmed out of the tent.

Pencil thin light beams from the crest of Montfaucon rose thousands of meters into the black sky. They flitted back and forth, searching. One caught the Gotha as it circled overhead, and just as quickly, two other beams honed in. Anti-aircraft fire from the crown of Faucon peppered the sky. The bombers luck ran out when the mid-section burst into flame. It rolled over in a slow swoop, trailing fire as it tumbled to earth.

"About time they got the bastard," said Hughes as he crawled back into the tent.

෴

On some supply runs Hughes and I were so exhausted we couldn't muster the strength to return to our bivouac. We just bedded down under the wagon, wrapped in a canvas to keep us dry. Dry, ha! Another quaint word. Most mornings I'd wake with a thin layer of ice over my tunic, still exhausted, but now chilled to the core. That doesn't even describe the gnawing hunger, because little food could be scrambled on a supply run.

I don't know where I found the capacity to keep going. Maybe the thought that my squad mates depended on me drove me on. It astonished me how none of the boys in the Squad proved wanting when their limits were tested. We just accepted the discomfort and danger. Like our horses, we were resigned to the job. The men of Second Squad performed as best we could—some more than others—I less than some.

Fannie and Hughes were the ones who kept me sane. Thinking of her and obsessing over her pictures became life-saving distractions. Hughes forced me to get my ass into gear, and that helped take my mind off the boy I killed. Yet, the strain of it all pushed my sanity toward the edge of a chasm. I wasn't alone in this struggle.

CHAPTER 36. Lost

October 22, 1918, Cierges, France.

Hughes and I returned around midnight from a supply run to Cunel and found Sedelsky waiting for us. We were back on night details; seems we had been losing too many crews during daylight deliveries.

"Lieutenant's ordered another run to Cunel. Afraid you'll have to go out again. Report to MontFaucon. Here's your requisition; load up, and get rolling."

"Hell, Sarge. We've been on two runs already tonight," Hughes carped.

"Not my call, Hughes. Now get on it."

With the artillery shells secured we began what should have been a familiar run to Romagne. Unfortunately, as we merged onto the Montfaucon-Romagne road there was a traffic snarl-up. Supply traffic ran all night on this road, and somewhere up the line an accident, a vehicle breakdown, or maybe a Kraut shell had stalled the advance to a crawl.

Hughes suggested that we could avoid the congestion by turning onto the Cierges-Nantillois road. I wasn't convinced this was a good idea; we weren't familiar with that route at night. Hughes argued that it was the route we'd taken just a week ago, when we stopped the ambush. I reminded him we would have to climb a steep hill in the dark, and I wasn't certain the horses had the strength for it. "We should stay with the congestion," I said. Hughes convinced me it would be a quick run with no traffic, and argued the horses had the strength to handle the hill.

The Cierges-Nantillois intersection was clearly marked on our map, and we confidently turned away from the congestion. There was no traffic, and the starlight helped us see the shattered remains of the village. The wagon rolled through Nantillois, and veered north to face the hill. Our horses struggled up the incline, and found the strength to reach the ridge. At the next intersection, we'd turn west toward Cunel, not more than half an hour ahead.

Forty-five minutes later the two of us were lost; totally disoriented for the first time. I don't know how it happened. The road was rutted and slow going, and we missed the turn. I suspected it was due to my exhaustion. I was so tired I couldn't think straight.

The wagon came to a halt, and I asked Hughes to check the map again.

The starlight outlined my brakeman as he retrieved a folded map and cigarette lighter from his tunic pocket. He tapped my leg, and I took the lighter.

I didn't have a lighter. Everyone else did. Yeah, I smoked, but I always bummed a light or carried matches. A drag now and then calmed my nerves. Not carrying a lighter was my crazy talisman. Made me different, and being different will save my life. Ha, more wacky thinking.

I flicked open the cap, spun the steel roller and watched the wick burst into flame. The flickering orange lit our faces and revealed the paths on the map. Hughes traced a finger along faint lines. "I think we're here. The turn's just ahead."

"What do you mean, 'you think?' Jeez Hughes. We should've stuck with the main road."

"Shit, Edwards, put a sock in it."

The tension between us was high tonight. I harbored a bad feeling about this run ever since Sedelsky ordered us out again. I can't pinpoint why. The road congestion, this alternate route, the fact we were alone, or just the depth of my fatigue.

Let's get this over with, ran through my head, as I snapped the lighter shut. The darkness closed in on me, and I experienced a momentary shudder of fear.

"Let's go," said Hughes, and I felt the wagon relax as he released the brake.

Tongue at the roof of my mouth, I snapped loudly, "tsk, tsk, tsk," and shouted, "Come on horsies." I whipped the reins at the same time. The animals tugged on the wagon pole, and the load of munitions lumbered forward.

The momentary flash, from German artillery rounds provided some light. But it didn't help much. Once gone, the outline of the road again disappeared into the black, and the feeling of isolation fed my apprehension. We encountered patches of deep mud, but they were passable. The rig moved forward for another twenty minutes.

"This ain't right, Edwards," said Hughes. "We should've seen the intersection long ago."

I pulled on the reins, and the horses came to a standstill. Hughes and I looked around, trying to get our bearings.

A voice came out of nowhere. "Who's there? Identify yourselves!" We nearly jumped out of our seats. The call surely spooked our horses. The starlight revealed the faint silhouette of a helmeted head protruding from the roadside ditch, maybe five meters in front of us. Hughes tapped my leg as a distant flash revealed the outline of a rifle.

"Private Edwards and Hughes, Second Squad, Third Platoon. We're on a supply run to Cunel. Think we made a wrong turn."

Why didn't he challenge us for a password? Maybe he wasn't on sentry duty.

His rifle shifted upward.

"There's no Cunel around here. Do you know where the hell you are?"

"Ummm, not really," replied Hughes.

"You're at the back end of the communication trenches. 'Bout five hundred meters from the front," the voice called back. "Me and six other gobs been hauling supplies. Had no idea who you were. Our supply wagons don't come this far at night. You'd better back-track out of here. Boche artillery is going be especially active at first light."

"Why's that?" I asked.

"Our boys go over the top at daylight," the voice responded.

"Shit! Anywhere to turn around?" asked Hughes.

"Go up about fifty meters. That's where our chow and supply wagons turn."

"Thanks," I said.

"You better get your cans moving. Not much time till daylight."

I shook the reins and the horses strained as the wagon inched forward.

"Pull up," said Hughes. "I think I see it."

He jumped off the buckboard and shuffled to the front of the team, taking the lead stallion's bridle firmly in hand.

"Looks wide enough, maybe twelve meters. Gotta be careful. Road's got a ditch on either side."

This won't be easy, I thought.

A hint of the coming morning emerged in the east. Hughes pushed on the bridle, and the horses stepped back. As the rig inched backwards, I watched the rear wheels over my shoulder, spied the edge of the ditch and yelled, "Stop," tugging hard on the brake. The rig halted. Hughes reversed, then pulled on the bridle, as I released the brake. The team stepped forward two meters or more, as he forced the animals into the turn. When he and the lead horses neared the far edge of the road, I heard him shout. "Brake now!" Back and forth we went, slowly turning.

We were almost around. I leaned over the side of the wagon, looking back, scanning for the roads edge. The roar from our guns suddenly shattered the stillness. Instinctively, I pulled on the brake handle, and looked up the road in the direction we'd come. Flashes sprang from the ridges and I heard the "whoosh" of projectiles as they sliced through the cold morning air high above us. Moments later, explosions flashed and rumbled as they landed. A gnawing panic grew in my stomach. The impacts were just a kilometer away. The entire sky toward the front glowed brightly in a confusion of brilliant orange strikes. We'd never been this close to the front.

Within minutes the Hun retaliated. His missiles flew in our direction. Some overshot their mark, bursting nearby with brilliant flashes, followed by sound shocks so strong they rattled my teeth. The ground shuddered. I watched with dread, and pulled hard on the reins and brake to maintain control. "Easy boys," Hughes shouted at the lead stallions, as their heads shook with fear.

"Come on Hughes, pull 'em round. Pull 'em round," I shouted, straining on the reins.

Over the din, I barely heard the gasp. "Oh shit," as Hughes nearly lost his footing at the ditch. He tugged hard on the bridle and the team turned into the straightaway. "We're clear," he yelled, while hooves escaped the far side ditch by centimeters.

"Get in! Get in!" I yelled.

He scrambled to the front of the wagon, leapt onto the buckboard and screamed, "Get the hell outta here!"

I snapped the reins. The horses eagerly stepped forward, as the growing daylight illuminated the route to safety. To our rear, the screaming German shells and the discord of their explosions marched on.

CHAPTER 37. Chlorine

October 23, 1918; the road to Cléry, France.

I watched as Edwards struggled to maintain control of the horses. They were on the edge of panic. The projectiles from the Boche guns crept closer to our fleeing wagon. They wormed into the ground and detonated with a skyward geyser  of flame, smoke and dirt. Searing waves of heat, along with the concussive power of the blasts slammed into us. I heard the shrill "whseeeech" of red hot metal fragments when they screamed by. Like the horses, I was on the edge of panic.

Edwards urged the rig forward and my hand gripped the front rail so tight my knuckles turned white. Damned if I was going to be thrown out of the lurching wagon. I scanned the road, and at the same time applied bursts of pressure on the brake handle in a struggle to keep the rig from slipping out of control.

All of a sudden the wagon lurched as a piece of shrapnel slammed into the upper edge of the sidewall. It tore a smoking hole in the wood. I glanced at the damage, and shouted to Edwards, "Wagon's okay." The sickening sound of a dull thud brought my eyes to the horses. The right rear stallion gave a hideous bellow of pain. Its head flailed upward, shaking side-to-side, teeth bared in agony. A shard of jagged metal protruded from its hindquarter, and pulsating red pumped from the wound. The Andalusia held its position, adding what strength it could to pull the wagon.

I yelled, my words now driven by hysteria, "Edwards, faster, faster!" But the cry was lost in the cacophony around us.

The animals drove forward in a blind frenzy. Our rig gained distance, now fifty, a hundred, one hundred and fifty meters beyond the turn-around. In another hundred meters we'd be safe. Something to the side and behind the wagon, caught my attention. A yellowish-green fog was spreading over the muddy earth. Its swirls rose higher forming a low-lying cloud that slid along the ground, as if chasing us. A moment later, my overloaded brain understood. I turned to Edwards, my mouth drawn in terror, and yelled, "Ga…," the word cut short by the blast.

The wagon rose in the air and time slowed to a crawl. I saw the surreal drift of feed bags and straw matting rising slowly past my head. Stainless steel artillery shells, released from the wagon bed, floated in the air. The shells rotated end over end in a graceful ballet, and sunlight from the distant horizon reflected a dazzling sheen from their polished surfaces. Lighter powder bags—thrown even higher from their locker—arched upward in a gentle trajectory. This is impossible, I thought.

A weightless wagon, horses, artillery shells, powder bags, supplies, Edwards and me helplessly drifted skyward. On the upward vault, I saw the reins tug on Edwards' hands, pulling him to the side, away from me, away from the wagon.

The moment ended, and I landed in well-churned mud. The impact opened the chin strap throwing my helmet away. I wiped mud from my face, then felt my head and searched for arms and legs.

"Jeez. I'm alive," I muttered. "What the hell happened? Edwards," I yelled. "Where are you?" There was no reply. I scraped mud off my hands, and quivered as I rose to one knee. Dizziness swirled, and I struggled to stand, only to fall back into the mud. My throat tightened and I retched uncontrollably. Sensibility slowly returned, and, gasping for breath, I became aware of screaming in my ears. Banging my head with my hand was a useless attempt to drive away the howling.

How long did I sit in the muck? A minute, maybe ten. A stunned man in shock can't judge time. The dizziness gradually subsided and I again struggled to rise, forcing myself into a shaky stand. Staggering to keep my balance, I again looked around, desperate to find my friend.

The overturned wagon, blown off the road, lay tilted at a bizarre angle; a tangle of splintered and burning wood. The once gleaming artillery shells were scattered in the mud. Burning powder bags released a grey-white plume of smoke, accompanied by golden sparks that winked in and out of the boiling folds as the smoke hurtled upwards. The heavier sparks spread outward, forming a glowing orange shower that tumbled back to the ground. I tilted my head to the side, enraptured by the near bizarre cadence of hissing sparks smothered in the wet mud.

A more gruesome scene abruptly drew my attention. The horses, still attached to the wagon pole, lay in a grotesque tumble of intertwined legs. A yellow-greenish mist wafted among them.

"Oh God," I uttered, unable to muster the will to look away. The horses' legs twitched in violent spasms. White froth oozed from flared nostrils. With frenzied effort, gaping mouths sought air but found none. Soon the agonized writhing stopped.

Fumbling at the chest pack to release my mask, I yelled, "Gas." A meaningless gesture. My mask in place, I again searched the seared surroundings for Edwards.

Finally, I spotted his boots protruding from the side of a shell hole. I struggled to step through the mud toward my comrade, and at the edge of the crater I could see that his immobile body lay just below the rim. His head angled downward toward a pool of putrid water at the bottom. At that moment, my eyes shifted to sluggish motion at the far edge of the shell-hole. I watched, with dread, a stream of yellow mist roll over the rim and ooze down the slope, slowly filling the bottom of the pit. Wispy tendrils of gas swirled and flicked upward toward Edwards' head. This horrible sight brought me to a halt, and fear quickly replaced awareness, summoning a terror-filled battle between mind and muscles to do the right thing, or just turn and run.

I kept my wits, leaned down and grabbed Edwards's boots, and tugged. He didn't move. Sweet Jesus, give me strength. In a few moments it will be too late. Straining harder a second time, his torso abruptly gave way, causing me to fall backwards as my friend came over the crater lip.

Edwards murmured, but he remained unconscious. Kneeling, I hooked my arms under his arm pits, and pulled his body upwards until we were chest-to-chest. With a downward twist, I positioned his frame across my shoulders and pushed upward to a standing position, then slogged through the muck toward the road.

The wagon continued to burn fiercely, and in the shimmering flames I saw the outline of artillery shells still attached to the bed. Shit, I gotta get outta here, ran through my head.

My heavy burden prevented me from stepping faster, and some distance beyond the burning wagon, a blast from behind drove me to my knees. I laid Edwards on the road, stood, and looked back. A yellowish-green mist from an exploded gas shell in the wagon bed slowly drifted in our direction. I frantically searched over Edwards. There was no gas mask pack. It must have come off when I pulled him out.

Suddenly, I remembered something I'd heard back at Redon; a casual comment made in a survival or first aid course. "Jeeze, you'll hate me for this, Edwards."

A handkerchief was removed from my rear pocket and the edges of the filthy cloth were untangled, opening it up. Hands fumbled with the buttons at the front of my pants and I lowered the handkerchief in front of me. A stream of piss soaked my hand and the cloth. When thoroughly wet, I folded the disgusting rag in half and placed it over my comrade's nose and mouth. His head jerked on contact.

An extra boot lace I carried in my jacket pocket was wrapped around Edwards' head and tied firmly to secure the filthy rag. The makeshift gas mask came just in time as the dispersed edge of the gas cloud grazed us. With Edwards' body again in the fireman's carry position, I continued the footslog away from danger.

To goad myself I repeated over and over, "Come on Hughes. Keep going. You can do this. Move... move, must save us." My exhaustion grew as the barrage gradually receded behind me. An audible wheeze with each breath now came from my friend. Coughing continued to occur in short violent fits, but all during this time he remained unconscious. I must have been near a half a kilometer from where our wagon was blown-up when I saw a line of vehicles cresting the distant rise, all with red crosses painted on their hoods and sides.

CHAPTER 38. Race Against Time

October 23, 1918; The road to Cléry, France.

Seven vehicles drove past, apparently oblivious to the fact I carried a wounded man. The last vehicle pulled over. A driver jumped out of the cab while a nurse exited the passenger side.

"Put him down soldier, carefully. What happened?"

I explained, and the driver asked, "Do you know what kind of gas he was exposed to?"

Gasping for breath, I could hardly speak. "Yellow-greenish stuff. He's been coughing off and on…last forty minutes. Started wheezing a while ago. Been unconscious since the wagon went up."

The back door of the ambulance opened, and I looked up to see the nurse remove a bag and blanket from the vehicle. She wore a white cap and a dark blue cape with a red cross emblazoned on it.

"How long ago did he breathe the gas?" She asked. "Did you put the handkerchief on his face?"

"Maybe forty minutes. Couldn't find his mask, so I soaked a handkerchief with pee and put it over his face."

"Probably saved his life, soldier." She leaned over Edwards and said to the driver, "John, roll him over."

She examined Edwards. "There's no broken bones or lacerations. Tell me what happened."

I repeated my story and added, "I landed in soft mud, but I think Edwards hit harder.

"That explains the bruise on his forehead," said the nurse. "Let's see if we can bring him round. Soldier, I'm Nurse Beurg. I'm curious, how'd you know uric acid neutralizes chlorine?"

"Uric acid?"

"Pee," Beurg said.

"Oh, remembered someone telling me once that a piss-soaked cloth cancels the gas. Jeez, it sounded, uhhh… gross."

"And it is! Would you remove the handkerchief for me?"

Beurg had John and I pull the unconscious Edwards to a sitting position, as she removed a small bottle and some gauze from her bag. Edwards's head flopped to his chest.

"John, grab his hair and lift his head. What's your name soldier?"

"Private Hughes, Ma'am."

"Okay, Hughes. You steady him."

Beurg poured several drops into a gauze square and placed it against Edwards' nose. I pulled back at the stinging smell of ammonia.

Edwards jerked, his eyes fluttered open. "Wh…What happened? Where are we?" This was followed by more coughing.

"Easy, Edwards," I said. "You took some gas. Nurse here's gonna help you.

"Where…. Where's the wagon? Where are we? How did I get here?" he stammered.

"That's enough soldier," Beurg ordered. "Breathe for me."

Edwards started to draw in, stopped, then coughed violently.

"Okay. Stop. Just short, little breaths. Don't force them. Let me see your hands." Edwards lifted his hands. "It's probably chlorine. I don't see any blistering."

"We were carrying chlorine shells," I offered.

"Ahhh," Beurg replied.

"Can I go back to my unit?" Edwards asked her.

"No. You're in no condition for that. You're coming with us to the evacuation hospital. The doctors will decide what's next."

"Can I go with him?" I asked.

"No. We've only room for the nurse, me, and the patients," John said.

Beurg looked at John. "We need to get going, get the stretcher."

"You must remain quiet, soldier," I heard Beurg say. "Breath as lightly as you can. You don't seem severely gassed, but the more you exert yourself, the worse it will be for your lungs. Force yourself to keep calm."

John and I lifted the stretcher and secured it to the center frame of the ambulance. I faced my buddy, "Good luck my friend." I held out my hand and he grasped it as our eyes met.

"Take care, Hughes," he said softly. "See you soon," followed by another fit of coughing.

Beurg closed the ambulance doors, and asked, "What about you?"

"I'm okay. 'Bout ten kilometers or so back to our bivouac. I can walk it, or maybe find a ride. Hey, you'll take care of him?"

"He's in good hands."

As the ambulance pulled away, I worried if I'd see my friend again.

Lieutenant Harden was on the field phone with his back to me, as I entered the tent.

Sedelsky looked up. "Hughes. Where've you been?"

Harden put down the phone and faced me.

I saluted. "Private Hughes reporting, Sir."

"What happened?" the Lieutenant asked.

As I started to answer, Sedelsky interrupted. "Where's Edwards?"

∽

October 23, 1918; Ambulance approaching front near Cléry, France.

I was wide awake now and struggled to follow nurse Beurg's instructions to keep calm. Coughing fits arose uncontrollably in short bursts.

John drove a modified Model-T with an extended rear bed that formed a compartment for patients. Stronger shock absorbers and wider tires were fitted for rough muddy roads. Unfortunately, no amount of fixes could smooth a ride in this battle torn land. At one point the nurse nearly hit the cab roof when we bounced over a mound of dirt. I'd have been tossed from the stretcher if I wasn't strapped in.

"How much further?" I heard Beurg ask John.

"Maybe half a kilometer."

John pulled over to allow the passage of ambulances returning from the front. The pause was a blessing. Every damn rut that driver hit wrenched me back and forth.

I could only see the dull army green of the canvas walls, and had to force myself to think of something other than the pain in my chest or forehead. The familiar sound of the four cylinder Ford motor brought momentary comfort. Unfortunately, every rut caused John to down-shift in order to retain traction, and his play with the gears worried me. Damn driver pops the clutch too hard. He'll blow the transmission, if he's not careful. Then where will I be?

Fear welled up, and I struggled to keep it in check. Jeez, relax, Harry! It's going to be all right. I'm good. I'm alive. Think of Fannie. I kept being overwhelmed by fits of coughing.

We lurched to a stop and a moment later the back door opened. "Where are we?"

"Be still, Edwards. We're picking up wounded," said Beurg, as she retrieved her bag.

The door shut. I heard muffled shouting and the shuffle of feet. Soon, the door reopened, and two litters were secured on either side of me. Two more litters were slid onto the overhead racks. I couldn't see the wounded doughboys above, though guy on the right moaned continuously. The nurse and driver returned to the cab, the engine sprang to life, and the ambulance backed up. With another shift of the gears we headed away.

John slammed on the brakes and we abruptly stopped.

"Don't they know we're transporting wounded?" I overheard an exasperated Beurg say.

"Nothin' to be done, Nurse. They're bringing up reserves. We'll just have to inch along till we're past 'em," said John.

Our lives depended on how quickly the ambulance got its cargo to the evacuation hospital, and the nearest—in Avocourt—was an hour drive to the south.

The man to my left had a gauze bandage wrapped around the stump where his lower arm had been. He tossed his head back and forth, moaning in obvious pain. Beurg heard his cries and struggled from her seat. Holding onto ceiling straps, she climbed into the rear compartment and checked the tag on his tunic.

"Time for another shot."

She shoved a needle into One-Arm's bicep. He fell silent as the morphine took hold.

"How are you doing, Edwards?" Beurg asked.

"Chest hurts somethin' awful."

We'll be there soon," she reassured, and returned to her seat.

Despite the bouncing vehicle and the sharp pain in my chest, I became aware that the man to my right wasn't in good shape. His torn shirt exposed a bandage taped over his left breast and his pant legs were cut open. The skin of his lower left leg appeared black and I guessed that was the source of the burned flesh smell.

He looked toward me and there was just enough light to see bloodshot eyes on an ashen face. His lower lip fluttered. Was he imploring me to do something? There was no voice, instead a trickle of blood seeped from the corner of his mouth, flowed across his chin and dripped onto his neck. I watched, horrified as he took three rattled breaths and sucked desperately for air. His restrained arms thrashed on the cot, violently pulling on the straps.

"Nurse. Nurse," I called, followed by a burst of coughs. Beurg struggled out of her seat again.

"I told you to keep still."

I gasped between coughs, hardly able to direct her and rotated my head as a pointer. She looked at the stretcher, leaned over and placed two fingers on his neck.

"He's gone." She checked her patients and returned to her seat. Her casual attitude caught me off guard. Shit, she's one tough broad. Damn, maybe I'm next, went through my head. A new quake of fear rumbled through me and panic throbbed just beneath the surface. How the hell am I supposed to keep calm?

CHAPTER 39. Outbreak

October 22, 1918; The Peterson House, Paxon Hollow Road, Marple, Pennsylvania.

I took the call from Albert and was distraught when I hung-up.

"Ella's ill. Albert says she's breathing heavily. He felt her forehead and she's burning up. He doesn't know what to do."

"Is it the flu?" Emily asked me.

"The newspaper said there was an influenza outbreak in North Philadelphia, but I don't know why it should be in Ardmore," I replied, then added. "Albert said he called the doctor, but he hasn't arrived yet."

"The flu is dangerous, Mother. It's highly contagious."

"I know Dear, but Ella's my sister. I've got to go to her."

Emily wanted to come with me, but I firmly told her no. She said they'd been studying the influenza in school. I told her it was too risky, but she argued, and started telling me what we had to do.

"We need to stop at a drug store and buy face masks, aspirin, disinfectant, and several boxes of tissues. The windows in Aunt Anna's room must to be kept open and at the same time the room heated and humidified. If Albert has a fan, it should be used to draw air from the room to the outside, and the room has to be wiped with disinfectant."

Emily did know more than me and I needed moral support. I agreed she could come. George got the car ready and drove us to Ardmore.

※

The first case of what became known as the Spanish Influenza was reported in March of 1918 at Fort Reily, Kansas. U.S. troops deploying overseas spread the disease to Europe, where the unsanitary conditions and troop concentrations at the Western Front quickly spread it along the trenches. From there it burst onto a wider world.

Death rates were as high as 20 percent, and between 40 and 50 million died from the disease. In the United States the greatest number of deaths occurred between October and December of 1918. Many counties declared a state of emergency and all public gatherings were closed. This included schools, churches, funerals, even the taverns. There was no vaccine, and on the home front treatment was hampered by the reduction in the number of doctors taken for the war effort. By mid 1919 the last influenza case was identified and the deadly illness disappeared as suddenly as it had appeared.

❧

At the front door a distraught brother-in-law was obviously pleased with my arrival.

"Oh, thank you for coming, Sally," Albert said. "She's not doing well. Doctor Braxton arrived a few minutes ago. He's upstairs with Ella now. I don't know what to do."

"We came as quickly as possible." Albert guided us to the living room.

"Did the doctor tell you what's wrong?"

"No."

That's when I heard the coughing upstairs.

"I want to see the Doctor. Albert will you wait downstairs, and open some windows, it's important to have air circulation. Oh, do you have an electric fan?" Albert replied that he didn't.

"Emily, come with me."

At the top of the stairs Emily stopped me. "Mother, we should put those masks over our faces before entering."

I tapped on the door and on entering the room we found the doctor sitting on the edge of the bed wearing a mask and rubber gloves. The curtains fluttered in a light breeze from the open windows.

"Doctor Braxton, I'm Ella's sister, Sally Edwards. This is my daughter, Emily. Is there anything we can do?"

"I'm glad you have those masks on. But don't touch anything and don't touch your face with your hands. When you leave the room, wash your hands and face thoroughly. Use soap and hot water. As hot as you can stand."

Dr. Braxton reached into his bag and took out several pairs of rubber gloves.

"You keep the gloves. I have more in the car. No one should enter the room without them. When you leave, wash them thoroughly, just like you were washing your hands. Place them outside the door."

"Is it Spanish flu?' I asked. He thought it was.

"Give Mrs. Long lots of liquids, and two aspirins as soon as she can swallow them. Repeat the aspirin every five hours," he said gravely.

I told Dr. Braxton that I'd brought several boxes of tissues with us, and he said to be sure Ella coughed into them.

"Flush them down the toilet afterwards," he insisted. "Tell Mr. Long he needs to keep the heat on in the house, and have him place trays of water on the radiators to humidify the room. Other than that, you just have to wait it out. If she wants to eat, she can sip clear soup."

I walked the Doctor to the bedroom door. In a hushed voice he said, "I don't like saying this, Mrs. Edwards, but to be truthful, your sister's condition is not good. You must prepare yourselves for the worst. The next forty-eight hours are critical."

I faced Emily and issued some instructions. "Emily, I want you and George to leave. You be sure and wash, just like the Doctor described. I'll stay with Ella."

"Is that wise?" she asked.

"Maybe not, but Albert can't take care of her by himself. He's too anxious. Now, you go, right now."

"I am worried about you, Mother"

"I know dear. Please, Emily, wash your hands. Have Albert bring the gloves back up and place them by the door. Get Albert to wear a mask and be sure George washes his hands also."

"Yes, Mother."

"Oh. Would you bring a pitcher of water, a glass, and the disinfectant, and place them outside the door?."

"I'll be right back."

Several moments later, Emily called from the hallway. "Mother, I've left all the things by the door."

I watched my children reach the car and called to them from the open window, "Tell your father I'll call tonight."

A soft voice beckoned. "Sally? Sally, is that you?"

"Yes it's me, El. I'm here. Albert and I are going to get you well again."

"Oh, Sally. I feel so miserable. I ache all over and it's so hot in here."

My sister remained semi-conscious over the next two days. I did everything to keep her comfortable, and at one point convinced myself the fever was decreasing. But it didn't. With little warning on October 24th, late in the afternoon Ella died. I was devastated, nothing I did made a difference. Emotionally drained, I couldn't even cry.

Albert made arrangements. The funeral home told him they were under civil orders to retrieve the body, place it in a casket, and bury it in the nearest cemetery. He was told that he could move her to a family burial plot after the emergency. I called home with the news, and asked George to come and fetch me.

Over the days I spent with Ella the paper reported that the flu had exploded out of North Philadelphia, engulfed the city, and seeped into the suburbs, reaching Media and Marple by early November. Albert concluded that Ella must have caught the flu when she took the train into the city a week ago to do some shopping.

Albert, George, Morris, Frazure, Emily, and I escaped the epidemic. I don't know how we were so lucky. Maybe it was because we followed Emily's directions carefully. Near the end of November many I knew were taken: Mrs. Levis, Harry's eighth grade teacher; my friend from Church, Mrs. Bradley; our mailman, Walter Houser; and Frazure's old friend, Mr. McFee. The outbreak came and went, and by December, 1918, there were no new cases reported.

Chapter 40. Evacuation Hospital

October 23, 1918, Evacuation Hospital Four, Avencourt, France.
An hour after we left the front, the Lizzy entered the grounds of Evacuation Hospital number Four. John braked hard. Through the thin canvas wall, I heard the crunch of running feet as nurse Beurg opened the rear door.

"One gassed, one missing lower arm, two gunshot wounds, abdomen and upper leg," she told an orderly. "All stable at the moment. The fifth one's gone."

The orderlies pulled my stretcher out, got a firm grip on the handles, and swung around.

"Hold up," Beurg shouted. "Good luck, Edwards. You're going to be okay."

I nodded in appreciation. Beurg faced her driver. "John, replace the litters and let's get going."

At a smart step, they carried me toward the hospital, where a sign over the entrance announced ADMISSIONS. I was transferred to a gurney, which the orderlies pushed down a long corridor to a room where they left me. I looked around. In front of me, two parallel pipes on the wall dropped from the ceiling, ending at a set of valves labeled *Chaud* and *Froid*. The spigots below the valves connected to a hose that terminated on a hand-held shower head, suspended on the wall by a bracket. Against the wall behind me was a small desk and chair and what looked to be a tall storage locker. Two bins identified as INCINERATE and REUSE lay against another wall.

A few minutes later, two new individuals pushed open the swinging doors and entered the room. From my gurney, I rotated my head and saw they both wore face masks and were dressed in full-length thin green coats. Their instructions had me empty my pockets. I removed my wallet, French change, a handkerchief, pen knife, and a packet of letters. They threw away the handkerchief, wiped down the rest, and placed them in a pouch. Without speaking another word my clothes were stripped or cut away and tossed in the INCINERATE bin.

"Lie back, stomach up," one instructed.

"Jeez. This thing is cold," I protested between coughs. The green coats didn't respond. One of them pushed my gurney over to the shower nozzle.

"We've warmed the water so you aren't shocked," he said.

The soothing pleasure of the water lasted only a moment, as they soaped me all over and began scrubbing every inch of my body with stiff brushes, and not gently. One coat spoke up, "I know this is uncomfortable soldier, but we have to remove all residue, otherwise you'll get sicker."

"Hold on, you're a woman."

"My, how observant" was her sarcastic reply. "Any problem with that?"

"No..."

"Close your eyes while I wash your hair and face." That got a strange stink of pee out of my nostrils. Where the hell did that come from? I wondered. Next they had me roll over to scrub my backside.

When finished, I was toweled dry, told to stand-up, and given green army pajamas to wear. The female aid dried the gurney top, spread a sheet over it. "Lie down" she ordered. That's when I realized the chill spreading through me. They pulled socks over my feet, and I was given a pair of flimsy slippers. With a pillow propped under my head, they covered me with a thin blanket, which didn't help my chill. After that, my tormenters removed their own coats and threw them in the REUSE bin.

I watched ceiling tiles and light fixtures slide overhead as the gurney rolled down the corridor. Forcing my head off the pillow I could see a set of double doors approaching with a sign that announced RECOVERY WARD D. On the other side was a large room with a high ceiling and huge windows. Many beds lay against each wall of the brightly lit room. It was a bustle of nurses, aids and doctors.

The gurney stopped in front of the only free bed. Fortunately, the ward was heated and with covers over me, the shivers I'd felt soon passed. Another coughing spell hit, and breathing felt more labored; the hacking seemed deeper. Over the next hour I coughed-up thick mucus.

A young American doctor whose name tag announced, "Doctor Paul Jensen," exuded complete indifference as he asked me to sit up. He tapped my chest with two fingers and applied a cold stethoscope to my skin, paused to listen, then advanced the Bakelite cup across my chest, holding steady from one position to the next.

"What do you hear, Doc?" I asked between coughs.

No answer, just a frown. He had me lean over; tapped my back and listened to my lungs again.

"Take a deep breath," he said. I drew a gulp of air, followed immediately by a fusillade of coughs that took several minutes to settle down. He repositioned the stethoscope and asked for another deep breath, with the same result. Doc entered some notes on a chart, and handed the stethoscope to a nurse. She repeated the whole examination.

Finally he spoke. "Well, Edwards, as near as I can tell, it's about ten hours since you were exposed. Everything points to chlorine, and the bubbling sound in your lungs confirms it. Your coughing is quite mild, and I don't see lung pieces in your phlegm. However, the gas has damaged your lungs and is producing mucous. I'm sending you to the Army Hospital for Respiration for further care. It'll take a day or so to get arranged."

"Where's that?"

"In Bordeaux!"

I wanted to ask another question but the doctor cut me off. "Meanwhile, nurse, see to it Private Edwards receives standard oxygen therapy. He's to breathe it for 30 minutes three times a day."

"Yes, Doctor."

"Soldier, you need to expectorate as much phlegm as you can. You need to stay in bed. No exertion. If all goes well, you may be out of the hospital in three weeks. You're lucky, soldier. Whoever carried you away from the gas likely saved your life."

I managed to ask. "Doc, what's expectorate mean?"

"You have to cough up the fluid in your lungs and spit it out."

"So, I'm not going to die?"

"No, Edwards, you'll live. Probably get out of this in fine shape. Good luck to you." He abruptly stood and advanced to the next patient. I felt so elated I didn't hear anything else.

October 25, 1918; Early afternoon, the Rail Yard, Saint Menehold, France.

In a drenching downpour, I climbed into a transport vehicle and was driven away from the Evacuation Hospital. Three hours later, with the rain stopped, five walking wounded boarded a hospital train at the rail yards in Saint Menenhold. For the next two days I headed south, toward the army's Tondu Hospital in Bordeaux.

October 26, 1918; 0115 hours, Layover, Tours, France.

"What's happening?" the man in the next bed asked. He hadn't said a word up to this point. "Why's the train stopped?"

"Hey. It's all right," I told him. "It's just a layover. We're in Tours." Jeez, I could hardly get it out between coughs. "I heard we're here for a couple of hours before the next engine connects. You okay? Want me to call a nurse?"

"No. No, don't do that. It's just, I can't see nothin'."

A large bandage covered his forehead and extended down across the bridge of his nose. I asked his name. "Tom Hoffer," he said.

"What happened?"

"I'm with the Fifteenth Infantry, Forty-Second Division. The Hun pushed back along our sector in early October. Least I think that's when. So many damn things going on, I can't keep dates straight."

"You got that right," I said.

"A counter attack's ordered; we pour out of the trench, and within fifty yards the Bosch's dropping mustard shells on us. I got my mask on, but not before some of that shit burnt my face. Doc says I wiped some of it into my left eye. Maybe the right as well. Can't see a damn thing no more."

"How you going to be?" I asked.

"Don't know. Doc said it only burned the outside of my eye, inside ain't hurt. Said it'd be slow, but I should recover.

"They say how long?"

"Maybe two months. I need re-evaluation at the base hospital. Can't believe those damn generals made us charge the enemy fire face on. We need some of them shits up on the line. Then, they'd start usin' their brains."

"You got it right, again."

"Otherwise, nothing else's wrong. What about you?"

"I'm Harry Edwards. In the supply section. Ran into chlorine on a delivery run. Doc says it's mild. Never guess it from how I cough."

"Nice to meet you, Edwards." Hoffer grumbled. "Jeez. I need a smoke bad."

"Say, I saw a YMCA Canteen through the window. It's just outside (cough). If you're game I'll lead you out. You could have a smoke and I could use a coffee. You up for it?"

"Shit, Edwards, that's the best thing I've heard in days. Let's go."

I tucked my kit bag under my blanket, waited till the nurse and orderlies were checking the next car. When all was clear I hustled Hoffer out of his bed and led him outside. I know I wasn't supposed to exert myself, but basic needs demand satisfaction. Coffee and cigarettes were basic needs. Hoffer got his smoke and I returned with two coffees.

Half hour later we crept back onto the train, and I returned Hoffer to his bed. We were never missed.

✄

October 27, 1918; Tondu Hospital, Bordeaux, France.

The train arrived in Bordeaux around noon. Hoffer transferred to the base hospital for burns and eye injuries. Four of us were transported by ambulance to the Tondu Hospital in the western suburbs. An orderly in the ambulance told us Tondu Hospital was once a prison. No missing that, the windows were still framed in iron bars.

I was settled on the ward after supper, and asked the nurse if she could find writing paper, a pencil and some envelopes. An hour later, a Red Cross volunteer handed me writing material. Said she'd pick up the letter tomorrow and deliver it to the post. The army had given me a top coat back at the evac hospital for the trip south, and I placed my personal effects in it. I had a few francs left from my last pay, but 'soldiers' mail' didn't need any stamps.

As I composed a letter to Fannie, an officer arrived at my bedside. He instructed me not to write anything about being gassed.

"Edwards, the army doesn't want the folks back home getting alarmed," he said.

"That's nuts. You want me to lie to them?" I protested.

"Those are the orders, soldier. You mention anything about gassing, the censor will black it out, and you'll get reported. Then, we'll both catch hell."

"What do I tell them?" I asked.

"Say you got a case of diarrhea. Tell them you got dehydrated or collapsed from exhaustion. I don't give a damn what you say. No mention of gas!"

That night I wrote to my father saying that Hughes and I were working so hard I didn't have time to drink enough water and lost strength from dehydration. I said I was getting better and mentioned the docs were real good and all the nurses were pretty. Asked him to have everyone keep writing me.

CHAPTER 41. Recovery

November 11, 1918; Tondu Hospital, Bordeaux, France,

"When can I get out of here Doc?" I asked for the umpteenth time during his morning rounds. "Soon enough Soldier. Soon enough." That's all he ever answered. Nevertheless, breathing oxygen over the last week had relieved my coughing.

The morning of November 11th began like all the rest. After breakfast, I sat up in bed with a pillow propped behind me, perusing a two-week-old issue of the *Washington Gazette*. Through the window next to my bed—which I kept slightly cracked to permit some air circulation—tolling bells suddenly broke the quiet. I looked at the wall clock, a little after 1100. A peculiar time for church bells, especially on a Monday, crossed my mind.

A commotion rose in the corridor, and a French nurse burst through the doors. "*La guerre est finie.*" She shouted. "*C'est merveilleux. La Boche sont défaits. La guerre est finie. La guerre est finie.*"

The guy in the next bed, covered in plaster from his right arm to his right leg, asked, "What's she saying? What's going on? Why are them bells ringing?" followed by a cascade of coughing.

"Douglas, calm down, breathe slowly. I'll see what's up."

I climbed out of bed, wiggled into my slippers, and hastened toward the double doors. Moments later, breathless with news, I burst through the doors to announce. "The war's over! Ended at eleven o'clock (cough, cough). The Krauts signed an armistice."

The realization spread around the ward from one injured man to the next. Twenty men in that room, from the ambulatory to the severely wounded, soon had huge ear-to-ear grins. I climbed back into bed, lost in thought as jubilation erupted.

My God, is it really over? Fannie, I'll live to come home. How are Sarge and the guys taking the news? Jeez, they must be dancing on the wagons. My thoughts were laced with happiness.

I wanted to be there. Doyle probably brought out that unopened bottle of schnapps he claimed he'd found on a dead German. It'd be drained dry by now, and Doyle would be swearing like mad he didn't get enough. Ha. I lay in my bed in a joyous stupor like every other soldier on the ward. I could only think, It's over; it's over. Thank God for all of us. The war is over; no one else will die…I'm alive. I'll soon be home to you Fannie.

"Edwards, your coughing is less severe. It's time to move around more. I want you to leave the ward for two hours every afternoon." This welcomed news was delivered by my doctor on his evening rounds. "Where do I go?" I asked the nurse. She replied, "Visit the canteen."

November 12, 1918; YMCA Canteen, Tondu Hospital, Bordeaux, France: The canteen on the first floor brewed real American coffee. It beat the strong, thick French brew served up for breakfast. Hell, just a few sips of it caused the "heebie-jeebies" that lasted all day. Now I could sit in the cafe, writing to Fannie, my thoughts lost in her and the luscious aroma of the Yank java. Contemplating my Fannie occupied more time than anything else. The more I thought about her, the more I missed her, and I wasn't sure I could miss her any more than I missed her before.

All the men obsessed over when we'd get home, and it formed the central point of all conversation. The opinions were fueled by rumors, all of which were true. They had to be, since a rumor always came from a reliable source.

A short stocky man, older than me, with a balding forehead, approached me with a coffee in hand. He looked familiar.

"It's Edwards, isn't it?"

"Yeah. Feel I should know you, but I can't think where we met. Damn, the war's ruined my memory."

"Know what you mean," he replied. "I'm MacKay. Jim MacKay from Harrisburg. Both of us were in the 315th back at Camp Lee and Redon. I was in Battery C, Fourth Platoon. We took instructions on working with horses together. I remember you 'cause you seemed to know your way about those animals. Hell, I'm a school teacher. Never been on a farm, and don't know a damn thing about horses. It didn't matter. They assigned me as a wagon brakeman, and our rig supplied shells to 75's in the Argonne sector. I've seen you down here a couple of times but couldn't place you till just now."

"Well, I'll be damned," I responded with a wide grin and an outstretched hand. "Hey, pull up a seat, come join me."

MacKay joined me. He took a sip of coffee. "Damn. This is good. Better than what they serve at breakfast."

"You got that right. Say, you been in Bordeaux long? What brought you here?"

"About two months. We went up to the front early the third week of September. About a week behind you guys. Saw action immediately in the central sector of the Argonne. We were delivering 75's to Le Mort Homme," said MacKay.

"Ha. We probably trudged up that damn hill together. So, when'd the gas catch you?" I asked.

"After Dead-Man's my platoon was bivouacked outside of Sepsarges. It was late September. The officers didn't realize it, but the gun emplacements were likely too close to the front. My driver and I were making a delivery, when we're caught in a God awful barrage. Shells falling all around. Christ, it was bad. The Krauts unloaded mustard, chlorine and phosgene, even threw-in high-explosive shrapnel: total chaos. Had everyone diving for cover. I didn't get my mask on right."

"I think I heard about that attack," I said.

"There's no safety in pockets or shell holes because of the gas. Damn shit killed my driver, wiped out the horse team, and damn near got me. I got a whiff, but kept my wits and managed to press the mask to my face to keep the seal. Doc's think it's phosgene. That's pretty wicked stuff. I've no memory of it. The next thing I knew, I was on my way to Bordeaux. They've brought me back pretty good. Tell me I'm shipping out next week, or the week after, but I still get these tingly sensations all over. Drives me nuts."

"Damn. Hell of a story. Say, I hope they're sending you stateside?"

"No such luck. The bastards are sending me back north. Doc says he's ordered to return all able men to duty."

"Jeeze, I don't want to hear that. I'm hoping they'll send me home."

"Don't hold your breath, Edwards." I laughed at 'hold your breath.'

"If you're being let off the ward, they're going to stamp you, "Fit-for-Duty." So how did you end up here?"

I told Mackay my story, at least what I knew of it.

"Guess we both were wearing lucky charms," he said.

Over the next week the two of us spent afternoons together.

"Say, MacKay. You get any mail from home?"

"Nope, only things I got are the old letters I carried in my coat. Captain said if I change mailing locations, my letters will most likely get lost or further delayed. You'd think the Army could get the damn post organized!"

"Been told the same. Some officer even threatened me if I wrote about being gassed," I said.

"I got the same swill. Stinks having the Army tell me what I can't write."

"You got that right. Hell, you should be thankful. At least you got some old letters. On the way here the train had a layover near Tours."

"Can't say as I remember any layovers," said MacKay.

"Any rate. I'm helping this blinded guy onto the platform to take a coffee break, couldn't have been more than fifteen minutes. Some creep broke into my kit and steals my razor, handkerchiefs, hand soap, all my toilet articles. The bastard took my pack of letters. So, I've nothing to read from my girl, sister, folks…nothing. They're all gone," I said. "I didn't realize they were missing till next morning."

"Jeez, what kind of a bastard takes a man's letters?" asked Mckay. " On a hospital train no less."

"I don't usually wish anyone ill, MacKay. But I pray this guy rots in hell. Should have been more orderlies on the train."

"Not very Christian of you," he replied with a grin.

"No, it's not. But it's been tough keeping the faith lately."

The Doc and his entourage of nurses entered the ward the morning of November 17th and started his rounds. I watched as he went from bed to bed, checking progress. Giving the nurses instructions and passing on reassurances. When he came to me, I got the usual, "ahhhs" and "hmmmmms," as the cold stethoscope roamed my chest. Could never figure if his grunts were good or bad. One of the nurses would listen for gurgles, then she'd render an opinion which never differed from his. Doc had me take a deep breath, which produced just one little cough.

"When do I get out of here, Doc?" I asked.

He glanced up from the chart and said that I'd asked him the same question twice a day for weeks. He wanted to know if I'd memorized his reply. He stared at me, as though waiting for an answer, and suddenly broke into a big grin as he handed me my release papers.

"You can leave in the morning," he said, showing me where to sign.

I took the pen and signed the pages, wearing an ear-to-ear smile. He added that I'd be on "light duty" for the next three weeks. Doc handed me a printed sheet of instructions and told me to show them to my commanding officer when I got back.

"Ahhhh… Doc, what do you mean "light duty" or "get back?" I'm… I'm not going home?"

"No, your injury isn't that grave."

"Ow, come on, Doc, you know I still get these coughing spells."

"You're only spitting up mucous. There's no infection and the cough will pass soon enough. Sorry, soldier, that's the way it is."

Later that afternoon, MacKay and I shared a last coffee. As I entered the café, a huge smile spread across his face.

"Jeez, MacKay, what's got you going?"

"Edwards, those docs changed their mind! Can you believe it? They're sending me home. A hospital ship arrives next Wednesday. I'm being transferred to it."

"You lucky bastard. I got my marching orders this morning. They're sending me back north, tomorrow. Doesn't that beat it?"

"Tough break, Edwards. But look, this means you've recovered. Jeez, Doc says I might've ingested some phosgene. My blood isn't right, and they don't understand it. Cripes! Doc says it could be nothing, or it could kill me."

I paused a moment. "I get sent north, back to my pup tent healthy, you go home with a problem, or maybe no problem. Not sure but that I'd rather be in your shoes."

"I'm not sure I agree with you." said MacKay.

CHAPTER 42. Back North

November 18, 1918; On the train heading north, France.
    I left Tondu Hospital and found my way to the Bordeaux train station. The scene at the station was chaotic. Troop redeployment since the armistice had strained all resources. Indeed, I was warned it might be difficult to find my unit. The 80th division, like all the other American divisions, had gone through substantial reorganization. Soldiers were pulled from the ranks and transferred to the Forty-Second Division. When Companies in the Forty-Second regained strength, they marched toward the Rhine as the Army of Occupation. At the same time the Eightieth Division consolidated units and prepared to relocate southward to temporary bases. With help, I identified a northbound train for the first leg of my return trip.

    The trip from Bordeaux to Souilly took three nights and four days. The overnight stop in Tours offered only wooden benches to sleep on. The YMCA Canteens in the *Gare du Nord* of Paris, and the station at Reims had cots set out. Their rest areas were away from the main concourse and reasonably quiet. At least, they dimmed the lights and I managed a good sleep. Thank goodness I had my bulky overcoat because the further north I traveled, the colder it got.

November 22, 1918; 0820 Hours, Souilly, France, 20 Km South of Verdun.
    An easy walk through the train station, and across the street, had me standing in a portico with large double doors. Two MPs at the entrance checked my ID and I entered. The 80th Division Command Post bustled with activity. An adjutant directed me to a room on the first floor. The operations room had at least fourteen desks, each with a soldier operating a clacking typewriter. I approached a sergeant who was shuffling papers on a desk near the entrance.
    "Sergeant, I'm Private Edwards returning from base hospital in Bordeaux. I need to find my unit and return to service."

"Speak up, Private. Can't hardly hear over this din." I repeated, louder this time.

The sergeant examined my orders and requested my identification number. When all seemed in order, he rose from his desk and approached a large bank of file cabinets. After about five minutes he returned, papers in hand.

"Bring this to Captain Chester in the Unit Locator Office. Room is to the right, as you came in. He'll help."

"Thanks, Sergeant."

The adjacent office had only four desks, the sign on one read: Captain Chester. Chester, an older man, sat hunched forward in his chair, staring intently at an open folder. His wrinkled uniform looked like he'd been in it for days.

With a salute I said, "Excuse me, these papers are for you, Sir. I am looking for my unit. Been away in hospital more than a month."

Chester looked up and returned the salute.

"Yes. Well, let me see those."

He looked them over, rose from his chair and walked to a large wall map. The map was studded with pins in different shapes and colors. As he scrutinized the map he asked, "What happened, Edwards?"

I told Chester my story. Said the hospital fixed me up, 'Fit for Duty.' I mentioned that it took four days to get here. The trains were jammed up everywhere with troops movin' all over the country.

The Captain glanced away from his map. "Heard the same thing. Travel's all cocked-up. You're lucky, soldier. I kept causality records before I was assigned here. Too many of our boys suffered from that damn gas. Most survived because of the mask. But there's plenty in bad shape. Lot of 'em didn't make it."

He paused, placed his finger on the map. "Yes. Here it is. The 315th is now holed up west of Sassay. Battery B has to be nearby. They're about forty-five kilometers north along the Mouzay road."

"How do I get there, Sir?"

Chester tilted his head down, and looked at me above his glasses.

"On your own, soldier..." He smiled and continued. "While you've been gone there's been a big change. Motorized trucks are arriving every day, and there're regular supply runs all the way to

Mouzay. Go over to the motor pool and ask around. You'll be able to hitch a ride." He handed my orders back.

"Thank you, Sir."

"And don't delay," Chester added. "The entire Division's pulling out of this sector soon and heading southwest to the Fifteenth Training Area. If your unit has relocated before you get back to them, you'll have a hell of a time finding 'em."

"Where's this training area, Sir?" I asked.

"Town called Ravieres, two hundred and fifty kilometers southwest of here. Rumor has it they've identified digs for all you gobs. Sure as hell it'll beat sleeping in pup tents the rest of the winter."

"It sure will be. Thank you, Sir." I saluted, and headed for the door, then stopped. "Sir, if I may, any word on when we head home?"

"Sorry, soldier. Like to know myself."

"Ahhh. One other thing, Sir. Is there a place I can get some chow? Haven't eaten in about twenty hours.

An hour later, with a full stomach, I hitched a ride on a supply truck. The driver knew of units located outside of Sassay. He'd delivered supplies to Battery B earlier in the week.

The truck driver had been in France only three weeks, and he never stopped with the chatter. I wasn't in a talkative mood, but did mention that I was returning from hospital; he mercifully let it be. Offered me a smoke but I told him I was off those sticks for now. Had to protect my lungs. Two hours later, the truck reached Sassay.

"We're here," said the driver. I thanked him for the lift, and walked toward what remained of a chateau. A large sign over the entrance said, 315th Field Artillery C.P. Inside, a lieutenant gave me directions to Battery B. I walked another three kilometers in the direction of Halles. The road must have been repaired, because it passed through a devastated landscape with shell holes and shattered trees. I soon came to a small cluster of houses that matched my instructions. A sentry checked my papers and pointed to the most intact building. I showed my papers to Captain O'Malley and yet again told the story of my recovery.

"Everything looks in order, Edwards. Glad you got out of that scrape. What's the hospital like in Bordeaux? I heard it's pretty cushy."

"You got that right. There were plenty of pretty nurses running through those hallways. Must say, I'd rather have been sent home."

"Wouldn't we all." He scribbled on a piece of paper and handed it to me. "Here's the direction to Third Platoon."

I saluted and left the building. The sun sat low in the sky and beams of sunlight skirted the trunks of dead trees. The light knifed through air cold enough to produce mist when I exhaled. As I walked the road, a feeling of melancholy surged over me. I longed to be home with Fannie.

Three large tents were in a clearing and alongside them were four rings of pup tents. Probably one for each squad. Hey, where are the horses and wagons? I wondered. Men milled around the camp or clustered about several fires. I spotted Ernie Gillespie and Phil Doyle. Jeez, it felt good to see their ugly mugs. Ollie Baker crawled out of his pup tent. Sarge sat by a fire talking, his hands moving back and forth in an animated manner. Joe Goldrick looked up, recognized me. Goldrick turned to Jake Osborn. "Damn, It's Edwards." The squad rushed over to greet me.

"Wow! Good to see you," said Charlie Powell. Doyle, Goldrick, and Nightlinger shook my hand, Gillespie gave me a hug and Jake Osborn and Ollie Baker patted my back. Sedelsky held out his hand. "Glad you're back son. We missed you. Lieutenant told us where you were. Had a bit of a vacation in the south. Warm there, eh?"

"Warmer than here, Sarge."

"Edwards, looks like you put on some pounds. They must have been feeding you good French food. Damn, I got to get me a hospital visit," said Doyle.

"It may be too late Doyle," I joked. "You'd have to suck some gas to be where I been."

Everybody grinned, and wanted to know everything at once.

Sarge cut through the commotion. "We kept your pack with us. It's over in the farm house. We'll get it later. You bunk with Powell for now. He's got a vacant spot. You okay with a tent mate, Powell?"

"Sure, Sarge. I need someone to snuggle up to!"

"No way," I said. "Say, where are Hughes and Adams?"

Sedelsky's smile disappeared and I felt a sudden chill.

"Whole Army's getting reorganized. Each squad gave up one man, and the Lieutenant picked Hughes. Seemed reasonable with you in hospital," said Sarge. "I hear tell his regiment marched north, week ago Wednesday. Part of the army of occupation on the Rhine River."

"And Adams?"

Sedelsky hesitated, and squared his eyes on mine. "He didn't make it."

"What happened?"

"He died after the Armistice, on a supply run, taking blankets up to Mouzay. With the war over, we let our guard down. You tell it, Powell," said Sarge.

Charlie Powell continued. "Adams wanted to stop, so he could take a pee. The guy was always shy about it. He walks off the road, twenty meters or so. There's a tree stump standing by itself. Hardly more than the trunk sitting there in this shot-up field. I see the jet of water splashing off the roots. He finishes, takes several steps back and BOOM. Never found anything, just blew him to nothing."

"What the hell!" I said.

"Stepped on a mine or an unexploded shell. Who knows?" said Powell.

Sedelsky added. "Powell led us back next morning. We found nothing. Not even his tags. Least he never knew what hit him."

"Jeez, the war's over, and to punch-out like that. Shit, the man had a wife and kids," I said.

"Yeah, we all felt the same," said Powell.

CHAPTER 43. Sassay

November 22, 1918; Sassay, France

Sarge sent Powell and me over to the farmhouse to retrieve my pack. On the way Powell resurrected the current rumor that we weren't going to be in these pup tents much longer.

"Sarge told us we'd break camp after Thanksgiving, head south to a place called the Fifteenth Training Area. I hope it's way south. Out of this damn cold and rain."

"It may not be that far," I commented. "When I came through Souilly a major at the divisional

command post mentioned that the battalion will soon shift to a town in the Yonne Valley, two hundred and fifty kilometers southwest of here."

"Don't sound that far south," said Powell.

"I only caught a glance at the major's map, so I'm not sure where it is."

"Say, mind if I tell the rest of the guys?" Powell asked.

"No. But I've no idea how true it is. Say, Powell what happened to the horses and wagons?"

Powell told me that two weeks ago the horses and wagons in the platoon were given to locals. The army couldn't care for them anymore. Farmers came from the other side of the river, where the land wasn't shot up, so at least they got a good home.

"Jeez, Edwards, it was tough for everyone to see them go."

"Yeah, I can imagine. What kind of shape were they in?" I asked.

"Pretty bad. We were about out of feed and they were lucky to find new homes."

Back at the pup tent, I opened my pack and removed my poncho and blanket. My bedroll needed airing bad.

"Jeez," I blurted after sniffing my blanket. "This thing stinks. How cold does it get at night? Do I need this blanket?"

"You'll need it. An extra one would be a good idea too. Check with Supply," said Powell. "They're plentiful now. Get two, and throw that stinking thing out." With Sarge's help I found the quartermaster and was able to requisition two new blankets, and a new poncho.

Later in the evening, the squad sat around the fire sipping coffee.

"Say, guys," I asked. "Did Hughes ever tell you exactly what happened to us? All I recall is being totally lost. Suddenly, we're tangled up in the communication trenches. We had to get the hell away, since there was an attack at sunrise. I remember turning the rig and hightailing it when Kraut shells started falling."

Goldrick interrupted. "Weren't you well behind the lines?"

"We got lost and were less than a kilometer from the front. The Hun started lobbing shells at the doughboys, mostly eighty-eights, and some two-ten monsters. Their aiming is piss poor, because suddenly shells are crashing down all around us. Dirt poured over the rig and the concussions damn near threw me off the seat. I couldn't push the horses any harder because of the road ruts. Even so, we were putting some distance behind us."

The guys were listening keenly; they'd only ever heard Hughes' version of the tale.

"Next thing I know, I'm lying in the middle of the road. Got this horrible stink of pee in my nose and my throat hurts like hell. I'm coughing in spurts. Hughes, some nurse, and an orderly are looking at me. My head's spinning something bad. They load me on a stretcher, shove me into an ambulance and hours later I'm at a hospital. That's all I know."

"Hell, Edwards," said Gillespie. "You told it just like Hughes did. But as near as I can piece together, you were knocked out when the wagon flipped."

I learned I was thrown from the wagon and that Hughes had carried me to safety, but not before I got a whiff of chlorine. They told me that Hughes used a piss soaked handkerchief as a makeshift gas mask.

"Jeez, now I know about that stink on my face. From what I'm hearing, the guy saved my life. Cripes, I can't even thank the bastard. So catch me up. What happened after I went away? Oh, wait, did our horse team survive?"

"They were killed by the same gas that got you," said Doyle.
I put my head down and sipped some coffee.

For the next forty minutes I learned about what the squad had done while I was gone. While I languished in hospital, with good food and a warm bed, they had it rough.

Lights out had me in the tent. My new blankets certainly smelled better, and despite a sense of sadness, I felt good being back with my brothers.

About a week before I returned from the hospital, the officers in Battery B had pooled their money and passed the hat among the noncoms and troops. With a good sized bankroll, they commandeered a staff car and supply truck, and set off for southern France on a secret mission.

Meanwhile, the squads in Battery B had scoured old German trench works for building material: wooden beams, planking, floor boards, nails, tools, or whatever else might prove useful. Everything of use was brought back to Battery HQ, where the engineers cobbled together a large enclosure. A mess hall rose out of the detritus of war to celebrate Thanksgiving. The searching and construction kept the boys busy, kept our minds off the war and ruminating about going home.

By the time I arrived in Sassay, four walls and the roof frame were in place. I helped lug boards from the trenches that the engineers used to lay a floor that would keep our feet off the cold dirt. Along one wall they built a huge fireplace out of reclaimed bricks and stones. Other platoons cut firewood for cooking. We couldn't wait for a taste of that Thanksgiving dinner.

On November 24th Sarge sent Second Squad out on another scrounging mission. We'd hiked a considerable distance north of the bivouac area along the muddy Halle Road. The countryside had its usual shot up appearance.

"Doesn't seem to have the same stench it had a few weeks back," said Baker.

After a while, we encountered a German trench that Phil Doyle was convinced hadn't been examined before. We climbed into the trough and split into two groups heading in opposite directions. After half a kilometer of negotiating ragged earthen works, we only found only the usual detritus of men at war: blood-stained boots, old mess kits, cartridge casings, a dirty towel, an old tee-shirt, a leather belt. Nothing out of the ordinary. Nevertheless, ever wary of bobby traps, we were careful.

I rounded a corner and came to an abrupt halt. A wall of rock and dirt blocked the path. I thought that an exploded artillery shell must have blown rubble into the trench. Charlie Powell noticed that several rocks along one side wall were wedged in such a way they revealed an opening from which poured a stream of cold air. Exploring the opening, Powell widened the hole by pulling away some smaller rocks. When large enough, he stuck his arm in, up to his shoulder.

"Wow," he shouted, "what's this?"

The three of us dug, exposing a much larger breach. Powell flicked his lighter and pushed his upper body into the hole and inched down the hidden steps. We should have been more cautious, but curiosity got the best of us. Gillespie and I climbed into the hole, behind Powell. The lighter revealed torches stacked near the entrance to a larger room. We lit one and it illuminated a large chamber, at least eight by six meters. More remarkable, the ceiling was high enough for us to stand upright.

"Wow, the room's ventilated. The torch smoke's flowing up the stairs," said Gillespie.

The bunker walls were lined with wood, and the creaking wooden floor was dry, despite a musty odor. The torch revealed chairs, a small desk, boxes, bunks and papers scattered over the floor.

"Damn, Krauts left here in a hurry," I said.

Powell spied it first. "Jeez, look at that."

Against the back wall stood an upright piano, scratched and battered, but intact. I lifted the cover to reveal dusty keys, banged-out a few notes—that, to my untrained ear—sounded pretty good. Powell came over and plunked out an old church hymn.

"This old girl's got music left in her," he said.

Ernie Gillespie examined the piano more closely and noticed an extra set of peddles. He fiddled with a sliding panel above the keys until it revealed a hidden mechanism.

"I thought so," he said. "She's a player. Hey, look around for some piano rolls."

I ransacked through the rubbish stacked along one wall and uncovered a wooden crate full of cylindrical tubes. "This what you mean?" I asked.

"Jeez, you found 'em. Must be a couple dozen," said Gillespie as he picked up several and read their titles with a horrible German pronunciation. "My uncle owned one of these. He'd let me operate it when my folks visited."

Gillespie lifted one of the rolls. "*Der La--ment des Gloc--en--spiels*," he sounded out.

Powell continued to explore the bunker. "Hey, I found a bench," he hollered, and carried it over.

Gillespie positioned the bench and sat down. He threaded the paper roll into the mechanism, fiddled with some leavers, and pumped the foot pedals. Damn, the roll started to turn, and next thing you know, holes in the paper were moving down the face of the player. The keys suddenly jumped and music poured forth. Powell and I stood there amazed. Gillespie's feet pumped away, as we swayed to the music.

I was as "wound up" as the roll of music. "Damn. We need this in the mess hall for Thanksgiving."

The three of us rushed out of the bunker to look for Sarge. When we found him, we led everyone back to the piano.

"Nightlinger, Baker, and Doyle stay here and guard the entrance. I don't want another squad finding this thing and stealing our bragging rights. Rest of youse men come with me. We need a truck."

Forty minutes later, I climbed into the back of a truck. With Sedelsky up front giving directions, the vehicle retraced the Halles road toward our precious discovery.

It was a hell of a job lifting that player out of the dugout, and pushing and carrying it along the trench to a place where it could be hauled out seemed nearly impossible. Damn thing weighed a ton, and with the mud it felt like we were pushing it through mush. It took the eight of us along with Sarge and the truck driver, to finally load it onto the truck bed. Back at the nearly completed mess hall, the Major's compliments were effusive. He ordered a search of the battalion for someone who could tickle the keys.

∽

November 28, 1918; Thanksgiving Day, Sassay, France.

The officer's secret mission returned with a truck load of dressed pigs and geese, ready for roasting. Nuts, and fresh turnips, cabbages, apples and pears were welcome additions. The boys in Battery B were served a tasty dinner. Cooks even prepared a French equivalent of cranberry sauce. Damn, they got it right for once. The pork and fowl were delicious. The secret mission had also bought back enough wine so that everyone tilted a glass. We all agreed—in total ignorance—it was a good vintage. Nightlinger thought it tasted like vinegar.

Okay, turnips and cabbage as vegetables weren't my thing. But the tables were set with plenty of butter, freshly baked bread and hot gravy. The meal could have used some mashed potatoes, but at least we finished with decent coffee and fruit pies.

Gillespie taught other guys how to load and unload player-rolls, and the music was nearly continuous with different men pumping the peddles. More important, the officers returned with a stash of disgusting, cheap Spanish cigars. We puffed enough to stink up the mess hall. A fitting finish to a mighty fine day.

CHAPTER 44. The Yonne Valley

November 30, 1918; Sassay, France.

The squad rose at 0700, had a cold breakfast, packed up the campsite and was ready to move-out by late morning. We assembled on the road, and walked toward the rail head at Dun.

A feeling of relief flowed through me at the thought of leaving the war zone. Hughes and I—of all the men in our squad—had come closest to anything you might call combat. I thought of the many things that had happened during the past six months as I walked in silence.

I relived the adrenalin rush of saving the lives of two men, if not more: Hughes up on the mast of the *Tenadores* during the squall, Ford when his leg got cut by the horse's hoof, and that company of doughboys at Nantillois Ridge. That thought caused new images to click in my head.

Click… There I was at Le Mort Homme, struggling with an artillery shell balanced across my shoulders. Where the hell did I get the strength to carry that damn thing?

Click… Will Adams, the last time I saw him alive. What a shitty way to get killed, and after the war ended no less.

Click… Now the horses. The conflicts of men meant nothing to them. I loved those animals, and they deserved better than a death from chlorine. What a waste of beautiful creatures.

Click… Nantillois Ridge. What would have happened if Hughes and I hadn't run along the crest and shot down those Krauts? How many doughboy families would've mourned sons who never returned to them? Was it really our providence to be there at that exact moment?

Click… Hughes and I had been through a lot together. He was a good friend, a friend for life. I missed him, wished he hadn't been picked to go north. What was he up to? Probably freezing his ass off on the German border. I needed to find his address. I'll ask Emily for it in my next letter.

Click… My gassing and hospital care. I'm still amazed I got out of that in one piece. Hughes saved my life on that one.

Click… That kid. How many times had I tried to force him out of my mind? I had as much success with that as holding my breath for five minutes. Would I ever shake those haunting eyes? Does sufficient guilt ever produce absolution?

Click… Then, most ironic of all, I recalled officers at Camp Lee lecturing us on the glory and honor of the Great Adventure. An adventure to last a lifetime. "Glory and honor," they'd say again. Who was I honoring and where was the glory? It was bullshit. There were a lot of men in the ground out there whose honor and glory came to a dead end… Jeez, what a stupid callous thing to think. What dominated everything for me in this war had been work. I never saw any 'romance' in my effort. I didn't experience any of that abstract stuff.

As we walked along other thoughts came into my head. At least I'm headed out of this hell hole. Jeez, how many boys didn't make it? Why had I survived? Was I just lucky? More than likely, being a wagon driver saved my life. Hell, was it fate that placed me in that assignment line back at Camp Lee? I hadn't planned on being a wagon driver, it just happened.

My thoughts deepened. Maybe chance is what life is about; being at a certain place at a certain time. Jake Osborn felt that none of us had any control over our lives. He emphasized we shouldn't dwell on what we can and can't control.

"There is no explanation for fate," he once said. "A man could spend a lifetime working to figure it out, and then play games to turn fate in his direction. In the end we all die just the same." Osborn believed that any effort to manipulate the forces of our life would fail. I remembered him saying: "The man who cleverly thinks he controls his destiny, and later realizes he can't, will likely end up bitter and angry. Hell, worse yet, frustrated, and unsatisfied. I don't want that. There's a better way. I'll learn from the things life throws at me. I can't fight them or change them, but the experience can better prepare me to deal with the unexpected next time around. I'll let the ebb-and-flow of events carry me along. For me, the adventure lies in the uncertainty."

Suddenly, something my sister had written flashed in my head; that Jake Osborn spouted some high-flutin' ideas at times. Well, I figure some of his ideas were hard to digest, but he wasn't cynical. Maybe more realistic than anything else.

That afternoon our platoon entered the Dun railhead where hundreds of troops milled around. I don't know who gave the instructions, but once sorted-out, I found myself in a passenger car. Jim Nightlinger took the window seat. I ditched my pack in the overhead rack and sat next to him. We adjusted the seats so they faced each other and Doyle and Powell sat across from us. On the other side of the isle sat Goldrick and Gillespie facing Osborn and Baker.

We dozed in our seats for an hour before I heard a "woosh" of steam, and felt the usual jerk as the engine applied power to the drive wheels. The Fifteenth Training Area, 250 kilometers south of us, as the crow flies, turned out to be more than 350 kilometers by train. From Dun we chugged southeast. Jim Nightlinger, pointed out station signs for Verdun and Nancy.

"Doyle, you still got a deck of cards?" asked Powell after we passed Verdun.

"What, you want a game? Would've thought you'd be gun-shy at the prospect of losing more money," Doyle responded.

"I'll take my chances again," said Powell as he retrieved his backpack from the overhead rack and used it to form a makeshift table top. For hours the cards shuffled before we tired of it. Charlie Powell smiled profusely, having cleaned the three of us of twenty-five francs.

After sunset Ernie Gillespie pointed to a well-lit passing sign with *Suisse* written on it.

"What's that?" asked Goldrick.

"We're near the Swiss border," said Gillespie.

We'd been riding for five hours. I had the feeling again of being lost, and the black of night outside the window made me feel even more isolated.

"Nightlinger, you got anything to read?" I asked.

"Why don't you ask Gillespie for his French dictionary? I hear it's a page turner," he replied.

"Very funny," said Gillespie.

"I got something you'd like," said Doyle. He reached into the overhead bin, opened a pocket on his pack, and retrieved a magazine, "*La Vie Parisienne.*" The cover showed two young women with smiles on their faces, posing on a beach in bathing costumes. Inside, Doyle's tattered March, 1917 copy of this risqué rag were other pictures of naked women in various poses. I leafed quickly through the pages.

"Where the hell did you get that?" I asked, as Nightlinger leaned in to catch a look. Powell's eyes were glued to the pages.

"Doyle has his ways."

Sarge hollered. "Okay, men, in five minutes we arrive at Belfort. Red Cross and YMCA has food and coffee set out. Leave everything behind; we'll be coming back here, car number thirteen. You've an hour to kill, not a minute longer."

I handed the magazine back to Doyle. "Can I see it again, when we get back?"

"Sure," he said, with a grin.

"Me too," chimed in Powell and Nightlinger.

"For you, Powell, it'll cost something. Have to earn my money back, don't I?"

"Aw, come on," groaned Powell.

December 2, 1918; Ravieres, France.

We detrained at a station called Nuits-sous-Ravieres mid afternoon, and then hiked across an ancient stone bridge spanning the Armançon River. A church spire in Ravieres, a kilometer away, signaled our destination.

More than eighteen months ago the army commandeered everything it could at Redon, our training base in Brittany. The same thing had taken place, here, in Ravieres. It served as another training base. The army vacated the town in late October of '18, as the last of the American contingents shifted to the front. Now reactivated, it held yanks relocating from the war zone. The town was larger than Redon with many multi-story stone buildings. At street level, shops and cafes peppered the street. It was the center of a rural area and surrounding the town were small villages. By the end of the war there were plenty of vacant buildings for us yanks to occupy. As we had in Redon, the platoons of Battery B were bivouacked in farm complexes outside of town. Second Squad found itself holed-up in a small building that had once stored grain. It had no heat, but lots of dry straw, and the roof showed no sign of leaks.

Nightlinger found a tub of nails and Gillespie, Powell, Ollie Baker, and I discovered a cache of wooden boards. Next day, Sedelsky showed up with a hammer, saw and roll of chicken wire.

"Now youse gobs can make some bunks and get off the ground," said Sarge.

We made bed frames, and stretched the chicken wire over them. With enough straw and blankets I almost felt warm at night. Almost! Sleeping for the past six months had been an abstract concept for most of us. A little less so for me, since I had that hospital stay. Despite the bed frame, straw and blankets, I never slept well from December through mid-March, mostly because the nights were bitter cold.

CHAPTER 45. Christmas

December 17, 1918; Ravieres, France.

We'd been at the new base for about two weeks and it was soon obvious that things in town were not good. What grabbed each soldier were the children. They were in a terrible state, with so many fathers gone, disappeared and likely dead from the war. Widowed women begged on the street, their dirty and disheveled children clinging to them. The local priest made a count and there were forty-two children between ten-months and sixteen-years old living in destitution. Another thirty-one children lived in the local catholic orphanage. We didn't know how the orphans fared as the nuns blocked our entry.

The men found little work; food was in short supply; buildings were run down; the roads beyond the town center were a wreck; and the sewers weren't working right. The whole social fabric had unraveled.

Our officers sought permission from the army for the battalion to pitch-in and help rebuild the town. A good idea, I thought, since the army had nothing else to keep us busy. It was granted and now we had an activity that felt good. The officers also hatched an idea that the battalion should chip-in and buy the kids Christmas presents. Everyone dug deep and collected over 5000 FF. Colonel Williams told the mayor there'd be a big party in the town square December 23rd. He told the mayor that all the children needed to be in the square so that *Père Noël* could give out Christmas presents. The Officers planned a surprise, like a good old Christmas morning back home. To help raise funds a drawing was organized to pick the squad that would buy the presents with the money collected from the whole battalion. But I wondered, where the hell are those presents coming from?

Goldrick burst through the grain house door so flummoxed he could hardly speak.

"Come on, come on, out with it." urged Sedelsky.

Goldrick struggled to regain his breath, then yelled. "We won! we won! I tell you, we won!"

"Won what?" Doyle hollered back.

"The Christmas present trip. We won. You remember the drawing?"

"You mean to buy presents?" Powell asked.

"Yeah, yeah, that's it. We won. They drew our squad."

"Do we all get passes for a whole day in Dijon?" asked Osborn.

"Right, a whole day, into the evening too!" replied Goldrick.

Everyone wanted to know when we were going.

"When Sarge arranges it," Goldrick said. "Has to be soon, the presents are needed by the 23rd."

∾

December 20, 1918; Dijon, France.

Sarge requisitioned a truck for December 20th, and we left camp just after morning chow and lumbered toward Dijon. By 1100 hours the truck entered the business center of town and drove along *Rue Victor Hugo*. Dijon appeared to have escaped the ravages of war. Large buildings lined the streets, and there was even a street car that followed tracks in and out of the town center. Christmas decorations, though meager, adorned every shop and café along *Victor Hugo*. We parked the truck and began our holiday mission. By the second shop an argument, erupted between Goldrick and Baker.

"Look Baker, you got nieces or not?" asked Goldrick. "Well, I do and I know they'd want dolls with eyes that open and close. It's lifelike, little girls will love 'em."

"Yeah, they might love them, but we could get three without blinkey eyes for the price of one "blinker." We got to stretch that money so that all the kids get something nice," responded Baker.

That argument swayed Goldrick.

By the time our shopping spree had concluded, we'd bought stuffed animals and rattles for the infants; dolls, toy cars and trucks for the younger kids, and board games, soccer balls, and construction kits for the adolescents. A stack of books were acquired for all ages, based on how the pictures pleased us. We'd even picked out an assortment of overcoats, jackets, shirts, blouses, dresses and pants in various sizes for the children and teenagers. Boy, our truck contained a heap-load of presents.

On the drive back to Ravieres we stopped at a bistro in a small village and enjoyed more than good meal. Each one of us was tipsy from the excessive flow of wine and that added to the good feeling we had when hitting the sack at 2130.

December 23, 1918; The Town Square, Ravieres, France.

The Christmas party warmed my heart. The children were all assembled in the town square as the regimental band struck up: *The Bells of Christmas*. Excitement ran high even though the children were unaware of the coming surprise. Suddenly an officer's touring car entered the town square. Everyone peered at it and the band broke into a flourish to accompany *Jingle Bells*. The top of the car was pulled back to reveal the occupant. An overweight *Père Noël*—the French Santa Claus—sat in the back seat and waved at everyone.

Jake Osborn told me the French Santa didn't look like that. He'd seen a picture of him in some French magazine. It didn't matter. Everyone stretched their necks to catch a sight of him. Behind the touring car was a horse drawn flat-bed wagon, loaded with presents. The kids waved at *Père,* and rushed to see what the wagon held.

Père Noël played his role beautifully. He handed out the gifts and talked with each child. They didn't understand a word, but they all laughed and giggled with anticipation. That's all that mattered. Jeez, those teenagers loved the clothes. Tears ran from mothers' eyes, and a few of us tough guys had some too.

The town folk set up holiday tables and our cooks had prepared cookies and cakes, which were set out and served by the First Platoon. There was plenty of food for all. Our band played old time Christmas favorites and everyone sang. The town mayor ordered a generator activated and the party went on into a lighted December night. Someone found a victrola, and dancing followed. The war was over. It was Christmas time, and the joy on those young faces blessed the season.

That German boy should be home for Christmas. Hell, I should be home giving my Fannie a Christmas hug.

December 25, 1918; The 315th Field Artillery Mess Hall, Ravieres, France.

The army let us sleep-in Christmas day, that is until 0900. I attended services at 1100 where there was singing by a nice French choir. At 1300 Sarge rounded us up. "Okay boys, time to feast on some Chrismaaaas dinner. I hear there's a surprise waiting for us," he said with his usual melodramatic style.

"A surprise?" asked Doyle. "What's her name?"

"They're serving dinner; that's the surprise," offered Nightlinger.

"I can always hope," said Doyle.

A half hour later, we all filed into the Mess Hall.

"Say, Edwards, you seeing what I'm seeing?" asked Ollie Baker. There it was, identified by the gouge on its side. Sarge told us the officers felt the French at Sassay had no need for a German player piano. It would have a better home with us in Ravieries, and was delivered here by the road convoy.

"You got that right," I said to Sarge.

We were seated, and within ten minutes piano rolls began spinning. Over dinner, tales of Christmas at home were swapped back and forth. I enjoyed Doyle's.

"I'm from a big Irish family," he began.

"Hell, all Irish families are big," interrupted Jim Nightlinger. "Nothin' special there."

"Okay. Okay, everyone knows the Irish like to do what makes lots of kids. Well, dinner was at my grandparents' house. On cue, grandfather, father, and my uncles would argue the whole time. It was always the same three things: our parish priest, Philly police harassment, and Philadelphia politics. My father couldn't stand our priest. He detested the man and I never understood why. Father Mahoney was certainly nice to me. As a youngster, I loved the arguments. No one gave an inch. Passions flared through dinner, and roiled into a shouting match during dessert. Uncle Patrick would get steamed, likely fueled by the Irish whiskey."

For some inexplicable reason Doyle started talking about the great dessert his mother and aunts always made.

"Hey, wait a minute," interrupted Ollie Baker. "What happened with the arguments?"

"Yeah. Finish the story," I demanded.

"Uncle Patrick. What did he do?" asked Osborn.

"Oh, yeah, Patrick. Well, he'd be hopping mad. All of a sudden, he'd jump up and yell, 'Marie.' That was his wife, my Aunt Marie. 'Get the coats on the kids. We're leaving.' Rude remarks would be directed to my father or uncles, and Patrick, Marie, and my cousins would storm out of the house. Never thanked anyone for dinner or their presents."

"Wow, never got that bad at our house," Charlie Powell said.

"Best part. Next family dinner, Uncle Patrick, the children and Aunt Marie would be back for another round. But sure enough, like a *déjà vu*, it all repeated itself."

We all got a laugh over Doyle's story.

The army, bless its heart, let us have French beer with dinner. Sedelsky knocked back more than a few and loosened up for the first time.

"Hey, Sarge, what was your Christmas like?" asked Goldrick. The Sergent was quiet, as if he wasn't going to say anything. But he did, maybe the beers loosened him up.

"When I was a kid my old man might just as well beat me Christmas eve as not." Sarge struggled to say more. "My mother'd put up some decorations." He hesitated again. "And unless she bought it, there'd be no tree. Christmas morning I'd be overjoyed if there were a piece of candy left for me. I never knew any other family. Didn't have a brother or sister and there were no aunts or uncles, at least none I ever met."

"Sarge, we're your family now," said Goldrick. Everyone nodded and tipped their glass to him.

"I guess you are." Did I see a hint of dampness in those crusty old eyes?

After supper, a piano player took over from the rolls. A fiddler appeared, and before I knew it, a square dance was underway. A guy in the HQ section knew the calls and got right into it. Guys paired up, formed squares, and started dancing. The dancing didn't last long, because you couldn't tell the women from the men. Confusion reigned and a heap of belly laughs came out of it. After the dancing a bunch of men gathered around the piano and sang Christmas carols.

The day made each of us long for home. The look on the faces of the kids, the stories of families at Christmas, the holiday songs plunked on an old piano found in a German bunker, the singing of carols; all were powerful reminders of what we were missing. Next day, I wrote Fannie.

December 26, 1918
Ravieres, France
Dear Fannie,

It is Christmas here in France and I am so lonely for you. Fortunately, there was a distraction. Us boys threw a big Christmas party for the children in the town. Everyone chipped in so we could buy presents. Those children were so thrilled that it warmed our hearts. The war was pretty bad on them. The boys in my squad bought the presents in a town called Dijon.

The Turkey the Army served for Christmas tasted terrible. Say, I'm joking, you can't find a turkey anywhere over here. Cooks prepared roast pig. It was juicy and fat, and served-up with thick gravy. Must admit, thought, the cabbage for a vegetable was chewy. We had lots of candy apples, and apple pie for dessert. Army even provided some beer. The YMCA gave out chocolate bars and cigarettes, or a tin of Prince Albert pipe tobacco for those who wanted it. Best fun was the square dancing after dinner. Turned into a disaster as you couldn't tell the man from the man who was supposed to be the woman partner. Utter confusion. What a laugh we had.

Trouble is, it didn't seem like Christmas. I missed being home. I missed you most of all. I wanted to find you under the mistletoe, and you know what I'd do then? I hope you had a nice Christmas and I promise I won't let you spend it alone again. I need to write Emily and the family now and wish them a good holiday. Hoping to be with you soon.
With affection,
Harry

The New Year came and went, and I felt more homesick than I had at Christmas. Everything I loved seemed no closer. I wanted to celebrate the New Year with Fannie, hold her tight, feel her head on my shoulder, kiss her at the stroke of midnight. No such luck for me.

Chapter 46. Old Dope

February 7, 1919; Ravieres, France.

In early February the army realized that they had to do something to keep us busy, or we'd go nuts with boredom. In their wisdom they decided to give us classes on subjects we could use back in civilian life. I considered that a sensible idea. Charlie Powell and I signed up for plumbing instruction and listened to plumbing lectures three days a week for two hours a day through January, February and half of March. All talk, offered by a couple of Master Plumbers found in the division. There was no practical application, but it was certainly better than nothing, and the lectures were rather good. Actually, I learned a lot. Powell less so; he wanted to study trains. The Army didn't have a railroad course and home-boiler installation was the closest he could get to large iron objects.

On February 10th, Lieutenant Harden asked Sedelsky to pick a man to work in the officer's mess hall. Seems one of the regular mess corporals had come down sick. Sarge picked me and I had no complaints.

After the officers ate, I bussed tables, swept the floor, and reset the chairs. I also dined on the officers leftover food, a real cut above our slop. Those bastards were served meat or chicken every night, mashed potatoes and gravy, and even the occasional green vegetable. Where the hell did the cooks get those vegetables and potatoes? Pie every night and occasionally ice cream. Even the coffee was superior to the gut-rot they served us. And every so often, I found a half, sometimes even a whole cigar left on the table. I'd take it home and share it with Goldrick.

About half an hour before lights out I'd give Goldrick a nod and the two of us would take a walk behind the barracks. I'd take my penknife, cut the cigar piece in half, and we'd both light up.

"Damn. Edwards, being around you is like going to heaven. How'd I get so lucky?"

"Well, I know you like these things," I said.

I wasn't a cigar lover, and whatever those officers were smoking, they certainly weren't Havana's. Goldrick, on the other hand, loved a cigar. He'd take a draw, hold the smoke in with his eyes closed to savor the taste, and then exhale. He'd look at me with the silliest, shit-eating grin you ever did see. All good things end, and within two weeks the sick corporal had recovered.

By late February I was back in the gobs' mess hall. Jake Osborn, Ernie Gillespie and I were peeling potatoes and washing dishes. We definitely had not volunteered for this duty. No more officer treats for me.

February 14, 1919; The 315th Motor Pool, Ravieres, France.

Osborn, Gillespie, and I were assigned to clean one of the officer's touring cars. We did such a good job that the lieutenant detailed us to clean the whole fleet of twenty-two cars. Fact was, most of their cars lay idle day-after-day. Osborn told us he'd identified the least used vehicle. With this information we schemed to pull some 'Old Dope,' the game played for dodging work.

'Old Dope' became an institution in Ravieres, and the plans cooked-up were often brilliant. Our plan, a little less so, was helped along by the fact that a new sergeant was running the motor pool. The three of us concluded he wasn't particularly bright. Osborn convinced him that the least-used car had a problem. That was the vehicle that gave us the best chance to pull some 'Old Dope.'

"Sergeant, Major Shaw returned his car yesterday and Gillespie, Edwards and I heard the engine as he parked. The damn thing wouldn't quit idling after he switched off the ignition."

"What'd ya mean, 'It wouldn't quit'?"

"Sergeant, the engine's dieseling. Cylinder's igniting even though there's no spark," I said.

"How the hell's that happening?" asked the sergeant.

"Carbon builds-up in the cylinders. Causes the wall to glow red hot, even for a while after the engine's off. The hot cylinder ignites unburned fuel. Dieseling could kick in for half a minute or so. Trouble is, it gums the carburetor and grinds down the cylinder rings." I didn't know if this was so, but it sounded good.

"Did the Major report the problem?"

"Not that we know, Sergeant. He left his car in a big rush. It should be taken over to the vehicle maintenance shop. Engine could freeze-up if not attended to," said Gillespie.

Osborn leapt in. "Sergeant, if the Major wants his car and she's not running right, you're the one he'll sound on. Hate to be in your shoes."

"Hmmm, okay. One of you boys run it up to the shop. Stay with it till it's fixed and, if it can't be worked on today, report back to me."

"Yes, Sergeant," we said in unison.

I cranked the engine and it started right up. Exiting the motor pool, I headed toward the maintenance shop. The plan was for me to circle around out of sight, collect Gillespie and Osborn at a pre-arranged place, then swing over to the wash station for Baker, who was on laundry duty. We weren't in an army base with a fixed perimeter, just scattered all over town and its immediate environs, so it was easy to just drive away.

Us four Media boys headed out of town toward Étivey, eight kilometers south. Rumor had it that a café there served an inexpensive, delicious lunch, with pretty ladies to comfort weary American Doughboys. We threw the top back and rode with the sun's rays drenching our skin. Fortunately, the car had more than half a tank of gas. The meal was wonderful, as were the ladies in the café. They certainly took a shine to us Americans and appreciated our generous tip.

Four hours later, with Baker back on laundry duty, Gillespie and Osborn snuck into the motor pool. Shortly thereafter, I drove through the entry gates. As I parked the car, the Sergeant confronted me.

"Private Edwards, come with me."

He led me to his office, not more than an oversized shack in the middle of the lot.

Gillespie and Osborn were already there. Off to the side, Major Shaw paced back and forth. The Major's driver stood behind him.

"Uh oh," I muttered to myself.

"Is this the man, Sergeant?"

"Yes, Sir."

"Your name, soldier."

I saluted. "Private Edwards, Sir."

"Edwards. I hear you took my car over to the shop. You say the engine dieseled?"

"Ahhh. Well… Not exactly, Sir."

"Not exactly. Not exactly, Edwards! Not exactly what?"

"I… I… took it for a drive to check it out."

"Were these men with you?"

I looked at Gillespie and Baker. What could I do?

"Yes, Sir."

"So you never got to the motor shop?"

"No, Sir. Turns out it wasn't dieseling."

"And that took four hours?"

The Major had me backed in a corner. No choice but to fess up. We'd been on a joy ride.

"You men caused me to miss an important meeting because you're pulling some 'Old Dope.' There'll be none of that nonsense in my unit." The Major didn't let up. "Only thing saving your sorry ass, Edwards, is you came clean. If you'd lied to me, you men, all of you, would be in the brig. You never went to the vehicle shop. I sent my driver to check. They never heard of you."

"Sergeant, report these men to Lieutenant Harden. I want them on KP duty indefinitely."

"Yes, Sir," he replied.

I couldn't have known, but the Major had missed his meeting with other officers in Saint-Rémy, another village with a great café. It was back to peeling potatoes and washing dishes, and now I wasn't even in the officers' mess.

I wrote to Fannie on March 1st and told her of my current predicament. I don't know what got into my head, but for the first time I signed the letter, "Love." Did I do the right thing?

CHAPTER 47. Dijon

March 3, 1919; Ravieres, France.

Sedelsky informed the squad that each man in the Regiment was granted a fourteen-day leave that had to be taken before the end of April. We slapped each other on the back at this good fortune.

"Army's being extra generous," he told us. "Youse gobs receive a two hundred Franc bonus, and—you'll be glad to hear—back-pay arrives this Thursday."

I was overjoyed since the army owed me back pay—around $144—for more than four months. With the exchange rate at slightly more than six Francs to the dollar, I'd put at least 860 FF in my pocket. Hell, with the bonus I'd have 1060 FF to frolic on.

Ernie Gillespie, Jake Osborn, Charlie Powell, Ollie Baker, Joe Goldrick and I decided to spend some time in Paris. From what we'd heard, Paris had the pizzazz. We talked of cafes, museums, entertainment shows, famous places like the Eiffel Tower, and boat rides on the Seine River. Gillespie wanted to visit the catacombs.

"What the hell are the catacombs?" I asked.

My needs were simple: a bed in a clean room with clean sheets and a soft pillow. A room with no mice, rats, roaches, or cooties keeping me company. I craved a warm bath, one I could soak in for an hour. Every pore in my body had dirt in it. Oh, and a beer would help. Well, maybe two or three to go with a nice meal of my new favorite: fresh calamari. A second meal of steak and *pommes frites* would also do my constitution a world of good.

In the end, only Gillespie, Baker, Osborn and I departed for Paris on March 11. The other guys decided on Marseilles. The warmth appealed to them.

At supper two days later, Doyle made a suggestion. "Say guys, I got something for us to chew on. Second Squad ought to be together.

You know, as a group. Go someplace. Kick it up a bit before we get back to the States. We'll still have a few days to party on after Paris or Marseilles."

"What you got in mind?" asked Ollie Baker.

"A friend of mine said his squad went to Dijon. They had a swell time. Seems there's fun cabarets with racy dancing shows and more."

"Wasn't Dijon where we bought the presents?" asked Nightlinger.

"Yeah. It's slightly less than eighty kilometers east of here," said Doyle. "A direct train runs from the Nuits station, three times daily. Costs only four francs-fifty round trip."

"Where'd we stay?" asked Osborn.

"That's the best part. My friend said there're plenty of hotels, all nice and clean. And not at Marseilles or Paris prices. Room's about ten francs a night for two, breakfast included."

"Hey. That sounds interesting. Let's plan on it, say for a couple of nights," urged Charlie Powell.

"Yeah. Could be fun," added an enthusiastic Baker.

"I'm in," said Osborn. A sentiment echoed by the rest of us. Then, we argued about when to go, and settled on March 27th.

Jeez, that trip to Paris was great. I went up the Eiffel tower. The view from the uppermost platform seemed to stretch forever. To be honest, the height scared the daylights out of me. There was only this thin mesh floor between me and my maker. But I was so sparked by being that high that, when I get home, I planned to take a ride in one of them airplanes, get really high. Gillespie convinced me to tour the catacombs. What a damn spooky place. What can I say about the sheets, warm bath and food? Well, I'll use the French: *"formidable!"*

On the 27th, the eight of us walked to the station, boarded the eastbound train, and arrived in Dijon three hours later. A working tram line connected the station to the center of town with a stop across the street from the *Hôtel Des Ducs*. Powell and I bunked together, and with breakfast included, it set us each back only five francs a night. The croissants at breakfast were hot and the blackcurrant jelly truly special. Supper at a bistro a block from the hotel served-up a delicious *calamari* plate. When we'd sufficiently digested our food, Doyle hailed two taxis, and Gillespie told the driver in broken French, he wanted the most risqué cabaret in town. The driver finally got the gist of it and broke into an big smile.

"Ahhh. Oui Monsieur, je comprends. I take you good place."

Five minutes later we're at the curb of the *Cabaret L'Escapade*. Once we were seated, Gillespie, Doyle and Nightlinger ordered a whiskey. Jeez, Gillespie never drank hard booze. The rest of us shared a bottle or two of Bordeaux wine. I recognized the name of a red wine bottled by Haut Brion from the last time Nightlinger picked the wine. I don't know how, but Nightlinger seemed to have a taste for good wine. I couldn't drink the hard stuff. Got a roaring headache if I did.

"Hey. They're dimming the lights," said Ollie Baker.

The curtain abruptly rose, and the gyrating shadows of dancers—hardly visible in the subdued light—spilled from the wings. The rush of sound from Offenbach's 'Can-Can' grew. I only knew the name because that's what Osborn called it. A moment later electric lanterns flooded the stage revealing five lovely ladies, wearing flowered bustiers cut lower than I'd ever seen. They kicked with first one and then the other leg, thrown high in the air, all in perfect unison. Each kick rose ruffled skirts to a height which nearly revealed all. The skirts ruffled back and forth as they rotated until their backsides faced us. At that point, they bent over and flipped the ruffle above their waist. The crowd shouted its approval.

"Hell. They're wearing bloomers," Nightlinger complained.

"What were you expecting?" hollered an exuberant Joe Goldrick.

The feathered plumes adorning their heads bounced to the music.

"Oh-La-La," shouted Doyle, his eyes lit like candles. All of us swayed with our eyes glued on the girls. It lasted six minutes, and I was exhausted when the curtain fell.

"This calls for a toast," said Gillespie, holding his glass aloft. Everyone "clinked," and our approvals echoed across the table. A comedian emerged from behind the curtain slit. His routine—in French of course—must have been good: the natives laughed their heads off. This was followed by a voluptuous lady who whirled onto the stage wearing a tight, white sheath dress that she must have been poured into.

She carried a large black feather that shook back and forth in front of her.

"It's an ostrich feather," said Jake Osborn.

"How the hell do you know that?" I asked.

Osborn didn't reply; his attention was riveted elsewhere.

When the pretty lady left the stage, she wore only the feather.

Osborn offered another toast. "Doyle, you've been a pain in my ass and I never, ever thought I'd utter these words, but God bless you, Irishman."

"You got that right," I added. The glasses clinked again.

Shortly after midnight, eight drunken soldiers hailed two cabs.

Gillespie, barely coherent, told the taxi driver, *"Le monsieur driver; Err... Monsieur chauffeur de taxi, Hôtel Des Ducs, s'il vous plait."*

"Jeeeez, Gillespie. I'm impressssed. You'ch beeeen readin' your dichhhionary," I eked out. Gillespie didn't answer, or maybe he couldn't.

We all slept late the next day and gathered in the lobby about ten thirty. We walked around town, took a ride on the tram, had another great bistro lunch, and Osborn insisted we visit a museum. The museum wasn't my cup-of-tea. The paintings made no sense. One looked like the artist just dabbed his brush on the canvas. I bought my mother a souvenir, a small brass container for face powder with "Dijon" etched on the lid. Mysteriously, Doyle disappeared after lunch. Said he'd join us at the hotel for supper.

Everyone but Ernie Gillespie and I were in on it. I didn't give it much thought when they kept insisting at supper that I have another glass of wine; then another, and yet another. I dismissed their insistence, or arrived at a point where I didn't care. Besides, weren't we here to have fun?

After dinner Doyle found us a different cabaret, not as upscale as last night's, but with a show that was just as entertaining. Our squad mates insisted Gillespie, and I try a special French concoction. Something blue, in a tall glass. It warmed my pallet, as it slid smoothly down the throat.

Soon enough, I was floating in a mild daze. Everything was wonderful. I looked at my friends and they were wonderful, as wonderful as the blue drink I nursed. Next thing I know, I'm in a cab being driven away from that wonderful cabaret. The wonderful taxi driver stopped in front of a building with a wonderful small sign over the door. How did I remember the wonderful name: *La Jolie Fille*? The rest was shrouded in fog with moments of clarity. I was inside, sitting on a sofa, in a garish parlor, and eagerly sank into its wonderfully luxuriant folds. I wanted sleep, but someone kept shaking me. Who? Jim Nightlinger? Ollie Baker? Phil Doyle? The walls of the parlor were deep red with a soft, wonderful feel of velour when touched.

"Upstairs, twelve francs," I heard. Someone took my wallet, removed the equivalent of two dollars, and replaced it in my trousers.

"Hey. What are you doing?" I was hardly in any condition to protest.

She led me up a flights of stairs, down a narrow corridor into a room. Who was this wonderful person guiding me?

There was an end table with a lamp beside the bed. The soft light cast gentle shadows on walls papered in the same wonderful velour as downstairs. She undressed me with great mastery of male garments. I tried to protest, but the blue drink didn't allow any objections. Besides, it was wonderful. Soon she washed me and led me to the bed. I stretched out, and watched as her wonderful clothes fell away, piece-by-tantalizing piece. It crossed my mind, as she wonderfully shed them that it was like the petals of an artichoke being peeled away. One-by-one, layer-by-layer, slowly, with great care, until the luscious core was revealed. Her hands coaxed me with practiced skill. I don't understand the French that flowed from those wonderful red lips. But the sensual words wonderfully soothed and reassured me. At the same time they added to a rising tension. She climbed onto the bed, and straddled me. I touched her skin, so wonderfully smooth and soft. Her movements increased and my head tilted back as I savored what I'd never felt before. Pleasure soon rose from the depths of my soul, and uncontrollably, I cried out, "Oh, how wonderful!"

When I returned to the parlor, I glanced sheepishly at Goldrick and Osborn. The look on their faces mirrored my own contentment. One-by-one, the rest of the guys wandered into the room. There was no talk, each of us lost in thought. Doyle asked the receptionist to call us a couple of taxies.

While we waited, new men entered the parlor. Their accents: Spanish, Italian, even Arabic mixed with the French. The world sought pleasure that night as each man discovered the wonderful delectations found on the upper floor.

My baptism taught me the wonderful rapture accompanying sensual delights. The need to return to Fannie took on an added desire.

CHAPTER 48. Crisis

March 10, 1919; Edith Worrell's House, Media, Pennsylvania.

Edith threw a party at her place Saturday evening and George offered to drive me, Fannie, and Frank Lewis over to her house. Frank was five years older than me and worked in the Media County Courthouse. The county supervisor requested a waiver for him from the Selective Service because he considered his job essential, and Frank ended up sitting out the war. I certainly enjoyed his company, but I thought him a little too quiet—not shy—but just quiet. He was a good dance partner, and Frank always brought something delicious to a party made by his mother.

George swung around to Third Street and called on Fannie. She sat up front, while Frank and I were in the back. Gossip and dancing were in full swing by the time we arrived.

Edith got her parents off to bed around 8:30 and now the real fun could begin. When the melodies of the Animal Dances were unleashed, Frank showed no interest whatsoever. Maybe the man had a moral streak. I couldn't do anything to bring him onto the dance floor. It was strange, because he was ready and able to dance to any other music.

Fannie and George were the couple who caught my eye. Most of the dancers rotated partners, but rarely those two. George seemed to be holding her hand every time I looked at them. What's she about? I wondered. Around 10:00 o'clock Frank took on a sudden sick spell and asked if I would mind if he stopped dancing.

"Frank, what's the matter, you look so pale."

"Emily, I am so sorry. I should have mentioned it, but I am just over a flu and the dancing has taken the pep out of me. Let me make it up to you with a soda at Payton's next week. Would that be okay?"

"Sure thing," I said. "Come, let's sit over here for a while."

A short time later, George and Fannie decided that they had to leave. Fannie said she wasn't feeling well.

The four of us bundled into the car.

"Emily, I'll drop you off first; it's on the way."

"Ahhh… Okay, George." I asked myself, why was he dropping me off first? Fannie's and Frank's houses were closer.

Mother and Father were in bed when I got home. I changed into my nightgown, brushed my teeth, washed my face, and, still excited from the evening, lay in bed, wide awake, thinking. I ran the party gossip through my head, hoped Frank felt better, and looked forward to having the soda with him later in the week.

I dozed off, but was awakened by a noise. A car engine idled in the driveway. It stopped and I heard a car door shut followed by fumbling with the back storm door. The loose boards on the back steps creaked, as George came upstairs. He walked quietly down the hallway and gently shut the door to his room. I switched on my nightstand light. The alarm clock said 11:50 p.m. That's peculiar I thought, It's only ten minutes to Fannie's house. What in the world took him so long? A disturbing thought flitted through my mind, but only for a moment as sleep overtook me.

Late April, 1919, The Peterson House, Marple, Pennsylvania.

A week ago I asked Mother if I could I have a dance party at our house on the first Saturday in May?

A few days later she responded, "Emily your father has agreed to the party, but he wants to invite a few of our friends at the same time."

"Mother, that's awful," I pouted.

"Well, it's what your father's agreed to. There's no changing it, once he's set his mind."

"Great. What do I tell my friends? There will be a bunch of old people at our party. That'll go over swell. Can't you talk to him, pleeease?"

"Father knew you'd be upset. He's asked George to buy a new victrola to replace our old one. We've been talking about this for months. He's also going to give you some money to buy a few new records."

"It's still unfair. This was supposed to be my party!"

Next day on the school wagon Anna, Edith, and Fannie said in unison, "Oh no!"

"I tried everything, but there's no changing his mind."

"Yes, but how many old people?" asked Fannie.

"My mother said two other couples and themselves."

"Guess we'll have to live with it," said Edith."

"It's either that or call it off. I want to dance with Frank Lewis again."

"I bet you do," said Anna. "But there'll be no animal dances with the old folks around."

"Well, Frank doesn't do animal. There's more. We're buying a new victrola and George will pick it up at Sears this weekend. It'll be one of those with the longer-play switch."

"Oh, that's nice. I'll be able to dance longer with George!" said Fannie.

Isn't she supposed to be waiting for Harry to come home? I asked myself.

"Father also gave me some money to buy new records. I'll be in town for the market with my Mother and Father this Saturday. How about we meet at Payton's and you can help me pick 'em."

May 3, 1919; The Peterson House, Marple, Pennsylvania.

On the day of the party a clear sky held the freshness of spring into the evening. George told us he was off to pick up Fannie and that he would stop by Frank's house and retrieve him too. I wanted to go, but Mother insisted I stay and help set the table.

"Hi, Emily, so nice to see you again," said Frank.

"You too, Mr. Lewis. Please, come in."

"Hi, Emily." You ready for some fun?" asked Fannie, as she and George "dance-stepped" into the parlor.

Anna and Edith arrived after that, and Edith brought a new friend, Wendell, who was handsomely dressed in his Marine uniform.

"My, but he's good looking," I whispered to Edith. "Where'd you find him?"

I watched Mother as she danced a slow waltz with George. She looked like she was in heaven, because my father was all feet on the dance floor. As the evening wore on, the grown-ups gravitated to the living room to sit and talk. I'm sure my father, Mr. Espey and Mr.

Moore were into politics or the situation in France, and no doubt my mother and the other women discussed recipes. My friends and I never stopped dancing—except to eat or have a drink. I hoped the new records wouldn't wear out, and the new victrola certainly produced a wonderful sound.

George announced that he had to get Fannie home early. She was traveling to Harrisburg on Sunday with her aunt and uncle to visit relatives, and they wanted an early start. Wendell agreed to take Frank Lewis home later. I bid Fannie good night, and returned to my friends. The party ended at eleven o'clock, and I was certain everyone had had a good time.

Mother and I were alone in the kitchen the next day and I've never seen her so angry.

"Emily, will you tell me what's going on?"

"What do you mean?" I asked.

"Every letter I get from your brother talks about Fannie." Just the thought of Fannie raised mother's agitation. "It's Fannie this and Fannie that. Meet Fannie's parents. What's Fannie doing? That I should get to know Fannie. It never stops."

"I get similar questions, Mother, " I said. "Surely you realize that Harry has great affection for her."

"And what does Fannie feel? Do you know?"

"She talks about Harry all the time."

"Last night, from where I sat in the parlor, I could see out into the yard where the buggies and cars were parked," Mother told me with a trembling voice. "I watched as she and George were ready to get in the car. George reached around and pulled her to him. They kissed." The anger in Mother's voice was apparent.

"I don't mean a little peck. It was like she kissed Harry at the train platform the day he left for the army. I... I just could not believe what I was seeing."

I listened in disbelief.

"What's that little hussy doing? Who is she playing with, Harry or George? She needs to stay away from your brothers. No good will come of this."

May 8, 1919; Providence Road, Media, Pennsylvania.

I decided to confront Fannie. "Fannie, would you get off the wagon at my stop? I'll walk with you to Media. We need to talk about something."

"Okay, Em. You sound so serious."

Fannie and I walked along Providence Road toward Media.

"I'm not sure how to begin." I said to Fannie. "It's awkward. My mother's upset with you. After you left the party last weekend she saw you and George kissing."

The look on Fannie's face changed abruptly, her brow furrowed, her mouth opened and she exhaled a long breath. With a nervous sweep of her hand she flicked a lock of hair off her face.

"W-W-Why's your mother so upset about that?"

"Why's she so upset? Are you serious? You know why."

Fannie nervously nibbled her lower lip. I waited.

"Goodness, Fannie. What are you are doing?"

"I don't understand, Emily." She was obviously upset.

"Every letter I get from Harry constantly talks about you. He does write you, doesn't he?"

"Yes. all the time."

"Do you reply?"

"Yes."

"Is your relationship with Harry serious? Steve Hughes writes me and says the same thing. He says you are all Harry talks about. Mr. Hughes also wrote that Harry has asked you to marry him, and that Mr. Hughes is going to be his best man."

"Mr. Hughes told you that? Well, he shouldn't have. It's not his business, or yours for that matter."

"Is it true?"

"Well…Yes. Harry asked me to marry him about a month ago."

We walked in silence until I asked. "Did you reply?"

"I…I don't know what to do."

She started to sob. "I don't know what to do." Fannie collapsed onto the grass beside the road, her hands covering her face. Her sobbing continued.

I looked down at my friend, a surge of emotion tinged with sympathy ran through me. I wondered, what the hell is going on here. Damn, she's been two-timing Harry. Hell, been doing the same to

George. Oh my, someone's going to get hurt here. Oh, Fannie how did you get into this mess? I wondered.

"We've been friends a long time," I said. "What's this all about."

Fannie took a hankie from her pocket, dried her face, and looked away.

"I don't know if you can understand," she said.

"Try me."

"When Harry left for the Army, I was in love with him. At least, I'd never felt about another man the way I did about him. But the last night we were together, I had this horrible feeling that I'd never see him again." Tears were streaming down her face.

"It's haunted me… nonstop… for nearly a year now. I was terrified Harry wouldn't make it through the war. With the war over I was relieved, but by Thanksgiving I was so lonely that when George started showing attention, I couldn't ask him to stay away. You know how wonderful his dancing is. But now, George never lets me alone. He keeps asking me to parties where none of our friends are, and when we are there, he sticks to me like glue. I like to talk and dance with others, but George does not allow that. And if I don't cling to George, he berates me about it. I like George, but I don't feel anything more. However, I don't think he sees it that way."

"Yes, George does seem relentless," I said. "But you could always say no!"

"I could. But he makes my loneliness go away. Worse yet, Harry doesn't understand how much I love the farm in Culpepper. He's so tied to your family that I'm convinced he'd never move away from Media. And I really want to return to the farm. Then, Harry's proposal arrived and I didn't know what to do."

Fannie and I talked some more and I think I understood her predicament. Regardless, I was angry as hell at her. She'd brought this on herself. I'd never been in love, but I understood the rules of loyalty, and she sure had broken them regarding Harry. I could see bad consequences of this, but didn't know what to do about it.

I was in the kitchen preparing for dinner when Emily arrived from school. I asked why she was so late and learned of her conversation with Fannie.

Later that evening as I lay in bed, thoughts kept running through my head. What's that girl thinking? Doesn't Fannie know she's playing with fire? Well, I'm sure of one thing. I don't want her near my sons. She's one heap of trouble. What would happen if Harry came home and found his brother involved with his girlfriend? This is bad. I must remedy the situation and protect my sons.

When Frazure came to bed, I told him of my concerns.

"I want you to stay out of this, Sally," he told me. "You'll only make matters worse. The boys have to work it out for themselves."

"I don't think I can stay out of it, dear." I replied. "I'm very worried and you should be too. That floozy could break-up our family."

"You're exaggerating this whole thing," he told me.

Perhaps I should have minded my own business, but Fannie had messed with my sons, and I was not going to let that continue! Emily explained to me how upset Fannie had been over Harry's departure for the army, and I hadn't realized that George kept inviting her to dance parties. Well, she didn't have to go with him, did she? Emily also told me that Harry had asked Fannie to marry him and that with George in the picture, Fannie was apparently at a loss over what to do. Well, things were certainly complicated but I knew what I had to do. I weaseled out of Emily where Fannie worked weekends. Like a predatory animal protecting her cubs I hunted her down, and gave her a piece of her mind! The arrogant little witch told me it was none of my business. Some ugly words were passed.

After that encounter, I was convinced that my son should not run off to a southern peach farm. He'll be quite happy right here in Marple. We need him on our farm. After all, Frazure and I aren't getting any younger, and someone will have to be around to care for us. I complimented myself on the good job I had done.

CHAPTER 49. Heading Home

May 13, 1919; Camp Meucon, Vannes, France.

The battalion departed Ravieres by rail and returned to Camp Meucon, in Brittany, where we had trained in September of '18. Two days later the whole regiment was ordered to prepare our uniforms for the next day's inspection.

Without announcement, Sergeant Sedelsky, Lieutenant Harden, Major Shaw, and Colonel Williams suddenly entered the barracks.

"Second Squad, ah-tenn-shion," Sedelsky shouted.

I tumbled out of my bunk and faced the officers. What the hell's this about?

"At ease," Harden called, followed by, "Private Edwards."

"Yes, Sir," I shouted.

"Front and center."

I approached the officers and saluted.

"Private," the Colonel addressed me. "At the Inspection tomorrow the General will bestow medals on the regiment. Seems, Edwards, you'll receive the Distinguished Service Cross." The Colonel, Major, Lieutenant, and Sarge were all smiles at my incredulous expression. My jaw went slack. I could hardly speak.

"Me…, Sir? How's that? I didn't do anything. Must be a mistake, Sir."

"No mistake, soldier. Officers in Company C of the 160th Brigade recommended you. It seems you prevented a German ambush and the injury or death of many men. On top of that you captured twenty-one enemy soldiers, along with those five children you and Private Hughes brought in. That's an impressive twenty-six Germans captured," said Colonel Williams, then added. "Private Hughes will also receive the same medal at ceremonies with his unit. At inspection tomorrow you need to join the other men at the reviewing stand. My

Adjunct will get you organized. Son, I want you to smile politely at the General."

I could barely reply. "Yes, Sir."

"Congratulations, Edwards. The Battalion's proud of you."

The Colonel shook my hand. I saluted and he asked Harden, "Where to next?"

Before they left, Major Shaw stepped up to me. "Edwards, it seems you are a better man than your 'Old Dope' episode."

"I hope so, Sir," I replied.

He held out his hand and we shook. We were both smiling.

Next morning, General Pershing and five staff cars entered Camp Meucon. The battalion officers and the General's staff dined sumptuously at lunch. That afternoon, under a brilliant blue sky, all the batteries and support companies passed in review. General Pershing addressed the assembled troops and told us that the Eightieth Division Artillery and Supply Sections were the only units in the entire Meuse-Argonne Campaign on continuous, non-stop duty. No wonder I was so damned exhausted. The General, then conferred battery service ribbons on unit flags, after which eight men—including me—were led onto the field with the entire regiment facing us.

Pershing and his entourage approached, and as he went down the line, his adjunct handed him a piece of paper and a medal. Now, he stood before me, and I felt nervous all over. His face had mottled features that carried tired, deep brown eyes that focused squarely on me. I watched his thick, graying mustache jiggle as his upper lip moved when he spoke. In my nervous state it suddenly appeared comical. What a crazy thought with the commander of the American Army about to pin a medal on me.

May 18, 1919; The Port of Brest, France.

Transfer to the Port of Brest was complete by the afternoon of May 17th. There were no accommodations, so the Army had us sleeping on the ground in the dock area. After breakfast the regiment boarded ship for the nine-day journey across the Atlantic. The Navy had commandeered a number of cruise liners from the German fleet. Ours, had been renamed the "USS Zeppelin."

Ollie Baker and I shared a cabin with real beds, soft mattresses and pillows, clean sheets, and fresh blankets. We were overjoyed by the adjoining bathroom with its hot water shower. These were decadent comforts after months spent sleeping in tents and dugouts, on the ground, or in a cold, damp, grain house, with only a stinking outhouse or worse. Okay, I'm forgetting Bordeaux, Paris, and Dijon.

"Yes, we deserve this!" exclaimed a happy Baker as the Zepplin steamed out of the Brest harbor into the Atlantic.

In a letter to Emily, I shared my excitement and enthusiasm about heading home.

> *The food is good and the ship's deck is huge. There's plenty of space to lounge, exercise, or play sports. You know I'm not good at sports, but I had fun with volley ball. Ollie Baker and I have a room with a soft bed. Feels good. The guys can't stop talking about getting home and seeing their girls. I can't wait to see Fannie. I can't wait to see you, Mother and Father, George, and Morris.*
> *Love,*
> *HCE*

I also wrote to Fannie.

The Zepplin berthed in Newport News, Virginia on May 25th, There was a new rail shuttle that whisked us from the docks, through Petersburg, and right to the front door of Camp Lee. Once there, Second Squad sat with nothing to do.

My pencil busied itself again, this time to George.

> *Say George, could you send me $10? I'll pay it back. The Colonel says we have to Parade in Richmond, a week from Saturday. I want to buy new spats and a fresh campaign hat. My spats are pretty ragged and the current hat crown is crushed and torn. I should look spiffy for the parade. Haven't received my pay yet and I'm about broke. Army says our pay should arrive any moment. Well, I've heard that before. Send the money insured, as I don't trust the mail here at camp, and right away. Besides, I may want to wear my uniform home.*

Fortunately, I could write whatever I wanted now, there was no more censorship.The entire 80th Division—and no one more than myself—were angry with the delay in our army release.

> "You know, George, this parade is bull swill. All show for the politicians. They already had the big one in New York. Why the hell does the division need to march in Richmond? More delay. Just get us the hell out of here!"

George sent the money by special delivery.

May 31, 1919; Camp Lee, Petersburg, Virginia.

Battery B was rousted out of bed in the early hours of Saturday morning. We had breakfast and left camp an hour later. The logistics of organizing trucks to transport 18,000 men twenty three miles and back in one day impressed me. Nevertheless, the parade began two hours late.

"Jeez, if they could get us up that early and have us here in Richmond by 0900, they could at least start the parade on time," I complained.

"Edwards, would you stop with the grousing?" chided Ollie Baker. "You heard, like we all did, that the Richmond officials were just poor organizers."

"Here, Edwards," said Ernie Gillespie. "Stuff your pie hole with this roll. That should quiet you for a while." He reached into his jacket pocket and pulled out a bun.

"Where the hell'd you get that?" I asked.

"I swiped it at breakfast."

"Well, Gillespie old friend, whoever said complaining never got you anywhere?"

"Jeez, Edwards. Shove it!"

The parade began at 1200. The Division marched up Broad Street, past the shops and new offices that had been built in the last decade, then turned right for two blocks down Fourteenth Street. Another right onto Main Street had us marching past the Capitol and State office buildings. The whole thing finished where it had begun in Centennial Park.

At many times during the parade, the regimental band played Sousa's military marches. The beat had the men stepping proudly, and the onlookers tapped their feet or waved hand held flags to the music. The Major would shout to the Master Sergeant directing the band, "March order Master Sergeant." The sergeant did a fancy reverse step, faced his band. He then shouted an order to prepare. The men marching behind the band smartened their ranks and came to order. Each man watched for the golden ball at the the upper tip of the band leaders' raised baton. The ball stroked up and down: once, twice, a third time.

On the down stroke of the fourth, the familiar notes of *The Stars and Stripes Forever,* or *The Thunderer,* or *The Liberty Bell,* or any number of Sousa's masterpieces blasted forth. In that moment, all the troops stepped out on the same foot.

Tens of thousands lined the parade route. Flags waved, people cheered and children were hefted on their fathers' shoulders so they could see everything. The crowd gawked at the One Fifty-Five Howitzers, now pulled by noisy tractors instead of war-worn horses. In front of us rumbled gun number four, the very howitzer I'd dragged through the mud of France.

After the war, when the silenced guns were refurbished in Ravieres, the gun crew had painted a label on the barrel in bright pink: 'The Grizzly,' with a cartoon of a fearsome bear standing upright on rear legs, menacing paws raised to reveal hooked claws. Adults laughed and the kids tugged on their fathers' pants to gain attention, excitedly pointing at the giant gun with its tractor and fearsome painted bear. The adults in the crowd knew the cartoon signaled the Grizzly Dance.

How many marshals, generals, and colonels had I passed in review in the last year? French citizens had cheered our parades, because they believed the Americans would save their country. After the war, they cheered again because we had. But the crowd in Richmond was different. They cheered because we'd done our job and were safely home. It felt good to hear their accolades, and it had an unexpected effect on me.

Back in the barracks well after midnight, our pleasure in the parade, and the coming end to our army life kept us talking into the wee hours.

"Did you see those kids jumping at the Grizzly?" asked Charlie Powell. "And those parents in the crowd, they knew the scoop."

Phil Doyle jumped up, formed his hands into hooked raised claws, like a Grizzly. "I can't wait to get back to the dances!" Joe Goldrick joined him, took the same stance, then placed his "claws" over Doyle's shoulders. The two of them began a side-to-side rocking motion from the hips, as we clapped to create a rag-time beat. Doyle and Goldrick exaggerated their rocking, and then added the 'in-and-out' action that pulled their chests together.

"*Beaucooop* dancing!" I hollered.

As the beat continued, Doyle and Goldrick suddenly stopped, rotated so they were back to back and and rubbed their backsides together.

"That's the Grizzly," shouted Ernie Gillespie.

Raucous laughter, whoops and whistles echoed through the room. Joe Goldrick stopped abruptly. The clapping ceased when he faced Doyle. "Damn it, Irishman, I need to get me a real woman to do this with."

"Me too. You just don't have the curves." Doyle glided his hands suggestively over his chest and waist. They both laughed.

The back and forth continued. Ollie Baker jumped up and said, "You know, I been saving something, and now's as good a time as any." He shuffled to his bunk, reached into his kit bag and returned with an unopened bottle of French cognac.

"Where the hell did you get that?" roared Jim Nightlinger.

"Been carrying it since Ravieres. Going to save it for a special occasion, and this is it."

A scramble for cups followed and Baker became the hero *du jour*.

Joe Goldrick with his cup in hand, said, "Hey, here's a toast to all of us. We made it home alive." Ollie Baker added, "And to all those souls who didn't." We raised our glasses and took a solemn drink.

Jim Nightlinger was less serious. "You know, when I get home, I'm going to take my war bonus, add some savings and set me up a bakery in West Philly. They're building a new trolley extension to sixty-ninth street. Figure that area should be a great market in a few years. My old man said he'd help out. What about you, Gillespie?"

Gillespie hesitated a moment. "I'd like to get back on a farm, but I don't have enough money to buy one right now."

"Just marry a farmer's daughter," laughed Doyle. "Hell, she might be ugly as pigs, but you'd get the farm." We all laughed.

"No. I'm getting hitched to Margaret. She's my heart throb, and she's pretty as a picture!"

"And her old man's loaded," I added.

We all laughed again. Doyle faced me and said, "I know what you're going to do, Edwards."

Everyone called out, "Marry Fannie."

"Yeah," I answered. "But I still want to study plumbing, get my license, start my own business," I said.

"You always liked cleaning crappers," interrupted Ollie Baker to a new chorus of laughs.

Jake Osborn took that awful pipe from of his mouth and asked. "Do you think things are going to be different back home?"

For a moment, everyone was caught short till Baker spoke up. "It'll be different for me. My grandmother and aunt both died from that damn flu. Momma took it pretty hard. What about you, Powell? You headed back to the railroad?"

"Sure am. I learned I'm good at figuring out routes riding them wagons. I'm going to apply for a dispatcher job. Routin' freight trains, that's where I'm going."

"Sounds good to me," I said.

"Hey, anyone got an idea of what Hughes is going to do?" asked Baker.

"Yeah, I got a letter from him a few weeks ago. He's been in the States over a month now. Says he got the little problem up in Scranton settled, signed some papers and it's gone. He's a divorced man," I added.

"So that's it, sign some papers and he isn't married anymore? Jeez, Edwards, it's too easy," said Jake Osborn. Osborn wanted to know what'll he do next?

"He wrote to me that he took training to be a fireman," I said. "Told me he liked it, the job had a thrill to it, was important. He's applied for work at one of them oil refineries they're building along the Delaware River."

Joe Goldrick spoke up, "Good for Hughes. But I'm worried over what my brother wrote. He said too many women are still pumping gas and changing tires. Even got factory jobs. We could have trouble finding work, if we don't take those jobs."

"I've heard the same thing, but we don't do some of those jobs. You know: typist, telephone operator, secretary, those sort of things," said Gillespie. A collective mumble of concern passed through the room.

"Hey, what you got in mind Baker?" I asked.

"Not really sure. Got to get a job so's I can eat, but I don't know what I want to do. Mostly, just forget the war."

"You'll find something," said Charlie Powell.

It was Doyle's turn. "I'm headed back to the docks. Going to get me a good job. If I'm smart about it, I may even try and move up in the organization."

"Yeah," said Joe Goldrick. "Make the big bucks being a corrupt Irish union boss!"

"That'd be okay by me," said Doyle with a grin. "And you, Goldrick, where you headed?"

"Can't say as I know. Been thinking of moving out to Harrisburg. My sister and her family live there. Told you guys I did some carpentry before the war. I like working with my hands, but I want something else. Maybe I'll go work for the state, in the capital, in Harrisburg."

"Jeez," I said. "Now we'll have a corrupt union boss and a corrupt state politician." We all laughed again, and Doyle and Goldrick offered me the universal sign of obscenity.

"Osborn, haven't heard a peep from you," said Powell.

"Well, I been thinking. First, I need to find me a curvy woman and settle down."

That surprised me, Osborn rarely talked about women.

"Now you're thinking, Osborn. I like the curvy part. But what's next?" asked Phil Doyle.

"Five years ago the government started that new income tax? Everyone hates it, but it's the law. It'll only get more complicated. I want to go back to school, become an accountant."

"You're full of surprises," said Nightlinger.

"Now, we'll have an accountant to cook the books of the crooked union boss and politician," I added to howls of laughter.

Jake Osborn frowned, and in a more serious tone said, "Hell, I left home as a kid, well, I don't see things or think like a kid anymore."

Doyle grinned, "Yeah, that's because you visited *La Jolie Fille.* Madame D'Agenville took real good care of you. You went in a kid and came out a man!"

"Come-on, we all visited the Madame. We might have been youngsters going into the war, but more than the visit to Dijon made men of us!" said Osborn.

"Yeah, we're certainly not the same guys who left home," offered Powell.

"Hell, like Osborn said. Who knows what we'll find at home?" added Ollie Baker. There followed another moment of quiet.

"Maybe my Fannie won't be the same as I remember," I said. My friends started shaking their heads followed by a chorus of disagreements. Gillespie held up his hand. "Look, Edwards, if half of what you said about Fannie is true, she won't be a dud."

"All I want right now is to get out of here. They've messed with us long enough. We've done our parade. It's time to go home. I didn't volunteer for this lousy war, nor did any of you." I hesitated, choosing my words. "Must admit, though, that parade made me feel good. Those people appreciated us." Then my voice rose, "But, I want out of here!"

"Edwards," Interrupted Jim Nightlinger. "I can't wait to get away from your carping, but I have to agree with you about today."

"Here, here," were the calls as we all enjoyed another hit of Baker's cognac.

"You know," offered Osborn. "I think I'll miss the excitement. Come on guys, admit it. Hell, we had a great adventure."

"You out of your damn mind?" said Gillespie. "I don't want any more excitement."

"I've had enough excitement for a lifetime," I added.

"None of us liked being overseas, but we can't change it. I got hope I can put what I've seen behind me. I think I can still be happy. Hell, we're the guys who made it home." We survived that damn war. We've a good life ahead of us. Maybe we get to use what we've been through to make us better, make those around us better."

"You're a heavy hitter, Osborn," I said.

The banter continued for another half hour until we finally collapsed into our bunks. Nightlinger crossed the floor and switched off the lights. "Good night friends," he said.

The parade in Richmond, the playful exchange between comrades, and the imminent end of this 'adventure' left me feeling good about myself. For the first time my future had a direction, and this new mood made me want to wear my uniform home.

The war had been relentless and intense. Every moment of the past fourteen months required effort to keep from going stark-raving mad. There were days peppered with terror and danger. But we had showed the Kaiser what us Yanks were made of. The horror I'd seen, and that young boy's lifeless eyes, the sadness of all those lost—especially the ones I knew—had revealed the value of my own life and that of those I loved. Nevertheless, I really had lived an adventure, and it would not be easy to return to the drabness of the farm and life as a plumber. In the coming weeks these ideas would haunt me. I couldn't turn them off.

CHAPTER 50. Culpepper

June 6, 1919; Petersburg Train Station, Petersburg, Virginia.

The army had finally discharged me and I headed home. I knew I wasn't the same 21 year old farm boy who had left for war 13 months ago. The fact is, I was trying to sort out who I was. I'd seen and experienced too much. There was only one certain thing, I couldn't wait to see my Fannie. With her in my arms, the world would be whole again.

I threw my meager belongings into a duffle and with Ernie Gillespie, Jake Osborn, and Ollie Baker boarded the evening north bound train out of Petersburg. Ernie and I sat next to each other and I landed the window seat. Jake and Ollie sat across the aisle. We were all completely talked out.

I felt the train gain speed and imagined belching black smoke and glowing embers spewing from the stack. Hot steam would be hissing from the release valves, and condensing into billowy white clouds in the cool night air. I gently rocked in my seat as we rushed northward and had just closed my eyes, when the conductor startled me.

"Welcome back, boys. I'm sure your folks are looking forward to seeing you," he said as he punched my ticket.

Two hours later, we stepped onto the platform at Richmond during a twenty minute layover and bought a sandwich and beer. When seated again, the train began its160 mile run to Washington.

With tickets checked, the lights in the car were dimmed again. We passed beyond the city and I gazed out the window as shadows of an unseen countryside flowed past. Occasional points of light penetrated the dark. Were they a distant farm window, or just the headlights of a car? Who knew? I only saw a spot of light on a jet black background. These spots appeared on the forward side of the window, then slid across the pane, some faster—some slower—to disappear on the opposite side. Those mysterious, drifting spots were hypnotic, inducing a mood that mixed memories and imagination.

In this trance-like state, an image flooded my consciousness. I recalled a Sunday afternoon in early June of '17, almost two years ago. Fannie and I had driven out to the McFee farm. Mr. McFee was an old friend of my father's. I approached the house, introduced myself, and then asked if it would be all right for my lady friend and me to climb Bowman's hill. I told them she'd packed a picnic lunch for my birthday. I imagined again Fannie and I climbing the hill. At the top she spread a blanket under the spreading limbs of a huge Linden tree. This single massive tree stood alone at the crest of the hill.

"Harry. This is so lovely. How did you know about this place?"

Without answering I laid back and drew her down to me. We kissed, but she pulled away.

"Harry, my lunch! It'll be ruined."

Fannie laid out her treats and we enjoyed her wonderful food and the view. In a playful mood after lunch, she asked me to get off the blanket, and tugged it out from under the branches into the sunlight. I remember being asked to lie down with my head in the blanket center. In the warmth of the afternoon sun she joined me with her body facing in the opposite direction from mine. Fannie wiggled around so that only our heads were adjacent to one another. In this position we watched the scuttling clouds. Their puffy shapes suggested to her an outline, which—for the life of me—I couldn't see. She couldn't recognize any of the shapes I saw.

Fannie suddenly giggled. "Harry, of course we can't make out what each of us sees. We're looking at things from different directions!"

It took a moment to get her point, after which I laughed at the obvious.

"You know, Harry, there's an important lesson here."

"What's that?" I asked.

"To see a thing clearly you sometimes have to look at it as viewed through the other person's eyes."

"Oh. I get it. See eye-to-eye."

"Stop. You're making fun of me."

Fannie soon tired of the cloud game, and rolled toward me. With an elbow on the blanket, she supported her head with her hand. I leaned in to kiss her again, but was gently rebuffed.

"I've things to tell you," she said. "You know my mother owns a peach farm in Virginia, and sells scrumptious peach jam."

Why's she telling me this again? I wondered.

"Well, I never told you why I'm here in Media. My mother started having babies at fourteen. By the time I came along at number twelve, she had no more energy. Papa wasn't much help. He saw raisin' children as woman's work."

I had never seen Fannie so serious.

"After papa died, momma became sickly trying to tend to all of us. When I turned eight, things were bad. The family finally stepped in and sent some of us away."

I rolled to my side and stroked her arm gently.

"Mamma's youngest brother is my Uncle Cliff. He and Janet agreed to take me in, so I came north to Media. When I first arrived, I hated being away from the farm. Media's so different from Culpepper. People seemed so distant, and the cold winters were awful," she told me. "But, I was the center of my aunt and uncle's attention, and they loved me as their daughter. My mother's better now, but she still acts strange at times. Several years ago, Cliff and Janet insisted I visit Culpepper each summer to keep connected with the farm. I look after my grandmother and help pick the peaches. I love the farm, Harry. I'm so happy there". She looked so contented with that memory. "Then, you came along, and I had a new happiness. But, I worry constantly that you'll be called-up for the war. I don't want you to go away. I want you to come to the peach farm with me."

I remembered leaning down and kissing her, and that time her arm circled my neck and held me there.

Gillespie muttered something and the distraction melted my scene.

"What'd you say?" He gave no response.

"Damn, you're talking in your sleep. Margaret will have none of that," I whispered to him, smiling.

I returned to my magic window and the hypnotic lights soon created a new kinetoscopic display in my mind. There was Fannie as the woman I knew over a year ago. I saw her laughter, her smile, and those darting eyes, coyly playing games with me. She had this way of seeing through me. There again was that seductive come-hither look whenever we danced the Grizzly. I sensed the outline of her soft body just as if she were nestled against me, and then remembered how she felt when pressed against me during the Bunny Hug. I could taste her inviting lips and sense the silk feel of her tummy. My mind escaped its bounds and went further. Since the trip to Dijon I knew what to anticipate with a woman. In Fannie I saw the story of my future written in the plural rather than the singular.

The image faded and my mind returned to the train coach. I had spent enough time dreaming about my life with her. Now was the time to make it come true.

CHAPTER 51. Homecoming

June 7, 1919; Mid-Morning, Media Train Station, Media, Pennsylvania.

I spotted Emily through the window as the Elwyn Local pulled into the Media station. She looked more like a woman in her spring frock than the sister I remembered. Emily saw me looking out and began waving and jumping, a grin of excitement on her face. George stood next to her, looking his handsome fit self. She warmly wrapped me in her arms as I stepped onto the platform.

"Brother, you're home, you're home! Oh, you look great." She grabbed me again with a big hug. I looked at George, and held out my hand.

"You get more than a shake," said George and the three of us clasped each other.

Ernie was right behind me and the scene repeated itself, as Margaret rushed to greet him. I jealously watched their embrace. Ernie and I chatted a few moments, and parted with a promise to get together soon. George picked up my duffle, and Emily inserted her arm into mine as we walked toward the parking lot.

"Where's everyone?" I asked.

"We all couldn't fit in the car, and we're not supposed to say, but there's a surprise for you at home," said George.

"A surprise, eh. Say, where's Fannie?"

"She's not here," replied Emily.

Okay, she's at home, I thought..

I spotted my Ford in the lot behind the station, its black lacquer finish gleamed in the morning sun. "Jeez George! She looks almost new. What'd you do?"

"I'm learning to repair and paint car bodies over in Thompson's shop. You remember him?" George bubbled with enthusiasm. "I'll tell you about it later."

"Sure, I remember old man, Thompson," I laughed. "Damn, that car looks swell. I need to drive. Outside of one caper in France, I haven't driven in over a year."

"What'd you say?" he asked. I remembered I had to face George and told him again I hadn't driven much in over a year.

"You remember how?"

"You kidding me?"

George tossed me the ignition key and Emily scrambled into the back. George pitched my duffle alongside her, and climbed in. I inserted the key, adjusted the gears to neutral, and prepared to crank the engine. "Hold up, Harry, she's got an electric starter. Just depress the clutch, tap the gas, turn the key further and hold it till the engine kicks-in," instructed George.

"What! An electric starter. When did you do that?"

Using my brother's instructions, the engine jumped to life when I toggled the key.

"Damn...," is all I could say. George's smile changed to a huge grin.

I backed into the parking lot, turned toward the exit, and shifted to first gear. Guess I was out of practice, because the clutch popped a little too soon as I depressed the gas pedal. The Ford pitched forward, and I panicked, stomping hard on the brake pedal. This jerked the car to a sudden stall.

"Yeoooow," shrieked Emily as her head snapped forward. George's hands flipped up to the dashboard to prevent a good head bump, and my chest slammed into the steering wheel. Embarrassed, I glanced at my passengers with a sheepish grin. I got the engine humming again, found my clutch-touch, and off we went, retracing the path that had taken me away thirteen months earlier.

I saw red and blue bunting twined through the white porch railings when the car turned into the driveway. A banner, painted with bright red letters, hung over the front porch. "WELCOME HOME HARRY," it shouted. George reached across me and pulled the handle on the horn, its raucous "Oooh-Gah" announced our arrival.

Aunts and uncles came around the side of the house. Morris ran to me, followed by my dog, Charlie. Morris gave me a big hug and Charlie barked at the excitement.

My aunts pushed and shoved to give me hugs and kisses and uncles shook my hand and patted me on the back. The look on Uncle Albert's face said it all.

"I am so sorry about Aunt Ella," I said.

"She would have loved to see you home, safe and sound. I miss her so," said Uncle Albert.

"I know, Uncle Albert. I wish she were here too."

Aunt Katie nudged me, "Your father's here."

I watched as he came down the steps, carefully negotiating each with his cane. A huge smile lit his face.

"Oh how marvelous, son."

His eyes welled with tears as we hugged.

The Moore twins burst out of the front door, bounded down the porch steps, and bounced up and down around me.

"Rachel, Mildred, you're both prettier than ever."

They glowed at my compliment. In the bustle, I glanced toward the house. Mother stood at the edge of the steps, her gaze fixed on me. She reached behind, untied her apron, hung it over the railing and descended. The group went silent and opened a path. I stepped toward her, and saw tears streaming down her cheeks as she grabbed hold of me.

"Oh, Harry. I...I... didn't think I'd be here to see you again, but I am and you are home. Oh my... my prayers were answered."

She regained her composure, and ushered her guests toward the backyard, holding tight to my arm.

"Is Fannie here?"

"No, Harry. Fannie returned to Culpepper two days ago. Her mother has taken ill."

I stared at her, speechless. It took a moment to collect my wits.

"That's terrible. Do you know if they have a phone at the farm in Culpepper?"

"I don't," she said. I felt suddenly drained of the homecoming joy.

"Harry, I know you're upset, but you can call Fannie later. All our guests are waiting for you. Don't you worry any about her. We have you here, that's what matters."

"They'll have to wait. Do you have Mr. White's phone number?"

"On the counter in the kitchen, near the phone, you'll see a red address book. Harry, can't you call later?"

I fumbled through the red book, found the number, and placed the receiver to my ear. It was dead. Speaking into the transmitter I hollered, "Hello, hello." Still nothing. "Anyone there?"

I called to Morris through the screen door, "Hey, Morris, how's this thing work?"

"Click the hook three times to connect to the operator," he shouted back.

"Hello, Janet White speaking." I announced myself.

"Oh. Hello, Harry. So good to hear your voice. Fannie told us you'd be home soon."

"Mrs. White, I just learned Fannie's mother is ill and that she's returned to Culpepper. Is it serious? Do they have a phone at the farm?"

"I don't know how serious, Harry. Yes, there's a phone at the farm, but you need to make a booking for a long distance call. It might take a day to get through."

"I do hope her mother's recovering," I said. "Say, how do I arrange a call?"

"Call the operator and tell her what you want. They'll get back to you with a booking time. The number is Culpepper, Virginia 214.

"Got it. How's Fannie?"

"Upset. You need to talk to her, Harry."

"Thank you, Mrs. White. When I'm settled I'll stop over to say hello."

"We'll look forward to that. Glad you're home, Harry."

Why'd Mrs. White say, "I needed to talk to Fannie?"

Later that afternoon, I took Emily aside. "I don't know the whole story, Harry," she said. "Fannie called me earlier this week. Told me she was returning to Culpepper. It was all rather sudden. I don't have any other details. Sorry I didn't mention it at the station, but I wanted to wait till we were home."

"Seems like she would have left a message for me. You sure she didn't say anything more?"

"No. Just that she was leaving immediately for the farm."

Emily seemed agitated by our conversation. Did she tell me everything?

It took two days before I got a connection to Culpepper.

"Hello Fannie, it's Harry."

"Oh goodness, hello, Harry. Wow, when'd you get home?"

"Just the other day. Say, I learned your mother's ill. Your aunt gave me the number and I wanted to call," I said nervously. "I hope she is better."

"Harry, thank you for calling. Yes, she has rallied somewhat."

"What is the problem?"

"The doctor isn't sure, but he's worried it might be serious."

"How are you doing?"

"Not well, Mother needs constant attention. Fortunately, one of my older sisters is here to help."

"What are your plans?" I asked.

"What do you mean?"

"When are you coming back to Media?"

"I don't have any plans to return. Mother needs my help: with her and with the farm."

"Fannie, I'll leave tomorrow. I should be there the day after. I can pitch in."

"No, Harry. That won't be necessary."

"Won't be necessary? What in the world do you mean?"

"Harry. It wouldn't be good. You would only get hurt."

"I'd get hurt! What are you talking about?"

"You have your life to live now that you've returned home. I have mine here in Culpepper."

"What are you saying? Did you get my letter where I... I... asked you to marry me?"

"Yes I did."

"You never replied!"

"Harry, I can't marry. My mother needs me here. Besides, I... I've been offered a job, teaching at a small school house out here in the country. I want to do it."

"Fannie, none of this makes any sense. I'll take the train tomorrow."

"No, Harry. Please don't. That's a bad idea."

We talked for another ten minutes, but she firmly rejected my entreaties to travel south and kept saying, "I'd only get hurt."

I was dumbfounded. My head swirled in a daze of confusion for a good hour after the call. Her words so upset me I could hardly remember the whole conversation. What the devil did she mean saying, "I'd only get hurt?" I couldn't sort out what had just happened. The realization came slowly, untill it hit me like a blast: Fannie and I were over. All those months in the hell of the Argonne spent dreaming about her, the expectations after Dijon, the letters from her signed "Love." What the hell was that all about? I had counted on Fannie. I believed she cared for me, and now this. It came out of nowhere. I felt as if I had been driving my car on a beautiful road and suddenly, for no reason, smashed into a wall. And worst of all, I never saw the wall coming.

Two nights later I was alone in the kitchen with Mother. I sketched out the phone conversation with Fannie, and told her I planned to take the train to Culpepper tomorrow morning.

"I don't think you should, Harry."

"I have to," I replied. "I love Fannie, I've asked her to marry me."

"Well that may be, Harry," she replied. "But have you really thought this through?"

"What do you mean?"

"Fannie may not be the woman for you." I listened as she went on. "Will she make you a good wife?"

"Why shouldn't she?" I asked.

"Just think about the way she was brought up," Mother said. "How she was taken away from her home as a young girl. It certainly must have had a bad effect on her. How could she properly raise your children after that?" My mother's comments were caustic.

"Is that the sort of woman you want to marry and spend the rest of your life with? I think not."

"I don't see how you can conclude that. You don't know any of her story and I'm sure you don't know Fannie very well." My anger at this conversation rose. "You only met her last October at the dinner Emily wrote me about."

"Besides a man like you, a war hero and all, you could do much better." My mother did not stop there. "She's just not the girl for you, Harry. It is best you forget her."

"That's a hell-of-a thing to say. You've no idea what I am feeling right now." Angry as all get out, I stormed out of the kitchen.

Without a shred of encouragement from Fannie or my family, I failed to find the conviction to leave for Culpepper. Maybe I was just frightened that Fannie would reject me and send me packing. I couldn't tolerate that thought.

As the days wore on, snippets of information emerged. It seemed that Fannie had attended lots of dance parties. Did she meet someone else? I questioned Emily, but she evaded my probing. I pressed George, but all he said was that he occasionally drove Emily and Fannie to parties. I harbored a deep suspicion they weren't telling me everything. My torment and anger grew, I couldn't make sense of anything. Fannie's departure, my interactions at home, my war memories and my failure to act did not mix well in my head.

PART THREE

CHAPTER 52. Something's Wrong

September 14, 1919; Presbyterian Church, Media, Pennsylvania.

After services on Sunday morning, Reverend Hartley sought out Frazure and me in the crowd mingling outside the church.

"Say, Sally, Frazure, can I speak to you for a moment? So glad to see you this morning, and this boy of yours, Morris, he's quite the handsome lad. And your Emily, what a lovely young lady."

Standing alongside us, Emily blushed, and a wry grin crossed Morris's face.

"Say, what I want to know is how Harry and George are getting on? I haven't seen them lately."

"Yes, Emily and Morris are both growing so fast," I replied, ignoring the second question.

Reverend Hartley persisted, "How's Harry doing? What's he up to? How long's he been home, about three months?"

"Sounds right," I said.

Frazure asked Emily and Morris to check on the buggy. "Put the hood up and place the curtains," he said. "It looks like it will rain."

Once the kids were out of earshot, Frazure spoke to Hartley.

"Harry's changed. He'll be working on his car, out in the barn or in the field, but his eyes are far away. He says nothing about the war. It's as if it never happened. He seems to be in this detached mood all the time."

"Reverend, it's downright strange," I said.

"Is he still going to the parties? Does he have a girl?"

"Well, that might be part of the problem," said Frazure.

"I'm worried something's seriously wrong," I added.

"Perhaps you should be, Sally. Elders in the regional Presbytery have been reporting similar stories cropping up in congregations across the district. That's why I asked. Many returned boys show lethargy, as if they're in a sort of mild shock or stupor. One Pastor thought that the events they witnessed overseas took the vim and vigor out of them."

"Sounds like Harry," said Frazure.

"Ask him to stop by and see me. Maybe I can sort out what's troubling him."

"I don't know if he will. But we'll encourage him."

September 16, 1919; The Peterson House, Marple, Pennsylvania.
I kept having this same horrid dream.

> *Lightning bolts flashed in a black sky and the shock waves from exploding shells passed through the driver's body as if it didn't exist. Oblivious to the chaos, the driver shook the reins. The horses stood their ground. A whip crack shredded the air without yielding even a flinch from the animals. One horse scraped the ground with its front hoof. Its leg rose, and came back to rest, swallowed in the mud to the fetlock. Beside the driver, another man jumped up and down in the wagon seat, waving his arms excitedly with equally no effect. The driver flicked the reins harder and cracked the whip again. The brakeman did his dance. The rear right stallion sluggishly shifted its massive head until bloodshot eyes stared with indifference at the driver.*

The bizarre dream scene dissolved and reformed.

> *The wagon lay on its side in the mud. A shaky voice desperately called to the driver. "Over here. Help me, I can't move." The driver crawled out from under the wreckage, and sought his brakeman. Finding him, the driver knelt in the mud, horror etched his face. The plea came from a severed head. A deep gash, spread across the cheek, from which no blood flowed. Quivering lips on a mouth that could hardly open, pleaded. "Help me, help me."*
> *"I don't know what to do. "I...I...I can't do anything."*
> *"Get me outta here," the head implored.*
> *"I don't know what to do."*
> *A hole in the ground appeared.*
> *"This is all ...," the driver said. "This is all... I'm sorry. Sorry." Trembling hands rolled the brakeman's head into the hole, then scooped furiously at the dirt.*
> *"No. No. Nooo...Please, Nooooo," pleaded the head, as mud filled its mouth. An unearthly still swept over everything.*

"Harry, Harry, wake up." The words entered my consciousness as Father shook my shoulder. My eyelids popped open and I sat bolt upright. My nightshirt was soaked with sweat and my head gyrated from side to side.

"You were crying out something awful," I heard him say.

"Oh God, I've dreamt again. Jeez, make it go away, please, please, go away!"

Father lowered his face close to mine, "Deep breaths son. Come on, deep. That's it, in… out…deep… slow."

Mother passed a cool damp cloth across my brow.

"The same dream?" Frazure asked.

"I can't shake it. It's horrible." I began to cry.

Returning from the dresser Mother said, "Here, Harry, change into this nightshirt. It's dry. You'll be more comfortable."

"I'm sorry I woke you. Sorry you see me like this. Did I wake the others? What's wrong with me?" I pleaded. "What's wrong with me?" as my fist slammed into the mattress.

"It's time to go see Reverend Hartley. You can't keep going on like this," Mother told me.

"We've been through this, Mother. I've nothing to say to him. Just leave me alone. Leave me alone!"

The realization came slowly. The War had indeed changed me. Trouble was, I couldn't sort out how or why. I understood how it had removed me from my rural life: separated me from my family, the farm, parties, my car, and the Animal Dances. If I once believed there was a God, that was now gone. Worst of all, it pulled me away from Fannie. I couldn't shake the notion that, if I hadn't gone to war, she'd still be with me.

For more than a year I'd spun in a web of something that was beyond my capacity to fully understand. Though I was home again, nothing felt familiar. Desperately, I wanted to share my feelings, but who'd understand any of the things that contributed to my anguish? How could I describe to Mother and Father, let alone Emily or George, the pervasive stench of decaying bodies that lingered in my nostrils? How could I explain to my little brother the gut-wrenching uncertainty I'd be blown to bits or maimed beyond recognition at any instant? How could I face any of them and describe the terror that rose from the terrible metallic taste of gas? And how could I look at George and tell him that most of the time my mind and body screamed at each other to hold my ground or just turn and run away? And could I tell anyone that I didn't deserve the medal? Worse, none of them would comprehend my tortured soul about that boy. Hell, to them he'd be just another dead German, a nameless slaughter among millions. How could I make them see that my lifeline in the Argonne Forest was Fannie? They just don't understand that I loved her above all else?

Loneliness overwhelmed me, and in the solitude of my room I'd call-out in anguish, "Fannie, I need you, I love you. Please come back." It was a call filled with pain and pleading. Call as I might, she was gone. My desperation slowly gnawed at my soul, and I could find no path out of that hell.

Chapter 53. Steve's Visit

September 20, 1919; the Peterson House, Marple, Pennsylvania.

426 Reed Lane
Marcus Hook, PA
September 15, 1919
Hello Harry,

Sorry I didn't write sooner. Been working for Sun Oil as an apprentice fireman three weeks now. The apprenticeship lasts six weeks and if I pass the test, they'll give me a full-time job. That would be terrific. Say, haven't been to your house to meet your sister and family. We need to catch up. Lots been happening. Need to tell you about it. Can I visit Media two Saturdays from now? Must give you the ring you wanted, hope you still need it. Don't have a car so I'll come up using the train. I'll get connection to Media Station. Should arrive at 11:30 Saturday, the 27th.

Harry, if this don't work call me at Marcus Hook number 1744. Or just drop a line. Look forward to seeing you.
Your Friend,
Steve Hughes

I rang Hughes and told him I'd meet him at the Media station on Saturday. We agreed that there was plenty of catching-up needed.

"Damn, it's good to see you, Hughes," I said.

"You too, Edwards, been a long time." We clasped warmly. "What, ten months since the cock-up back in November?"

"Sounds right. Say, you're looking great. Civilian life hasn't put any pounds on you."

"No it hasn't. Got a new gal. She keeps me fit."

"Hmmm. What is it, she likes to walk a lot?" I said with a sarcastic smile.

Hughes gave me the strangest look. When he got what I was driving at, he laughed with me.

I picked up his valise and we headed toward the car.

"So when'd you know they'd sent me to Germany?" he asked.

"After I returned from the hospital, just before Thanksgiving."

I told him I had bunked with Powell.

"Didn't Powell bunk with Adams?"

I wasn't sure what to say next and to gain time to steady my thoughts, I changed the conversation.

"You know, I hate using last names. It reminds me too much of the war. Can I call you Steve? I'd like you to call me Harry." He agreed that we'd grown out of that, and he drew me back to Adams.

"Steve, Adams didn't make it," I said when seated in the car.

He was pretty upset as I filled in the details. After a point I didn't want to talk more about it.

"So, who's this new gal?"

"Ah, Stella. I arrived in Scranton, maybe a month before you got home, signed some papers, and I'm finally divorced. Gotta tell ya', it's a sack of coal off my back."

"I bet. Come on, more about Stella," I said.

"Now, don't rush it," he said, teasing me. "My momma died in late '18 of the flu. Tore me up bad because I wasn't there. When I got home, I found she'd left everythin' to me. The property, house, bank account, the whole lot. Not that there's that much. Took me several months to empty the house, finally sell it, and sort out the rest of the estate. I think I told you my Dad died several years earlier."

"You didn't want to live in Scranton?" I asked.

I hit the ignition, shifted gears, drove out of the parking lot and turned onto Baltimore Pike. I thought Steve might say something about the automatic starter, but he just kept talking.

"Hell no. Nothin' to keep me in that two-bit town. Be damned if I'm goin' back to the mines. I'm sure I wrote you and said I studied firefighting."

"Yeah, you did. So, what happened in Scranton?" I braked at the intersection with Providence Road, waiting for the newly installed traffic light to change.

"Everythin' in the house reminded me of my mother and father. It got me down. Hell, Harry, it was more than just cleanin' out all that stuff. After I got home, I had trouble concentratin'. Couldn't keep focused, didn't sleep well. Crazy as it sounds, there was no one to talk to and my mind kept wanderin' back to what we'd been through. I kept relivin' all I'd seen. It wouldn't leave my head. The damn war left a mark on me, Harry. Inside, here," Steve tapped his chest. "It's in a place where I can't seem to throw it away."

"I know what you mean."

"After a few weeks holed-up by myself, some friends badgered me. They insisted I get out. They damn near came to physically carrying me to a party. That's when I met Stella. This ray of sunshine falls out of the sky, and damn if she ain't one free-spirited woman. Still amazes me how we connected. I don't know what got into my head, but as I'm leavin' the party I up and asked her to a picture show the next weekend."

Steve told me that after the movie they stopped at an all-night diner.

"I told her about the house, packin' up all the clothes, sellin' the furniture, how I inherited Pop's old car. She wanted to know more an asks me how I felt about cleanin' out the house, throwing out all my parents stuff? Harry, the woman was amazin'. She nodded, like she's takin' it all in. I talked about my mother dyin' from the flu, I talked about the guys in the squad, and she's laughing at my stories. Harry, the woman was sittin' there listenin'. I mean really listenin'. Top of that, she's asking me questions, as if she's tryin' hard to understand."

"Well, she ought to, you being a war hero and all!" I injected.

"Oh yeah, that was a surprise. We'll talk about it later."

"So, back to Stella." I accelerated down Providence Road.

"We kept talking for more than two hours! At one point I told her I was itchin' to get away. Plannin' a trip up north, to Canada where I can hear French again. She asked me why's that so important. I told her that I didn't know." I said, "It's just somethin' I gotta do." Steve looked at me all serious like. "Stella tells me that I'm trying to recapture a dream. Harry, would you believe it? She just up and asks if she can join me on the trip. Seemed she was living alone and didn't like her job. Said she had saved some dough."

"Well, that's free spirited," I laughed.

"Yeah, guess you'd say that. Anyways, we spent a month together tourin' Quebec, explorin' Montreal. The French talk's not as smooth-sounding, but the food's good, an nothin' costs much. Damn if the two of us didn't hit it off swell. More than swell, if you get my drift."

"Yeah, I see where you're drifting! So, where's Stella now?" I asked, as I turned onto Paxon Hollow Road.

"She's back in Scranton. Soon as I get settled at Sun, we're fixin' to get hitched. It's the reason I wanted to see you. Want you to be my best man."

"Are you serious? Wow, congratulations, I'd like that. When's the date?"

"Early December, if the job goes well. Hey. Enough of me. How's the family and Emily? She got a man yet?"

"They're all fine, survived the influenza, though not without some scary moments. Emily's got a fancy for our new mailman. He's called for her a number of times."

Steve said to me, "Well, hopefully he'll deliver the goods!"

I laughed. Damn, same old Hughes. We pulled into the driveway and I parked in front of the barn.

"And how about you?" Steve asked. "You're probably plannin' a weddin' 'bout now. Say, I brought the ring you wanted. Got it right here." He patted his jacket pocket.

A pained look must have passed my face.

"What, Harry? Somethin' wrong?"

"Come on, let's meet the rest of the family. I'll tell you later."

Steve hit it off with Mother, but she did not let him smoke in the house. After he left, Emily told me he was as cute as his pictures. However, she was put off by his occasional swearing, a laugh that was too hearty, his waving arms to make a point, and the way he kept reaching out to touch people on the arm. All silly issues, but I thought it was best she stay interested in the postman.

After supper Steve wanted a smoke so we retired to the back porch.

"Harry," he said. "You gotta tell me, what the hell happened between you and Fannie?

"I don't know what happened," I replied. "I asked her to marry me. Wrote it in a letter about a month before I got home. She never replied."

"You seen her?"

"No. She left for the peach farm the week before I got back. Her mother took ill."

"Well, wasn't her fault her mother took a turn."

"I know. Spoke to her on the phone, couple of days later," I added.

"And ...?"

"I told her I'd leave immediately for Culpepper. She said no, that I'd only be hurt. She had to take care of her mother and the farm. Said she'd been offered a job and wouldn't be coming back north. Said she knew I wasn't really interested in living in Virginia, that I needed to be loyal to my family. When I hung up the phone, I knew we were through."

"Damn, Harry, just like that?"

"You know how I dreamed about that woman, Steve. I miss her something awful. Her leaving, and the damn war, got me all messed up."

"How you mean?"

"I have this bad dream, same one, over and over, and I feel washed out. I can't get any gumption, haven't even restarted my plumbing training."

"When'd this begin?"

"After Fannie left. Worst thing is, I can't shake the dream." I had trouble looking at Steve. "I wake up in a cold sweat. Momma tells me I cry out in my sleep. They keep trying to get me to talk about the war, but I can't."

"Know what you mean. The only ones who understand are those that were there. I've got it locked away, Harry, I can't even talk to Stella about it. Lord knows, she wants to share my experience. Tells me it'll make us closer. She's bein' genuine, but I don't know how to talk about it."

"Yeah. it's how I feel. The words don't come. And there's that kid I shot."

"That's part of it, eh? You know, maybe you and I can talk some of these things out."

I stared at him. "You'd be willing to do that?"

᳇

My war experiences were so bottled up it created a pressure cooker inside me. One thought after another swirled and I could not grasp any one of them to try and make sense out of the past year. Most memories were horrid, and I had convinced myself that if I shared what I'd been through, I'd subject others to my pain. But with Steve's help over the ensuing weeks, I started to put it behind me. More importantly, I started to see my feelings for Fannie in a different way. Perhaps I had blown our relationship out of proportion. Maybe she was a soldier's fantasy fed by the anxiety of war. But, if I really believed that, I would have to conclude that what I felt we had between us was all a sham. I knew better.

I soon learned that Gillespie, Osborn, and Baker suffered this same inner torment. The five of us began to meet for a beer, maybe once a week. We talked about everything. By opening up with each other about the war, we slowly pulled each other back. My own abyss of despair was perhaps the deepest, because it mixed-in Fannie. With their help, the world gradually gained a semblance of order, and with timid feelers I began to look toward the future again.

In December I called Mr. Morell and asked if I could return to my plumber training. He agreed, and I started with him three days a week. He paid nothing, but I was learning the trade. Steve did me another favor. In March of '20 he called and said Sun Oil was advertising for steamfitters. I filled out a form, got an interview, and in April I started a real paying job. Made enough money to consider moving away from home. I used the long commute as my excuse for the move, though Mother was quite distressed by this possibility.

CHAPTER 54. Dorothy

March 12, 1920; The Peterson Home, Marple, Pennsylvania.
While I explored the steamfitter's job at Sun, an unexpected letter arrived.

The Herr family had managed a farm on the lower end of Paxon Hollow Road. They had twin boys, Wilber and Amos, who were my age. I knew those boys well, and as youngsters we had played together regularly. Mr. Herr, a farm manager with a good reputation like my father, never had a problem finding a property to settle on. The Herr's had moved-out in the spring of 1913, when the property changed hands. On occasion I'd bump into one or the other twin, but in recent years I'd lost touch with them. According to Ernie Gillespie, who kept in contact with the boys, they'd enlisted in the Marines in '17. Ernie learned they saw action in Belleau Wood where Amos got his leg shot up bad. He recovered but walks with a limp. Wilber came through unscathed. The Herr's also had a daughter, Dorothy. She couldn't have been more than ten last time I saw her. That would make her seventeen now, and I wondered what she looked like?

Mrs. Herr's letter invited me to visit the family. "Come out for a weekend, stay with us overnight," she wrote. They now lived between West Chester and Downingtown, fourteen miles west of Marple.

I didn't answer. Didn't mean to be rude, but I had little interest in socializing. Worse, I worried that those Herr boys would ask me questions that I wasn't ready to answer. Toward the end of March another invitation arrived, and this time Mother insisted: thought it would be a good idea for me to visit. She told me I needed to meet folks, get out more. I wrote Mrs. Herr and said I'd come up the second weekend in April.

❦

April 10, 1920; The Herr House, Dowingtown, Pennsylvania.

I remain amazed at how impossible it is to anticipate the events that change your life. The Herr visit being one of them.

Over that weekend, I reconnected with Wilber and Amos. Since I'd been talking things out with my buddies, I felt more at ease swapping war stories. It was Dorothy who caught me off guard. She wasn't the little Dorothy I remembered, but now I saw a very pretty young woman.

During Saturday dinner, Dorothy didn't say much. But she kept eyeing me with this sly look. She's too young to look at a man that way, I thought. I couldn't help stealing looks back. Our eyes met at one point and created a connection. She smiled.

Mrs. Herr served up a nice leg of lamb for dinner, and I asked, "Did you treat the meat with some sort of marinade? Has a unique taste, I like it."

"You're right, Harry. But Dorothy's the star here. You tell it, dear."

Dorothy explained how the lamb sat overnight in a dandelion wine sauce.

"I kept rotating it every few hours, so the marinade would seep into the meat."

"You were up all night?"

"Well, not all night… But Momma wanted to make a nice meal and that's what it took."

"Well, your effort's certainly appreciated by this farm boy." We didn't have wine, but I lifted my water glass in a toast, and everyone else joined in.

"That's right nice of you Mr. Edwards," said Dorothy.

"But tell me, what's this dandelion wine?"

"Mama makes it in the spring. She uses the dandelion flowers and leaves. It has to sit all winter to brew just right."

"I don't drink it, Harry," said Wilber. "It's just too strong for me."

"But it's perfect for cooking," added Dorothy.

"Certainly adds a different flavor. Can you copy the recipe for making the wine? Strikes me as a thing my sister would enjoy."

Out of nowhere, Dorothy asked. "Mr. Edwards, Amos said you received a medal during the war. Could you tell us what happened?"

"Dorothy, that's very impolite," admonished Mrs. Herr. "Maybe Harry doesn't want to talk about it."

"I'd like to hear, too."

"Now you hush-up, Amos."

"Hold on Momma, General Pershing don't give out medals for nothing," said Wilber.

There was an awkward moment. All eyes were on me.

"Well. I don't usually say anything 'cause it never seemed that important. My buddy and I certainly weren't heroes that day."

"Come on, Harry," said Amos. "Make me feel better about getting my leg shot up. Remind me that someone over there did something right."

They insisted, so I told my story. Mr. Herr listened carefully, asked a few questions, and arrived at an insight.

"Harry, you're right, I don't see where you or your friend's life was in danger. No, that's not it." Mr. Herr paused a moment as if organizing his thoughts. "You boys saw a disaster brewing, knew you had to respond, and acted without hesitation. The medal recognizes your action."

His comment took a moment to digest. "Must say, Mr. Herr, I never quite saw it like that."

"No, Harry," he said. "You were too busy fussing over the medal being undeserved."

"Well, your view makes it sit better."

Mr. Herr's interpretation of Nantillois Ridge lifted something troubling off my chest. A huge something. A piece of my guilt left me. Just like that, up and gone! But something else, even more important occurred during the weekend. It was Dorothy. How grown up she was, and so bold to ask a man such a question. Suddenly, I saw her as a woman, confident and strong. Hell, I'm a sucker for a woman like that.

After dinner Dorothy asked, "Momma, can I show Mr. Edwards Mary Jane?"

"Sure, if he's interested in a walk."

"Mr. Edwards, come with me. I want to show you something lovely."

"Well, I would certainly love to walk off your dandelion wine. But who's this Mary Jane?"

"Dorothy's pride and joy," said Wilber.

"Well then, let's walk, but since you asked me such impertinent questions, you should call me Harry. Mr. Edwards is too formal."

"I'd be pleased to, Harry."

Dorothy led me out the back door. "Come on, come on," she implored. She grabbed my hand and led the way. As we walked a tree-lined path, she wrapped her arm around mine and inched closer to me. Our light conversation soon had me laughing.

"So tell me Harry," Dorothy began. "Do you like working on the farm better than being a plumber?"

"Hmmm, never thought about one verses the other," I said. "But since you ask, guess I'd prefer plumbing."

"Why's that."

"Doesn't depend on the weather."

Dorothy laughed. "Well, that's one way of seeing it."

I liked her cheeky style. As I said, I'm a sucker for a woman like that..

At the pasture gate Dorothy stopped. I reached for the latch, and she said, "Wait." She tilted her head down and looked intently at me, "No, don't open it. Just watch."

I grappled with that seductive look as she placed two fingers in her mouth, and with no warning, let out an ear-piercing whistle. I heard a whinny and shuffling of hooves off to our right, as Mary Jane trotted over and nuzzled her head into an outstretched hand holding an apple. The handsome mare glanced at me, saw no treat and looked back at Dorothy. I scratched behind her ear while she munched the fruit.

"Isn't she beautiful, Harry?"

"Yes she is. But never mind that, where the hell'd you learn to whistle? I never saw a girl do that before."

She glanced at me again with that trademark, sly, head-tilted stare. Damn, this girl has one come-hither look, crossed my mind yet again.

"Harry, we girls can do lots of things you gents'd be surprised at. Like marinate beef with dandelion wine." A smile spread across her face and she returned to Mary Jane.

I suddenly found myself asking, "Say, do you think we could take in a picture show in Downingtown some time."

"You asking me out?"

"Well, ought to sound that way."

"Oh! I haven't been to a picture show. Do you really think we could go? When? You got to ask my Daddy. I don't think he'd mind if you're escortin' me. He dislikes boys around me he don't know."

"I'll ask before I leave."

"Oh, please do, Harry." Her eyes jumped with excitement.

October 30, 1920; Downingtown Methodist Church, Dowingtown, Pennsylvania.

I went to work at the Sun Oil Refinery in April of 1920, completed the steamfitters trial period, and had a full-time job by May. I was now a man of means with a steady job and a future to consider. With Mr. Herr's permission I had called around for Dorothy all during that spring and summer. In August I popped the question and she said yes!

Dorothy and I were married on a Saturday in late October of '20. My new wife—and mother-in-law—organized a lovely day. Steve served as my best man, and Gillespie and Osborn vouched for me. Emily brought Mr. Miller, our mail-man, to the reception at the Herr house, and Morris danced with all the young ladies. George stayed home. He seemed out of sorts, and Mother wondered if he was coming down with something. Amos and Wilber sure enjoyed themselves, and I sensed that Mr. and Mrs. Herr were pleased with their new son-in-law. My mother seemed especially happy.

We took a three day honeymoon and drove out Route Thirty to an inn between York and Gettysburg. The fall leaves were still turning a lovely golden yellow and burning red. To be truthful, it wasn't the leaves I was interested in.

CHAPTER 55.
Children and the Bonus Army

November 20, 1920; 144 Cedar Street, Marcus Hook, Pennsylvania.

Shortly after we were married, Dorothy and I moved into a house on Cedar Street in Marcus Hook, two blocks down from Steve and Stella. Cedar Street consisted of a long row of modest twin houses owned by Sun and rented to its employees. Luck broke our way and we qualified for a two-story, two-bedroom house.

We cobbled together some furniture and old household items from the barns or attics at the Peterson and Herr houses. After they were repaired and cleaned, they looked pretty good. Trouble was we slept on a rope bed that, according to my father, had belonged to my great grandfather. The mattress was terrible, and, as soon as we could afford it, a new bed was going to be our first purchase.

Sun paid $1.25 an hour, or $55 a week. Jeez, we were rolling in dough and I had lots of opportunity for overtime. Refinery operations expanded along the Delaware River, and overtime paid time-and-a-half.

Dorothy made curtains and found some second hand electric lamps for the living room and bedrooms. She ordered coal for the fireplaces and cooked with a wood stove. Our house had an ice box and electricity, but no appliances. Every other day the ice man delivered a large ice block, which Dorothy cut in half for the fridge compartments.

On weekends, we drove into the countryside and hunted firewood. Dorothy loved the fresh air. The girl had a bounce about her, and she laughed at every joke I made. Seemed everything I said was an excuse to give me a hug. I even let her drive my Ford. How that woman squealed with delight to get her hands on the steering wheel. And she learned to drive right quick. Surprised me how easy gear shift and peddle action came to her. Every second week we'd drive out to the farm so she could ride Mary Jane.

Dorothy shopped for fresh food at a nice market four block from our house, and the lady proved to be an artist at the stove. I told her often how good her cooking made me feel. During supper she'd ask me about my day. She'd want to know all the details. Then, I'd ask what she'd been up to. We shared everything. Well, not quite everything: I didn't talk about the war.

We took long walks together around Marcus Hook or down to a walking path along the Delaware River. Dorothy loved watching the huge cargo ships on route to berths in Philadelphia or the oil tankers that docked at Sun. She'd dream of the exotic oceans those ships would steam on. More than once she'd see one and ask, "Harry, is that the kind of ship you went to France on?"

"No, bigger," I'd always reply. "A lot bigger."

Other times we'd drive to Ridley Creek and hike through the woods along the river bank.

"Harry, I want to try skipping stones again," she'd say.

I'm sure glad I taught her the trick, because it came with benefits. We'd find a particularly large pool or straight stretch of creek, and she'd send me off searching the bank for a skipper.

"Look Harry, I had five skips." If I only had three or four, she'd dig at me with how she was better at skipping than me.

"Looks that way." When I agreed, she'd run up and give me a big kiss, and add, "I want to go home, right now."

Why skipping stones got to the woman is beyond me, but, hey, we gents needn't question such things. Trouble is, we couldn't afford a new bed yet, and I'm forever tightening ropes on that awful thing.

Steve and Stella, and Ernie and Margaret, were married in 1920, and later that year Ollie Baker moved away to take a job near Baltimore. Jake Osborn was dating a girl named Ethel. She certainly was a pretty thing, and they married in '23.

Occasionally, on a Friday or Saturday, we'd get together with Stella and Seve, and have a swell time. When invited to Steve's place, Stella often brought-out the cards and poker chips. Where'd she get this nutty passion for poker? She claimed that now that women had the vote, they could do anything. Mind you, I'd never played poker with a woman. It felt strange. With men it's stogies and beer. But with Stella at the table there were no stogies and only an occasional beer. Oh my, that woman could play a hand. She took on a stone face, became a person I didn't know: a cold, ruthless player. Dorothy learned the game, though she couldn't keep her composure. She'd look at her hand and giggle. Stella would chastise. "Dorothy, stop it. You've got to get serious to beat these boys."

In March of 1921 the local steamfitters union elected me Shop Steward. Guess the guys liked me, or maybe that medal from Pershing played a part. Must say, I felt good about it. The best part was I got an extra $1.75 a week in my paycheck.

The union pushed for wage increases, and by May of 1921 I was making $1.95 an hour. Taking home nearly $4,200 a year with another $350 in overtime. Stella and Steve also did well. Stella's a skilled typist, and she was working in the Sun shipping office.

By the summer of '21 the Hughes' kitchen had all the latest appliances. A Kelvinator refrigerator meant no more ice deliveries. Gas lines were installed down Cedar Street that year, and Stella insisted on a gas stove. She also pushed for an electric washing machine. Steve planned to install it on the back porch, so it would drain into the yard.

"What are you going to do in the winter when it's freezing?" I asked. He gave me this surprised look, like he hadn't thought of that. They didn't flout their success, but Dorothy noticed the additions at every visit. On top of all that, Stella announced she was expecting.

By late 1921, the Hughes' purchases were driving Dorothy nuts with envy. She kept nagging me to improve our place. "Harry, you're making good money. Can't we try to make my kitchen easier to work in? Please?"

"We've talked about this. Do you want to start a family or fix up the kitchen?"

"Stella has all those nice things. It makes her life so much easier. With a baby comin', I'd be able to pay more attention to it."

"What? Whoa. What do you mean 'a baby coming'?" She rolled her eyes with her seductive signature, then gave me the sweetest smile.

"I only learned yesterday," said Dorothy. "Spent all last night thinking how I was going to tell you. Didn't expect it to work out this way."

Dotty was a summer baby in '22, and baby or no baby, my wife remained persistent. She wanted things. I didn't know how to appease her. We bought small items, a toaster, a new rug. Unfortunately, the washing machine, gas stove, and fridge were beyond us. I needed more money. If I took on more overtime, she'd complain that I needed to be home with Dotty.

"You don't want to neglect your daughter do you?" she'd ask.

April, 1923; Sun Oil Company, Marcus Hook, Pennsylvania.

As Shop Steward, I did more than just collect the dues. I had to be sure we followed the union rules to the letter of our contract. My job was to check the work orders from the foreman, and assign jobs to the men. I had to check to be sure the jobs were completed on time and with a quality of work that would keep the foreman and his bosses off my back. I also had to keep the peace between the men, and make sure they never got into a direct altercation with the foreman. All their complaints had to go through me. Sun provided us our tools and I kept their inventory. There were always items getting lost or broken. We were installing a pipe line over at the docks when an expensive wrench fell in, and it took some explaining to tell the foreman what happened so we could order a replacement. Oh, and I had to dole out the overtime duties. That proved tricky, since everyone wanted overtime, and I couldn't be seen favoring one guy over the next, or favoring myself for that matter. Dorothy helped me create a ledger where I rotated overtime from one man to the next. But it could get complicated if the next man up was out because of sickness. However, I made every effort to run a fair shop and the men saw that.

Tony Lorentini was a member of my shop of 15 guys. A vet like me, he'd served with the 77th Division in the western sector of the Argonne during the Oise-Aisne Campaign. Tony was a good worker, and the rest of the guys got along with him. I didn't learn—till later—that Tony was running with some bad fellows on South Street in Philadelphia. He owed the numbers boys a sizable sum.

It started in April of '23 with small things that went missing: welding rods, tubes of sealing grease, blades for cutting tools, nuts and bolts with their washers, and steel hangers to support pipes. Compared to the quantity of supplies we used, it was just a tiny blip. Problem was the blip grew, so that by June, the foreman took me aside.

"Edwards, the stockroom tells me your guys are signing for an unusual amount of supplies. You aware of this?"

"No, I'm not," I told him. "I check the guys carefully, so that they have what they need for each job. I don't think anyone's up to no good."

"Hey, I'm not saying anything's wrong," said the foreman. "Your guys do good work, and you've run a tight ship. It's just that the stockroom called this to my attention. Keep your eyes open."

I spoke to my men and told them that if they were pilfering supplies, they were putting all our jobs in jeopardy. By August there were new reports of excessive requisitions, and the foreman again expressed his concern. In September bigger tools began to disappear: a pipe wrench, bolt cutter, even a welding torch.

Two of my crew, Sean Dalman and Kurt Weinen approached me toward the end of September with a story that implicated Lorentini in stealing tools. They were worried that if he got caught, their jobs could be at risk. When I confronted Lorentini, the man went to pieces before me.

"Harry, I'm in hock to the numbers boys and I've been using the money from selling the Sun stuff to pay 'em off. I'll stop, ask my brother for some dough and get those creeps off my back for good. Jeez, don't can me, Harry. I need the job."

"Yeah, you should have tapped your brother right away. Hell, we all need a job," I replied. "What do we do about the stuff you took?"

"If my brother helps out, I'll save money from my pay. I'll buy replacement tools. Harry, you can say they were lost on a job and that we just found them."

"Not sure that will work," I replied.

"Come-on, Harry, cut me some slack. I've always been a good worker. Besides us vets need to stick together."

Against my better judgment I did cut Tony some slack, and no more tools disappeared for the next month. I hadn't realized it but the foreman requested plant security to watch my shift, when we left the plant. I don't know where they got the tip-off, but in late October security did a spot check as Tony left the plant at day's end. They found tools in his lunch box and a pipe wrench tucked under his work jacket. He was fired on the spot and security was planning to bring charges on him. My whole crew was interviewed, which I thought was more to intimidate than anything else. When Dalman and Weinen were questioned, they said they told me of their suspicion about Tony, and that as far as they knew I didn't do anything.

I was called back for another interview.

"Mr. Edwards, you told us that you did not know that Mr. Lorentini was pilfering supplies or stealing tools," said the chief of security.

"Ahhh, yes, that's what I said."

"Well, why would two of the men in your shop tell us they approached you with their suspicions concerning Lorentini?"

Jeez, those guys ratted on me, I thought.

I tried to explain that Lorentini was in deep with the numbers boys, that he had a plan and was going to replace the missing tools.

"You were protecting him, weren't you?" said the investigator.

I had no excuse. I was protecting a crook, and it didn't matter to Sun that he was a vet, or needed the job, a crook is a crook. Next day I was fired.

May, 1923; The Peterson House, Marple, Pennsylvania.

Dorothy cried for a week when we left Marcus Hook. She was incensed at my behavior. I tried to explain I had honorable intentions. But that didn't go down very well. I felt so ashamed. What the hell was I thinking? Worse, I didn't have the fortitude to tell my mother or father what happened, let alone the Herr's. Hard, honest work was my only atonement, and through it I hoped to regain a good life for Dorothy and little Dotty.

The three of us moved into the Paxon Hollow Road house. My mother and Emily loved having Dotty to play with, but the close company frayed edges.

Morris came out of vocational school with plumbing skills and after an apprenticeship had his license. He'd developed a successful independent business over the next few years and could hire me as a plumbing assistant. With his encouragement I soon qualified for my license. In the summer of '23 Dorothy found an apartment in Media, and the three of us moved again.

With my brother's shrewd business sense, I soon had a higher income than when I was at Sun. There was plenty of work, as the need for plumbing facilities exploded in our rural community just as I predicted years ago. Morris and I developed a reputation for excellent service, and he soon made me his partner. We worked together nearly four years.

April, 1927; Walnut Street, Morton, Pennsylvania.

Dorothy and I scouted out Morton Township—an area seven miles north east of Media—in the spring of '27. Morris had heard that the lone resident plumber had recently retired, leaving a catchment area with no service. So, I decided to tell Morris I was opening my own shop. Dorothy, Dotty, and I pulled up stakes and moved to Morton. We bought a place on Walnut Street, a modest four-bedroom, three story house.

Dorothy and I did some inside painting to brighten the rooms, equipped the kitchen with an electric stove and refrigerator. The ample cabinet space for dishes thrilled my wife. I repaired the oil heater and fixed one of the gutters. The back yard was big enough for Dotty to play in, and next spring we planned to put in a garden. We were proud of our house. I advertised my business in the local hardware stores, fire halls, taverns, post offices, libraries; heck, any place I could find a bulletin board.

Margaret came along in late September of 1927; another bubbling, healthy child. My business thrived to the point that I hired a couple of vets desperate for work, and Dorothy finally had her new clothes washer. By the spring of 1929, we had a substantial bank account. But I'll be damned, another tike was on the way. Then, all hell broke loose in October. Thank goodness I didn't have anything in the stock market.

Evelyn joined our family in December of '30, and there were now five mouths to feed, with the Depression rearing its ugly head. Nevertheless, we managed to more than scrape along. I'd developed a loyal clientele, and plumbers were a "needed" trade. There were always stopped-up drains and blocked toilets. Like a mortician, I never ran out of clients.

Everyone suffered in the depression, but I kept food on the table and maintained the mortgage payments. By 1931 money was tight. I let my help go. It hurt cutting those guys lose: they needed the work. The same year we caught a break when I renegotiated the house loan. It gave Dorothy a little more to spend each month.

Steve and Stella fared okay. Sun still needed firemen. Unfortunately, Stella had been dismissed. Gillespie worked for the county and he held onto his job. The depression, however, took Margaret Gillespie's beauty shop. Now, she was home raising two-year old Johnnie. Jake Osborn kept his teaching post in Malvern. Morris was doing fine. Like me, he never lacked customers. George's body shop limped along and Emily worked off and on as a secretary and handled George's customers on the phone. The secretary job folded, but she found work at the Media 5 & 10 Cent store as a salesclerk.

In October of 1931, Dorothy announced that she was pregnant again. How did that woman get so fertile? Well, I'm to blame, I can't keep my hands off her, and there's never any opposition. That's fine and dandy, but how do I feed six with the depression full-on? In June of 1932, Charlie Frazure Edwards came into the world.

July 2, 1932; Walnut Street, Morton, Pennsylvania.

Saturday afternoon Steve brought Stella and their daughter, Helen over for play time. Stella loved to play with our new baby. A perfect time for Steve and me to get out of the house. Osborn, Gillespie, Hughes and I were soon sharing a beer at the Irish Pub in Morton. After a few sips of the first round we were on the topic of the war bonus.

Five years after the war the government had authorized a payment in the form of a bond for War Vets. Congress, in its wisdom, stuck it to us. The bonds couldn't be redeemed until 1945, thirteen years away. Jake had calculated the compound interest and figured that it would be worth nearly $1500 in 1945.

"Wheeee," I whistled. "I sure could use the money. You guys know if you can cash in early?"

"Yeah, me too, Margaret's been pestering me to fix the roof," said Ernie.

"Government says we can't collect till '45," Jake added.

"That's true, but I read in the paper about those vets in Washington, call themselves the Bonus Expeditionary Force. They're demandin' Congress pass a law so we can cash-in now," said Steve.

"Yeah, read the same thing," I added. "They plan to march on the Capitol Building, try to force Congress to change the law."

"When's the march?" asked Jake. "Maybe we ought to join 'em. The lousy government knows we vets need the bonus." The more we talked, the more steamed-up we became.

"Walter Winchell said on the radio a couple of nights back that Hoover's been calling the Washington vets communists," offered Jake. "Hoover argued that no man who served his country would march on the Capitol Building."

"Hell, Hoover's got no idea what's happened to us working stiffs," added Ernie.

"Vets ain't communists," said Steve. "Just guys wantin' to keep food on the table. Hoover's done nothing to make jobs."

"Dorothy never stops bugging me about money, and my youngsters are costing plenty," I said. "That bonus would sure help. We should join the march."

"You got a point, Harry. We ought to drive down and camp with them gobs for a few days," added Ernie.

After some thought, we concocted plans for the last week of July.

"It might all be over by then," offered Jake.

❧

"Dorothy, I really have to go. If Congress changes the law we'll get over $600. We need the money. Could think about a new car, a new appliance. Hell, if we have leftovers, I'd take us on a trip."

"Harry, I just don't want you away," she pleaded. "Taking care of the girls and now Charlie. I'm worn out. I'd ask my mother to come down, but she's got her hands full taking care of my father."

"Sweetie, Dotty's twelve now and she's a help. You and the girls and Charlie will be fine for a couple of days. Look, I promised the boys I'd drive. I'll only stay for the march? Say, two days?"

"I don't want you to go away. Two days'll stretch into three or more. I need you here."

July 27, 1932; Anacosta Flats, Washington, D.C.

Jake Osborn had rung the local American Legion Post, and they assured him there'd be plenty of space available on the Anacostia flats. We'd drive to Washington Wednesday, camp overnight and Thursday it would be a brisk walk across the Eleventh Street Bridge to the Capitol Building.

The four of us were on the road early Wednesday morning. Steve, Ernie, Jake, and I told jokes and stories or sang all the way. Each of us had brought something to sleep on. I had a big canvas sheet, some rope, sticks and stakes to set a lean-to. I stowed a pot, and Osborn brought plates, coffee mugs and some knives and forks. Steve brought a small portable gas cooker. Three cans of spam, a loaf of bread, a tin of crackers and coffee for a drip coffee maker would keep our stomachs from growling tonight. A toothbrush, bar of soap and a wash cloth made for a simple kit. I packed several jars of fresh water. What else did we need? The four of us were rough and tumble guys again. Were we reliving our war days? Perhaps, but we ignored the fact that was fourteen years ago.

I found a place to park and we hiked half mile to the flats, where as many as twenty thousand vets were camped. It surprised me how many came with families, and most of them lived in makeshift cardboard or corrugated tin shelters. What a horrible place for a family, and some had been camped there for several months. From what I guessed, they'd nothing else.

Thursday morning the four of us assembled at the base of the Bridge, as part of the group walking to the Capitol steps. By eleven o'clock the Capitol Building was in sight. Gillespie's backpack carried peanut butter sandwiches that Margaret made. Steve's carried vegetables diced by Stella and a small bottle of olive oil to make a salad. Dorothy, despite her misgivings, baked a tray of brownies that I carried in my pack. Jake's contained a couple of thermoses filled with coffee. We sat on the steps with thousands of others and ate lunch while listening to speeches.

Around two o'clock a rumor spread. Hoover had ordered the D.C. police to evict veterans from several government buildings. Another rumor swept through the crowd. The cops had clashed with vets outside the Department of Labor and in the melee, two men were killed.

I didn't see any police where we were. However, around three-forty a U.S. Army cavalry troop, four tanks, and a company of infantry approached us from East Capitol Street. They were coming toward the Capitol, in strict order, about half a mile away.

Someone yelled, "Here are our boys, comin' to support us." The troops halted at First Street, three hundred yards away. I watched in dismay as they fixed bayonets, and resumed marching on us at an even pace, guns outstretched from their hips. I heard the yell. "They're comin' for us! Everyone out of here."

Panic broke out. Thousands of folks ran toward Constitution Avenue, beating a retreat toward the bridge. Women, children, and vets slipped and fell. Many helped the fallen, others were run over in the melee. The troops shifted direction and followed the crowd. We funneled onto the Eleventh Street bridge pressed by the horses, tanks and soldiers advancing on us from behind. The horses suddenly charged, women and children screamed, men grabbed at the cavalry, and some troopers were pulled off their mounts. Far more marchers were trampled.

In our dash for safety Jake slipped, and as I grabbed for him a horse charged past, grazing his arm, and spinning him to the ground. Disoriented, he struggled to rise. Ernie and I grabbed Jake and helped him up. Dodging horses, we tumbled off the bridge onto the flats. Back at the lean-to, Steve was waiting for us.

"Sorry, we got separated. Hey, what the hell happened? Jake, you all right?"

"Yeah, I Think so. Got raked by a horse. My arm hurts like hell."

"Give a look." Steve gently pulled up his sleeve. "Yeah you're gonna have a damn good bruise."

"Hey, look there," said Ernie. "Up toward the bridge, troops were demolishing the camp. They're setting fire to everything."

"We need to get outta here," said Steve.

"Grab the stuff. Head for the car," I hollered.

By early evening we had made our way into Maryland and following the map, reached the intersection with Route One. The car turned north, taking us home. I pulled into the driveway well after midnight.

As I removed my jacket an hysterical Dorothy confronted me in the kitchen. "Harry! Harry, where have you been? You weren't here." She trembled all over; something was terribly wrong.

"Dorothy. What is it?"

"He's dead," she sobbed. "Charlie's dead."

I looked at Dorothy in disbelief. My heart skipped a beat and I couldn't catch my breath.

CHAPTER 56. Reconciliation

August 2, 1932; Media Cemetery, Media, Pennsylvania.

We buried Charlie five days later in the Media cemetery, where my grandparents lay. Thirty-five folks came for the service. When my turn came to say words, I couldn't get them out. Steve stepped up, spoke for all of us, short, and to the point.

"We never overcome the tragedy of a child passin' before its time. Leaves a scar and a lifetime of strugglin' over what might have been." He looked at Dorothy and me and continued. "Dwell on your grief, Dorothy and Harry. It'll ease with time, and you'll bask in the beauty that lives on in your girls. You remain blessed with them, and they will give you the strength you need." How had the man found words so clear and simple?

But they did not ease Dorothy. Her grief festered in her mind, as she convinced herself that Charlie'd be alive today, if I'd stayed home. The doctor told us that sudden unexpected infant death had been known for centuries, and that its cause was unknown. Dorothy wouldn't listen when he told her no one was at fault, that this was a tragic event that happened with no rhyme or reason. After the funeral She pretty much stopped talking to me. It was like I ceased to exist in her mind.

It took a while for me to piece together the events that preceded my return from Washington. Charlie had an early evening feed Wednesday, he sputtered a bit after a burp, and Dorothy placed him in the bassinette, on his back, and tucked him in. Around 2:30 a.m. he fussed, ready for another feed, and a little after three he was asleep. This time, Dorothy thought he'd sleep better on his tummy.

Dorothy awoke when the girls were climbing on the bed early next morning. She thought it strange that no noise came from Charlie. Usually, he'd be crying for his morning breakfast. She played with the girls for a while, before getting up to check on the baby. Charlie looked grey, and when she leaned over to touch him, his skin was icy cold.

I shudder to think of her reaction, likely torn between screaming and trying not to alarm the girls. She told me she went to the phone and called our family doctor, the police, then Stella and her mother. The police arrived and pummeled Dorothy with all sorts of awful questions.

Satisfied with what happened they advised Dorothy to contact a funeral director and have Charlie taken away.

By October of '32 there was nothing I could do to lessen her misery. The first civil words she said to me in months cut like a dagger.

"Harry. I've decided you need to move into the spare room on the third floor. I don't want you in the bedroom with me."

"Dorothy, we need to work this out. You know there's no fault in Charlie's death. Not yours, not mine. The doctor said some babies just stop breathing in their cribs. No accounting for why. You didn't do anything bad. It's just one of those awful things. Look, we need to stay together for the girls' sake."

"Don't you sweet talk me," she said as the pent-up anger exploded. "I can't get the thought out of my head. You just upped and walked out. I asked you not to, but you ignored me. Didn't matter a damn to you I was left home with three children and a baby. No, you had to have your fling with those old war buddies. I've said it a hundred times, if you'd been home Charlie'd be alive. I can't forgive you."

I moved to the third floor. Dotty—now twelve—saw a problem between her mother and father right away. We hid it from the younger ones, but they soon realized something wasn't right. Steve, Ernie, Jake, Emily and Morris knew the score. They encouraged me to divorce Dorothy. I wouldn't put the kids through that, and never thought seriously about it. The girls were the thing I lived for, and I had convinced myself I still loved Dorothy.

By 1933 my marriage lay in tatters and for many months a forlorn mood played on everything I did. Dorothy never directed a word to me. She cooked supper, but never asked what I'd like. She made no response if I complimented her cooking. All communication with me was conducted through a third person.

"Margaret, ask your father to get the milk out of the fridge," or something to that effect.

We stopped socializing because it became too embarrassing. Dorothy behaved as though I wasn't in the room, and while I tried every means to get through to her, she just ignored me. If it weren't for my daughters, I'd have succumbed to loneliness in my own house.

During 1935, a crazy idea grew in my thoughts. All the miserable things in my life were due to the war. I kept ruminating on the Bonus March. The government released its troops on us veterans. If there had been no war, there'd have been no march and I'd have been home. Who knows, maybe Charlie would be alive. But there was another unsettling thought rattling in my brain, and I had little success suppressing it. Had I caused the deaths of two children?

In April of 1936 Congress overrode President Roosevelt's veto and passed the Adjusted Compensation Payment Act. It provided an immediate pay-out of the war bonus. I cashed in, and received a check from Uncle Sam for nearly eight hundred dollars. We bought things for the house, and new clothes for the girls and Dorothy. I bought some replacement tools for my work, and had enough left over to take us on a vacation during the summer.

In August we drove to Ocean City on the Jersey shore, and stayed a week at a place called Fox's, a block off the beach. The girls, were now fifteen, nine and seven, and we had a wonderful time. I had to drag them out of jumping in the surf, and I surely tired of building sand castles. Dorothy came along, I guessed for the ride. Certainly not to accompany me. She did play with the girls though.

October 15, 1938; Walnut Street, Morton, Pennsylvania.

There are events in life you remember with a clarity that never fades. Like that Saturday morning in October of '38. I was up a bit early, and entered the kitchen to make a pot of coffee.

"Good morning, Harry," Dorothy said.

I halted in disbelief at the kitchen door. What's it been, six years since she's spoken to me?

"Ahhhh. Good morning." I pulled out the chair from the kitchen table and sat in confused silence.

"Can I make you scrambled eggs?"

"Ahhhh," I again stammered. "That'd be nice."

"Would you like the radio on?"

I regained my composure, "Dorothy, what's going on?"

She struck a match to ignite the stove burner, broke two eggs into the skillet and scrambled them. Three minutes later, Dorothy scooped the eggs onto a plate.

"You'd like some coffee? A piece of toast?" Dorothy asked.

"That'd be nice," I replied.

The eggs were set before me and she poured two cups of coffee, set one next to the plate and the other across the table at her seat. She removed a bottle of milk and butter from the fridge, set them on the table, and sat across from me. I eyed her continuously. Deep in thought, she poured a tad of milk into her cup, added a teaspoon of sugar, and staring at her coffee, slowly rotated a spoon in the cup. Her head rose and she looked directly at me. We hadn't made eye contact in years.

"You know I've been walking the girls to the Methodist Church on Sundays. We got a new minister about six months back, and I've been talking with him for several weeks now. He's a wise man. Helped me understand some things I didn't see before. I've been a foolish woman about you and Charlie. You were right all along. Charlie's death had nothing to do with you being away. My minister has opened my eyes to your loyalty all these years."

I stared at my coffee cup and listened. The woman now trembled as she spoke. "I can't believe you stayed with me. I'm not sure I deserved it. I... I'd... Like to see if we can sort this out."

The room was silent for a moment.

"I don't know. I'm hurt real bad," I replied. "I wanted to leave, but couldn't, 'cause of the girls. I don't know if I can give it a try again."

She rose from the chair, crossed over to me, and placed her hands on my shoulders. The first touch of a woman in so long.

"I know I hurt you bad, and I can't change it. Please help me, I want to fix this."

A week later I moved out of the third floor back to the second. Civility returned to our household, but my marriage never regained its old passion.

CHAPTER 57. The Circle Closes

August 22, 1951; Walnut Street, Morton, Pennsylvania.

The economy was booming in the summer of 1951, and my business grew to the point that I couldn't respond to all the service calls. I hired an assistant and that helped considerably. Nevertheless, the need for plumbing often slackened in August, perhaps, because folks were on vacation. With the post-war economy going great guns, more families could afford a summer holiday. Evelyn was the only one of my daughters that still lived at home, and she was working full-time in Philadelphia.

The phone call from Emily arrived Wednesday morning, just as I was walking out the door. Evelyn hollered, "Hey, Dad, wait-up, phone's for you. Its Aunt Emily."

I took the handset, "Hi Em. You're up early."

"Brother, I wanted to catch you before you left for work. There's some news in the morning paper, in the obituary section. Clifford White passed away two days ago. There's a viewing this Friday and the funeral's Saturday noon; it'll be at Rigby's."

"Oh, what unfortunate news. Did it say anything more?"

"The obit gave a summary of his life. It mentioned, Fannie. At any rate, I just thought you'd like to know. You always spoke well of Cliff. Oh, I learned from the paper, his wife, Janet died a few years earlier."

"I had no idea. Remind me, where's Rigby's? What time's the viewing?"

"It's on West Baltimore Pike, just as you enter Media. Wait, let me look again... Yes, the viewing begins at seven o'clock this Friday."

"Thanks, I may go."

I told Dorothy of the death of an old Media acquaintance, and that I wanted to attend the viewing. Told her I knew him from many years ago. I'd never talked of Clifford, and Dorothy didn't make any connection with Fannie. I told her he taught wood shop at Media High, and I always liked him.

"Do you want me to come along?"

"No, you won't know anyone there. I'll hardly know anyone myself."

"Okay, but tell me all about it. Does Emily know him?"

"Yes, she knew Mr. White quite well. She can't make the viewing, but she'll go to the funeral Saturday."

"We haven't had Emily over in ages. I'll give her a call and invite her to dinner sometime in the next two weeks. You okay with that?"

"Sounds good," I replied.

August 24, 1951; Rigby Funeral Home, Media, Pennsylvania.

I approached an attractive looking woman from behind. Her conversation was so focused she had no sense of my presence. Eventually, she faced me. Our eyes locked. I smiled, and she looked surprised.

"Hello Fannie," I said.

"Harry... Harry Edwards. Oh, my goodness."

I gave her a hug and kissed her on the cheek. It seemed the natural thing to do, and she returned my gesture.

Fannie, took both my hands in her's. "How long's it been?"

"Thirty-three years," I replied.

"Oh goodness, that's a long time," the revelation seemed to startle her. "Did Emily tell you about Clifford?" she asked, regaining her composure.

"Yes. She saw it in the paper."

"You always liked Cliff. I wondered if you'd be here."

"I did. How long will you be in town?'

"At least several weeks. Cliff made me the executor and I'll be settling the estate. I don't know if you knew, but Janet died a few years earlier?"

"I didn't till a few days ago. Are you here by yourself?"

"Yes." I had thought about the possibility of this encounter for the past three days.

"Fannie, do you think we could get together next week? I could take off work. We could have lunch somewhere and catch up. You have a lot of people to talk to here and I don't want to take more of your time."

Fannie looked at me, thinking for a moment, and said, "I'd like that, Harry."

I nodded, "How's next Thursday, say around 12:30. I'll come pick you up. Where're you staying?"

"I'm at Edith Worrell's old house. Do you remember where she lived?"

"Yes. I'm pretty sure. So, see you on Thursday?" I asked.

"Yes. That'll be nice, Harry. Say, Edith is over there," and Fannie pointed.

"I'll be darned. I'll say 'hi' to her."

She leaned in and gave me a peck on the cheek, and then shifted her attention to other mourners.

While driving home, I marveled at how good Fannie looked. She'd kept her figure, and in our short encounter I saw mannerisms and expressions as I remembered from all those years ago. Yet, I wondered what I'd got myself into. What am I going to talk to her about. All sorts of things, totally boring and mundane crossed my mind. Things I couldn't give a damn about. Come on Harry, I said to myself. Be honest, you know what you're after. Yes, I do, but how do I broach it?

August 30, 1951; The Media Inn, Media, Pennsylvania.

A week later Fannie and I were seated at the Media Inn.

"This is so nice, Harry. I remember the Inn when I lived here. Cliff and Janet would bring me here on special occasions, like their birthdays."

"I took my mother and father here many years ago, but haven't been back since they died," I said.

"Oh, I didn't know. Was it recent?"

"A number of years ago."

"And George, is he still fixing cars?"

"No, George died from a heart attack in '48."

"Oh my, I'm so sorry. I remember him as a remarkable dancer."

"I've had ladies tell me the same thing more times than I can say." Fannie smiled at that.

We sat in a secluded booth, and as we looked at the menu I asked, "Are you married?"

"Yes, Matthew and I were married in '22. My last name is Forbes. Matt's the Superintendent for the Culpepper school district. I'm a teacher in one of the grade schools. That's how we met."

"Children?"

She nodded. "Two girls. Catherine's 29 and Elizabeth's 25. The oldest is a nurse and Liz works on the farm."

My conversation felt awkward, and perhaps, it was the same for her. I talked about my daughters, Dorothy, my job. Fannie told me more about her students and how she had inherited the peach farm. I mentioned that Emily never married, and she said they'd been out of touch for years, but had talked on the phone yesterday. They were going out together later in the week. We both ordered an iced tea and lunch. The chit chat continued, until I found the courage.

"Fannie, after all these years this may sound silly, but I must tell you. I always hoped someday we'd have the opportunity to meet again. You've held a place in my memory, even my heart, all these years. And to hear life has been good to you, it's what I would have hoped for."

Fannie smiled that same alluring smile I remembered from long ago. "What a lovely thing to say," she responded.

My comment relaxed us both, and over the next hour the conversation bridged topics, casual and more intimate. It seemed as if the thirty-three year gap didn't exist. At one point it was suddenly easy for me to say, "Curiosity is driving me to explore something that has troubled me."

"What's that?"

"I came home from the war and found you gone. And, when you said you did not want to see me. I was totally confused. Well, the more truthful word is 'devastated.' The stress of the war, my hopes for us, and the thought you never really cared for me, left me hollowed-out. I concluded you were just a soldier's war-time infatuation. Yet,

I've always wanted to know what happened all those years ago? Was there any truth in those letters you sent to me?"

When I finished, her hand moved across the table to cover mine.

"Harry, I didn't want to hurt you. You've also lingered in my heart these many years."

"I always felt I had missed part of the story, as if there was something I didn't know about," I added.

She searched for words while I patiently waited.

"It's been so long, Harry. I'm not sure I can stitch it together to make sense."

"Try," I said. "It'd bring closure, perhaps for you too."

"Harry, can you recall the time we were picnicking on Bowman's Hill? I think it was around your birthday in 1917."

"Vaguely."

"You told me you could never work in Virginia, that you wanted to remain close to your family."

"I don't recall that, but why was that bothersome?"

"I thought you understood how much I loved the peach farm and Culpepper. The fact that you could never live there distressed me."

"I never realized."

"There's more, much more. The last night you were home, before leaving for the army, I had a horrid thought that the war would take you. That I'd never see you again. That thought haunted me."

My facial expression must have changed and Fannie asked.

"What Harry?"

"When I left next day on the train and you came running to the station, I wondered if I'd ever see you again."

"Amazing, our anxieties came true," Fannie said. "I agonized over you being killed. It fed my loneliness. My Aunt kept insisting I go to the parties. Told me I needed something else to think about."

"So, you went?"

"Emily also kept insisting, and by early October I relented. But there were no men around, at least not any I'd like to be seen with. One evening George drove Emily and me to a party and he asked me to dance again and again. He was such a heavenly dancer. I felt relaxed with him. After all, he was your brother, how could I get in trouble?"

"So, I still don't see a problem. You just danced with him," I said.

"George kept asking me out and I didn't say no. During this time your letters became more intimate, and the more I felt for you, the worse became my fears. But, when I was with George, I was able to forget my fear."

"How long did this go on?"

"Through the late fall, winter, and into the spring of 1919. I was relieved about your safety with the war over, but couldn't stop going to the parties. It was such fun, and a needed distraction from my loneliness. I was at your house in April for a dance party. George had driven me there, and I don't remember why, but I had to leave early. George and I were in the driveway, in front of your car. He grabbed me. Initially, I pushed back, but he overpowered me, and in my state of mind I gave in. Your mother saw our embrace through the parlor window."

"Uh oh," I said.

"About the same time your letter arrived asking me to marry you. I planned to reply immediately, but my mother took ill. I was worried about her but couldn't leave for Culpepper, because it was near the last week of school with exams and graduation coming. That's when Emily confronted me and accused me of two-timing you. I felt awful, because she called it like it was. I didn't know what to do."

Fannie hesitated as if collecting her thoughts. "My heart belonged to you, Harry. I never had deeper feelings for, George. Next thing I know your mother confronted me. About a week later."

"My mother? How did she get involved?"

"I don't know. I always suspected it was triggered by something said between Emily and your mother, egged on by your mother seeing me and George out by the car after the party."

"But what did my mother have to do with anything?"

"Harry, your mother and I did not have a very nice encounter. She told me in no uncertain terms to stop seeing her sons. She called me a hussy, said no good would come of it."

"Really!" I could hardly believe what I was hearing.

"It got worse. With my dander up, I told her to mind her own business. Your mother called me a name. I'm sure I replied. She said the word again and stormed off. It's the last I saw of her."

I sat in stunned silence and Fannie just stared at me. I didn't know how to react. Fannie continued. "You were coming home in a few weeks, and I was scared of what might happen between you and George, and what your mother might do."

"Yeah. I guess I'd be plenty upset if I'd known all this."

"When my mother had a relapse, I saw an escape. Right after graduation I ran to the peach farm. You know the rest."

"But why didn't you let me come to Culpepper?"

"Truth is, Harry, I wanted you to defy me. But you didn't."

"No, I didn't. My mother kept putting things in my head, and I felt so down-in-the-dumps I couldn't act."

I shook my head, sending Fannie a message that I regretted my foolish inaction. It was a moment in my life where I failed to think for myself. We sat, looking at each other, lost in thought, until I sat back in the chair and broke into a smile.

"Wow, that's some closure! The pieces all fall together."

Fannie waited for me to say more.

"We were young. I came home from the war with horrible memories and a weight around my neck. I had killed a German soldier who turned out to be just a child. In the vast scheme of the war it was nothing, but the event has haunted me, even to this day."

I hesitated again, regrouping my thoughts.

"Fannie, Emily never got married, nor did George. My father's health worsened, and by 1920 or '21 he no longer worked the farm. George's body shop business was growing and Emily worked in Media as a secretary. Morris had a successful plumbing business, and I was making good money, so the four of us decided to build a place for Mom and Dad."

I paused for a sip of coffee. "We chipped in, bought some land on Providence Road in Media. George, Morris and I built the place, did enough of the work ourselves so that we could afford it. Mom and Dad moved into the house in 1924 and lived there the rest of their lives. George lived there till he died, and Emily's in the house now. But there's another snippet I remember. My mother always said it was her children's job to take care of them when they were old. She didn't harp on the theme, but it came up more often than not as I grew up."

"So where's this going, Harry? That's the way people thought back then, children were supposed to take care of their parents when they grew old. There was no Social Security yet."

"Well, that's right. But the worry over old age security plagued my mother. If I fill in the blanks from what you just told me, I suspect my mother was frightened I'd marry you and move to Virginia, depriving her of her security. Chasing you away solved the problem."

"Do you really think that's it?" she asked.

"There's more. After I moved away, I'd hear stories of relationships Emily had over the years. They never seemed to work out, and Emily eventually became the nursemaid to my folks. I wonder if my mother chased off her beaus too."

Fannie had a startled look on her face. "Could that be?"

"Yes, I think so. You know we ought to write a book on the follies of youth."

"And of meddling parents," she added quickly.

"Jeez, you got that right." We both laughed.

As we talked a new friendship blossomed, and Fannie and I agreed to keep in touch. I now understood what happened all those years ago. My encounter with Fannie had reaffirmed my belief in the fickleness of life, filled with unexpected twists and turns that could never be anticipated.

CHAPTER 58. Friends Grow Old

March, 1968, Walnut Street, Morton, Pennsylvania.

Dotty met a soldier on leave at the Morton USO club and they married in '43. I wasn't happy. "She's too young to marry," I told Dorothy. Dotty's husband, Chet was educated on the G.I. Bill after the war, and worked for an insurance company in south Jersey. My anxiety for my daughter had clouded my judgment. Chet's a fine husband and father, and they're happily married.

Margaret—always the wild one—announced in late 1945 she was marrying a guy a year older. She'd just turned eighteen. We knew Kenny from high school, a nice boy, but not very ambitious. He had avoided the draft because four other brothers were already in the war. I objected again, but they married anyway. Kenny did car maintenance work out at one of the post-war dealerships on the Baltimore Pike. Four years later, he was elevated to a salesman. Surprised me, but he turned out to be good at it. Hope Elaine, my gorgeous first granddaughter came along a couple of years later.

Evelyn lived at home till she was 23. That's when she moved out to an apartment in Philadelphia to work as a secretary. Evelyn's the one with the good head, and after night classes in accounting, she became a bank teller. She got hitched to a co-worker in '56. I wasn't sure about Jeff, too Republican for my taste, but he'd have us laughing around the table at a holiday dinner. Dorothy adored him. Evelyn was promoted to branch manager, which was unheard of for a woman. Probably the classes she took was a good idea, but as I said, she has a good head. More grandchildren eventually arrived.

As I aged, I came to see how precious and beautiful my own children and grandchildren were. They occupied a unique place in my life. I luxuriated in them, relished their company, and loved them with the fullness of my heart.

March 10, 1968; Walnut Street, Morton, Pennsylvania.
Ernie phoned and reminded me that May of 1968 would be fifty years since we had arrived at Camp Lee. He suggested that it'd be nice to see the guys again: said he'd try and put something together. He called in April to say he had booked a restaurant in Philly, a place famous for seafood. I asked him who else had responded and he said everyone was planning to come except Bill Ford and ole' Sedelsky. He mentioned that Doyle had died in 1959.

"Died! What happened?" I asked.

"I talked with his son on the phone. Told me Doyle got in a fight with an Italian over a Teamsters' issue. Seemed the Italians were trying to muscle control of the Dock Workers Union. Shots were fired; Doyle took two in the chest."

"Damn, that's terrible."

"They caught the guy and he's serving life."

"How about Sedelsky?" I asked.

"He's holed up in a place for old soldiers in the Adirondacks. The sod'll be ninety-two this year. I called, but they said he couldn't come to the phone. Told them why I was calling and the nurse said he doesn't remember people anymore."

"Hell, that's terrible. And Ford?" I asked.

"I found his phone number in the division registry and called. He lives in Florida, on the west coast and is now retired. Said he can't easily travel and won't be able to make the reunion. Harry, I'll say more at dinner so all the guys can hear."

"Jeez Ernie, where'd the years go? Seems like yesterday we were boarding that train for Camp Lee."

"I feel the same. Oh, there's some uncertainty about Joe Goldrick. He's not been well. Spoke to Joe's wife, she said he's determined to join us, but it's up in the air for now."

May 25, 1968, Bookbinders Restaurant, Philadelphia
Pennsylvania.

Steve and I arrived at the restaurant and were directed to a private room upstairs. There they were: Ernie Gillespie, Jake Osborn, Jim Nightlinger, Ollie Baker, Charlie Powell, and Joe Goldrick.

"Damn, you bastards are still alive and kickin'," said Steve. Handshakes and back slapping hugs were shared by everyone.

"My God, Charlie, I'd recognize you like it was yesterday," I said.

"You're not looking so bad yourself, Harry."

"Well, thanks. But sadly, the ladies just don't look my way anymore."

"Hey. You're not the only one," said Charlie, as he patted his extended belly.

I felt a tap on my shoulder. "Hello, Harry."

" Joe… Joe Goldrick. So glad you made it."

In fact, it took a moment to recognize Joe. His face was pale and hollowed out. He appeared very thin. His illness must be serious, entered my mind..

"I wouldn't have missed it for anything," said Joe. "Hazel drove me in from Harrisburg with a couple of girlfriends. They're having dinner in the outer restaurant. Hazel said that if the gents had a night out, the ladies would do the same."

"Hey, smart wife, Joe. Be sure I say hello to her when we break-up."

Ernie interrupted us and spoke up. "Grab a seat guys."

I sat between Jim Nightlinger and Charlie Powell, and after our drinks arrived Ernie raised his glass.

"Gentlemen, here's to Will Adams, Phil Doyle, Bill Ford and the good Sergeant Sedelsky. Oh, and to Lieutenant Harden, wherever he is, may he stay there." We laughed.

"To them all," and we raised our glasses.

The appetizer came and went as did our main meal. I had a calamari dish. It tasted good, but not the best I've had. Around the time for dessert, Ernie announced Jim Nightlinger had something to share.

Jim stood, held up a bag and removed two bottles. "Gentlemen, these bottles of Kentucky whiskey are unique. Like us, they've survived." We all laughed.

"Bought a case of this in '25, during prohibition. Label says it was bottled in 1918. Been saving these last two malts for a special occasion. This is sipping whisky, gentlemen."

A whoop of cheers broke out as Jim reached back into the bag and withdrew a box.

"You boys remember those shitty cigars we puffed back at the Thanksgiving dinner in 1918. What was the name of the town?"

"Sassay," hollered Joe.

"Yeah, that's it. I remember those damn things stunk me up something terrible. Well boys, we're going to celebrate this well-aged booze with these Havanas. Hell of a time getting 'em out of Cuba. But I know a guy in South Philly."

"Oh yeah," shouted Joe. "This man makes me happy."

"These goodies come with a price, though. You boys have to tell what you been about the last fifty years. Afterwards, I'm going to tell you about something I've saved a long time."

Jim reached into his jacket and took out a carefully folded, yellow paper.

The waitress brought glasses. Jim passed the box along accompanied by a cigar cutter. I watched Joe take one. He cut the end, sniffed its aroma, and broke into a knowing smile. "Doc says I shouldn't, but hell, no one lives forever."

"Okay, Ernie, you first," said Jim.

"Jeez Jim, give a guy a chance to think," and he sipped his drink. "Oh this is smooth. Well, Margaret and I were married in the summer of 1920. Harry was my best man."

I nodded my head.

"A year later Margaret's cousin tells her he knew a guy in the Works Department over in the county seat who heard from his brother there's an opening coming up in the County Commissioner's Office in Media. I applied and was offered a job in the Procurement Department. Worked my way up, and by '40 I'm Assistant Procurement Director. Eventually, the commissioners appoint me head of the department. I had charge of purchases for the county: everything from school supplies to road equipment. Had to run a tight ship. There were always venders ready to sweeten the deal, if you get my meaning."

"Come on, Ernie. You telling us you're a boy scout?" laughed Jim.

"Yes, I am. Kept my nose clean. Hell, I don't want to do time. Retired in 1963 with a nice pension and Social Security. Margaret studied hairdressing and opened a shop in Media. Did okay, but along comes the Depression and it's all over."

"Kids?" asked Charlie.

"Yep, boy and a girl, Oscar and Marjorie. They're both married. Live out in Chester County. Marge's a stay-at-home mom. Oscar manages the A & P store in Kennett Square. Both done okay. Got three grandkids, 11, 14, and 19. The younger one's a pip."

I took another sip. Oh, it warmed the gullet nicely. The room slowly filled with smoke. Thank goodness for the exhaust fan. Maybe my clothes won't stink so much, I thought.

"What about you Charlie?" asked Jim.

"Maybe you guys remember that I loved the railroad."

"How could we forget?" yelled Jake. "It's all you talked about."

"I got a bug for dispatching trains from the war."

"Aw, come on, Charlie. Where's the connection?" asked Steve.

"Came from reading them maps and figuring how to get a wagon from here to there."

"Well. Seems like a twisted path, if you ask me," added Jake.

"Any rate, worked my way up. Served as a freight dispatcher with the old PRR and then moved to CONRAIL. Dispatched trains for twenty-nine years. Loved every minute of it. And never had an accident! I retired in 1964. I had married, Leslie back in '23, and we had two kids; a girl and a boy. My daughter's name is Jeanne and my son was called Joe. Named him after Joe Goldrick."

"Charlie asked me to be his godfather," said Joe. "I watched the little Joe grow into a fine young man."

Charlie suddenly became serious. "Joe was killed in the Battle of the Bulge. Leslie and I are as over it as we'll ever be. We count the twenty-one years we had him as a blessing. I'm damn proud of my kid." Charlie choked back a tear.

We were silent for a moment, until Jake stood, raised his glass, "Here's to Joe Powell." We all stood and tipped our glasses.

"And how about you, Joe?" asked Jim.

"I came home from the war, had a rough time of it for a while. Memories of France wore heavy on me. I couldn't shake some of the things I'd seen. Did odd jobs in carpentry, lived at home. Gradually, I got real down. The war played in my head and I couldn't get over it. It took a couple of years, and it's hard to recall how it all came about. In 1924 I got involved with an old high school friend. He's running for state senator here in Pennsylvania. I went to meetings, addressed envelopes, canvassed door-to-door. He asked me to edit his speeches, and then I started offering suggestions. I guess they were good, because damn if he didn't win. The new state senator asks me to join his staff in Harrisburg. Wouldn't you know, he's got this good looking secretary named, Hazel."

"Ah ha," among the guys was audible.

"I hit it off with her and we tied the knot a year later. Well, I liked working in Harrisburg and soon was doing research for other senators. Built it into a consulting business. It's still active. Hazel and I had two kids. Bill is forty-four this year and Ben's forty-two. They both went to Penn State; did civil engineering. They're involved in construction work around the state. Don't know if you heard. I'm fighting some bad stuff in my colon. It's a tough time, but I'm going to beat it."

Each of us were taken back by those last words. No one knew what to say. Jim broke the silence, "We're all with you Joe," and we toasted him. "So, how about you, Steve?"

Steve thought for a moment.

"Charlie, I'm sorry to hear about your son. War's tore us all up in one way or another."

Steve sat silent for another moment. "Joe, I also had a tough time of it, when I got home."

With the pause, Steve leaned over to Jim. "Jim, can you top me up?"

"Sure can," and out spilt a generous dollop of that golden liquid.

Steve sipped and regained his thoughts. "You guys know the army sent me off to Germany. We were just sittin' around in the ungodly cold. Suddenly, the army decided to offer us classes. I took this course in firefighting. Gotta tell ya, I loved it."

"You always sought the excitement," I chimed in.

"Maybe I did. I saw it as a challenge, me against the fire," Steve explained. "I got a job in the fire company at Sun Oil. Worked my way up the ranks to assistant chief. The chief retires in '36 and I'm passed over. Some runt-faced kid, who's related to the Sun's Director of Operations, gets offered the job. The fire section ain't unionized so there's nothin' I could do. I'm pissed. All those years loyally workin' for Sun. Gotta tell ya, put a real sour note in my head."

"So what happened?" interrupted Jim.

"Stella—she's my wife—gets wind that they're looking for a chief in the volunteer brigade over in Springfield Township. I hustle over, make an application. Jeez, if they don't offer me the job. Don't pay as well as Sun, but hell, it's a job, and the chief's a full-time township appointment. Over the years I built the department into one fine unit. Had to do fundraising and got pretty good at it. I'm still the chief, but it's getting' time to retire."

"So, who's this Stella?" asked Jim.

"Met her in Scranton after the war. The woman was a pip when I met her and still is. She's a secretary in a law office over in Springfield."

"Any kids?" asked Ollie.

"Only one daughter. The girl reminds me of her mother, just as smart. She won a scholarship to college."

"What's her name?" asked Jake.

"Helen. She's married to a real ambitious guy. They do nothing but work all the time."

I lit another cigar. Damn, I've never smoked two of these things back to back in my life. I'll stink like hell when I get home.

"And you, Ollie?" I asked.

"I worked outside Baltimore, place called Woodlawn. Sears and Roebuck opened a big store on the Baltimore Pike. Worked in the Shipping Department until retirement in 1966. I married in '30, but it didn't turn out so well. Caught her with another guy and it ended in a divorce. I remarried and Marie and I are doing just fine. We saved enough to buy into the Presbyterian Village out in Oxford, Pennsylvania. Two years ago now. It's one of those new retirement villages, and we love it."

"Any kids in your story, Ollie?" I asked.

"No. It never worked out that way."

I took a deep draw on the Havana.

"Who'd I miss?" asked Jim. "Oh yeah, how about you, Jake?'

"Like some of you guys, I struggled for a number of years after I came home. Couldn't shake things from the war. I was listless, hadn't a clear grip on life," said Jake. "My father kept insisting I go back to school. Gradually, I managed to piece things back together and began studying biology at West Chester Teachers' College, eventually becoming a high school biology teacher. I love working with the kids, find it rewarding."

"Sounds good to me, Jake," I said. Jake continued his story.

"I found the last good woman, gentlemen. Her name's, Ethel. We married in '24 and had two boys." Jake seemed to search for the next words. "The older boy, Marcus, perished in the hell of Okinawa. After Marcus died, Ethel and I were in a bad way. Fortunately, Thomas came along too late to be drawn into the second war. I think our loss prevented Ethel and I from giving our second boy the attention he needed. Marcus left home after school, drifted around for years, had run-ins with the law," Jake hesitated for a drink. "We haven't heard from him in a while now and worry about him all the time."

"I know too well about losing a kid to war. You never get over the waste of it," said Charlie.

I was about to take another sip, when Steve stood up, "Let's toast again to Marcus Osborn."

The room was silent for a bit before Ernie spoke up.

"Hey Jim, what you been about?"

"Yeah, what have I been about? Well, that's a long story," began Jim. "I married later than some of you guys. Like many of you, the war played with my head in a bad way. For a number of years I couldn't shake the image of all those dead men I'd seen. Luckily, by 1925, I managed to get myself sufficiently back together that I opened a bakery out near Sixty-Ninth Street. The shop went great guns, even three years into the stock crash of '29. That's when it all collapsed. No one had money to spend on fancy desserts, and I got to the point where I couldn't pay the rent or the help."

Jim paused for a draw on his cigar.

"Frances and I lived with my folks for a year or more, surviving sometimes off soup kitchens. The Depression proved a mean time for us. Desperate, in '34 we moved to Nevada where I got a job working at the Hoover Dam construction. We're living in a shithole of a place called Ragtown. To make more, I took a job as a highscaler. I couldn't tell Frances, it would've scared the hell out of her."

Ollie interrupted. "You mean you were one of the guys working on the canyon walls?"

"To quote one of us, Ollie, 'You got that right.'" Laughter flitted across the group as they looked toward me.

"Wasn't that dangerous?" Steve asked.

"You might say so. Any rate, to shorten the story, one day I make a suggestion to the foreman, and next thing you know, I'm in the safety office working on things today called hard hats. I got the idea from those tin hats we wore in the war. It seemed so obvious that I was always amazed it hadn't been thought of before for this kind of work.

Fran and I hang on at the dam till operations wind down." Jim stopped for another cigar puff, and then he continued. "We came back east, to Philly. Fran had family here and my dad was still alive. I got a job working on the installation of the railroad flanks on the Ben Franklin Bridge. It was exciting work if not dangerous."

"Aw, come-on Jim, you're makin' up this stuff," said Steve.

"No. All true. Long story short, Frances' father dies, and she's left an inheritance. She lets me use the money to open my own company, a small metal fabrication operation in North Philly. That was in '40. It was something I'd been thinking about since the episode with the 'hard-hats.' The war comes along, and the army gives me a contract. All at once, the shop's making small special parts for the tail section of B-17 bombers. The work's good. I bid on more contracts, and gradually expand the business. The boom of the postwar years carried me right along and we now make parts for Boeing in those 707 jetliners."

We learned that Jim was still working, though, like Steve, he realizes retirement is looming. He also told us that he and Frances had seven kids. Seeing a look of surprise on our faces, Jim explained.

"Hey, she's a good Catholic girl. They're all grown now, and there's eight grandkids. But I've bored you guys long enough. How about you, Harry? I got a suspicion what I'm going to hear."

Old memories are tenacious. As if on cue, the other guys in the room echo, "Marry Fannie."

Another sip loosened my tongue.

"Well..., that's not quite how it worked out. I got home and Fannie's not there. She's returned to the family farm in Virginia. Her mother took sick, and I never saw her again. At least not till 1951."

Even after fifty years, I could see the looks of surprise.

"What happened?" asked Charlie.

"It's complicated. My older brother passed in '48 and my folks were gone by then. You may recall I had a sister, Emily."

"Hell, yes. She was a looker, Harry. I remember the pictures. Think I had a thing about your sister once," said Jake.

"She never married. Still lives in Media."

"Such a waste," said Hughes. "I think I still got a picture of her in a box in the attic."

I took a hefty sip of whiskey. I needed the help.

"I didn't learn the truth about what happened with Fannie until we met again in 1951 at her uncle's funeral in Media. There's Fannie, as beautiful as I remember her. She stayed in town for a couple of weeks to settle the estate, and I took her out to lunch."

"Aren't you the suave one. Lunch..." said Jim.

"Well, I still need to please the ladies. Any rate, that's when I learned the whole story."

"So, what's the scoop?" asked Charlie.

I told a shortened version, noting how she went to dance parties with my brother, and was afraid it would create a disaster in my family if I found out after I came home.

"Didn't she write all sorts of romantic stuff to you?" asked Jim. "And all the time she's screwing around with your brother!"

"I don't think it went that far. My mother confronted her about messing with her sons, some bad words passed. Fannie's all confused. A month before I came home I wrote and proposed to her. Not very romantic, in a letter and all, but it was what I did. Just before I'm home, she returned to Virginia to take care of her sick mother. We talked on the phone a few days later, and that was when I knew it was over."

The room fell silent. I talked on, about Sun Oil, how I met Dorothy, the girls, baby Charlie's death, my plumbing business. Told them Dorothy died three years ago, and that I now lived alone. Everyone took a good sip and the guys just looked at me nonplused and silent.

"Damn, Harry, that's a story," said Jim, breaking the spell. That's when Jim withdrew the yellowed paper from his pocket, and carefully opened it.

"I have another surprise. You guys remember the night in Camp Lee, after we returned from the parade?"

There were a few nods around the room.

"We were all saying what we'd do after the war. Next day, while heading home, I wrote it all down, least as best I could remember. Saved this paper all these years. Here it is."

He held up the yellowed page, and its contents became the center of conversation. Jim's note tied it all together despite the late hour.

"From what you guys said after our victory parade, and from what I heard tonight, it didn't quite turn out as we expected, did it? We've all had some difficult times, but we're still alive and can laugh together," said Jim. "I wrote something else down. Something Jake said, fifty years ago. Stuck with me all this time. When I was in the dumps, I'd re-read it."

Jim read. "I got hope I can put what I seen behind me. I think I can still be happy. We all have a good life ahead of us. We're the guys who made it home. We survived the war. Maybe we get to use what we've been through to make us better. Make those around us better."

I stood up and raised my glass. "Here's to Jake." We all stood and took a swig.

The reminisces continued. Steve told the story of our adventure on the "Nest" of the *Tenadores* during the storm. The guys were amazed. They'd never heard that one before. Joe reminded us of how Sarge warned him about ground bugs the first time he camped in the pup tent.

"When the hell was that?" asked Jake.

"The first night while we were on the road to Camp Meucon. After we left Redon," said Joe.

"The whereabouts of Sarge came up and Ernie shared what he knew. Sarge stories were swapped, and we all agreed he held a cherished place in our past.

"Anyone know about Doyle?"

Ernie spoke again. "I talked with his brother," and he related his rise in the union and the shooting on the docks.

The memories flowed. We were "feeding the fish" again on the Atlantic crossing; reliving all those strange new sights our first day in France.

"Look, Edwards, you were trying to cheat on me during that swimming race at the canal," said Jim.

"Hell, I knew I'd never beat you any other way." My candor produced a good laugh.

"You remember Doyle yelling at them young women, and us facing 'em, naked?"

"Yeah. Say, didn't one of those ladies faint? I think because she looked at you Joe." I said.

It took a moment, but soon enough our recollection kicked in from that time we were swimming in the canal back in Redon. We all chuckled, except Joe.

"My most vivid memory is of the first day at the front. We were driving along on a crowded road and a Kraut plane strafed us," recalled Joe. "Steve, you were going nuts thinking every plane had you in their sights. I was about to crap in my pants, I was so scared."

"We were no heroes," offered Jake. "Just kids."

The stories went round and round. I didn't say much.

Of course, our dalliance with the ladies of Dijon found its way into the conversation, but only briefly. Seemed no one was inclined to go there.

Steve mentioned how our wagon got blown up, and how clever he was to use a handkerchief on me as a makeshift gasmask. I thanked him, but added I didn't appreciate the piss-soaked rag wrapped around my face. Using as much sarcasm as possible, I told Steve that I still smelled him in my nose. That got a good laugh out of the guys. Steve also commented on Nantillois Ridge and how we saved a company of doughboys from an ambush. He certainly sent praise my way on how quickly I realized we could run along the ridge to a spot where we could shoot down on the Germans below.

"Ok, you're forgiven for the handkerchief," I said and everyone laughed again.

"Do you guys remember those Animal Dances?" asked Ollie. We all nodded. "They just disappeared after the war. Right about the time we got home. Damn, I missed those moves."

"Yeah, you're right, Ollie. The parties were never the same again. At least till the roaring twenties," said Jake.

"Hey, Harry, you remember anything special?" asked Charlie.

I was about to say something when, at that moment, three ladies popped through the door.

"You boys going to talk all night? It's past eleven. Some of us ladies need our beauty rest. And it's a long drive."

We cheered Hazel, Joe's wife, and her friends. By now we'd been sipping whisky for over two hours. Jim invited them in, offered 'em a cigar and a shot. But the hour was late.

Steve and I relived the evening as he drove me home. Then, both of us were quiet—lost in our thoughts—till he broke the silence.

"Harry, I been thinking. This may be the last time we see those gobs all together."

"Jeez, 'gobs,' haven't heard that in years," I laughed. "What do you mean?"

"I'm just amazed at how each of us walked different paths, some expected, others less so. As I've been driving, it occurred to me each of us shared a common voyage for a tiny slice of our lives. One that that burned itself into our memories. Another thought got to me. It's hard to say it, but for the eight of us in that room tonight, our journey's comin' to an end." I had to let that digest for a moment.

"Old friend, you've amazed me at times. I thought Osborn was the thinker, but you can be a rival. Reminds me of something that's stuck with me all these years. We're up on the mast of the *Tenadores*, the day we got caught in the squall. Hell, I still see the scene. It's a beautiful sunset, and the ship's running with the wind. There's hardly any sound and the mast is rocking gently. Out of nowhere you wondered if God had forgotten us. Confused, I asked if you meant the two of us here in the nest, or everyone 'out there' in this war. Do you remember that?

"Ahhh, no." Steve replied, and changed the conversation. "I know what was in your head tonight, Harry. Just before Hazel came in. Do you think you could have said it?"

"I don't know. Maybe I should have, it might have gotten something off my chest. But, it didn't work out. You'd think after all this time I'd put it away. But I can't. It doesn't go away, ever."

We drove on in silence, the whirr of the tires the only sound.

EPILOGUE

Could my life have been different? Hard to say. I came out of the Great War convinced I never controlled my fate, just flowed with it. The rest of my life was much the same.

I followed Beatrice in the news and occasionally her name might be mentioned in a story featuring Alice Paul. Fannie writes me occasionally, and we've had phone conversations. I'm glad we've kept in touch: she was very kind when Dorothy died.

Emily never married. She kept the books for George's business till he passed, and tended to Mother and Father as they aged. She now lives alone in the house on Providence Road. Morris was the most successful of the four of us. His business thrived, and he married in 1939 to a kindly lady named Betty. They have two lovely daughters, who I should see more often.

My girls are all grown now, and there are six grandkids. They light my life, and I get visits most weekends. I can't wait to hear the door chimes ring.

I think about the dinner at Bookbinders. Those guys and I had amazing travels through life, and for a fleeting moment, our ships sailed through a common passage. A passage that permanently branded us. I may never see them together again, but they, and our voyage live in me.

January, 1969; Walnut Street, Morton, Pennsylvania.
When the nights are freezing, I burrow into the covers of a cold bed, struggling to find sleep. It is in that moment that the scene unfolds again in my mind. The Hun stands there, taking aim. What a confident bastard he is. The fool's totally exposed, has no idea what the next moment will bring. I tighten my right index finger. Slowly, ever so slowly. "Crack," the rifle butt jams into my shoulder and in that cold bed the memory makes me shudder. Like the day it actually happened, I see his hands as they flail to the sky. Watch his rifle as it flips upward, falls and clatters on the hard stones. His body arches backward and disappears. The child disappeared from my sight, but never from my mind.

I've come to realize that echoes from the 'War to End All Wars' will depart my soul only when my heart no longer beats. Was it the same with all the young men who left their youth on another shore so long ago? Does every war burn permanent scars into those drawn into its hellish embrace? Perhaps I dwell on it too much. However, there's one thing I know for certain. I survived the war, but I never again found the Animal Dances of my youth.

1973, Morton, Pennsylvania.

Harry Edwards died in 1973. The death certificate indicated respiratory failure from obstructive lung disease. The coroner, knowing nothing else, assumed it was from smoking. He was wrong.

THE END

Acknowledgements:

I wish to thank Cassandra Hirsh and Greg Frost for guiding me in the struggle to change from the reality world of science writing to the imagined world of fiction. Thanks also go to Professor Peter Holquist who introduced me to the historical facts about the First World War. The critical comments of Roz Warren added greatly to the story flow. The editorial contribution of Joshua Isard assured a readable text. Special thanks go to Gayle Joseph who contributed many excellent line drawings to the chapters. I greatly appreciated the creative talent of Dwayne Booth in the front and back cover design. Special thanks go to Donna Cavanaugh at Shorehouse Books. Her encouragement and enthusiasm arrived like a ray of sunshine.

Along the way many others, in no particular order, contributed to my effort; Dupont Guery, Elaine Goldberg, Alan Rosenquist, Leonard Warren, Larry Palmer, Gershon Bucksbaum, and Radley Smith. Special thanks to the encouragement of my brother Tom and my two sons, Brett and Drew. Further, to all the luncheon and dinner guests who suffered through endless depictions of Harry's adventures, I say thank you. Each of you helped shape the story.

Finally, again to my partner in life, Elaine. Your sharp eye kept me from making countless dumb mistakes, not only in the book, but in our half century adventure.

The skeleton of Animal Dances is derived from the 163 letters written home by Harry C. Edwards while serving in the army in 1918-1919. They were written from Camp Lee, Virginia, from towns in France, and from the Western Front during the Muse-Argonne Campaign. The letters were dutifully saved by his sister, my wife's Aunt Emily. The skeleton had meat placed on its bones by the wonderful and vivid descriptions in the 315th Field Artillery Regimental History, published in 1921 (Authored by Regimental Members: Edited by a Regimental Committee. (1921). *History of the 315th Field Artillery, September, 1917-June, 1919*. John & Pollock, Inc., Baltimore, MD, pp 192.). I was fortunate to find this rare book in an antiquarian book shop in San Francisco. Some of the Chapter drawings, acknowledged below, by William J. Moll and W. W. Crapo, were reproduced from illustrations in this History. All the names in the book were once living persons and Harry refers to them frequently in the letters; their depiction in the book is, of course, fiction. Using their real names is my way of honoring those soldiers of a century ago.

Credit for Cover and Chapter Pictures.

The cover picture is part of the material in the Harry C. Edwards collection. Rear Cover: Modification from the painting titled "The Cortez" by Lester Ralph at: https://imgc.allpostersimages.com/img/print/ lester-ralph-dance-the-cortez_u-l-psa7du0.jpg?src=gp

Chapter 1: https://willisweaver2.com/category/ship-lyon/

Chapter 5, 12, 20, 24, 34, 35, 44, 45, 49, 54, 55: 57 From material in the Harry C. Edwards collection

Chapter 2: https://www.pinterest.com/pin/ 169870217167446761

Chapter 6: https://en.wikipedia.org/ wiki/ USS_Tenadores_(1913)

Chapter 7: http://www.nationalgeographic.com/content/ dam/environment/ photos/000/002/270.ngsversion.1487025002214.adapt.1900.1.jpg

Chapter 9: Drawing by William J Moll, In: History of the 315 Field Artillery Regiment,1921, Kohn & Pollock, Inc., Baltimore, MD, pg. 83.

Chapter 10, 13, 19, 23, 25, 29, 30, 33, 39, 46, 58: Drawing by Gayle Joseph, 2016. See below on how to contact Mrs. Gayle Joseph.

Chapter 11: Unknown Artist, In: History of the 315 Field Artillery Regiment,1921, Kohn & Pollock, Inc., Baltimore, MD, pg. 5.

Chapter 14: https://de.wikipedia.org/wiki/7,92_%C3%97_57_mm

Chapter 16: Drawing by W. W. Crapo, In: History of the 315 Field Artillery Regiment,1921, Kohn & Pollock, Inc., Baltimore, MD, pg. 67.

Chapter 17: https://upload.wikimedia.org/wikipedia/commons/thumb/b/b0/ 155mmHowitzerUS1918TravelingPosition.jpg/800px- 155mmHowitzerUS1918TravelingPosition.jpg

Chapter 21: https://americangallery.wordpress.com/category/raleigh-henry- p/

Chapter 22: https://www.google.com/search?q=unloading+wagon+from +flatcar+wwI&tbm=isch&tbo=u&source=univ&sa=X&ved=0ahUKEwj7l aG-zYfVAhVHyT4KHWR7B8kQ7AkILg&biw=1152&bih=566#imgrc=XDOT- X6H0V9hE

Chapter 23: Drawing by William J Moll, In: History of the 315 Field Artillery Regiment,1921, Kohn & Pollock, Inc., Baltimore, MD, pg. 84.

Chapter 26: http://www.ddoughty.com/boy-soldiers-ww1--ww2.html

Chapter 27: https://st.hzcdn.com/simgs/1681ff4b023c52b2_4- 7926/farmhouse-dining-room.jpg

Chapter 28: https://www.pinterest.co.uk/pin/323625923202468461

Chapter 31: Philadelphia Inquirer – Philly Edition, January 23, 2017.

Chapter 37: http://chronicles.dickinson.edu/studentwork/ sheridan/steese/WWIPics/wwi10.jpg

Chapter 38: http://history.amedd.army.mil/booksdocs/wwi/fieldoperations/ ch6fig44.jpg

Chapter 41: https://i.pinimg.com/736x/2c/4d/a9/2c4da9e0d9 d0fd32316a94117c93422b--tribune-newspaper-newspaper-headlines.jpg

Chapter 42: Modified from the cover drawing of the pamphlet titled: *When you Go Home*, Distributed by the War Department, Commission on Training Camp

Activities. Published by The U.S. Public Health Service Division of Venereal Diseases, 228 First Street, N.W., Washington, D.C., 1919.

Chapter 43: Figure modified from;
https://fineartamerica.com/featured/regina-player-piano-ira-shander.html

Chapter 47: https://i.pinimg.com/originals/48/8f/46/
488f467dd2dbb1eabd3a80e28759ef38.jpg

Chapter 55: https://historicdistrict.files.wordpress.com /2012/02/bonus-army-poster.jpg

Chapter 57: http://1.bp.blogspot.com/-
9CNjVdqDf2E/UyX9vArKYDI/AAAAAAAAAa4/
uwly7-tk3Es/s1600/1d+Media\+Pa.+Media+Inn+c.1940+pc.jpg

If you wish to communicate with the artist, Mrs. Gayle Viale Joseph, please contact the publisher.

Author Biography: The author is a retired Professor of Otolaryngology, Physiology and Neuroscience at the University of Pennsylvania. He is a graduate of Ohio Wesleyan University, and holds advanced degrees in Experimental Psychology from Connecticut College and Sensory Psychology from Princeton University. Faculty appointments were held at Monash University in Melbourne, Australia and the University of Pennsylvania in Philadelphia. His career was recognized with the Claude Pepper Award for outstanding research from the National Institutes on Deafness and other Communication Disorders, the Christian R. and Mary F. Lindback Distinguished Teaching Award from the University of Pennsylvania, and the Dean's award for outstanding Leadership in the School of Medicine. He has spent extensive scholarly time in Perth, Australia, Stockholm, Sweden, and Bordeaux, France. Major scientific efforts produced an extensive bibliography depicting the biological mechanisms of normal hearing and hearing loss. Today, he continues to lecture on the topic of Hearing Loss in the Elderly and is active on the Board of Trustees of the Hearing Loss Association of America, advocating for those with hearing loss. An avid fisherman, kayaker, stamp collector, and world traveler, he relishes in telling of his adventures from circumnavigating the globe and exploring the Australian outback. The families of his sons enrich his life. He lives with his wife in a century old house in the Philadelphia suburbs and is currently working on a novel set on Cape Cod in 1943.